Praise for *Nothing Is Terrible* by Matthew Sharpe

". . . as funny as Céline's 'Death on the Installment Plan' . . . an upbeat existential childhood nightmare." —Kim Gordon, *BookForum*

"Having committed us emotionally to the action of his debut novel, the exhilarating, transgressive Sharpe also has rung some important bells in the house of contemporary American fiction." —Peter Wolfe, *St. Louis Post-Dispatch*

"Sharpe manages to imbue his young protagonist with the perfect mix of sugar and spice." —Jay MacDonald, *Fort Meyers News-Press*

"As Nabokov's 'Lolita' marked an aging Russian emigre's fascination with his newly adopted America, Sharpe's novel wonderfully illustrates a young urban author's response to the grand fictions we grow up with." —Richard Carter, *Times Record News*

". . . at its heart, *Nothing Is Terrible* is a testament to [the] phenomenal use of language . . . Matthew Sharpe hits with dead-on accuracy the center of this girl's thawing heart." —Jennifer Gilmore, *Time Out New York*

"The novel, sometimes strange, often shocking, delivers a rollicking good time."—Kristine Huntley, *Booklist*

"Warped and oddly touching, *Nothing Is Terrible* is brain candy for the bright and jaded." —Christine Muhlke, *New York Times Book Review*

Praise for *Stories from the Tube*

"Sharpe's stories are wildly effective—and often touching—collisions of the banal and the surreal." —Mark Rozzo, *L.A. Times*

"Sharpe is a witty, unpretentious and occasionally moving writer in the tradition of Barth and Barthelme."—Lev Grossman, *Time Out New York*

"... remarkable fiction debut. ... Layers of humor, horror, tenderness and social critique are at work underneath the surface, more than redeeming the stories' base inspirations. Anyone who can craft a story like "In the Snowy Kingdom," which Raymond Carver would have been proud to call his own, from an antiperspirant commercial is definitely someone to watch."—*Forbes FYI*

"With a force that moves lithely beneath the words and resists detection, Sharpe's writing recreates the surface ritual of our day-to-day lives while simultaneously undermining that smooth surface to reveal the often strange beauty and wild sadness at its core." —David Agruss, MSNBC.com

"'Stories from the Tube' reads like a 'Canterbury Tales' for the modern-day ad age." —Anderson Clifton, CNN.com

"Matthew Sharpe's first collection of fiction is unnerving, haunting, and dark, dark, dark." —*Philadelphia Weekly*

"... a prose maverick." —Lisa Shea, *Elle*

"Matthew Sharpe is exploring the way in which the modern television through its instantaneous and widespread domination of a culture has become a new formula for myth-making." —Jere Real, *Richmond Times-Dispatch*

"... hilarious, nerve-wracking, heartbreaking ..." —Sara Miles, *Wired*

"It does seem a little disingenuous for a writer to trash the medium that provides his sales hook." —Debra Goldman, *Adweek*

Jamestown

Also by Matthew Sharpe

Nothing Is Terrible
Stories from the Tube
The Sleeping Father

Jamestown

a novel

Matthew Sharpe

Soft Skull Press • Brooklyn, NY

2007

Jamestown
© 2007 Matthew Sharpe

ISBN: 1-933368-60-8
ISBN-13: 978-1-933368-60-3

Published by Soft Skull Press
55 Washington St., Suite 804
Brooklyn, NY 11201
www.softskull.com

Cover Design by Goodloe Byron
Book Design by Anne Horowitz

Distributed by Publishers Group West
www.pgw.com 1-800-788-3123

Printed in Canada

Library of Congress Cataloging-in-Publication Data

Sharpe, Matthew, 1962-
   Jamestown : a novel / Matthew Sharpe.
      p. cm.
   ISBN-13: 978-1-933368-60-3 (alk. paper)
   ISBN-10: 1-933368-60-8 (alk. paper)
   1. Jamestown (Va.)--Fiction. 2. Smith, John, 1580-1631--Fiction. 3.
Pocahontas, d. 1617--Fiction. 4. Powhatan, ca. 1550-1618--Fiction. 5. Rolfe,
John, 1585-1622--Fiction. 6. Colonists--Fiction. 7. Powhatan Indians--Fiction.
I. Title.

PS3569.H3444J36 2007
813'.54--dc22

                                                                    2006100994

For Lore Segal

One

Johnny Rolfe

To whoever is out there, if anyone is out there:

Today has been an awful day in a run of awful days as long as life so far. The thirty of us climbed aboard this bus in haste, fled down the tunnel, and came up on the river's far bank in time to see the Chrysler Building plunge into the earth. The grieving faces of my colleagues being worse to look at than that crumpling shaft of glass, brick, and steel, I used my knees to plug the sockets of my eyes, put my fingers in my ears, and clamped my nose and mouth shut with my thighs. All main entries to my head remained sealed till Delaware, where I looked up in time to see John Martin vault his seatback, steak knife aimed at George Kendall's throat. Kendall, bread knife aimed at Martin's throat, said, "How dare you say that!" Some great, quaint pre-annihilation philosopher described the movement of history as *thesis, antithesis, synthesis*, whereas I've seen a lot more *thesis, antithesis, steak knife, bread knife*. John and George jabbed each other's arms once each before a couple guys broke up the fight, not because they didn't want to see George dead, or John dead, but because we'd signed a contract with our employer stipulating no murder on the bus. Murders off the bus must be approved by a majority of the bus's five-man board of directors. We don't yet know who those five are: their names are sealed in a black box we're meant not to open till we pass from Maryland into Virginia—that is, from civilization into its counterpart, if indeed civilization's what to call what we're fleeing, or exporting, or both. I am this trip's communications specialist, having taken a degree from the

Manhattan School of Communications Arts, where I received certificates in linguistics, diplomacy, typing, modern dance, telecom, short and long stick.

A mile into Delaware a log or rock got lodged in our tank tread and we came to a halt. We'd passed a trading post a mile back and all of us but three set out for it on foot. Our home having cracked sooner than we'd thought it would, we left without a lot of things we need. Those men walked up the road with what they had to trade for food: small electric things, copper, beads, knives, love; scarcity reveals the nature of exchange.

The driver and mechanic fixed the bus while I sat here and called to my thoughts. None came. I gazed out the dirty bulletproof window at two plump red hares, creatures one sees none of on the island of my birth. "Say *bullet-resistant glass* not *bulletproof glass* because there's no such thing as bulletproof glass and while that may be a technicality I wouldn't want to sell this glass to you under false pretext however slight," the used bullet-proof glass salesman said to me in my role as this trip's communications specialist, back at home, three days before the earth swallowed the tower. "What will you be using the glass *for*?"

"For not dying," I said, and put my fist in contact with his chin, the punishment for poor sales technique in modern-day New York. Stepping over his prone form, I put as much glass in my cart as would fit. Don't judge me, if you exist. Show me a man who goes to sleep each night integrity intact and I will hit him in the chin with my fist and take his glass.

I continued to console myself with the two red hares gently munching grasses in that roadside field—though what was road and what was field was not so easy to discern. Two weeks into spring, the hares seemed unperturbed to find the trees around them dead, all leaves brown and holed and half-mashed in the earth. I liked the hares and wished them all the best, but they were plump and I was starved enough to risk ingesting what toxins they might have contained. I pulled my bodkin from my sock and stood when two brown rodents big as the hares entered the field. So low to the ground were these two new beasts that I couldn't see their legs above the brown and desiccated grass; they seemed to glide along this stiff, brown lake of blades. They tapered at the back end into bushy tails, and at the front end into meager heads each of which came to a point in a weapons-grade black nose. Their tone was frolicsome. They signaled to the hares their wish to play. The hares seemed angry. The brown rodents approached and were rebuffed, approached and were rebuffed, and by now the hares' fiery fur stood on end while their bodies shook in place. The hares were puffed up very big and red and I sensed a miscommunication between these species of dumb beasts that looked like other miscommunications I'd sensed or made. Never have I seen a hare open its mouth as wide as did the red hare who now bit the small head off the brown thing, whose red blood stained the stiff, brown grass. The second brown thing fled along the stalks, but not in time to not get caught by hare two and sheared in half. That was when I turned away and opted not to hunt the hares.

The mechanic, Jack Smith, bounded up the bus's stairs. He gave me a thumbs-up that transitioned into a wave. "Johnny! How you doing? We got the bus fixed. What's with the sick, morose look?"

"Did you see what those hares did to those—other things?"

"That's what you're upset about? That's like being upset about earthquakes, or asteroids falling into the sea, or war, or having to breathe to stay alive. Think happy thoughts."

"And what would be a happy thought for you?"

"That I'm alive."

"Great."

"Don't be so pessimistic. We'll get down to Virginia, trade with the Indians—"

"'Trade,' right."

"Maybe someone like you'll meet a nice Indian girl and fall in love."

"What's someone like me?"

"Someone who believes in love."

"You don't?"

"Love's like me, it does its dirty job. People like you think love's a virtue in itself. That's why I like you."

"When people say 'That's why I like you,' they're either about to swindle me or they're laboring under a grave misapprehension."

"'Laboring under a grave misapprehension,' that's cute. You contemplative types are such a gloomy bunch of freaks," he said, and pinched my cheeks and kissed my ear and stepped down off the bus.

The other guys returned. Their clothes were torn and fouled, their faces bruised. George Kendall, whose throat John Martin had tried to cut, was not among them.

"What happened to Kendall?" I said.

"The less you know, the better," Martin said.

"Did you finally succeed in killing him?"

Martin lunged at me and Jack Smith, the mechanic, blocked him. The driver started up the bus as Smith knocked Martin to the ground. "Now get up and I'll give you a hug," he said.

Martin stood, hugged Smith, and tried to stab him in the gut. Smith took his knife from him and sliced his forehead open. Night fell. We drove slowly down the blasted road. Smith stitched Martin's head and dressed the wound and fed him soup and laid him down to sleep. I don't like a bus of guys. Is there any bus of guys on which a man can hug and feed another soup without first having sliced his face?

Pocahontas

To the excellent person I know is reading this:

Hi! My name is Pocahontas and I'm nineteen, but Pocahontas isn't my real name. I will never say my real name. If I say my real name you will die. Anyone who hears my real name will die. Pocahontas is my nickname, it means "person who cannot be controlled by her dad." My dad didn't make up my nickname, my mom did, before she died, and he's kind of mad that that's my nickname because every time someone says it—which is any time anyone says my name because anyone who says my *name* name will die, which has been proven, but right now I can't talk about that because in English, which is not my mom tongue, you can talk about only one thing at a time, at most—any time anyone says my nickname they're also saying my dad can't control his daughter, and that's bad for my dad, my dad claims, because he's chief of our town and a bunch of other towns in this general area—Superchief, I think y'all might say in English.

Oh English! How I love to write to you in English, even though it is so slow to do anything in English, because English moves at the speed of talking, whereas my language moves at the speed of thinking. Thinking in English is beautiful sort of in the way it is beautiful to have smoked a big bowl of busthead. When I think of the world in English, or look at the world in English, it moves so slow, like English, and that feels good cuz life's so short! Like when I look, in English, at my two little cousins, Opechancanough and Steve, throwing a ball back and forth between them in a meadow or former parking lot, the ball slides along the air as a snail slides along the sand, and leaves a furrow of air in the air as thoughts of you, the excellent person I know is reading this, leave the faintest furrow in my brow.

I want to tell you all about the sweet but kind of weird and sad day I had today, okay? After I spent the morning working in the cornfields with my gal pals I was running around and around and around my dad's house. My dad's house is pretty neat, and contains many a mansion! It's shaped like the lower-case letter n, but as if you had a very tall stack of papers and each one had a great black letter n in the exact center of it, so that there was a big stack of n's all kind of connected to each other, and then you took a very sharp knife and cut away all the whiteness of all the paper surrounding the n's, and were left with about five hundred black n's stacked on top of one another, and then you tilted the stack so the n's were standing on their feet, so you had a tunnel of n's, which you lived in with your wife, who bore you a girl when you wanted a boy, or thought you wanted a boy, but you found you loved the girl so much you let her disobey your rules, and so on, so that's what my dad's house looks like, which I was running around and around, a thing a girl my age won't do for much longer, it just ain't right, who knows why, gonna have to find another place to run, and maybe not around but through.

Well so I'm running when this guy, my favorite second cousin, Stickboy, came up to me and asked me to take a walk with him in the woods, and I said yes, why not, it's always good to spend time with him.

Stickboy's smart, and knows things no one else knows, but few acknowledge this. His dad was killed before he was born and his mom, who is the cousin of my dad, came to live with us, and gave birth to Stickboy in our n-shaped house. Like I said, my dad had no boy, i.e., heir, so Stickboy is supposed to take over the family business, which is executive-level politics, except for the little problem that no one thinks he's up to the job. "Doesn't kick," my father said, with his hand on his cousin's womb a month before Stickboy came down the tunnel of her cunt and out into this vale of tears. "What kind of politician doesn't kick in the womb?" And many years later—now—when my father enters a room Stickboy is already in, Stickboy, without thinking, brings his hands up to his chest as if to defend his heart from a barb my dad would fling at it, and my dad says, "What are you doing, covering your breasts?" and both man and boy wince, boy cuz he wants my dad to love him, man cuz he knows he flings the barb at the heart of his adopted son cuz the boy's weakness reminds him of his own and he's therefore, in a sense, flinging a barb at his own heart. Isn't life sometimes complicated and sad?

I walked with Stickboy out into the woods. I want to write a fabulous description of the woods for you in the exciting language of English, but it's going to be hard. I don't know the English names of woodsy things. There's a kind of moss that's soft and green and smells like the neck of my mom, who died when I was one. I guess I'll call this moss mom's neck. Mom's neck drips or droops from the branches of the trees. The branches have leaves that fall off in autumn and grow back in spring. The leaves in the spring are green and round or spear-shaped or heart-shaped or radiant. The air in the woods this time of year is wet and green. When I open my mouth in the woods it fills with green. When I speak in the woods my words come out green. If I think of someone I love, my thoughts are green. The woods also have the remnants of a defunct civilization that thrived on this very spot, so for every couple dozen trees there'll be a brokedown edifice of years gone by. The woods have deadly creatures too but I'll not say their names right now.

Deeper and deeper into the forest went Stickboy and I. "I think we will not marry after all," he said, which stopped me in mid-stride.

"What?"

"I think we will not marry after all."

"What will prevent us?"

"The future."

"Why, whenever you talk about the future, do you sound as if you're describing a country where only sad people live?"

"To counteract the nostalgia for the future that you and everyone else around here seem to feel. To counteract the naïve idea that what makes the future good is that it's the future."

Well it hit me pretty hard when he said that about him and me not getting married, an event we'd been planning since we met at birth. I think he's right but I don't know why. Maybe he's right because he said it. Does that ever happen in English, where saying something makes it true? That happens in my language all the time so people have to be careful what they say but no one ever is, enough.

Then some time passed in the woods that I don't remember anything about, a little wedge of life that's disappeared. And then he said one more thing to me, a single word that caused a single feeling in my breast. The feeling I remember well, but not the word that was its maker. Ugh, I wish I hadn't written this. Too late now.

Johnny Rolfe

To the one whose existence I doubt:

We parallel the river's southward course. Our progress is glacial. Long swathes of the old road are gone. Often we know we're on what used to be the road only by the signs that remain on what used to be its side: FARM-LAND-FRESH PRODUCE, BUMPER-TO-BUMPER AUTO PARTS, FRIENDLY MOTEL, MOOSE LODGE, CHRISTIANA CHICKEN SHACK, SHAFT OX CHIROPRACTIC, OASIS CAR WASH, MIRACLE DELIVERANCE TABERNACLE, SPEED LIMIT ENFORCED BY AIRCRAFT, DRUG-FREE SCHOOL ZONE: linguistic detritus of history, voices from a past we hope to reclaim, lonely notes our forebears wrote in code to tell us how to find them. WHISPERING PINES MOTEL, MASON-DIXON SPORTS COMPLEX, CRAFT EMPORIUM, SELF-EMPLOYED HEALTH INSURANCE, OTHELLO, BAIT AND TACKLE, TEMPERANCE, WILDLIFE REFUGE, FREE WATERFRONT CATALOGUE 7000 FEET.

We passed another trading post today. Everyone but Jack Smith, the red-haired mechanic, who'd had to slice John Martin's face, shunned this one. We stopped for lunch; Smith removed a red wagon full of paltry trinkets from the trailer of supplies behind the bus and went to the post alone on foot. I gazed through the scuffed-up glass at the most compelling sign of all:

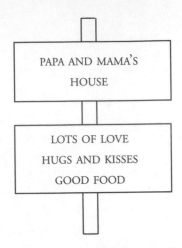

I would have risked my life to find who made that sign, but the house it stood before and described had become a house-shaped square of ash, so I stayed put.

An hour later Martin, whose face there was a little less of now, said, "Let's leave without Smith."

"I'm not going anywhere," the driver said.

Others said:

"Let's wait an hour, then go after him."

"Let's wait an hour, then leave."

"Let's kill him when he gets back, if he isn't already dead."

"Let's go after him now, he's been gone long enough, something bad's happened." (That was me.)

"Let's send you in after him alone," Martin said.

I said, "I know it stings to get punked by someone of a lower social station, Martin."

He came at me along the bus's wide central aisle, a blur of bandages deep brown with dried blood. I removed from my pocket the very handheld device on which I'm now describing this and jammed it in his knee. He howled and fell and howled. He wouldn't walk again for hours at least, and thus I'd saved him from a dozen fights, a munificent gesture, almost as if I'd used this thing to communicate something of value.

Against my own best sense, I want to know John Martin—not know him tactically to know what he'll do next so I can do it to him first, I mean I want to know him in the useless way people know. He's small and pale, fine-boned and quick, a meticulous dresser and a dirty fighter with a high, elegant forehead. With his speed and size, his wont to bite and scratch, he fights well in a cramped space. The syllogism of his inclusion on this trip: he's good at number crunching, he'll bite off the finger of his assailant, let's include him on this trip. And Martin's a born executive—one of that class of men who make or know the secrets that define the contour of our lives without our knowledge, secrets one hundred molecules of which the rest of us inhale with every breath. You can tell he's one of them by how he wears his suit. Even when it's soiled and scuffed, stained with blood, and stinks of fear and rage, Martin's suit attends his body as the air attends an eagle's wing.

We on this bus are brothers by default. We breathe each other's breaths, fumes, and farts. That a flake of Martin's shed skin, while riding the currents of the bus's inner wind, should land on my lunchmeat is a likelihood too great not to make my peace with. The enmity of my neighbor is rent I pay for life on earth. I love the man who hates me and I know that if what I need badly enough can be obtained in no other way I'll kill him for it.

Darkness has arrived. I'm reclining on my bunk on the starboard side of the bus, caressing the small, soft qwerty keys of my wireless device. Diagonally across from me, lit by candlelight, the forlorn-faced, bloody-foreheaded Martin runs the front of his wounded fingers lightly over the set of brass balls even an adversary must admire.

"What are you staring at?" he says.

"I'm not your enemy, Martin."

"Yes you are."

"What do you want?"

"What?"

"What do you want out of this trip?"

"Same as everyone: live long, get rich."

"At any cost?"

He doesn't answer me, the question is evidently too stupid.

"What about ensuring the survival of the community?" I say.

"That's a little grandiose for me, let me think about it."

I've observed that if I beat a man in a fight in the afternoon, he will give my ideas serious consideration in the evening.

"Well," he says, "I haven't killed you yet and you haven't killed me yet."

"I think a civil society means you can go to sleep not having to be actively thankful no one's killed you since you woke up."

"What the hell are you typing?"

"Our conversation."

"Type this: fuck you."

"Thanks, I just did. Do you love anyone, Martin?"

"What?"

"Is there anyone you love?"

"You cripple me and ask me that?"

"Yes."

"Yes. I love a few people. But I already know them. I don't see the point of loving anyone new. All new people are just variables, stand-ins for each other, it doesn't matter who they are or how you treat them."

"That sounds like a recipe for unhappiness."

"Like you're so happy, Rolfe. Hope you don't get murdered in your sleep. Good night. Up yours."

"Where do you think Smith is?"

"Also up yours, I would guess."

Pocahontas

Dear person who by reading these words will know me deeply and truly,
Hi, I've had another interesting day! I gathered wild rice and acorns in the
morning. Just roasted and ate a turtle for dinner, it was yummy! The sky is
now the color of a day-old bruise. I have a tumult in my ovaries. That's what
our family doctor, Sidney Feingold, says: "You have a tumult in your
ovaries." He's a funny man, our family doctor, not funny-laughing but
funny-sighing, he's like a figure in a bad painting who wishes it was in a
better painting. I'd like to tell you all about our family doctor but there are
other things I need to tell you first, about my ovaries, and again I face the
problem of the delicious slowness of English. In the supersonic tongue of
my mentally agile people you'd already know about our family doctor and
about my ovaries, and Joe, and Stickboy, and my desires, and the sexual
mores of this town. If I were writing to you in my people's language that
moves faster than time itself, you'd know about things that haven't happened
yet.

"You have a tumult in your ovaries" is another way of saying I'm nineteen
and don't have my period yet.

> Blood oh blood oh careless blood
> Come flooding down me if you would

That's a rough translation of a song girls in my town sing while skipping
rope. You can't get married till you bleed in these parts. Not that I'm in a

rush to get married but I am in a rush to fuck. I'm nineteen and god I'd really like to fuck someone. I *could* fuck someone—premenstrual, unmarried—if I didn't mind being shunned, but, being the chief's only and favorite girl, I'd mind being shunned more than I mind not fucking, at least for now. If I were shunned I'd have to leave this town that's surrounded for hundreds of miles on all sides by forests, rapists, murderers, thieves, brokedown highways and quondam strip malls, mutant beasts whose skin is made of stuff that if it touches you, your own skin will turn black, crumble, and fall off your body.

And not only would it suck to be shunned, but the chief's daughter's recalcitrant ovaries are delaying a potentially important political alliance. You see I've got this other, dad-approved suitor named Joe. Stickboy is weak, Joe is strong. Oh Stickboy. When I think of Stickboy a sweet sadness fills my belly and spreads out like a light invisible gas inside me. I'd gladly fuck Stickboy. We'd be like two clouds who slowly collide. We'd burst and rain on the earth.

To appease Dad, I take walks with Joe a few times a week. Joe is heroic and, like I said, strong, if you like that kind of thing, ugh! "How are you?" he usually starts our walks off with. There are a hundred ways to say "How are you?" in the language of my empathetic people, and the way he chooses literally means "How is your digestive tract?" but everyone knows it really means "What is the status of your reproductive system since last I saw you?"

"From the nutritious lining of my womb / To the wallpaper of your baby's room," I chant at him, and slap his face hard and run a circle around him. At the start of my walks with Joe, I treat him as I treat the other pompous men I know: with insouciance and aggression. I say things I hope will upset him, I don't listen, I wander off, I interrupt him, I slap him and spit at him and knee him in the groin. But after ten minutes of walking with Joe I give up; most of what I know about the world and what's good about myself retreats deep into the interior, far from the surface of my body, so far in I can't see it or feel it; I don't hear from it for hours, sometimes days, and I begin to doubt it's still alive. Sure, I'm the irreverent scamp, "Pocahontas," and I'm the girl with the secret, killer name, but I and all the girls of my town were also given an inaudible name at birth, a synonym for *girl*, really, "she who'll be shunned if she fucks before she bleeds." So there you are: my inaudible name, my corresponding silence.

I have a recurring dream in which everyone I know is gathered in the town square, all their heads craned back. They are looking at two small, delicate ruby earrings, my ovaries, dangling from the top of a thirty-foot-tall white pole. Down the side of the pole the word EXPECTANCY is written in enormous letters with menstrual blood. Well, really, I've never had that dream. But I feel like I could.

I took a walk with Joe today, in case you couldn't tell by the gloom that pervades this letter to you! He didn't even walk me through the woods, he walked me around town, in plain view of all the women out in front of their n-shaped houses making stews or baskets or sewing winter clothes or shaving the right side of their men's heads.

On our walk, Joe kept putting me on his left side, and I kept moving to his right. The women in the lives of the men of my town shave the right side of their men's heads so their hair won't interfere with the shooting of their arrows. The hair on the left side of the men's heads grows long. Some men have their women braid trophies into their hair. Joe gets his mom to. His latest is the desiccated hand of a guy from a town a few miles up the road, a guy I dated when I was thirteen which makes it extra creepy and sad. So I tried to walk on Joe's right side, which affords a perfect view of Joe's soft, tawny ear wax, black scalp stubble, and pale, flaky scalp skin—gross but not as gross as that guy's hand—but Joe, strong, agile, quick, maneuvered me repeatedly to his left.

"The look on his face when I killed him was a shame," he said, apropos of the hand in his hair. "I've trained for twenty years so that if I should be in a position where I'm about to be killed by my enemy—and I'm not saying that would happen I'm just saying *if*—I wouldn't cry and beg. I've had nightmares since that raid though. *Damn* it, why do you keep moving to that side? Get over here—ow! Cut that out. My point being by the time a man turns twenty, he should be in control of his own face."

"Which do you prefer," I asked, "the beauty of inflections or the beauty of innuendoes? The blackbird singing, or just after?"

"What? You're changing the subject."

"Which do you prefer, steel or intimation?"

"Well I've been having these nightmares about killing that guy, only in the nightmares I look down at his face, which is full of tears and snot and fear, and my stomach goes all queasy cuz it's not his face, it's mine! What do you think that means? Never mind, I don't want to know. I'm going hunting with your dad tomorrow, so that's cool. Did I tell you what he said to me after I killed that guy?"

And that's when I disappeared into myself, stopped trying to change the subject or kick him or maneuver to his right side so I wouldn't have the dead hand in my face. I continued to be unhappy but did nothing about it. To know and not to act is not to know.

Want to know something awful? I'd like to fuck Joe. His body's tall and hard like a big erect penis. I want to throw it down on the ground and climb on it and go at it. That's disgusting, I know, the worst, so wrong, and yet the part of me that wants to fuck is not a student of ethics. I'd fuck Stickboy, I'd fuck Joe, I'd fuck a dozen other guys in town. My dad'd be pretty bummed if he found this diary. That's why I write it out in this corn shack in the middle of this cornfield under the twilit sky that looks like a day-old bruise on the thigh of a woman whose body is five hundred times bigger than the world. I write it all down on this wireless device, keep no copy, send it off to the ether, from whence it goes directly to your mind.

Now the sky is black. I like to be out in a cornfield under the black sky, invisible to everyone I know. This place and time let me come back to myself after fleeing on a walk with Joe. Here I am! There I are! I hug myself and give myself a long, soft, gentle kiss, missed you, love you.

Johnny Rolfe

Dear air:

That night I dreamed a dog lay in the road at the edge of a wood. The road was like the real road this bus is rolling down: hot, bright, cracked, dry, dead. The wood the dog lay at the edge of was soft, green, dark, and smelled good. The dog lay half in each world, its head and upper self in ours, the rest in the dark wood. We walked toward it, a few of my bus brothers and I. It looked at us. Its eyes were clear, its tail wagged, a healthy, happy-looking dog, but something was wrong. Someone's ill health or bad luck lurked in the dream. A few men walked toward us from beyond the dog's tail, inside the shadows of the wood. They were forms more than men. Their intentions weren't clear, though they didn't seem to mean us harm. Then came a light, high whine, from the dog, I guessed, but not from his mouth, which was closed. Then came my first glimpse of the faces of the men from the other world. They seemed eager, though eager for what I did not know. The rhythmic insistence of the light, high whine that came from inside the dog seemed to amplify the feeling that produced the look of what I thought was eagerness on the faces of these men who, I realized, in the dream, came from where our bus was taking us. We gathered round the dog, and then I saw it, the source of the light, high whine: the dog's slick and bright pink penis, standing up from its lower thorax, hard and gorged with blood. As if sated, or drunk, the dog smiled, and from the slender hole at the tip of its cock came the gooey wet pups, about an inch apiece, one after another, ten seconds apart, eyes closed, two, three, four, five, six pups, seven pups, eight, ten, thirteen, a small, blind army of baby dogs. All the faces looked bewildered now. The weapons all came out at once, as if we all had guessed we'd have to kill someone to exit from this dream alive. I came up into waking life in time to see red-haired Jack Smith, a gash on his head, drag his whiny-wheeled red wagon down the wide aisle of the bus.

The wagon was loaded with bottles of booze. Smith stopped in front of my bunk. The new, wide, red, vertical scooped-out area of his forehead was level with my eyes. It's poignant to see a fresh wound in the head of someone you're beginning to care about. My heart went out to the wound and the stoic face of Smith below it, over which blood slid not alarmingly but steadily, and mixed with the coarse red hair of his beard.

"The trade was not made under the best conditions and I didn't get exactly what I wanted," he whispered. The sun was not yet up and most of the men were still asleep, though I saw our driver, Chris Newport, ease his wide girth out of his bunk at the front of the bus. "I'd have preferred food, water, tools, knives, guns, and, you know, *fuel*. No one wants what we have. Whose idea was it to bring jewels and gadgets?"

"No one's idea."

"You get laughed at when you bring bracelets and walkie-talkies to a trading post around here, and then you get punched, and then you get stabbed—at least you get one guy stabbing your forehead and you don't want to hurt him too bad but you do have to make an example of him by hitting him hard with the sharp edge of the walkie-talkie you happen to have in your hand because you'd just been trying to show his friends how sleek and effective it was so they would give you food or fuel or guns, but they weren't buying it, so you end up hitting *this* guy with it till he's out and then you hit him some more so at least his friends who don't want your walkie-talkie or your pearl drop earrings and are annoyed enough to kill you for showing up with nothing better will sit back for a minute and think about what to do next so you have time to lift the gun off the guy you've smashed and point it at his friends and kind of ease a wagonful of their booze out the door of their sad little concrete kiosk and on down the road. Like I said I'd've rather had water but I can see where booze could be a language I could talk to these guys in, but a language I *don't* want to say anything to them in yet is this." From his belt he pulled out the pistol he'd taken from the gentleman and threw it on my stomach. "You hold onto that and just remember once you start talking with it you may be committing yourself to *parlez-vous* twenty-four-seven, *vingt-quatre-sept* if you get my meaning."

I was about to object to the gun on the top of my shirt when the first few bullets hit the back window of the bus. As our friends woke up, Chris Newport ignited the engine and the bus began to groan down the road, or what was left of the road. Bullets continued to hit the bullet-resistant back window while angry men rode the door and tried to break it down. Soon they fell off, and a plume of exhaust enveloped our pursuers, and the bus eluded them while they continued to express their frustration by shouting and firing their guns.

Moments later two big men—an army twice the size of Smith's—appeared on either side of him and grabbed his arms. I don't know their names. They're among the fifty percent of men on this trip in the Early Release Convict Program, two tall muscle men in white underwear with no meanness in their faces, just tired and dutiful stares, big men doing a skilled job—put the cuffs on Smith's thick wrists, the ordinary business of physical force and restraint.

Smith did not resist. A man named John Ratcliffe, who, like John Martin, belonged to the executive class, stood up from his bunk fully clothed and told Newport to stop the bus. "I'm placing Jack Smith under arrest for bringing unapproved contraband on board."

"I'm not stopping this shit with a bunch of guys back there ready to kill us. I put thirty miles between us and the guys with the guns before I even think of stopping."

"Fuck you," Ratcliffe said, the universal epithet of impotence. His plum-colored blood ascended his peach face from neck to hairline. Ratcliffe is a soft and petulant man. He's not old, but the skin of his face has already begun to loosen from the bone in preparation for the kind of oldness it is his ambition to acquire—the one that comes with a cook, a valet, a bodyguard, and well-defended water, food, and fuel supplies. His mother being the concubine of the Manhattan Company's CEO, he's a contender for succession, despite his lack of skill at anything.

I watched Ratcliffe scan the bus to see whom he might call on to outrank Newport. His eyes brushed past John Martin, whose knee I'd undone. I saw Martin give Ratcliffe a *not-now* headshake that bespoke an alliance I hadn't known about, just as I hadn't known Ratcliffe controlled Jack Smith's under-wear-wearing jailers. I also didn't see anyone object to Smith's arrest, a passivity that may not have been engineered by anyone, though it can also happen on this bus—and elsewhere—that man wakes man in the night and offers him something he wants or can't say no to: food, drugs, strength, will, loyalty, friendship, threat, sex. The political landscape of the bus is as volatile as the physical landscape of the town we saw swallow its tallest building a few days ago, an event I described in a previous entry in this venue, which you may not remember since you don't exist.

It has been our custom in the morning to throw open the windows and deboard, to let oxygen and smoky earth-scent replace the air of this close space that is dense with the smell of men who eat bad food and don't bathe. But now, gunmen behind us, we rode on in the thick stink through the gloom of a damp day. Smith stood stock still in the aisle, as did the men who'd cuffed him and continued to pin his arms. Most men stayed in their bunks and dreamed or did nothing. A few sat in chairs and ate gruel. No one talked.

Newport stopped after noon. We got off and stood beneath a semi-tent of trees that didn't quite keep the stinging rain off our necks while the two big boys brought Smith to the cargo trailer attached to the back of the bus by a steel armature. It surprised me that Smith didn't fight but I assume his quiescence was strategic. He and I exchanged a wordless set of looks in which I asked if I should try to free him with the gun—the only firearm on the bus, as far as I know—and he said no, thank Christ, so he was set down on a hard chair inside the trailer, his legs shackled to its, his hands still cuffed behind him. His big wagon of bottles of booze was also placed in the crammed trailer, also shackled. We reboarded and rode on. Over the course of this day I've made my first ally and he's been imprisoned.

Pocahontas

Dear special person out there getting to know me:
Nothing much "happened" today, so I guess here for your delectation is a typical day in the life of Pocahontas aka Not Telling Or You'll Die.

I'm out in the cornfield again. It's really late, way past midnight. Air's pretty cold. I've got a blanket but I'm shivering enough that my fingers hit the wrong keys on this tiny thing and I have to go back and erase the words I got wrong and re-type them. I live to shiver, it makes me feel so alive! No I'm just kidding. I said "It makes me feel so alive!" for a goof because I think it's so dumb when people say that something that feels bad makes them feel alive. "I like stubbing my toe because it makes me feel so alive!" "Please punch me in the face because it makes me feel alive!" "Joe, walk me around the town with your dead hand in my face and silence me with your long, aggressive, boring monologues because of how alive it makes me feel!"

I tell you this because I feel like I can be honest with you and because I feel like if I were to lie or dissemble in English you would know right away because every English sentence goes by so slowly that you have all this time to examine it and decide if it's true. I used to always speak my mind in my language too but that's getting harder the older I get. I guess holding your tongue is kind of built into my language what with that business of secret names and that other business of being a girl. So anyway I'm going through this real confused period (but not *period* period—if I were going through *that* I wouldn't be here writing to you now, I'd be under Joe, who'd be driving down into me like a madman, what fun! Can't wait! Woo-hoo! Just kidding!)

No but here's why I like to shiver: goosebumps. I stick my arm outside the blanket and my arm goes from calm lake to choppy sea. To me that means you can become different very fast. So whenever I feel stuck in my life or myself, I try to shiver or remember shivering.

Everyone in town is asleep now but me, out here in this little shack on stilts where the cornfield meets the world, my own special private place at night. Oh, I know something that happened today. I was in the pantry alone in the late afternoon, separating the skin of a squirrel from its meat for a squirrel custard for the big pre-hunt banquet tomorrow night, which I will tell you more about later, when who should walk in but the Big Cheese or Chief, my father. "Daddy!" I said, and flung my arms around his neck. Though we're both too old for it, he encircled my upper arms with his massive hands and swung me around the pantry. My feet swept three skinned squirrels to the pantry's dirt floor. "Daddy, precious, could you do your Pocahontas a favor and fill the squirrel-rinsing bucket with fresh water?" He gave me a look that said, "I'm the commander in chief of an army of five hundred men." I gave him a look that said, "I know, but it'd be really sweet if you would, it'd make me feel special." He gave me a look that said, "It's already a compromise for me to visit you in a pantry." I gave him a look that said, "Pretty, pretty please?" He filled the bucket. I rinsed the squirrels. He said, "How are you?" I told you there are a million ways to say *How are you?* in the phatic language of my people, and yet my father chose your basic bland *How are you?* to signal he wasn't there to put pressure on my ovaries, though why he *was* there I didn't know, and still don't.

"I'm good," I said. "How are you?"

"I'm good." You're probably going, "Why's she telling us they said how are you I'm good to each other?" but you have to understand how every little thing my dad does is always at least a little bit awesome, this enormous guy, king of all he looks at, Dad, so much more different from the air that surrounds him than are most people, who walk down the street and allow the air that's in front of them to become them, even as the air in back of them ceases to be them. My dad is so not the air; it parts for him. Whatever he is standing near—sky, trees, houses, people—seems to organize itself in space around his body.

"Well, I'm maybe not so good," he said.

My dad is not so good! Remember just now when I said how enormous my dad is? Well sometimes he's so enormous that it's like I'm inside him, which means that when he's not so good, I'm not so good. "What's the matter?"

"I'm tired, I'm tired, I'm tired of the hunt," said Dad. "Can it all amount to something good?"

"It could."

"Are you answering me in rhyme now?"

"Are you really asking me the question?"

"Yes. I don't know. No. I'm tired. Another hunt. More running, throwing, shooting, stabbing, carrying, running."

"Why don't you ride a bike instead of running?"

"I'm *emotionally* tired, is what I meant. Something bad is going to happen. Not on this hunt, maybe, but soon. We should be saving our strength for what's coming but we can't, we have to go on the hunt. The hunt is inevitable. What will follow the hunt is inevitable. Our fatigue and unpreparedness for what follows the hunt are inevitable. We are free to choose what to do, and our freedom is real, and our destiny is open and free, and each decision we make is inevitable."

"Want a neck massage?" I went to my dad and stood on a stool beside him and massaged his giant, hard neck, which was like massaging a cliff. "You smell sweet, like lavender," I said.

"You smell like dead squirrel meat," he said.

My dad's chief advisor, Dr. Sidney Feingold, the one who I know you remember I told you said I have a tumult in my ovaries, and reminds me of a guy in a bad painting who wants to be in a better painting—that guy—entered the pantry.

"Lots of big important men in the pantry now," I said.

He winked at me in a somewhat creepy but mostly avuncular way, and said to my dad, "Time to meet with Frank and Joe."

"Thank you for listening," my dad said to me.

"Dad," I said soberly.

"Yes?"

"I'd like to change my name to Tiffany."

He laughed. It must be hard to have fun when you're commander in chief of an army that kills lots of people. "Sing me a song," he said.

"Oh powerful Powhatan, I'm sad to see you sad. / You'll always be my daddy, you'll always be my dad."

"Bye."

"Bye."

Do great and powerful men where you're from say they're sad and use words like *emotionally* only when talking to women? I mean I love my dad and everything but what was that visit to the pantry about, anyway? What did he mean to tell me? Does he think I'm a receptacle for his delicate girly feelings? I ain't no receptacle.

Johnny Rolfe

Hello again, in a sense—

In my mind I watch each word of this hurtle upward, bounce off one of earth's half-atrophied prosthetic moons, fall back down, hit my crown, and break into its constituent letters, which slide down my neck and arms, through the bus floor, and are crushed by its tank treads into the earth, where each then merges with the genetic material of the single-celled organisms those pre-annihilation Cassandras warned would be earth's sole post-annihilation forms of life.

There is a window at the front of the supply trailer behind the bus, made, I think, for folks like us who like to see their stuff while hauling it from place to place, and a window at the bus's back, so people on the bus who wanted to could keep an eye on the air that touched the window that touched the air that touched the window that touched the air that touched the redoubtable body of Jack Smith, shackled to a chair, and his liquor, trapped in glass. The two underwear-wearing men who'd grabbed Smith sat in the back seat facing the trailer, erect in their bespoke suits of taut muscle, their unrelenting vigil on Smith controlled by what form of payment the soft and petulant Ratcliffe had convinced them they'd receive. How, then, did Smith do it? How'd he undo the chains, open a bottle of booze, take a nip, close it, arrange the boxes in the trailer to resemble a bar, find glasses in the boxes, arrange them on the "bar" in a come-hither style, return to the hard chair he'd been chained to, and put his feet up to mimic what a bartender might look like? Half the bus was at that back window by the time Smith was recumbent.

"Who would it hurt to have a drink?" someone said.

The mass of purple blood billowed up inside the silky face of Jack Smith's keeper, the mean, ambitious, talentless John Ratcliffe, when one after another of my travel companions shouted, "I'm thirsty!" and, "I need a stiff one!" and, "It's whiskey o'clock!" Chris Newport didn't stop the bus, at least not at first. Ratcliffe was grateful to him for that, though I doubt Chris drove to please Ratcliffe. I know nothing of Chris but that he's older than the rest of us, lost an arm in a fight, and has a wife who makes up for the arm—such at least is my idealized view of wedlock. Another thing I know about him now: he has a thing for young and handsome men. I know because we have a man like that aboard our bus, a fun and tireless piece of ass, or so I've heard: Happy Lohengrin, whom I've seen exert his will as guile to get his way. So once he sat down side-saddle on Chris's lap while he drove, and explained to him roughly how much fun a drink would be, Chris hit the brakes and we got out. The two big men who'd shackled Smith turned to Ratcliffe, cocked their heads, and shrugged, a three-second ballet of abdication that Ratcliffe joined by empurpling from sole to crown. And so seems to go the trip and the world: one man's relief's another's pain.

We drank, sang, and wept. The driver and his friend went off and fucked. We slept and drank and slept. Ratcliffe made the muscle men shackle Smith back up. We started on our way.

In the best of times, if there is such a thing, a certain kind of man will not be content with a drunk that lasts a day or two. In times like these, if there are times like these, no one will be content with anything. Chris Newport, for one, was not content to let his shame remain within his breast, but had to distribute it over the population of the bus, which he did by driving as fast as he could, without letup, while the men yelled at him to stop for another drink. And red-haired Jack Smith was not content to stay bound a second time, nor was he content not to put on a second show for the crowd of men at the back of the bus, in which he drank a double shot of rotgut and pantomimed contentment by laughing, smiling, hugging himself, swaying side to side, and opening his mouth in the shape of the word "Ahh." And one man was not content to let a moving bus not let him reach the booze of which he'd not yet had enough.

That man was Happy Lohengrin, who'd used and cast off Chris—though, a ventriloquist of agency, he made Chris feel *he'd* done the casting off. The back window being sealed, Happy slipped out the port side and onto the bus's warm metal roof. He climbed down the back and tightroped along the steel armature by which we were hitched to what had become the bar car. When he was midway across, Chris—a man whose great, grizzled, one-armed body easily converted shame to rage—braked hard. Happy lost his balance, and would have plunged beneath the bar car's wheels had he not dived for and caught a rope hanging from the bus's stern. The men who watched made a noise in awe of his valor and skill.

Happy climbed to the roof of the bar car. Smith swung open the door at its back. Happy, supple as quicksilver, slid off the roof and into the arms of red-haired Smith, whom he tried to french. Smith shoved him away, wiped his mouth with his sleeve, cocked his head at Happy, and shook a shame-on-you finger at him. Happy threw his head back and laughed, Smith poured, they clinked and downed their shots, Smith poured, they clinked and drank again, Happy tried to cuddle Smith, Smith shoved him away, they drank and laughed again, the two performers angling toward the window that framed them and was framed by our window, which in turn was framed by our eyes.

There followed several days on which Chris drove the bus in a nonstop snit from dawn to dusk and a man who wanted a drink in that time had to take the Happy route out the port, over the roof, down the stern, across the armature, over the trailer, and into Smith's waiting arms. Chris begrudged this silently, Ratcliffe did so noisily, Smith enjoyed it cannily; the other men were men, who'll slake their simple thirst by drastic means if nothing else will do.

A man called Herb went over, or tried. He was called Herb for the hydroponic crop of weed he grew and sold in jail, being another of the early-release convicts who constitute half the population of the bus. While we'll be paid—if we survive—in water, food, and fuel, the convicts, for the trouble of taking this trip, receive the trouble of taking this trip. Nor has it been lost on Herb and his mates that this bus differs from jail only insofar as it's more crowded and volatile, smells worse, and what surrounds it makes most of what goes on in jail look like a walk in a field of poppies. Herb climbed to the roof, down the stern, and was crossing the fast-moving space between bus and bar car when Chris braked for a crack in a road that's more crack than road. Herb dove for the rope Happy had dived for, missed, and was crushed beneath the bar car's tires.

If you're past the age of two these days you've seen somebody die before his time, if time may be said to belong to the living. Herb, unlike Happy, or Smith, had no attributes, physical, mental, sexual, or otherwise that any of us felt we needed, so his death on his quest for a drink met with little interest. Still, none of us liked removing from the trailer's tires and wheel wells the bits of Herb we'd all have rather seen remain a part of Herb, nor did we enjoy interring as much of him as we could manage in the roadside's bone-dry dirt that was so obdurate against our efforts to make a Herb-shaped hole in it. We made an epitaph for him, and since we didn't know his surname we gave him one that did for his current incarnation what his first name had done for the previous: HERE LIES HERB MANGOLD, WHO WANTED A DRINK.

Pocahontas

Dear fellow human:

On this evening's menu is me telling you about the pre-hunt pep rally that just happened and that always happens around a fire in the center of town on the night before all the guys in town—most of the guys in town—the popular guys in town—the physically strong guys in town—the aggressive guys in town—the normal guys in town go on the hunt.

The enormous fire gets built by the women, and many excellent dishes of food get prepared by the women, and the sun goes down, and everyone in town sits on the ground in a haphazard circle just beyond a dozen ceremonial state-sponsored log sculptures that surround the fire. The sculptures are about eight feet high and made of unsculpted logs except at the top, where a hunting-type face has been carved. Each face is different from the others and means something, since people here don't only say things in words, we say things in faces, too, and now I will translate each log sculpture from face language into English. 1. The one with meanly slanted brows, nose so sharp you'd cut your eyeballs just to look at it, thin lips, sharp teeth, and wicked smile is the sculpture of *vengeance.* 2. The one with a face lax and devoid of expression, eyes open wide, nostrils unflared, lips closed and sensual (our current state-sponsored sculptor-in-residence knows that the mouth is a place on the human body where sex is both longed for and spoken of and I, who am nineteen and have not yet had my period, know this too) is the sculpture of *marksmanship.* 3. The one with semi-closed eyelids, red flared nostrils, parted lips, scratches on its flushed face, and tousled hair damp with perspiration is the sculpture of *just made love to the wife of my enemy in the dirt against her will while her husband lay freshly murdered not ten feet away.* I'm probably editorializing on that one because of what happened to Stickboy at the pre-hunt banquet earlier tonight that I'm about to describe as I sit here alone in this cornfield's small thatched shack on stilts. Anyway I'm sick of log sculpture descriptions, so in the waning light of the dusk that precedes the day of the hunt, the people of my town gathered in small groups, laid their hempen pallets on the ground, and ate their turtle stews. There was a feeling of boisterousness in the air, while beneath it in the ground there was a feeling of receptivity to human blood. Boisterousness, receptivity, doom of birth, dessert was served, women bussed the plates. Everyone who was not a wise old man or a strong young man—women, girls, sick people, weak people, fools— gathered round the logs, whereupon the huntsmen rushed in shouting toward the fire.

Three old men hit their drums each in a different rhythmic pattern. The hunters, inside the ring of logs, across the fire from the drummers, danced, arms on one another's shoulders. They kicked their legs up high: all those bare, muscular, oiled legs pumping up and down in a long arc in the firelit night like a row of synchronized penises, a machine made for the frequent and varied sexual initiation of an eager novice.

The hunters stepped back and formed a semicircle along the inner perimeter of the logs, stopped dancing, clapped and swayed. The men then stepped forth one at a time, did a brief solo dance, and answered a question posed, as in olden times, or so they'd like to think, by the old men. First up was my buddy Joe, who, if a man could dance and have a heart attack and an orgasm all at the same time, would resemble that man.

"Who are you?"

"I am Joe. The day I was born a dark cloud split in two and the sun shone between. Seven mothers gave birth that day and all their children died but me."

Joe then recounted the salient—i.e., valorous—i.e., violent—acts of his life, which I'm too bored by to duplicate here. Vigorous applause. Next warrior, Frank, friend and co-conspirator of Joe, the brains of the Joe-and- Frank operation—not a hard-won accomplishment—shorter and more sinewy, does not stomp the rhythm of the drums into the dust, as Joe does, but wedges himself between the beats with his head and shoulders and hips, comes up into the rhythm from beneath it as if tunneling up into water from beneath the ocean floor.

"Who are you?"

"I am Frank. When I was born, lightning hit my house, which burst into flame," etcetera, and then all the other hunting guys went, and then my sweet and thin friend Stickboy jumped up and did his bobbleheaded crazy-leg dance that makes him look as if his bones are long chains of paperclips, and though no one asked him, he said, "I am Stickboy, also known as Poor Common Bill, Colicky Baby Bill, Bill with the Footspeed of a Cock, Bill with the Cock of a Gnat, Depressed Bill, Weakened Bill—"

"Get him out of there!"

"When I was born, a cur whimpered and curled up in the corner to sleep. I was one of the six babies to die the day Joe was born. When I was fifteen a spider wove a web of cares in me. We will be defeated on the hunt and I will cower."

Joe and Frank lifted Stickboy by the arms and threw him out of the circle. The drumming increased in volume and speed. The people of my town lined up in two rows that faced each other. Each warrior, starting with Joe, ran wailing down the line. When Joe passed Stickboy, who stood in the line, he hawked and let fly a thick wad of spit in his face. Frank was next, and spat on Stickboy too. No one made a move to stop them, not even my dad. When the next man came down the line and was about to spit on Stickboy, I leapt up and stood between them. The man looked at me, and looked at Stickboy, and looked over at my dad, who watched all this from his fancy chair, and after a long pause gave his head a little shake as if to say, "Don't spit on him," so off went the guy, and all the other guys, one by one; none stopped to spit on my friend.

I know I put my dad in the awkward position of having to defend Stickboy and me in front of the whole town, but if a girl's called Pocahontas you just got to expect certain shit to happen.

As for Stickboy's performance being first allowed, then criticized in the unequivocal language of spittle: I suppose that is our town government's way of regulating dissent. Our town government is a meritocracy in which

33

one important form of merit is who you were conceived by, and other forms include success in battle and compliance with the sanctified rites of official power. Merits that accrue no political capital include satirizing the sanctified rites of official power, loving well, being humble, giving expression to useless but beautiful thoughts. I wonder if there's a town on earth where such acts and qualities confer authority on one who performs or possesses them.

Johnny Rolfe

To You, to whom I tell this, if indeed there is a You to tell, an I to do the telling, a This to tell about, and a Telling to bring You, I, and This together in the mystic wedding of communication:

After we buried the bottles of booze with the Mangold body in hopes he'd get the drink in death he could not have in life, Ratcliffe, the would-be executive, made the two muscle men beat Smith's face and ribs and shackle him again. Several days have passed since then, and many things have happened, most of which I won't describe because I'm tired and don't feel like it. *I'm tired and don't feel like it* has itself become a tired phrase in my life, it can keep its eyelids up hardly better than I.

Newport stopped the bus today and said we'd soon arrive. Shall I describe the dread I felt when hearing this? I shall not; dreads these days are a dime a dozen, a dozen a day. To describe it is to have it twice; to endure it once is quite enough. We all, except for Smith, got off the bus. Chris, the driver, brought out the black box that contained the names of our board of directors and president, that is, the five men who would govern the rest of us, or so it was supposed to go. He blushed and said he'd forgotten the combination to the box's lock. The air was musty and cool. The ubiquitous greenish cloud or fog hovered above us, reducing the height of the sky and making all the world seem to be a low-domed arena built for the purpose of bloodsport.

Ratcliffe tried the box. Martin tried it. A few guys tried to wedge it open with knives, screwdrivers, hammers. The two big men, Bucky and Bill, their names turn out to be, took a crack at it with a crowbar. It was suggested Chris Newport run over the box with the bus. Newport said the bus's tank treads were designed to demolish any three-dimensional thing they rode over, that they would break the box and rip the paper in the box to shreds. It was then suggested the box be run over with just the bar car, on the grounds that if it alone was enough to break open the body of Mangold but not smash up his bones too bad, the box might break, the paper might be spared. So that was tried, and failed, and Chris, sensing the kind of impatience that precedes mutiny, ran the bus over the box, which broke open, a lot.

The four legible names were John Ratcliffe (President), Chris Newport, Father Richard Buck, and Jack Smith; the bus had chewed the fifth. Ratcliffe's first act as president was reluctantly to order Bucky and Bill to unshackle Smith. His second was to hold the chewed-up paper to the light and claim to see John Martin's name on it.

Smith, cracking the dried blood in his red beard with his fingers, stepped toward Ratcliffe and suggested that it was a bad idea for him to begin his tenure as president of this little group of guys out in the middle of nowhere by shoehorning his own guy onto the board with the ridiculous lie that he could somehow read his name on a piece of paper that had been violently sandwiched between a jagged stretch of road and however many tons of bus. Smith then put forward my name as board member five. "So let's all discuss this like gentlemen, Ratcliffe, and choose the fifth man the decent way, the fair way, the democratic way, via civil fucking discussion."

Ratcliffe's face bore the trace of a brief skirmish in his heart—or whichever body part ambition commandeers for its home office—between conciliation and force. The latter won. Ratcliffe sicced his two guys on Smith again. Six or so of us, bolstered by the shred of paper from the broken box, surrounded Bill and Bucky such that they'd have to dispense with us before they could get to Smith. Ratcliffe, purple billows ascending the flesh of his face, said "You *idiots*, I'll *ruin* you if you don't do what I tell you *now*." Bill and Bucky looked at the six hungry, exhausted guys surrounding them, looked back at Ratcliffe, shrugged, gave him the finger, stood down. And then I must have missed Ratcliffe's cue, but saw and heard the guns Martin and a half a dozen other guys produced, cocked, and aimed at the six of us who'd defied

Ratcliffe. I felt the hard tube of "my" gun along my thigh, and let it stay there. Apparently I'd been wrong about possessing the only firearm on the bus, and there's a fitting epitaph for me: APPARENTLY HE'D BEEN WRONG.

Martin, *it was then decided,* would be sworn in as the fifth man on the board, and was. Toward the end of the swearing in, I saw a bit of worrisome rustling in the high grasses we were standing near, but said nothing. As we readied to board the bus again, a raccoon leapt from the field and attached itself to the ear of John Martin, who, you may recall, if you exist, was already cut in the head by Smith and inconvenienced in the knee by me. Since I was nearest him, I removed my bodkin from my sock and stabbed the coon. It died, and was then pried, with some difficulty, from the ear, a piece of which it had succeeded in disconnecting from his head with its teeth. Martin seemed saddened. I should have tried harder not to laugh.

On the bus, Smith dressed Martin's wound. Later, an hour ago, I told Smith he's a good man.

"What makes you say that?"

"You bandaged Martin."

"So? If I hadn't, someone else would have."

"But you did, and not for expediency but because it was the right thing to do. That's the difference between you and Ratcliffe. That's why I don't like him."

"Who cares who you like and don't like? Not liking Ratcliffe is babyish and pointless. It accomplishes nothing. And you don't know him enough not to like him."

"Yes, I do."

"Bullshit. You use the same thimbleful of knowing on everyone and everything you see."

"Why the attack on me? What did I do?"

"Nothing."

Pocahontas

Dear fellow grown-up:

My life has undergone a drastic change that I can't wait to tell you about! On this cool spring day when all the men in town who hunt were gone, I sat in a shack in my favorite field extracting last night's corn from my teeth with a poplar toothpick and reveling in the company of my own animated thoughts when who should happen to wander by but our family physician and my father's chief advisor, Dr. Sidney Feingold, my uncle by habit if not by blood.

"Mind if I join you?"

"Yes."

He climbed into the shack on stilts and banged his head on a beam. "How do you—ow!—How do you—Do you see that raccoon over there?"

"No."

"How do you know it won't attack you?"

"Do you really want to know how I know or are you going to use my answer to evaluate my state of mind?"

"A man can't inquire about a girl's raccoon knowledge to make sure she's not going to get a toe bitten off while out here picking her teeth in the middle of a cornfield?"

"I've been coming here alone since I was five. Why the sudden concern?"

"I've always been concerned, just been shy about expressing it."

In the relative dark of the corn shack he looked at me with eyes half hooded by thick and heavy lids. I feel permeable when I'm with Uncle Sid, like without touching me he's bypassed the border of my hair and teeth and skin, he's used his eyes, which hide behind those lids, to pry open my soul. But I trust him. Want to know why? Because he's sad.

"Don't pretend to be stupid and harmless and avuncular," I said.

"Who's pretending?"

"I'll tell you something about yourself—"

"Okay."

"Shut up. I'll tell you something about yourself, and this evening when you're in your easy chair *chez toi* enjoying a little pipe of sweet tobacco and busthead, and Aunt Charlene or one of your nubile servant girls is massaging your feet, or whatever type of total catering to Feingold goes on *chez* Feingold, you can idly reflect on how my description of you earlier today out there in the cornfield with the toothpick bobbling at the edge of my mouth was really more of a reflection on my own mental state than on anything having to do with you."

"Go ahead."

"Shut up. See, I think you were very ambitious when you were young. You had good leg speed and you were a good hand-to-hand fighter and an above-average bowman, but you figured out early on that your physical skills, good as they were, were not commensurate with your ambition, and you also found, to your chagrin, perhaps, that you really didn't like fighting that much, you didn't like being in that position where if you don't immediately kill an opponent you've rendered helpless, you may have to spend the next six hours suffering the humiliation and unimaginable agony of being tied to two trees while watching chicks from a town up the road scrape all your skin off with sharpened mussel shells. But you also noticed that you had a keen intellect, not only in terms of sucking up book learning and making sense of it and developing your own original ideas that didn't come from any book, but also in terms of being able to read people as well as you read books, to perform the same operations in your people-reading as in your book-reading, namely, to read into the person, read beyond the person, know things about the person that the person not only does not tell you but that everything about the person's seemingly straightforward presentation of herself to the world and to herself is very elaborately trying to cover up. So there you are, there's young, ambitious Sidney Feingold, strong young Sidney Feingold back when he had a full head of lustrous brown hair, with his pretty good physical skill and his very good scholastic skill and his *singular* skill at seeing through the shell of the person not just to the person's intentions but to all the wishes and fears and memories and stray thoughts and unfelt feelings that inform the person's intentions without the person even knowing they're informing them, and I think—you know what I think?—shut up—I think you got so turned on by your own skills and your own ambition that you did the most obvious and stupid thing with them and didn't even stop to consider what else you might have done with them. Now don't even—I know what you want to know, you want to know what I think you might have done with your skills and ambitions besides use them stupidly to become what you are today, and the answer is nothing, have you ever thought of that one? Maybe doing nothing with your wondrous abilities except having them and reveling in their intrinsic beauty and taking them out for long, leisurely, peaceful, pointless frolics in the forests and meadows each day would've been the most worthwhile thing. The moment you discovered your excellent intellect is the moment you betrayed it, began monstrously to deform it, and here's another thing I think. I think at a certain point, I don't know when, exactly, not long ago, I suspect, you woke up to the fact of the wholesale betrayal of yourself by yourself, a treason against the self for which the penalty is death, and what's going to be really horrifyingly interesting is how you, the only person in all of Feingoldia authorized to do so, mete out the punishment."

"You seem angry."

"Really? What gave that away?"

"Do you really think that's an accurate description of me?"

"No."

"Then why'd you say it?"

"Because it's an accurate description of you."

"You're mad about last night."

"Duh."

"I do not think your description of me is accurate. I think it's an adolescent fantasy of how adults have ruined the world."

"Adults *have* ruined the world."

"What would you do differently?"

"I wouldn't jog up the street every month or so to kill, rape, kidnap, and pillage."

"That's not all we do."

"It's the worst thing you do and you do it often."

"And what would you recommend, sit around and wait to be killed, raped, kidnapped, and pillaged?"

"Are those the only two choices?"

"You'd be surprised."

"How about talking? How about economic and cultural exchange?"

"You know we do those things too."

"Badly."

I saw a nasty little movement in his face as if a bat had bit his cheek.

"Oh," I said. "I get it. *You're* the one who's angry at *me*. Why, because I stopped the guys from spitting on Stickboy?"

"Why did you?"

"He's my friend."

"And loyalty to your friend supercedes loyalty to your dad?"

"That depends. In cases where my dad so obviously has his head up his ass and my friend hasn't done anything wrong? Yes."

"Your friend disrupted and mocked a state occasion."

"The state shouldn't have such occasions."

"The state needs them to survive."

"Then the state shouldn't survive."

"Fine, the state shouldn't survive. What about your friends and family? Should they survive?"

"Is me making sure Stickboy doesn't get coated with too much of the saliva of my friends and family going to kill them?"

"Maybe."

"Do you not see how fucked that is? I was just protecting my friend."

"Social relations can be enormously complicated and sometimes require difficult sacrifices from individuals."

And then the strangers came to town. One minute I'm lounging carefree in the corn shack shooting the breeze with Sid on this and that topic, the next these guys roll down from the north in a massive golden armored freak machine, which five of them climbed down out of one by one looking and smelling, sorry to say, somewhat less nice than dog poop. The five of them stood blinking in the sun. Who else was in there? We didn't know. Here was us, young girl and old man alone in a field, confronted by a rolling petroleum-run thing the size of a blue whale, all the fighting men in town gone for days. We leaned back in the shadowed recess of our stilted shack, slid our hands back along its rough, uneven floor, and let them rest lightly on the bows and arrows all such shacks contain. We did not know what they meant to do, but we knew that in a half a minute we could put an arrow in an eye of each of the five, tumble out the shack's back hatch, and be lost among the tall stalks.

We waited. They stood blinded by the nothing that hung between the sun and their eyes. A gentle late-spring breeze carried their grim scent to our nostrils. Nearest us stood a rounded, petulant man with silken, purplish face; next to him, a little man who seemed mean, with tall forehead and part of one ear chewed by a coon, I'd guess; a mild-looking glasses-wearing man in a suit of black but for a square of white at his throat; a short fireplug with a thick red beard with bits of dried blood caked in it; the biggest guy, in under-wear, muscled, dumb, the requisite big dumb guy in the greeting party, not the guy you use your first arrow on.

More waiting. Silk-faced man raised a hand, palm toward us, and said, in (you're not going to believe this!) English, "Hello. Do you speak English?"

"NO!" I said.

Sid looked at me wide-eyed and whispered, "Let's not assume the foreigners will understand your bilingual sarcasm."

"Judging by the crudeness of them, I'd say they'll understand little."

The one with the silken face had a quick talk with his four boys and they all raised both hands to head height, palms toward us. Their fingers went up and down, like flowers quickly opening and closing. I think that meant they wanted us to think they bore no arms.

I stuck my scuffed bare foot into the sunlight beyond the shack door and, sole toward the strangers, mocked the movement of their fingers with my toes.

"Uh, do you speak *any* English?" Silky said.

I giggled. They heard me and seemed to relax. Sid and I exchanged *what the hell* glances, and slid down out of the corn shack to greet them. We've got a number of standard ceremonial greetings of strangers and the one we decided on was the Friendly Greeting with Understated Caveat. It's a synchronized step-to-the-right, step-to-the-right, slide, twirl, step-to-the-left, step-to-the-left, slide, twirl, arc-with-the-left-toe, arc-with-the-right-toe, I-fake-a-roundhouse-kick-to-Sid's-chin-and-he-blocks-it, vice versa, a few more like moves, and then we hugged each one of them—despite their stench—a warm embrace, quick weapons check, and initial assessment of each one's potential in hand-to-hand combat.

They looked confused. The short, stocky one, who not only had blood in his beard but looked as if he'd been punched in the face, whispered something to the silk-faced one, climbed into the vehicle, and climbed back down a minute later with a new, tall and willowy guy, dark-haired, the first one of them to be remotely handsome, though he had sallow skin, was bone-thin, and smelled like poop. And something was amiss about his face, as if fear and sadness had long done the work meant for seeing, hearing, smelling, tasting, and touching. I was surprised, then, at what he did next, watching Sid and me all the while. He put his arms over his head and swayed slowly from ankles to fingers like an oak tree in a strong wind. He fluttered from place to place on tiptoe. He became small and dense and round and seemed to float back along the hard-packed dirt. He balanced on his head and spun around, slowed himself by extending his arms, sped up by retracting them. He stood again, held his arms out, and went into a kind of my-hands-are-oak-leaves-shimmering-in-the-sunlight-near-a-fast-running-brook tableau. Then he hugged Sid Feingold. Then he hugged me, and when he did, something in me broke. It hurt like hell. I made a noise, a gasp or shout. I tried to comprehend what he'd done, where I was hurt, what part of my body he'd injured and how, but I couldn't localize the pain. And it wasn't pain. Sid had him by the throat. The guy raised up his arms, drew his elbows together, and jammed them down on Sid's wrists to make him break the grip on his neck. The guy kicked Sid in the chest. Sid fell down and came up with a knife in his hand. I rushed between them and told them to stop. The guy gave me a queer look, maybe something strange had happened in him too. A flicker passed across his face, the shadow of a seagull's wing, an escapee, perhaps, from the place in him where all the moods were jailed.

"How many more guys you got in your, um, thing?"

"Twenty-five."

"Tell 'em to come out."

Some signals passed among them and a grim bunch of guys descended from the thing.

Silken man said to me, "Do all of you here speak English?"

"No, just me," I said. "Come to town with us and we'll give y'all some stew and definitely a bath, you stink."

While Sid walked them to town the long way, I ran ahead and told my girlfriends of their arrival. We prepared for them.

Hospitality, as you may know, is an intoxication of the senses, so by the time the bedraggled foreigners arrived, bright damask cloths had been laid atop the folding tables in our town's central square; mosquito-repelling torches, soaked in mint and busthead paste, had been driven into the ground and lit; two man-sized vats of deer stew cooked on open fires; my nubile homegirls were oiled, scented, painted, polished, pomaded, and loosely wrapped in few thin skins. What man after a long, hard journey on a bus could take all this in and not feel his body's loveblood drawn down to his dick?

The men sat at tables and were served a big bowl of stew apiece, which they devoured, and were given a second, which they devoured. Most ate too fast, or weren't used to stew, and puked. The less couth among them puked in place, which signaled the end of the meal.

As is custom in my country, thank god, ovarian retardation kept me from joining in the next hospitable activity, the bathing of the strangers. So I watched from afar as the stinking men were disrobed by my galpals while their penises stood up straight in the cool moonlit air. Some girls carried the men's nasty clothes to the laundry house. Others led the men to large, open-air bathtubs. Clothes and men were shoved in vats of hot soapy water and held beneath its surface till the first bits of dirt, dried sweat, dried blood, and congealed grease broke apart and floated from their hosts. The girls scrubbed the men, rinsed them, helped them from their baths, dried them, oiled their naked skins, and slowly stroked their dicks until they came. Three men demurred from this capstone: the fat, old, one-armed, bearded one; the short red-haired one who'd been punched in the face; and, glad to say—not sure why—the one who broke that thing in me.

The foreign men, dazed, glazed, and amazed, were helped into fresh, shapeless hempen gowns and led to n-shaped houses, where we meant to let them sleep.

"No," the silk-faced man said. "You've been kind to us but we have to sleep somewhere fortified, company rules. We'll return in the morning for our clothes and we'll bring you gifts."

And so the men tiptoed off into the woods, crying out in pain when their bare and tender feet touched something sharp. We bid them adieu with jeers: "Smelly out-of-towners!" "Little-penis men who won't sleep over!" "Ejaculate and split, thanks a lot!" We didn't really mean it, just having fun as is our wont with men who spurned our offer of a bed.

Well, one more thing to tell you. Can you guess? I'm really sleepy now, I think I'm anemic. Now can you guess? So I came out here to my lonely little corn shack to contemplate and tell you all these things about my day, and I felt something itchy-tacky, you know, *down there*, in the tippy-top-of-the-thigh-type place, and I casually reached down to give a scratch, I withdrew my hand, found it wet and sticky, I looked at it, and the darkness of the corn-shack notwithstanding, there's no doubt but that's blood on my hand, so either I'm hemorrhaging to death through my pussy or—yes, beloved English speaker—I'm having my period! Which is also the word y'all use when you want to show you've come to the end of what you have to say, for now.

Johnny Rolfe

To nothing that is not there and the nothing that is:

The road dead-ended in a field. That was it. We'd arrived. The only thing worse than the journey is the destination. I looked out the window at the tall bulbous stalks we were surrounded by. Beyond them lay dark woods like the ones in my dream of the dog. The predatory sun devoured the field and had begun to eat my eyes, so I turned my head, bent down in my seat, pressed my knees into my eyes, and tried to let myself be soothed by the black behind my lids. I vaguely sensed the bus door open and the men who represented us step down to what awaited them. Maybe they'd be killed. I often think that death would bring relief but, fearing change, haven't sought it out.

I sat in the brown, foul air of our armored container while time passed on its hands and knees. Someone punched my shoulder. It was Smith. "We need you."

"Fuck off."

"Don't be a baby. You're the communications officer and we've got a communications situation. There's two people out there, a girl and an old guy, and they just did some kind of ceremonial greeting, and we haven't got squat, and this could be a make-or-break moment for the mission, you know, a greeting test, so get out there."

"I'm shy."

He grabbed me by the hair and lifted me. That was interesting. I got in a couple hard shots to his solar plexus before he grabbed my fist with his stubby fingers and squeezed it so hard tears came to my eyes.

"What do you want me to do?"

"Give them our ceremonial greeting."

"We don't have one."

"Make one up."

"Do they have weapons?"

"Don't know."

"This is idiotic."

"No one made you come on this trip. Now you're here. Greet them."

He still had ahold of my hair. I jammed my left heel down on his right foot as hard as I could. He released my hair and drove his fist into my throat. He was kind enough to wait till I could take a breath. We limped off the bus arm in arm.

The sunlight was killing. I felt faint. I breathed poorly and my throat hurt and my arm was sore and my hand was sore and my hair was sore. The sweet, hot smell of rotting vegetation made me want to puke. A girl and old man stood by a wooden shack on stilts. You don't see much wood or many trees where I come from. The man was lean and had a pointed face with semi-hooded eyes, like a buzzard's. The girl was spectacularly ugly. She was short and thin and of an unnaturally reddish hue. Her face was wide as it was long, with big, thick cheekbones and pockmarked skin. Her black hair came halfway down her arms in two dense, gobbed-up plaits that looked like a pair of large, dead rodents hung in the sun by their tails from the top of her head to cure their meat. The need to stare at her I felt as a force my eyes succumbed to while the rest of me looked on in dread. She laughed at me. Her teeth were yellow stubs. She had a smile that showed more gum than teeth, and the only part of her face less nice to look at than her teeth were her gums, which were soft, pulpy, red, and seemed designed to show us we were making a mistake. I closed my eyes and felt something hard and sharp—Jack Smith's finger—jab me in the ass. "Do a nice greeting dance," he said.

With this girl's teeth and gums in mind I crouched into a ball and made myself become a kind of dull and ugly tooth. I allowed my fingers to flutter up behind my back like waving dendrites. I was at a disadvantage for not having seen the dance the girl and man had done nor having ever seen or done a dance like this. I sensed I'd had a bad start by imitating a bad tooth.

I pondered what our greeting should represent about us and our intentions: that we were an open people eager to make friends; that we were pragmatic, tough, hard-headed, couldn't be provoked or taken advantage of or victimized or fooled; that our indomitability had not entailed a sacrifice of thorough self-knowledge, nor an unceasing awareness of and striving for the loftiest potentialities of the human spirit. Meantime I remained crouched like a bad tooth. With one eye open, I peered up at the ugly girl, who peered down at me with one eye open, laughing. I laughed too, which made my body shake. I still was in a lot of pain, and drenched in sweat. My body resisted my attempts to control it. I feared I'd puke or pee or crap. I tried to become an ice-cold mountain stream of clear water running over smoothed and rounded pebbles. I stretched out in the dirt at the feet of our potential hosts and let the unwilled trembling of my muscles make of me a continuous series of rushing waves, and wondered if I didn't look more like a beached and dying fish than the happy body of water it had stupidly leapt out of. I shook on the ground till I was exhausted. I knew I couldn't just lie there on the ground like a corpse because that, too, might send the wrong message. I stood and closed my eyes and gathered my strength. I felt myself swaying back and forth and nearly fell over several times. I opened my eyes and found myself standing an inch from the girl. Without meaning to, I touched her hair with my hands. The red hills and planes of her unappealing face were inches from my eyes; pockmarks troubled the landscape. I had entered the atmosphere of the body of this alien girl and discovered there a medley of unexpected smells from home—varnish, chocolate, gasoline, bubblegum. Her arms and neck were taut and scuffed and soft. I circled her in my arms and pulled her toward me. She screamed and I came. Then the old guy's surprisingly strong hands were around my sore neck and I broke his grip by slamming my elbows into his wrists. He pulled a knife. Jack stepped in and took the knife from him. The girl looked at me as if I'd just murdered her father.

Smith exhorted all of us to calm down. He gave the old man back his knife, removed a flask from his coat, and gave him a sip. The guy nodded his head in approval and whispered something to the girl, who then invited us to her town in oddly accented English, and issued this warning unaccompanied by words: she reached out to one of the man-high bulbous stalks that grew everywhere around us, broke it off, and held it up above her head; a small arrow, which had evidently been shot from a concealed location, seemed to materialize inside it.

Smith dragged the rest of the men down off the bus. The girl signaled us to walk behind her through the woods to the south of the field. I hadn't ever been in woods and didn't want to go in these today. Today I didn't want to do or be. A temporary hiatus from doing and being would have been my preferred way to spend the afternoon but you can't have everything—you can't have anything—and here was this peculiar-looking, smelly girl who'd made me come for the first time in a year, two years, five, ever, a savory blottoing of consciousness to be grateful for. The romance of being beckoned by her into a dark wood was not lost on me, so I followed her, as did my thirty companions.

She frolicked through the woods, running back and forth across the trail. She ducked behind trees and re-emerged. She shouted—in English, her own tongue, both, or gibberish I could not say. She came to me and whispered in my ear what sounded like, "When on my couch I lie in vacant or in pensive mood, I think of you and come," and then she disappeared.

An hour later, we arrived at a clearing in the woods, where, as if in a dream or porn film, a group of almost naked young women awaited us, carrying huge steaming platters. Less like a porn film and more like a dream, all the women were ugly, with lumpy faces, pocked and cratered dark red skin, and hairy arms and legs. The men let out a loud group moan.

Night had come. No moon shone. We found ourselves in a meadow whose upper half was made of stars. Torches burned and gave off thick and soporific smoke. I wished to sleep, or weep, or die. Beyond the fire I saw large, dark mounds that must have been their homes. The platters the girls held were piled with steaming towels. "Towel? Towel? Towel?" the girls all said, like giant, stupid, landbound, rust-hued birds. None of us had been offered a platter of towels before and we didn't know what we were meant to do so we just stood there. The girl who'd done the dance I didn't see peeled a towel off a pile and placed it on her face. As if to see the stars, she tipped back her head, but let the towel lie across her eyes. Hot water dripped down her tawny, muscled neck. "Mmm," she said, "mmm, mmmmm." The men plucked towels from the piles and looked up at the stars and draped the towels on their mugs and said, "Mmm, mmm, mmmmm." The girl took the towel off her face and showed us how to clean our hands with it. The men of course did not see this because they were standing there, skinny and filthy and dumb, in the clearing of an alien forest, in the dark, humming or moaning in voluntary blindfolds, necks exposed, waiting to let their throats get slit, though somehow, as you may have gathered—you to whom I call out from the depths—we seem not to have been slaughtered yet, for here we are now, as I write this, returned to the bus again, thank the lord, sliding back into our greasy beds for another excellent night's sleep than which only death itself could be more restful.

But earlier tonight, in that strange meadow, with signs and grunts, the foreign girls coached our brilliant guys to wash their hands and sat them down on folding chairs arranged around circular wooden tables. There seemed to be a girl per man, and now each girl fetched a bowl of stew from a big vat and tried to fork-feed her assigned man its contents. A lot of us didn't take well to the pointed tines of forks, held by aggressively smiling foreign girls, coming at our heads, stew or no. What was with these girls' glee? These were some very glad girls, sitting on our laps with few clothes and sharp forks, happy hostesses who shrieked and had acne and tough, manlike arms and legs and bare, soiled feet. Thirty fork-centered wrestling matches ensued. The girls were strong, and we were weak. They pinned us to our chairs and jammed stew in our mouths. The stew seemed to contain real flesh, which none of us had ever had, since non-human flesh is hardly to be found up north, and if it's found it's likely to be sick or sickening. Some of us puked, others wept and acquiesced. A few resisted. Several tried to kiss their girls and were slapped in the lips. Most of the men—not Smith, not I— were docile when they led them to their baths, scrubbed them, dried them, oiled them, jerked them off, swaddled them in hempen shirts and pants, and then sent all of us back to the bus sans shoes in total darkness. If those are that town's girls, I'm not so sure I'm keen to meet its boys.

Pocahontas

Dear ??

First thing I did as a woman was the dishes. Oh no wait, that's not true. First thing I did was watch two boys fight, and try to break them up, and fail.

Last night, after I told you about the advent of the menarche, I kind of went into a swoon and passed out in the corn shack and woke up at dawn with a killer backache. I eased my red ass down out the back flap of the shack so as not to be seen by the guys on the bus, in case they were awake, and I tiptoed, real quiet, Indian style, through tall corn stalks all dolled up in dew like girls in rhinestones. "Hello, you glorious young woman," they said to me. Corn loves me. Plants in general love me. Soil, rich with human blood, loves me. Clouds love me. The sky loves me, though I know she wouldn't hesitate to crush me dead. So anyway I'm trying to skip and frolic through the field but I've got this wicked backache—welcome to womanhood, Pocahontas; thanks a lot, womanhood—so I'm sort of half-frolicking, half-hobbling through the field, stumbling now and then upon a half-dead block of concrete of days of yore. When I got to the edge of town, I saw two things. First, I saw the girls hadn't done the dishes, strange, dirty dishes and stewpots everywhere, big tables still unfolded with scraps of meat and soggy crackers on their damp tops, sick and scary coons and rats gnawing at the meat. People here never leave food out. I leave town for a few hours, become a woman, return, and things don't make no sense no more, as if that little bit of blood that leaked down my legs was knowledge, and every month from now on I'll lose a little more of what I know, and ten years hence, when I am in the full flower of my womanhood, I will have attained, through no effort of my own, a supreme state of idiocy.

I threw rocks at the rats and coons and they dispersed. As I walked toward the mess, I saw two boys; the first sat on top of the second, who lay face-up beneath him. The first was punching the second repeatedly. They both seemed calm, nonchalant, bored, two boys doing boywork, no choice in this, it's what you do if you're them, you get down in the dirt at dawn amid the vermin and the uncleaned mess of the feast and you go at it for much longer than some woman walking by thinks you ought to or need to, punch, punch, punch, chest, throat, chin, mouth, nose, eyes, ears, skull. Getting tired? Take a quick break; bottom boy, roll over and get clobbered in the spine awhile. The boys were both my cousins, by the way, Opechancanough and Steve, ten years old. Opechancanough is big and strong, Steve is thin and weak. Neither seemed to notice I was there. Punch, punch, yawn, sigh.

"Get off him already," I said.

"Yeah, get *off* me," Steve said, mechanically, more, it seemed, as if the line were in some unseen script than because he wished for that outcome.

More punching plus invisibility of me in Opechancanough's little world of total domination of his cousin.

"I said get off him.'"

"She said get *off* me."

"He stole my lollipop."

"So? One lollipop, one punch. Not one lollipop, five hundred punches."

"He stole my *last* lollipop."

"Get off him."

"Get *off* me."

A few casual punches, pace slowing. More punches, pace picking up.

"Get the fuck off him, now."

"Ooh, 'Get the fuck off him.'" Punch, punch.

I could've kicked him in the head but would've sort of undermined my point. I grabbed him by the hair instead. He came up when I yanked. Steve lay there pee-oh'd, like a man whose plate has been removed before he's done eating.

"I think he knows now not to steal your lollipop."

"Get off me," Opechancanough said to me.

"You're done."

"If I stop now, he'll steal again. You don't know him."

I twisted his head around by the hair so my face was in his. I admonishingly held my forefinger up to his nose. He tried to swipe it away but I pulled it back and replaced it as soon as he'd finished his swipe. He swiped again, I dodged it, he swiped again. I was in this thing now too, whatever it was: not stopping it, not changing it, just in it, as ineluctably as Opechancanough and Steve. I felt the boredom, too, of the player of the violence game that none of us couldn't not play just then. I let my mind float away, and watched my body put its finger in my cousin's face, and him swipe at it, and so on. Finally, I tossed him back down on his cousin, whereupon he resumed punching, and his cousin being punched, and all was set aright. A year ago, a day ago, this would have happened differently. What power I had over boys had evidently retreated to my uterus. Onward to the dishes.

Johnny Rolfe

To the one I hope receives this, though I'm not sending it:
Sarcastic hope is a mask made in the shape of the hopeful man's face before the lead pipe of experience fashioned him a new one. My wireless device is gone. I'm composing this by hand on humankind's flimsiest and least likely invention, paper. Hope of reaching you I've never had. Some other type of hope I still must have, I guess, or else I wouldn't make these notes at all, and now I'm going to let this hope alone: scrutiny's corrosive effect on hope has been demonstrated down the ages on folks who started out with far more hope than I.

We're on this bus again against our will, a bunch of guys on a non-moving house-sized bus in the middle of a dark, alien field. The bus we thought would take us to our new home may turn out to be our new home. This stinking, fetid, airless bus may well be where we spend our final days, which may well be tomorrow.

We woke up in a good mood, collectively. I suppose a hot meal and even the sort of swift and businesslike erotics most of us underwent had had a healthful impact, moodwise. So a lot of us were thinking what an excellent idea it had been to take an interminable bus trip that had almost killed us, if it meant ending up in this beautiful new land where people eat real meat, and which we would soon lay claim to. And everyone was eager to start scouting for food and a worthy place to build a provisional town.

We all got off the bus and stretched and shook our limbs, and were dazedly taking in the singular and vivid *hereness* of the place—the warmth of the clime, the less-intensely greenish tone of sky, the field of *corn*, I think she said it's called, and other things I can't describe. Some guys slapped each other on the back, some guys laughed, some guys talked about looking for water and food, and then, in a sense, we met the local men.

A guy named Matthew Bernard—nice young guy, good guy to have around for his cheerfulness, and who cares if he's a little stupid?—felt what he first thought was a stomach cramp, and looked down to find the back half of a short arrow sticking out of his lower abdomen. I think the wisdom on these things is that you're not supposed to yank them out. Would you have remembered that if you were him? He yanked it out and moaned and said, "Oh no."

Then a lot of things happened at once. Other arrows sprang into being in other guys' body parts—hands, beards, knees. Some guys scrambled for the bus. The guys with guns removed them from their hidden sheaths and fired in various directions since no one knew where the arrows were coming from. Richard Buck, our priest, laid Matt Bernard on the ground and said to him, "Okay, let's lift up that shirt and have a look at that, it's probably not all that bad, even if it hurts like hell." Matt sobbed. What we saw then—Richard Buck, kneeling over the first victim of our new hosts, and I, standing above him, not helping and in harm's way—was a sort of second bellybutton an inch below the first, darker, more inward, more bottomless, oozing a thick, unthoroughly mixed red and brown goo. I don't know much about anatomy and physiology but the goo didn't seem like something that ought to happen to anyone, least of all a nice young guy like Matt.

I looked around: no assailants, just arrows, visible not as they flew through the air but only as they hit or missed their mark, and not many missed. I guess a field of tall and densely-planted grain is a good place from which to launch an arrow attack against a group of hapless guys getting off a bus. I envied the shooters. They did with their bows what I'd been trying to do with my wireless device: send a message, instantly and invisibly, across a vast amount of space. I removed my cloth bag from my shoulder and now touched my wireless through the bag, held it, my sad and stupid wireless. An arrow came from nowhere and hit the bag, which flew from my hands and landed beyond my sight. I dropped to the dirt to look for it. I saw instead Matt Bernard's aggrieved face, which I was now crouching above. Father Buck was down by his feet. "Lift him, Rolfe, for Christ's sake, how many times do I have to tell you, hello? Gently, don't shake him." We eased him up into the bus, and all the while I thought of my wireless on the ground. Maybe without me its luck will improve.

Our guys shot, hid, shouted, and ran, while Dick Buck made do with me as surgical assistant on the floor of the bus. It was nice and not-so-nice to see how shiny-clean and sharp the tools were. Buck cut a short red line in Matt's belly. The line grew into an ovoid hole. Matt howled and passed out. I tried not to let the stench make me retch.

"Try to stay with me here, Rolfe, I can't do this by myself. Clean that out."

"Clean what out?"

"That."

"How?"

"Do you think I've ever sat on the floor of a bus and operated on a guy who's been shot with an *arrow* before? Don't be a dead weight."

I did my best to clean him up. He's still alive, though febrile, tonight, here, next to and slightly above me, as I sit on the floor of this bus writing this, glancing up at Matt, thinking of my lost device.

The arrow attack didn't last long. Newport, our driver, stopped it with an automatic assault rifle. (Again the emphatic wrongness of my previous assessment of who on the bus had what weapons. Wronger and wronger I grow day by day.) With his single arm he wasn't too precise with it, but didn't have to be to get his point across. The particular wisdom of the assault rifle is the wisdom of abundance and speed. But any of our guns, really, seem gross and stupid compared to their lean and intelligent arrows, with the assault rifle earning the prize for the stupidest gun of all. It takes no intelligence or skill to use it, and it took not only no intelligence but a willful negation of intelligence to have invented it, though I do think it took a certain kind of imagination to invent it. To consider the imagination it took to invent the automatic assault rifle is not a happy or controllable activity. I wish I hadn't started to think or talk about it or its user or its maker or its effects. I wish I hadn't seen its effects, or known of its existence, or been born into a world in which people use, make, think of, or are shot by automatic assault rifles.

Pocahontas

How sad I seem to me today, you who know my inmost thoughts and dreams. I'm bleeding, I'm bloated, I'm nostalgic for my snuffed-out girlhood and ambivalent about becoming an adult on the side of the dish-cleaners whose words and deeds mean nothing to the ugly sex whose words and deeds make up the world.

Tell me, as ah mopes along the forest path with mild back pain, what's missing here, besides you, whoever and whatever you are. Give up? Look carefully at me. What am I not doing? I am not tapping out these thoughts on the keys of my wireless device. I am screaming them into you but not with throat or mouth. I'm screaming them inside my head. Did you catch that thing I just screamed and beamed directly from my head into yours, receptive vessel of my thoughts? The beloved wireless device is no longer in my possession. Here's how that happened.

So there I was, spread languidly on the divan in the Family Living Unit of the vast congeries of n-shaped dwellings that constitute my father's house, minding my own business, and minding the business of the large looking glass on the wall opposite the divan, which is the business of the secrets of the world revealed by looking twice, once forward and once backward. And to my hardened, dirt-caked feet, and to my skinny legs and scrape-scarred knees, and to the rough and colorless garment that covered my sylvan torso, and especially to my dented and inquiring face—whose eyelids drooped not so much in languor as in the lids' attempt to shield the eyes from the full-on assault of seeing—I asked, "Who are you?" and "Who are you?" I asked back at me.

As if in answer, my dad entered the room, trailing his advisor, Sidney Feingold. They loomed above me. "How'd the hunting go?" I asked, and breathed my father in, and tried to hold my languid pose, which hardened in his gaze. Dad—sweaty, dirty, bloody, the musk of the hunt in his unwashed skin and clothes—stared down at me in silence. The divan I was on was long and comfortable and beige, and in the middle of the otherwise even surface of its cushion was a modest lump made by a small non-divan element wedged between the cushion and the frame, about which much more quite soon. Sid glanced at the door. I sensed whoever spoke would lose control word by word. I leapt up and threw my arms around my big, odiferous dad, and so, by the way, did the girl in the glass. I clasped my hands behind his neck, and swung to and fro across the immoveable column of his body while my double swung fro and to, and each time she swung out, the edge of the glass cut off her legs, and each time she swung back in it sewed them on again: cut and sewed, cut and sewed, cut and sewed. I took a big final swing out and let go and hit the dirt. Now in the room in the glass, which was the sole bright thing in the real, dark room, my father and his friend existed and I did not.

Their mouths, the mirror said, were straight unbroken lines. "No, really, Daddy, what's up? Why so grim?" I talked to "them" instead of them—I hoped to find more giving there, I guess. Still more silence and grimness and immovability from my father, while Sid looked at the wall to see what I was looking at, discovered his own face, paused, looked back at me. I sensed his face dismayed him, but he didn't let his eyes show it, his eye management skills being superb.

No one talked. Minutes passed. I lay down again. Time crept by the divan in the mirror of the Family Living Unit in the Kingdom of the Forest that day, while I aged. To try to make time run I said, "Pops, you stink. Couldn't you get someone to hose you down when you're done hunting?"

Tick-tock, tick-tock.

"Did it go okay? Did you add another town to the State, and if so, does that feel worth having risked the lives of a hundred of our best guys for? And by best I mean most good at killing. I'm not making idle chatter here. I'm in the mood for serious philosophical dialogue on the meaning of modern warfare. Come on, Daddy, engage your favorite daughter in a vigorous debate."

Nothing.

And that was how things were in the living room where time congealed: the men loomed, and loomed again, while I, on the real and unreal divans, cowered twice. Older we all got. I slept and woke and slept again. I dreamt I lay on a divan in a dark and smelly room whose one bright spot was a looking glass that contained a dark room whose bright spot was invisible.

Someone spoke: "You must give us the wireless device now."

"What wireless device?"

They stood and stared and didn't speak. Hours passed.

"I don't have it," I said.

A year went by.

"I have it but not on me right now."

Continents cracked. Fish grew legs. Stars were born, shone, died.

"Everything I've written there is private. You haven't read it, have you?" I said, after which it was too late not to have said it, and even a child would have been able to decipher what their silence and expressionless stares meant: *we know everything*. Talking is dangerous. Writing more so. Best not to. They left. I might have thought I'd dreamt this whole event if not for what happened next.

Joe came in. Remember him? Warrior, oppressive conversationalist, dimwit, government-approved suitor of the girl with the divan attached to her back?

He stood above me. This is what men do: they stand above me.

"You're not as good at looming as my dad."

"What? Gimme the thing."

"You're not so good at grooming, too."

"Come on, I'm here for the thing. Gimme the thing."

"You smell terrible. My dad smells bad after he hunts but he doesn't smell like he shit his pants."

"Gimme the thing."

"What 'thing'?"

"The device, the wireless communications device."

"I guess you were absent from school the day they taught diplomacy."

"It's better if you give me it but I'll find it and take it if you don't." His gaze wandered the room but didn't land on the lump in the divan and he's pretty obtuse so I thought the 'thing' would be safe. Why they wanted it I didn't know but guessed.

"I guess you were absent the day they taught subtlety. I guess you were absent the day they taught likeability. I guess you were absent on the days when they taught intelligence, ethics, decency, charm, good looks." He fumed. In the air above his head, thin, moist, English-language fume lines hung. "You're better at fuming than you are at looming. You're better at looming than you are at grooming."

He sighed and sat down on the edge of the divan with his large, muscular, squared-off buttocks. He would have sat on me had I not moved. His square buttocks depressed the cushion that was slightly depressed from below by the sleek wireless device. He sighed again. It saddened me to hear him sigh. I'm one of those girls who think men's sighs are sad. Note to self: it does you ill to be saddened by the sadness of men; if you don't believe me, believe your own repeated bitter experience.

"Oh man," Joe said, and put his head in his hands.

"Who do you think is sadder, you or him?" I said, and extended a languid forefinger toward the glass, in which he appeared to be a creature with a young woman's torso and head growing from its right hip and a young woman's legs and feet growing from its left hip, and a divan growing out its ass.

"Look," he said.

"I'm looking."

His face, which, since my body was behind his body, I could see only in the glass, became a mask of anger, and then, again, a mask of woe.

He said, "I like you. You know that, and you take advantage of it by being cruel to me."

"Who takes advantage of who?"

"Please just give me the wireless device. After that we can have sex. Your dad told me you had your period or whatever so it's okay for us to do it now."

"What?!"

"You pretend not to like me but I know you want me. I'll make you feel really good, like you've never felt before in your life."

English-speaking person or whoever the hell I'm talking to inside my brain right now, do you want to know something really fucked up? His saying that made me want to have sex with him, and his saying that made me hate him and vow never to have sex with him. Oh why, why do I have a body when my life would be so much easier without one?

"I see you staring at my ass," he said to me through the glass.

"I'm not staring at your ass, I'm looking at—"

"What?"

Oops, huge oops. Dim-witted as he was, all that hunting had made precision instruments of his eyes, and he noticed me look at the lump in the divan. Obscenely, he parted the cushion from its frame, shoved his hand in between, and pulled out the device. He held it aloft in his hand, feral satisfaction in his eyes as if he had just ripped the bloody heart from the chest of a rabid wolf.

I stood up. "I don't like you and I'll never fuck you!"

He laughed and slid the wireless into the large pocket of his cargo pants.

I recalled the dream of his own violent death he'd told me of a few weeks back, and tried to say the thing I thought would hurt him most. "You'll die," I said, "whimpering. Your enemy will take your weapon and cut you open with it, and scoop out your organs and throw them on the fire he made you build before he cut you open. You'll blubber like a baby, and then you'll die, and then you'll spend the rest of eternity in the special place in the afterlife where warriors go who were humiliated by their enemy and used their last breath to scream like little girls."

Joe stopped laughing and stared at me. He seemed about to cry. I looked past him across the room, where I saw him, from behind, in the glass, become a statue of a strong man poised to strike his foe. He turned and ran toward the glass, as if to jump through it to unite with his double. As he grew in the glass, what light there was in it receded to its edges, and disappeared. The bottom of his hard, cleated hunting shoe flew toward its reflection, cleat met cleat, foot kicked foot, the room broke and went dim. He picked up a shard, crossed the room, grabbed my hair with his free hand, and held the shard to my neck. He gripped the shard so tightly that a line of blood of increasing thickness flowed along the thin line of glass that dug into his palm.

I spit in his face. People of my culture spit in one another's faces to communicate contempt, English-language speaker to whom I am now telling, I hope, all the worst things I'll ever know.

Joe yanked my hair back, forcing me back down to the divan. Oh divan, what horrors you've known. He used the shard to cut apart my dress, and in so doing he cut into the flesh of the arm of the person who is now telling you he cut into the flesh of her arm. I kicked him in the balls and he didn't react so I kicked him in the balls and then kicked him in the balls and did it again and then again. He stood up slowly and looked sad again, and moped toward the door. I didn't pity him this time. Well maybe a little. Not much. Not at all. A tiny bit. Unwise as it may have been to do so, I entered this world with a promiscuous heart in my chest which, acknowledging its owner as one of the lowly, ugly, pitiable creatures of the earth, compels her to seek out others of like constitution and mix with them.

"You'll die," I said to his back as he left, to let him know I cared. "You'll die, you'll die, you'll die, you'll die, you'll die."

I lay in the dim light and looked at the black mark on the brown wall where the glass had been. I thought of the death of Joe. I thought of the death of my dad, the death of all the men my dad commands, the death of Feingold and Stickboy, the death of my mom, the death of my aunts, cousins, and friends; we'll make a fine, high hill of corpses, weeds growing skyward from our eyes, cunts, and mouths. I got up and went to look for my dad.

The bright light of the sky dazed me. Blood still ran from the place where Joe had sliced my arm. I guess I walked along the forest path with a torn dress and a gash in my arm. Now don't go all porno on me, dirty-minded English-speaker, my breasts were not exposed, and even if they were you mustn't think of them right now, you must think of how it feels to have a cut. Think of how it feels to walk among the trees of the woods with the egregious inconvenience of a fairly deep cut in your arm that you got from a guy who sliced you with a piece of a mirror he'd broken while trying to rape you—a guy, I might add, sent by your own dad to steal something precious from you, a guy your dad may even have pimped you out to a little bit, no doubt with the best of intentions, by implying it was okay to fuck you now that you're bleeding from your vagina or whatever.

On I walked in the afternoon sun, dizzy, confused, sad, mad, surrounded by trees and concrete quondam walls and dangerous wild animals, until I came to a clearing where I saw a thin man with a wound in his head. That man was Stickboy, if you'll pardon the contradictory nomenclature. Other men surrounded him, the same men who'd just hunted and who, before the hunt, had mocked him and would have spit on him had I not stopped them. They convened on the ground in this grassy place for the post-hunt sit-down, future corpses of the Chesapeake. My dad sat above them on a time-smoothed tree stump or partial tree corpse.

I stood in the woods with a tree in my eye and listened to all that was said. And I bled, and smelled the blood of dead men on the live men on whom I spied. And the sun, which one day will explode, dried up all the blood on the skin of the men in the grass, while my blood, on and under my skin, in the dark of the trees' shade, remained wet.

"What happened?" my dad said to Stickboy.

"I don't know. I was sitting there and a tree fell on my head."

My dad sighed.

"I saw it," said Frank, the man my dad says is the best tactician in the group, a cunning man one hundred percent smarter and two or maybe three percent more likeable than Joe. "It happened after that one-armed guy used his machine gun to try to kill everything—corn, trees, insects, us. He killed an ash tree by slicing through its trunk with bullets. The top half fell over and landed on Stickboy's head. But, Stickboy, what were you doing near the foreigners' vehicle just when we happened to be attacking them?"

Stickboy answered Frank as my dad and Sid had answered me when I tried to start a conversation from my place of weakness on the divan, forever ago: with silence. It seems my dad and his men had meant to strike fear into the foreigners and got struck themselves by a big and unexpected gun. The men surrounding Stickboy on the grass responded to his silence with a silence of their own, and it seems twelve silences obliterate the single silence they oppose. Or perhaps, in silence, kind and not number is what determines strength, and each time a man kills another man, the killer absorbs into himself the eternal silence he's caused in the man he's killed, and can then use it to win a conversation, as Frank and my dad and Sid and their men now did with Stickboy. Stickboy, too, has killed, but only rabbits and deer, and the silence of a dead deer is as nothing to the silence of a dead man.

"Get out of here now," Frank said to Stickboy. Stickboy neither spoke nor moved.

"Go!" my dad said, and extended his arm toward the head of the trail that led back to town.

Stickboy stood up slowly. His knees and eyelids wavered and he sat back down. The other men looked at Stickboy with *go!* in their eyes. He stood again and swayed, just as the trees around him now swayed in the wind that had just arrived from the north and was cooling off the air.

My dad was about to speak again, and even though it's hard to think kind thoughts about him now that what was then about to come to pass has passed, I don't think he would have made Stickboy walk back to town alone. But I will never know because I stepped from behind the tree that had been hiding me and said, "Can't you see he's hurt?"

Dad, on his throny stump, leaned down to Sid in the grass on his left and whispered something to him—"Get her out of here" would be my guess, but I'll die before I know what men say when they know girls can't hear them.

Sid came toward me. I tried and failed to punch him.

"Easy now, sweetheart. Your cousin got hurt and I want to ask you to help him back to town so he can lie down and heal."

"*Now* you talk to me? Move aside so I can talk to my dad." I shoved him in the chest and he grabbed my arm but I shook it loose but it was my same arm that Joe had cut so now I had a cut that stung my upper arm and a bruise rising to the surface of the skin above my wrist in the shape of the strong and bony grip of Sid.

Again my father's mouth was like a line. Tired, he looked, and what else? Ashamed of how he'd behaved toward me that day? Of having let Joe know I was now a woman, if he did? Of his daughter's disobedience? Or not ashamed at all, but some sentiment I'll never know or comprehend. Do other daughters know their fathers more than I? To hate one's dad's to know him not at all.

Well. Well, here's what I said to him, forgetting and remembering that talking is the mirror of life: "The guys from the north will rise up against your pitiful little army. They'll outnumber you, they'll outarm you, they'll outwit you, they'll outmaneuver you, they'll defeat you, they'll reduce your dominion to nothing, they'll rule over you, and slowly, over years, they'll kill every last one of us, till we're nothing but a story passed from the mouths of parents to the ears of children, and then not even that."

My dad's head became gray ash. His chest and limbs turned to ash and fell upon the thronelike stump he continued to sit on in human form. The wind that swayed the trees and cooled the earth swept the pile of ash that was my dad into the air. The dad of mine who hadn't turned to ash looked at me and said, "You'll go now, and not let me see or hear you again as long as I live."

Did I say talking is the mirror of life? Talking *is* life, and death. Why must people talk? I opened my mouth and Frank shoved a slab of wood in it and held the slab there with the palm of his hand, and continued to hold it as two other men carried me a hundred yards into the woods. And two more men carried Stickboy. They placed us next to one another on our feet, draped his arm across my shoulders, shoved us down the path toward town, and barred our way back to the clearing where my dad and his ashes still were. And then I saw a look pass between Frank and Stickboy that seemed to signal understanding and complicity, a look that caused a germ of thought I can't give voice to yet to settle in my brain.

The sky, which the leaves of the trees in the thick woods broke apart, had been late-afternoon chartreuse, but now was made gray by the dense ash of my dad blown by the stiff wind. I spat Frank's slab of wood to the ground, invited him to fuck himself, slung Stickboy's arm across my back, and waded toward the town through ash, which grew upon the ground like snow. A clump of ash in the shape of an eye stuck to a nearby tree and stared at me. A mouth of ash entered my mouth and fell down my throat. I gagged and spat and resumed the limp homeward with my friend.

"What *were* you doing out there?"

"Out where?"

"Out by where my dad was making war."

"Guy can't walk in the woods without a reason?"

"What were you doing?"

"What were *you* doing?"

"Just now?"

"Mm."

"How's your head?"

"It hurts."

"I'll make you a busthead-cayenne-arrowroot poultice when we get back."

"There is no back, there's only forward now."

"Crap."

"So what were you doing?" he said.

"I asked you first."

"What were you doing?"

"I came to curse my dad."

"What did he do to deserve it?"

"Nothing."

"So, for no reason—"

"No, not for no reason. I had a reason but it was wrong. I shouldn't have done what I just did."

"You can't suck back a fart."

"Shut up." I shrugged out of Stickboy's arm and he fell down. I sat by him on a rock and took his hand and pulled him up next to me.

"Sorry," he said.

"I can't believe what I just did. I opened my mouth and changed the world. I didn't understand. I didn't understand."

We sat on the rock in the woods while my dad's ashes swam around our shins. I cried, and ceased to cry, and felt myself become more like the rock on which I sat. "He sent Joe after me," I said. "He sent Joe to defile me and take away my . . ."

"What?"

"I don't know, maybe he didn't send him to— but I had a— I had . . ." Stickboy quickly looked away from me.

"What?" I said.

"Nothing."

"I had a wireless device that I was writing in and Joe commandeered it."

"I know."

"How do you know?"

He paused in such a way as to make that germ of thought grow in me, though it's still too small to see. "I overheard them discussing it," he said.

"What was that look between you and Frank?"

"What look?"

"You know what look."

"There was no look."

"So why were you out there where that tree fell on your head?"

We were sitting side by side on that rock and my bony friend turned to look into my eyes. Did I tell you Stickboy has the saddest eyes in the world, a superlative for which there is considerable competition among the people of my melancholy race, and that that is one of the reasons I love him with an intensity I sometimes find unbearable? The red of his wrapped forehead wound brought out the red in his sad eyes.

"They were returning," he said, "from the hunt. It had gone badly. Kills on both sides. No spoils. Conquest in doubt. And who should they run into on the way home but that golden tank with the men inside whose faces look like swarms of ants. Your dad and his men shot at them, not to try to wipe them out but to let them know that setting up shop in this area would be inconvenient for them. They might have killed a few, I don't know, I saw one get hit in the knee, one in the hand, one between the navel and the cock."

"Stickboy?"

"Yes, Princess?"

"What are you not telling me?"

"Nothing."

"No. I've asked you a question several times that you haven't answered."

"What?"

"What were you doing in that place at that time?"

"Nothing."

"I don't believe you."

"What's to believe? I was there because I was there."

I understood I was asking him the wrong question. The right question has not yet taken form in me. But I know there is one because I saw the meat flicker in the very small red dots at the inner corners of his eyes, one small entry in the body's voluminous lexicon of revelation that thwarts its owner's efforts to conceal.

"Please tell me."

And this was his response: the sound of the wind on the land, the same wind that blew the ash that clogged my ears. A friend who won't respond to what a friend can't ask is like a looking glass in which you cannot see yourself.

Two

John Ratcliffe

Dear President Stuart:

Please allow me to begin by letting you know how honored I am by the confidence you have expressed by appointing me Executive Vice President of the Virginia Branch of the Manhattan Company. I will do my best to execute your intentions, to the extent I understand them.

We have arrived safely, and have begun scouting the area for a suitable location on which to begin construction of regional headquarters. As surely you must know, our departure took place under less than ideal circumstances due to the unanticipated urban infarction of which you were also no doubt a recipient. (I trust you have found safe ground, Sir, and are prospering!) We are therefore somewhat less than adequately equipped as regards certain basic items such as food, water, weaponry and munitions, tools, building supplies, spare automotive parts, and fuel, to name but an incomplete list. If all goes as per planned, as I am confident it will under my leadership and with the cooperation of the group of fine men which you have handpicked in your wisdom, Chris Newport will, after a several weeks' exploratory excursion into various of our neighboring territories in these Southern Parts, return to you on the Autobus Godspeed and will—after sufficient debriefing as you see fit, and rest—in a slower and more deliberate manner than the hasty and haphazard manner in which we made our first departure for the city, re-depart for the Southern Region fully stocked with aforementioned supplies of which we are now in exceedingly short supply.

And now, Sir, a brief account of events since our premature departure from Manhattan. As you wisely anticipated in planning meetings and in the series of memos subsequent to those meetings—all of which I have here not only as practical guides as to how to behave in the face of the various vicissitudes which we face on a day-to-day basis in these Southern Parts but also, if you don't mind my saying so, as, collectively, a bible, if you will (and I hasten to add: a secular bible, so as not to give you the impression that I am blaspheming, but I still cannot think of a better word than bible to express my sentiments vis-à-vis your memos, some of which I read daily), of how to survive, in moral terms, the vicissitudes entailed by interstate travel in our difficult age—as you wisely anticipated, we have encountered certain difficulties on our journey and subsequent to our arrival, and yet I am also able to transmit to you some good news regarding the kind of data we

One minute I'm writing a business letter and the next my sphincter is open wider than it's ever been and my last few remaining thoughts are pouring out of it, whew! And speaking of surprisingly large anal radiuses, I wonder if Jimmy Stuart will notice how far up his ass I am in that letter. I just don't know if I can finish it with a straight face. Maybe I'll wait till we've had this sit-down with the Indians (what's with the red skin?) that the bespectacled Judaic-looking one of them tiptoed over here balls out the other day to arrange in broken English. Beside that one peaceable gesture that I don't trust, the Indians are turning out to be a major pain in the ass, and vicious, and more formidable than you'd expect a bunch of savages living out in the woods to be, which is why I've got these two big shit-for-brains guarding me while I take a dump, which I hope they're far enough away that they can neither see nor hear nor smell what's going on here, this is one of the least beautiful experiences I've had, and I've had some doozies lately in terms of lack of beauty, like that whole bus ride, one non-highlight of which was getting buggered by that superhumanly strong race of businessmen in Delaware, wow did we ever not do well in *that* trade, though some of the fellows, and I know exactly who and how much, judging by the looks on their faces, enjoyed the event more than such an event ought to be enjoyed by people on a mission no less serious than the economic revitalization of the Manhattan Company, and this is the sort of information—who among one's employees gets pleasure from what illicit activity—one needs to keep in the safe, dry storage area of one's head for a rainy day—and it rains daily—and I just hope I haven't shat out half my memories in the last five minutes, Jesus my thighs are burning, how long can I hold this position? This is the sort of moment one hopes one's mother did not foresee for her son when she changed his diapers and ran her warm hands up and down the length of his infant body, which sent shivers of delight coursing through it. I wonder how Mother's doing now, my God, I hope Jimmy Stuart's keeping her safe, a man can barely concentrate on his leadership duties on a deadly journey to the south when he's so worried about his mother, *bastard* Jimmy Stuart, I hate to think of him with her at night, perverted frog-faced bastard, or in the morning, Mother, how could you, I know how you could, I know *exactly* how you could, which taught me as a boy never to spy on you in your boudoir or kitchen or living room or basement or attic, you do what you have to do to survive, I know that, I do too, kisses to you, Mother, and health—ooh—I hope this is the last of that Indian stew. I'm still Penny Ratcliffe's hopeful son, Mother, and I'll make my promise to you true, you and me and my future wife and the ashes of Father all living comfortably on a fortified country estate, soft white lace curtains billowing in the fresh mountain air, mornings I dictate letters to the shareholders, afternoons I write my memoirs, evenings I play croquet with the rosy-skinned future Mrs. John Ratcliffe whoever she may be as you watch and drink a lemonade and dandle the heir on the knee of your still-youthful leg. Ooh, Christ, this is really starting to burn, am I done? I think I'm done, thank God I'm done.

"Hey, Musclehead, you, Tweedledum, Ace, Buddy of Mine, Hello!"

"My name is Bill Breck, Mr. Ratcliffe, for the hundredth time."

"Less lip and some toilet paper, please."

"Toilet paper?"

"What have you got?"

"Nothing."

"Anything."

"Leaves?"

"Not leaves, did you see what happened to Martin's ass after he used 'leaves'?"

"Mr. Ratcliffe, it's good we have Mr. Martin along, we learn from his mistakes."

"That's not funny, *Bill*. It's a little funny. Now, Champ, we've got to work together on this ass-wiping project. One hand wipes the other's ass, it's a good thing I've got your undying devotion, boy am I a mess right now. What have you got for me to work with?"

"The Virginia Branch Charter."

"No."

"Your pants, which you left with me to hold."

"No."

"The Oath of the Virginia Branch Board of Directors."

"No."

"Your own shirttails."

"No."

"Bandages from the first aid kit."

"How about *your* pants?"

"How about President Stuart's memos?"

"Anything else?"

"A mustard seed."

"Approach with the memos."

"Mr. Ratcliffe, with all due respect, sir, did a chipmunk crawl inside you and die?"

"Mr. Funny doesn't want to keep his job, I guess. Come here with the memos. Closer, I can't reach. Oh stop with the nose-holding, you big musclebound sissy. There, that's it, just a little—ah, Christ, I almost fell in, stop fucking around and just give me the damn—Oh, this is hilarious, look at this memo—don't walk away, I'm talking to you, look at this memo—Stuart, what a clown—'Instructions by Way of Advice . . . Find a safe, dry patch of land upriver from, and at a higher elevation than, potential attackers.' Well, this memo sure is finding its way to an upriver patch, but not a dry one."

"Mr. Ratcliffe, I don't think I can effectively guard you in such a densely-wooded area if I'm standing this close to you."

"This memo's in a densely-wooded area."

"Sir, you're delirious from dehydration. When you're all, um, done, please take a sip from my canteen."

"That swampwater's what's making me so sick. We've got to find fresh water fast. When are we scheduled to meet with the Indians?"

"Fifteen minutes."

"How much ammo has Newport got for the assault rifle?"

"Not much."

"Who's got the wireless thing we commandeered from Rolfe?"

"Bucky does."

"Who's Bucky?"

"My brother, the guy you grew up with."

"Oh, him. I wouldn't say I *grew up with* him. I can't believe your mother named you Bill and Bucky Breck. What kind of mother—"

"Sir, I'll have to ask you please not to talk about my mother, or I'll kick your ass into the hole you just shat in."

"You're right, good rule: no mothers."

Penelope Ratcliffe

I am the ceiling fan whose spinning above the bed is caused by the motion of the feet of an anonymous employee of Jim's in a dark room somewhere in this building. I do not know that the room is dark but I like to think it so because I prefer not to picture the face of the man whose fall and summer hours are organized around the daily pedaling that turns the ceiling fan that keeps Jim and me cool as we make love. The purpose of my job is to ensure that my son, John, a boy of modest talent, will never have the job of the faceless man who pedals. That my job and I would come with violent pleasure I did not expect: it's no accident, I've found, that Jim Stuart is Manhattan's king: he drives me down into the bed with such force that I float up like this to the ceiling when he gets off, and remain here, sometimes an hour, reassembling my own face, which I also find more bearable to let disappear in the act. I see, in a blur, the whole periphery of the room once per second as I spin up here and let my face reconvene in its own time. The return of my face is always heralded by the appearance of John's. His appears and mine asserts itself within it. We share a face, just about. Almost anything can make my face blush, such as, for example, sex, or the thought of it, or being spun and spun and spun up near the ceiling by a motor run by the feet of a man whose face does not exist. I want, most of all, John's happiness. Absurd, I know, to expect more than survival and the slaking of the body's basic needs. But slaking itself can, I have discovered, be a higher good, an art form for which one may have a native talent, as I do: savory and sweet foods of many textures, a hard bed and soft chairs, cream-colored walls and aubergine drapes, an unobstructed view of Hoboken and the green sunset in which my son's face appears . . .

Father Richard Buck

Dear God, am I the path on which your seed is to be eaten by the birds? The rocks from which your seed springs up, is scorched by sun, and dies at dusk? The jealous thorns who take your seed among themselves and choke it as it grows? Could I be the fertile soil in whom your seed becomes a crop, a hundred times what was sown? And must being good feel quite so bad? Well, Lord, never mind, I know the answer to that one. And I know that being bad feels bad as well. And if I rarely know the difference between good and bad now, I know I'll have the eternity that follows death to figure it out, though my puny mortal mind can say *eternity* without knowing what it means.

Lord, I come to you with all my doubts; if I did not you'd know them anyway. In spite of all, please grant this one modest request: welcome to heaven the soul of Matthew Bernard, in whose lower intestine an arrow has made a hole. Lord, by the way, if you don't mind my saying, what were you thinking with regard to the flimsy construction of the human form? Oh, sorry, Lord, let me try to put that more respectfully. For what mysterious purpose hast thou made men such weak vessels of thyself? Really, why'd you make his middle so soft and arrow-pervious? Look at him lying here dead in the dank and miasmatic air of this bus. On an upbeat note, the mind of man is one of your beguiling inventions, being both material and not. I try, I try to make mine one of your successes. I hope you've noticed how much I've encouraged it of late to produce hopeful thoughts. I see, for example, in the upcoming meeting with the Indians, the potential for positive results for both sides, though I don't kid myself that the results will be so positive that there won't be *sides*, that from this or any future meeting between us and them there could arise an understanding so thorough as to result in the abolition of *us and them*. Lord, do you remember, from that brief time when you had a body, how good and evil scream so loud from every cell of it, and how this internal cacophony can drown out the world's other sounds, many of which are not constructed along principles as uncomplicated as *good and evil*, as, for example, when an individual becomes aware that in all conflicts between one group and another there are claims on his conscience besides *good and evil*, such as *which side is my mother on?*, or *that jackass of questionable morals saved my life yesterday*, or *that jackass of unequivocally lousy morals will more likely end than save my life but I grew up down the hall from him, and his mother and my mother are friends?*

That I might appear to be explaining things to you, Lord, as if you didn't already know them, I hope you'll bear with. I think tainted water and lack of food have made me delirious as I try for the twenty-thousandth time to understand you, and feel free to give me some kind of sign, preferably something I can perceive with one or more of the five senses you've blessed me with, that would be a nice crossover moment of spirit into flesh, just shoot a clear communication on over from the non-corporeal part of the universe where, I can't help thinking, you spend most of your time. Amen.

Johnny Rolfe

I hereby refuse to begin this missive with a salutation to you as it is being written not only by nothing, to nothing, for nothing, with nothing, and about nothing, but also *on* nothing, my paper being used up and my wireless device having been commandeered for a purpose—if so dignified a word may be applied to so absurd an activity—to which I will now address myself.

Bucky Breck, with a pistol, stood in the door of the great hall, watched by Chris Newport, who stood with his rifle at the edge of the woods, ten yards from the door. John Martin, crouched behind a bush, guarded Chris with a gun. Happy Lohengrin, with a gun, high in the branch of a tree, guarded Martin. Guarding Lohengrin with a gun was Bart Gosnold, in a hollow log. Guarding Gosnold was the noiseless, patient spider he'd displaced. The spider was guarded by a gnat. The gnat was guarded by God, who invented the gnat and the gun, for reasons that shall remain unknown to us until the sea falls into the sky.

Why the hall itself had to be so dark I cannot say. Can a people have developed the wireless communications device and not the window? Or the gun? Or perhaps, like us, they've borrowed all they have from the past and are quickly using it up. Several fires burned; smoke replaced air. As all their buildings seem to be, the great hall is shaped like a lower-case letter n. It is twice my height, forty feet across, one hundred feet from end to end. Their chief or president or king, it seems, receives foreign dignitaries while reclining on a high and massive oaken bed, eyes two-thirds shut, cooled by great feathered fans swung back and forth by concubines, wives, aunts, cousins, daughters, slaves, or, for all I know, several of these in the same person. While my lungs ached and a steel vise of oxygenlessness squeezed my head, I asked myself: where is the oxygen in this room? Answer: in and being shepherded by feathered fans into the great bellows of the king's lungs. Bed, girls, air, men, hall: this sleepy big red man was lord of all.

Their top ambassador, a Judaic-looking man with hooded eyes called Sit Knee Find Gold, by signs, showed us how to greet the man: pass along his left flank and briefly grasp his outstretched hand. None of our hands were big enough for the job; his enveloped each of ours and lightly crushed them one by one, except for Smith's. Smith used his two hands to encircle and vigorously shake the king's one, enough to send a ripple up his arm and even to flutter his long gray hair, which hung down over the side of the bed and grazed the hard brown dirt—"just to let him know someone had shown up at his extremity he'd eventually have to reckon with," as Smith later said; the left eyelid of the king peeled back; the eyeball rolled left to see what had caused the modest perturbation at the end of his arm, and took in Smith before the lid descended over it again. I wouldn't recommend it, but the lying-down greeting in the dark and smoky hall was regally discomfiting, like being greeted at the bottom of the ocean by a blue whale lying on a bed of soft coral.

Two long folding conference tables stood facing one another in the center of the hall, behind each of which were five mauve office chairs on wheels. Sit Knee Find Gold directed us to sit in them and to place what used to be my wireless device, and now was evidently ours, before the chair of the man who would operate it—me, not because anyone trusted me with the rhetoric of diplomacy but because I could type seventy-five words per minute; I knew the typing elective would be useful to me one day.

How much more bearable this all would have been had the ugly girl who made me come been there.

The Indians' first question, composed by Sit Knee Find Gold in his language on his wireless device, and translated into English by software whose author's no doubt long dead, appeared on the tiny screen of the device before me:

"From where do you come?"

As John Ratcliffe leaned toward me and whispered in my ear, compelling evidence suggested he had not had time, in haste to leave his crumbling New York home, to pack a toothbrush. "Tell him we're from Manhattan, an island 300 miles north of here." I did.

"Where are you going?" came the reply.

"We do not know where we are going, for that is how it is with going," Ratcliffe told me to write, and I wrote it, with a qualm.

Smith hugged Ratcliffe's neck in the crook of his elbow, and smiled, and said through greenish smiling teeth, "Just how soon would you like us all to be slaughtered, John? Ten minutes from now? Five? Three seconds?"

"Get your fucking arm off my neck."

"Why'd you say 'for that is how it is with going' to them? We're not writing a poem here, we're trying not to get killed."

"'All warfare is based on deception,' Sun Tzu, *The Art of War*," Ratcliffe said, and reached into the left inside breast pocket of his soiled suit coat.

"If you pull out your paperback edition of Sun Tzu I'll shove it up your ass," Smith said.

"No you won't," said Ratcliffe, who pulled out a handkerchief, once soft and white, now brown and stiff, and blew his nose.

"Please we ask that you do not plinuckment," came the response on the screen from Sit Knee Find Gold, along with a scowl from across the hall.

The translation program evidently did not have an English word for the Indian word *plinuckment*, and while Smith and Ratcliffe continued their struggle for the soul of the Virginia Branch of the Manhattan Company, I typed "What is 'plinuckment'?"

"Toyn," Sit Knee typed back.

"What is 'toyn'?"

"Gavagai."

"What is 'gavagai'?"

"According to the employment of the language of metaphor use, 'rabbit slices,'" Sit Knee said, via his inscrutable plinuckment. Jack and John continued to embrace. Each whispered imprecations in the other's ear. And both of them were oiled down with grime, and both of them were skeletal and grim, and both their mouths were lip-lined rotten eggs, and how they were was how all of us were: not wealth, not power, not a gun or a knife, not a happy childhood or a promising career, neither a decade of good deeds nor one of ruthless conniving exempted any of us from foul corporeal odor. Decrepitude is egalitarian, and it warmed my mind to see Smith and Ratcliffe inured enough to one another's stink to embrace like brothers, even fratricidal ones.

"Sorry, your last message was not fully intelligible," I wrote, and wondered which English words were unknown in their tongue. Are there, in their world, *you* and *I*? If yes, then there must also be *message* and *sorry*.

"One is there who badly thinks of it," they said, via Sit Knee, his machine, and mine.

"What?"

"There are one, who thinks badly of it."

I looked to see who *one* might be. Their chief, who seemed sad or drugged or both, on his bed? In the dark and smoky room, a darker darkness clung to him. Foreshortened by my viewing angle, he was compressed and condensed, except his left arm, which hung at full scale off the side of his bed. Sit Knee Find Gold looked at him, and I sensed communion between them, but of what kind I could not say since neither spoke nor made a sign. He typed, "It is compelling that we know your intentions."

Smith and Ratcliffe had suspended their squabble and sat on either side of me, and wheeled in close on rollered chairs. Their bodies were a festival of deliquescence; I breathed them freely. Ratcliffe read the screen and said, "For Christ's sake, back at home we're running out of fuel and food and guns. Every day our enemy in Brooklyn attempts to advance on us and we can hold him off for only so long. We drag our dead off Brooklyn Bridge and bury them at night. Let's just tell them how bad our situation is and ask them for their help." Ratcliffe swept his sodden, enervated hair from his eyes and it fell back into them, and he seemed to find this alone cause for despair.

"Ratcliffe?" Smith said. "Is this the imperious Ratcliffe I know who had the blood beat out of me for insubordination? What has happened to you?"

"I know, I know," Ratcliffe said.

"You know?"

"I don't know."

"Hasn't your Little Red Book of Sino-Fag Military Tactics told you you can look weak only if you're strong, but if you really are weak, which we are, you have to appear strong?"

"I don't care," Ratcliffe said.

"'We are in the area on a mission that is both fact-gathering-oriented and diplomatic. We are interested in an exchange of resources and ideas.' Type that," Smith said to me.

"What the hell does that mean?"

"Type it," he said, and firmly pressed something—gun, finger, knife— against my back. I typed, but slowly: the smoked air of the great hall by now had molassesed my brain.

"We wishes you in the end in the most specific order," Sit Knee typed.

"I don't understand," I typed.

"You we wish for the most specific account."

Ratcliffe, while breathing on me, said, "It's madness that our lives depend on this."

I said, "Our lives always depend on this."

Smith said, "Johnny, don't get philosophical on us right now, please. Let's get through this, gentlemen. No philosophy and no freaking out. Level heads. Strategy. Cunning. Think: how do we use the fucked-up-ness of the machine to our advantage? I think this guy's saying he wants us to be specific about what we're doing here, so I say we feed into the machine specificity that we know will get lost in translation."

I said, "What about we tell them what we're really doing here, which they'll figure out eventually?"

Ratcliffe said, "But they're not expecting us to be honest, so if we really *are* honest about how desperate for their resources we are, they're going to look at that and think, 'Well, what they're really doing here must be pretty horrendous if *that's* what they're using to veil it with.'"

Smith said, "Tell them we're looking for a trading partner, we need fuel and food, and can supply protection and technological know-how in return."

"Oh, great, we and our technological know-how," I said.

Smith poked my back again.

"Cut it out," I said, and typed, "Where's the young woman? She knows English."

Smith poked me again. I ignored him.

Sit Knee seemed to speak my query to the king, along whose foreshortened torso a ripple of dismay ascended.

"The young woman at this time is indisposed," Sit Knee typed.

"We are an advanced society facing a shortage of key resources, chiefly food, water, and fuel. We would like to engage in a mutually beneficial exchange of ideas, information, and goods," I typed.

His reply: "It is our habit, around all exterior-to-control-towers of, which with us demand congress, to perform a series of examinations physical and moral."

"Where?"

"In my office."

"Only if we can examine your people in the same way," Smith told me to say.

"I'm the communications officer so stop telling me what to type, and if you poke me one more time with whatever you've been poking me with I shut down the machine and walk out of here."

Smith sighed. "I think it would be judicious," he said as if speaking to a child, "to require of them what they require of us, for the purposes of both information gathering and negotiations equity. What do *you* think, Rolfe?"

"I think we should be ready to ask for something else if they say no."

"There's a boy, Rolfe. I didn't think you had it in you." He lightly slapped and pinched my cheek. I felt and feel if anyone can save us it's him. Whether the world will be a better place with us saved or dead the biological imperative prevents me from considering too deeply.

Across the hall's congealing air I floated Smith's reply. I could barely breathe by now, and had brought up and swallowed several tablespoonsful of bile since we'd arrived.

"No," was Sit Knee's reply.

"Why's he have to type that one?" Ratcliffe wanted to know. "Why doesn't he just shake his head?"

I typed, "Then we'll hold one of your best archers until the examination is complete."

"All right," he typed.

Negotiation ensued regarding where and how to make the exchange. I explained to them what a handshake was, and suggested we meet between the tables to perform one. Sit Knee tactfully encouraged us to improve our cleanliness and smell. Smith, Ratcliffe, and I walked toward the center of the room, as did Sit Knee Find Gold and two other officials, or guards, or thugs, or friends. Each of us shook a hand of each of theirs. For reasons I cannot enumerate, I surprised Sit Knee with a hug. "Bring the young woman tomorrow," I whispered. He pushed me away in disgust. His eyes watered. He retched and puked at my feet, which, since vomit needs no translator, caused me to puke. Ratcliffe, also sick, ran for the door but puked instead on Bucky's feet. Bucky ran to the woods but only got as far as Newport, at whose side he puked. Newport leaned over the nearest bush and inadvertently puked on the head of John Martin, who was crouching behind it. Martin puked on himself, and the sight and stench of all the puke caused Happy Lohengrin, on the branch of his tree, to let hurl his, which also fell on Martin's head. A brook of puke whose source was Gosnold's mouth flowed along the runnel of his hollow log, and drowned the spider and the gnat, whose last acts on earth were to puke on God, who is everywhere, and on whom creatures great and small have therefore unremittingly puked since the fateful hour he'd created a man in his image and a woman from the man's rib.

Sidney Feingold

An hour on the bike and here we are at our *pied à terre* with light pouring
in through the windows and a relatively fresh breeze blowing in off the
Atlantic. Charlene rides shotgun and fends off predators with a blowtorch
and throwing knives. Her dexterity keeps the marriage exciting, a woman no
longer in the full flush of youth who can hit a leaping coon in the eye,
though she gives me endless grief about my poor bike-riding technique too,
remarks that are of course at this point in our relationship mostly by way of
kibitzing—repetitions, as farce, of the near-tragic fights of the early post-
connubial period. How many times, in the early years, did I not know
whether a fight with Charlene would end in murder or in the fiercely ath-
letic lovemaking that was more like killing and being killed than any but
those activities? Whether the scratches I often bore on my face and neck in
that dozen-year period resulted from the fights or the sex I was in a state of
ongoing uncertainty about.

With someone like Charlene on the team, too, an aging couple gets a
surprising variety of tasks accomplished with a blowtorch. Nor is your typical
Algonquian schoolchild trained in the use of the blowtorch; few such instruments exist; use of them is thought profligate, what with the energy crisis. We
have one and can fuel it and use it whenever we wish because we are the
chief's kid sister and his chief advisor, respectively. The blowtorch and
smidgeon of fuel a week are perks, the bike's a perk, the beach house is a perk,
the inner place I can arrive at at the beach house where the violent, headache-
producing thoughts stop coming quite so fast and hard is a hard-won perk,

and of course the peace-of-mind-enabling fresh—in relative terms—air is a massive perk, in the sense that something of almost no mass can be said to be massive.

I love the quiet of the beach house. I hear hardly a peep from the neighbors, Japanese folks, fishermen and hunters, throwbacks, really, to a gentler time. (A gentler time: a constant myth since man began to prey upon the earth; nostalgia is optimism in reverse chronology.) The ocean's one big toxic vat of death, aquatic life has dwindled down to almost nil, yet season in and season out they pull from freshet, pond, and sea robust fauna girdled in tasty meat. They do the same with beasts that roam on solid ground or hover in the air, and with plants that spring up against the odds from the earth's infected soil. You've got to give the Japanese their due: they know something we don't. They have processes to draw the poison from meat and stem alike. From the quiet of their town you'd never guess their central role in the greater Chesapeake economy. They supply and purify our food, Powhatan distributes it and protects them and their way of life.

We threw open the windows—this is how people with beach houses open their windows, by throwing them—and we brought the damask-covered cushions out to the front porch with the sea view. We unfurled the cushions, we lay on them, we stripped down to our dark underwear, I removed our pipe from its cushion pocket, and we passed an herb-softened bowl of ginger busthead twice between us to take the edge off the ride.

"You wouldn't believe what a day I had," I said.

"Before you tell me, clean the gutters."

"Now?"

"They're dirty."

"They'll still be dirty after I tell you about my day."

"Do it now."

"I don't make enough money that you can pay someone?"

"'I don't make enough money that you can pay someone?'"

To be mocked by Charlene is worse than receiving a blow to the throat with a blunt object administered by her.

"I wish you'd asked me this before we smoked. I'm mellowed out now."

"I'll get the ladder."

"'I'll get the ladder.'"

"Oh good, you get it, and I'll do a little grocery shopping."

I climbed the ladder till my nostrils had reached the gutters' level. They stank with multiple seasons of clotted leafmeal. What's in there? A stray arrow, desiccated; fossilized fish heads; sand; hardened air poison residue; crushed bird fetus skeletons; dust; hair; a hundred other things that once had names. In the world we failed to inherit I imagine there was a branch of science devoted to extrapolating whole societies from a single rain gutter long uncleaned by a lazy husband. In case we continue to exist and such a science is revived, a lazy husband may leave vital clues for the future of the race. As I completed this thought, Charlene came in low shoulder-first against the ladder. It tipped and I hit the dirt from ten feet up. I tried to breathe and clutched my left foot in pain. As I lay on my back, she slammed her knees down on my hips and swatted at my face and head not lightly but with an open hand. I tasted blood and my nose filled up with it, while my lungs emptied of air. She tore off my shirt and created a freeform lattice of deep scratches on my shoulders, neck, and chest. With her knees she continued to drive my hips into the hard-packed ground while pistoning my kneecaps with the pointed tips of her cowboy boots. She screamed and spit flew from her mouth into mine. I gagged. I hadn't breathed since I hit the ground. She rolled me and fore-armed the back of my head till my face and the earth were one. I ate and breathed an acrid mix of blood and dirt. Having yanked and torn my pants, she wedged open my ass and drove something stiff up me till it hit my prostate as the steel ball hits the bell at the he-man booth of a traveling carnival. I yelped and came and spun up and smacked her in the nose. Surprised, she sat with mouth agape and legs splayed, like a little girl who's just seen her father beaten. I squatted, sprang at her forehead fist first, nailed it. She collapsed backward and came up dazed. I grabbed her hair, whirled her down, laid her flat face-up beneath me. I put myself in push-up form, crotch above her mouth. She sucked like a hungry infant till I was stiff enough to penetrate her crotch. We had our sweet and tender missionary sex till she came for her usual minute and a half and I for my millisecond.

"I wonder when those idiots will catch on that English is our language too," I said, afterward, lying on the ground.

We dragged each other to the porch cushions, collapsed onto them, lit the dreg of busthead there, shared it, quietly dreamt awhile. I saw a gull at the shore drop a clam on a rock, fly down and pick it up, float up and drop it again, and so on, like a yo-yo. Char, from her cushion, half awake, strung a crossbow and shot the gull from the sky so we could nap and not wake up with our eyes plucked out. I woke in early evening to a heavy, fevered face of hardened blood, like a hot raspberry pie filled too full of fruit and baked too long. Char lay to my right, similarly indisposed.

"We're getting too old for this," I said.

"It's nice once in a while. Did you have a hard day you want to talk about now?"

"The chief's depressed."

"And?"

"Pocahontas cursed him and he banished her."

"What'd he say?"

"That he never wanted to see or hear her again."

"What was her curse?"

"Annihilation of us all."

"Oh."

"He's a good strategist but still primarily a man of action. In his mind words cleave to what they're meant to name; the word *hammer*'s a hammer to him, its purpose is to drive a nail into a piece of wood. So it's hard for him to see his teenage daughter's curse as merely the expression of her profound disappointment in him, her sense that he violated her, her heartbreak and rage."

"Merely?"

"Yes. Fathers and daughters should be able to bounce back from this kind of thing."

"He's a fool."

"He's also a great man."

"I used to think so."

"Our lives are easier, thanks to him."

"We live in a perpetual state of war."

"That's because he understands the alternative is our death. And that's why his daughter's remark—which she made to him, by the way, in the presence of the entire war council after we'd suffered a humiliating defeat in a battle with these idiots from up north—was unbearable to him."

"He stole her little gadget that she cherishes for that stupid event you staged today in which all of you pretend you don't speak English and therefore need to communicate through translation software. Do you think the northerners were fooled by it?"

"They're pretty stupid."

"I mean he sent Joe to steal it. My God, Joe, there's someone who should be killed in battle."

"How do you know this? Have you spoken to her? Where is she?"

"Her father gave Joe permission to have sex with her."

"No he didn't."

"Yes he did."

"Were you there?"

"Were you?"

"Yes," I said.

"You were there when he instructed Joe to take the device from her?"

"Yes."

"And did he say anything to Joe about her, I don't know how you people would put this, her status as a woman?"

"No."

"I don't believe you. He wants them married. He wants the alliance with Joe's people down in Durham. I don't believe you."

The sun had gone down. We lay on our backs on adjacent cushions, looking at each other's eyes. A breeze had come up, causing gooseflesh to cause my scratched skin to ache. Charlene knew I was lying and knew I knew she knew. This is the sort of event that would have enraged her twenty years ago and now did not. I don't know her well enough to know what my untruth made her feel. Well not an untruth as much as the most honest way I could stay in the conversation and not breach my loyalty oath, an oath which at times in talks with Char requires me to make remarks that bruise her wish that love transcend all else, including politics.

"So Powhatan could barely move today," I said.

She did not respond.

"He was so depressed. We had to prop him up on a bed in the great hall and pretend that's how he always receives foreign dignitaries."

"I don't want to hear about this elaborate deception of your opponent."

"Your opponent too."

"Are you sure?"

"Pretty sure."

"I'll go start dinner."

Charlene Kawabata Feingold

Deep in the den of the beach house I abide. Having battered and buggered my husband, during dinner I brooded. My brethren are a botch he's built and bought into. Am I better? Barely—badly. I suffer fools, not gladly, but know no one who isn't one, myself at the top of the list. What can I do? Abrade, make my life a goad of self and world. I try, am beaten down, get up, try again, am beaten down, try again. At a stage in life when bone growth has come to a halt, I stay down to rest awhile, love the rest, hate myself for loving it. All the while I know what stands between myself and doom is my own botched brothers. Our doom's our neighbors' coup, and they're as botched as we. The only proper remedy for all of this is doom of all, which my body's will will not allow; I muddle on.

Who is there to count on here? Sid for love but not for truth. Princess P for outrage but not for programmatic action. She too blithely inhabits the present for the latter, too much enjoys the peaks and troughs of exuberance and melancholy that are the purview of the privileged teen. But I love her the most. She lives a bit like me but without the self-imposed burden of trying to live as if for all. But when I saw her tonight after dinner I saw a different girl. The first menarche tells a secret to a certain kind of girl she can't ignore and can't but act upon. And so she's cursed her dad and run away; but not far away; not away at all, in fact; she runs along the margins of the world she's always known. We met in a hole in the woods beneath the stars. At the bottom of the windless air, we lay close on the ground, which smelled of dirt and blood. I like to lie near her strong young form that I've watched grow from that soft initial mass. Her face is dark and broad, its pocks that night an homage to the sky's stars.

"He hates me."

"He loves you."

"You weren't there. I told him that thing I shouldn't have. More than told. I made something happen by telling."

She cried. I kissed her face and held her close. The ground's gore seeped through our clothes, through our skins, stained our hearts.

"I like your bony arms," she said.

"Soon all bone, no arm."

"Wow, you're a downer. What should I do?"

"What do you mean?"

"I mean I want advice about what to do."

"Go to him, talk to him, apologize."

"I can't."

"Yes, you can."

She grabbed and shook me. I think I knew what she meant.

"My advice is inadequate, of course," I said. "I think you understand that what you really want to know I can't tell you, nor can anyone."

She kicked my shins. I kicked hers back twice as hard.

"If kicking me is your advice," she said, "don't bother, I already know that one."

"Don't trust Stickboy."

"What?"

"You wanted more advice? There's some."

"You're out of your mind."

"I'm in my mind. There's something wrong with him."

"Who isn't there something wrong with?"

"You know what I mean."

"I have no idea what you mean."

"I can't be specific. Just be careful."

"And how about you? Should I trust you?"

I had an answer to that question that was comforting and I had an answer that was true. Neither was correct.

"You give crap advice."

"Don't stop loving him. Just don't believe him."

"That's enough advice. No more advice, please. What happened to your face, anyway?"

A figure emerged from the dark. "Poc, Char," he said, an old joke of his to which the girl was meant to respond by poking me, but instead lay there. He approached from the side of her I was not touching, sat, took her hand in his. "How are you tonight?"

Her answer was her baleful starlit face.

Stickboy said, "What happened to your face, Char?"

"Seagull. How's your head?"

"I brought you food," he said to her, produced a parcel of rough cloth, and unfolded it on the balding grass. "Arrow arum patties with a scallion trout paste."

"No thanks."

"Drink water, at least." He brought a skin of water to her lips.

She pushed it away. "Is this rancid?"

"No!"

"How come we gave those guys from New York bad water? Why can't our strategy be kindness and generosity?"

"Why you asking me?"

"I'm not."

"Then who you asking?"

"The stars." She took the water from her cousin and drank.

I stood. "I'll leave you two."

"Watch out for attacking seagulls," he said, from which I inferred he'd heard me speak of him.

"And you for falling trees, and stars," I said, and walked away.

And crept back, and lay behind a bush to hear what he would say, and peered between its stems to see what he would do.

"I'm glad that bony witch is gone," he said.

"I'm not. I have this feeling as if my body extends all the way out to the edge of what I can see, so anyone who walks into my field of vision, or out of it, bursts my skin. All arrivals and departures hurt. I wish everyone would stay put."

"It's she who's betraying you, not I."

"Shut up!"

"You need to hear this. She pretends to be your ally—"

"Really, don't say this, I can't take it."

"She tells Sid what to tell your dad."

"Are you not listening to me?"

"You need to hear this. Who do you think came up with the idea to steal your communications device?"

"You're awful."

"And do you know why she did?"

"Don't tell me why."

"Because—"

She punched him in the head. "I forbid you to tell me this, whatever your motive."

"All right, I'll let it go."

"You have to do more than that. Take it back."

"What good will that do?"

"Take it back."

"I take it back."

"Say it wasn't true."

"It wasn't true."

"You're a liar."

"But you—"

"You were right, you can't suck back farts, and rescission is a poor perfume for them. Farts plus perfume smell worse than farts alone. Like when you and Frank were conspiring about something in the woods that day I cursed my dad, and I asked you about it and you said it was nothing and now you can't take that back. Everything everyone says is false. Everything everyone does is false."

"I'm sorry."

"Liar."

"I meant to comfort you but then I heard Charlene lying about me so I— I'll leave now."

"She wasn't lying about you. You're up to something with Frank and you're not to be trusted, but don't leave," Pocahontas said to Stickboy. "That would be worse than if you were to stay."

He stayed.

The night was dark, my eyes were swollen halfway shut, and my view was obstructed by the clumped stems of an unnamed bush, so what I saw was a blurring movement of two dark bodies.

"Touch me here," I heard her say.

"There?"

"No, here."

"Really?"

"Really, fakely, I don't care."

And so he did, or so I imagine, try as I might not to. Just then I wanted to relieve myself of the burden of form. Instead, I tried and failed to stand.

"Stop, it hurts," she said, to my relief.

"But I wasn't even—"

"I said *stop*. What part of 'Stop, it hurts' don't you get?"

"I thought maybe you were just kidding."

"What's the matter with you?"

"Well a minute ago you said everything everyone says is false."

"Shut up."

She said this affectionately, and hugged him, or so it seemed to me from where I lay with standing up in mind. I'd told her as best I could. What she'd heard and what she did I couldn't control.

Powhatan, my half-brother, lay on a bed a room. I laid my body parallel to his along the bed. Everyone I knew was lying down: my husband, my niece, her cousin, my brother, my neighbors, me. I pictured all humanity on its back, an attitude from which you'd think it could do least harm.

"How are you?"

His planetoid form seemed to draw all smaller forms in the room toward it.

"Children say things they don't mean."

"She's not a child."

"Do you mean if she'd cursed you last week, before she 'became a woman,' you wouldn't have taken it to heart?"

His response was a deeper kind of lying there, a fuller habitation of stasis, a rehearsal, it seemed, for the lull between the frenetic struggle of life and the unwilled busywork of decomposition.

"Adults say things they don't mean too," I said.

"She has a history of undermining me."

"A history? She's nineteen."

"That I love her most is a sign that I desire my own subjugation."

"So you've been talking with my husband the psychiatrist. Anyway, what's so bad about subjugation? Women face it every day and we think it's just swell."

"I'd rather die than submit to these bumbling New York asses."

"Oh, them."

"They think we have oil. If we had oil, wouldn't we already have driven up and killed them for theirs?"

"So why don't you kill them now that they've saved you the inconvenience of travel?"

"They have better weapons than we do."

"But they're stupid, they're slow, and they're careless. You could pick them off two by two and be done in a week."

"This is a turnaround for you."

"I'm just saying."

"We can make better use of them alive."

"And yet they're who your favorite daughter has predicted you'll be defeated by."

"That was no prediction. That was a curse. And *we*. *We'll* be defeated. If I'm defeated, so are you."

"And again I report to you from lifelong experience that defeat isn't the worst thing that could happen to a person, or a people."

"What is?"

"Victory."

"Your sense of humor is charming."

"Look at you. You're what victory looks like."

"No, this is the result of a defeat urged on me by someone whose remarks I can't ignore."

"This is also the result of your having banished her from your sight."

"Yes, that's true."

"What decision of yours of the last twenty years has not been predicated on the fear of defeat?"

"So?"

"The victor is completed by the vanquished. Victory and defeat are each other."

"This is sophistry and I'm tired. The crucial difference between me and my defeated enemy is that he's dead and I'm alive. He's enslaved and I'm free. What he owned is now mine."

"You should go to her," I said.

"She should come to me."

"Is that all it would take?"

"Is that all *what* would take?"

"For you to forgive her."

"I'll never forgive her."

"Why should she come to you then?"

"Because she's my daughter. Daughters attend to their fathers."

He closed his eyes and lay inert, and so did I. And so we joined all humanity, in resemblance if not in fact.

Pocahontas

To the edge of the world I am running
Beyond the land, beyond the sea
I evade my predator with cunning
And so does my virginity

So that's a rough translation into English of a song I am singing to myself in my real language. Singing and trying to pretend to be insouciant are what I'm doing to strive against the leaden heaviness of my heart and neither is working but that song is taught to generations of my town's girls by their moms and aunts with a somewhat different purpose than the one I'm using it for, namely, to evade a neighboring town's hunter in the sexual predation phase of his hunt, during which he's looking not only to use the body of one of his enemy's girls to slake his rage and lust, but to humiliate the girl's brothers, uncles, cousins, dad, and mayor, and to get her pregnant toward the ultimate goal of making everyone everywhere into more of himself: rape in battle is an economical activity, and lots of guys do it who wouldn't under normal conditions. Thus the song, and ain't it ironic that I'm using the song to help me flee from guys whose humiliation-by-proxy the song is kind of meant to make not happen?

I'm still a virgin, by the way. I almost "gave it up" to Stickboy last night but no, I continue to be beautifully intact. He and I did some light touching and that was definitely something I'd like to do more of but I got overwhelmed—too much else going on—and had to ask Stickboy to stop, plus my Aunt Charlene was lying behind a nearby bush looking, listening, and breathing, and what girl wants her first sexual experience to be witnessed by an aunt, even a cool one? Not I, thought the princess whose dow'r's now her mind.

Oh English speaker, why does ah persist in thinkin to if not fo you in yo pretty but lazy tongue? You're probably as bad as my guys are, or worse, and yet I can't but think for two—me and you—to try to use my brain to know and say at the same time. I feel like my head is about to crack open; what would you find in there? Eggs and jelly.

I am reclining in one of the many stilted corn shacks that constitute my diffuse home in this grim passage of my life. There is a vernal crispness in the air that my bosom feels as gloom, and here comes Frank, whose nickname is Knifeface, and whose face does indeed seem to want to cut your eyeball just for looking at it. Out the back chute of the shack I go, and am running low along the stalks of corn. What the corn thinks of this it won't say. Wish I'd seen Frank coming sooner. Teach me to daydream toward someone who may not exist, English-speaking bastard.

"Hi Frank!" I have just shouted, over my shoulder, to let him know I'm running away from him not because I'm scared of him but because I don't want him to rape or otherwise hurt me.

"Hi Pocahontas!" he has just shouted back very recently—I try to report this as it is happening but please forgive me if sometimes there is a delay of several seconds as I trip over a disused brick or concrete block while transforming event into experience and experience into message all with the glorious engine of thought, ow, twisted my ankle, crap, not slowing me down, not slowing me down.

"Back off, Frank!" I have shouted back to him and am now diving over a low stone wall built by the European settlers of this land many hundreds of years ago, the start of all the trouble, or such is the role they've been assigned, someone had to start it, may they be cursed and the rest of us spared, though we are them and they are us by now. I somersault and come up and run and "Oh, hey, Frank, I thought I said to back off!" I shout. My ankle hurts, I wish he'd quit it.

"I just want to talk!" he shouts.

"About what?"

"Things! Nothing special. Relaxed conversation."

"Why should I believe you?"

"Because I'm a man of my word!"

"No you're not!"

"With you I always have been!"

Let me test his last remark against a lifetime of memories of him. There was the time when I was a girl and he saw me kissing Stickboy and said "I hate you!" That was true. There was the time when I was a girl and he saw me kissing Joe and said "I hate you!" That was true. There was the time when I was a girl and he kissed me and said "I love you!" That was true too. God I'm so embarrassed about how traditionally girly my memories are that I'm using to figure out whether to trust Knifeface Frank. It's hard to think beyond custom while running with a sore ankle from a man who might mean me harm.

I feel raindrops on my skin and they hurt, not because I'm going through a period of heightened sensitivity but because sometimes when it rains each drop contains a fire that burns the skin. What moments ago was vernal crispness is now shifting over to vernal blur, vernal pain, vernal fear of the fiery rain. One drop won't kill you. Ten drops won't kill you. A hundred drops won't kill you. Ten thousand drops could damage you a bit, and I don't know if you've ever counted how many raindrops land on your skin per second even in a light drizzle but they add up fast, so now I'm running away from Frank on a bum ankle and considering his overture of aimless chat while I look for shelter from the wounding rain.

"I have a spare waterproof garment!" he has shouted.

"Shove it up your ass!" I've shouted back.

We've entered the forest now and are heading for the river. The trees, whose leaves are nearly full, protect us from the rain. He has stopped running, and brief strategic glimpses over my shoulder suggest he is putting on a kind of portable sausage casing for his body. So now it is only I who run toward the river's edge. Can I say that I am chased if no man pursues me? How much longer will the leaves protect me from the rain? What will I do when the trail I'm on dead-ends at the river? Here he comes, suited up, and I've been running all the while as fast as I can, which makes me think that he could already have caught me if he'd wanted, and hasn't. Why?

"Could you have caught me if you'd wanted?" I ask, running.

"Yes."

"Why haven't you?"

"Want you to trust me."

"So you can extract information from me for my father and then defile me?"

"No, I want to have an open and honest exchange with you."

It creeps me out when men say that. What can I do? He'll outlast and out-run me, my ankle hurts, my skin is being injured by the rain. I am stopping now. He is next to me. We breathe hard, standing side by side by an ancient nonfunctioning partial grocery store. He rolls his eyes toward me and looks me up and down. He faces me, our heads a foot apart. "Turn your head the other way," I say.

"Why?"

"I don't want to breathe in the air you breathe out, it stinks."

"Want that waterproof garment?"

"No."

"Umbrella?"

"No."

"Why not?"

"Turn your head away still, please." He turns his head, he pulls his large umbrella from a quiver that also has arrows. He opens it. It protects us. Here we are, breathing and standing and not getting rained on and listening to the rain and thinking.

"How are you, anyway?" he asks.

Though I cannot see it and am not literally touching it, I can feel the angularity of his face. I smell the fresh sweat on it, and the musky, darker residue of older sweat beneath. The tautness, the leanness, muscular strength and strategic know-how of his body, as well as his body's documented viciousness, are all right here next to me in the dim light and light rain of a spring dawn, and I'm trying not to be interested in them or impressed by them or annoyed or scared or anything. I'm just me and this is happening and after this happens something else will happen and I'll continue to be me or one of several things I call myself, unless I die, in which case no big deal, is how I think you'd think it in English.

"I'm fine," I say. "You?"

"Good."

"Neat."

"Nice weather."

"Yep."

"You being sarcastic?"

"I wish you weren't in such a hurry to reveal your intentions."

"My intention is to befriend you."

It sounds nice, doesn't it? And that's just in English. That same phrase in my language strokes the little bones in the ear that make perturbations of the air sound like speech. And yet because someone you've known all your life standing next to you in the forest stroking your ear bones with a remark about how his intention is to befriend you is just so very screwed up in this certain kind of way, I am now grabbing the umbrella away from him and poking him in the eye with its tip and running, the worst part of which is how demoralized the expression on his face is as I glance back to see how effective my violence has been. That poor man. Did I blind him? Violence sickens me.

And on I skip on this strange morn, skipping along through the stinking, rain-singed, fucked-up forest I know so well. Trees, trees, trees, trees, dirt, water, air, fire, Pocahontas, and in the sky a little light, which means I haven't died in the night. What's this? That man, the dirty, stringy, greasy one, the one who broke that thing in me a while back, the foreigner and barbarian who arrived on a golden armored bus and is ambiguous. "What are you doing, fair man?"

"Just out here."

"This weather could kill you, you know," I say to him in his native tongue, and stand warily at a stone's throw from him.

"Ya, we have this same type of weather in New York."

"So, you know, really, what are you doing out here?"

"The bus is worse than this."

"'Bus'? Remembuh, mah English ain't too good."

"The bus is the armored vehicle where we still stay in bad weather while our fort gets built and waterproofed, which may never happen given what bad carpenters we are. Your English is very good, though strangely accented."

"Fort?"

"A fort is a place where—"

"No, I know what a fort is, I'm just surprised you're building one. So what are you people doing here anyway? And stop walking toward me."

"We're building a —"

"And before you answer me you should know that we kill people who try to deceive us."

"Do you expect to die if *you* deceive?"

"Yes, and if we don't deceive, too."

He wears a yellow rain hat, the young interloper, from under which droops his oily hair and his thin, dingy, greased-down face.

"You should bathe," I say.

"Don't you want to know why we're here?"

"I know why you're there. Why wouldn't you be there? You look sad."

"I miss home."

"Where is home?"

"My mind."

"Do you have a girl there?"

"Yes, but she's not real. She's an advertisement."

"What is an advertisement?"

"It's when a manufacturer makes a picture of a beautiful woman who is using its product and you fall in love with the woman and the product."

"What does she look like?"

"She's dancing."

"How?"

"Accurately."

"Where?"

"In the driver's seat of a bus."

"Show me."

He is trying to show me.

"Her mouth is open like that?" I ask.

"Yes, but her lips are fuller than mine."

"Is she licking them?"

"No, I've just licked mine to try to make them shiny and wet, like hers."

"Is that a smile?"

"It's a look of concentration. She's concentrating on her arms and shoulders, which are moving robotically, like this, and on the side-to-side wavelike movements of her body, like this."

"She looks as if she enjoys dancing."

"Very much, that's what I like about her, and she's wearing a hat."

"What's it made of?"

"It's fuzzy."

"Like a raccoon?"

"Softer, as in a morning sunrise, and pink, like her lips. A cap with a brim, an old-fashioned cap."

He dances awhile as the girl.

"I think I understand the girl but I still don't understand 'advertisement.'"

"In an image or a series of images, a woman becomes a kind of stand-in for the thing you're meant to buy."

"And what's the thing you're meant to buy?"

"This trip."

"I feel as if we're speaking two different languages."

"Every day, see, for several hours, the Manhattan Company, my current employer, broadcast on an enormous screen in Times Square a moving image of the girl in question, dancing in the driver's seat of the Autobus Godspeed—the bus we now live in—floating past palm trees swaying in a gentle breeze against a deep blue sky. Text appeared beneath her that said *food* and *ease* and *return to past lifestyles and values.* But mostly the girl dancing."

"What is a moving image?"

"A flat picture that is a record of a certain space and time."

"Can anyone make one?"

"No. It requires complex machines and a lot of fuel. Only the company that controls our very limited resources can make moving images, and even they must be careful how many they make and how often they show them. All moving images must be both purposeful and beautiful. That's why we're here, by the way."

"Why?"

"To increase our fuel supply."

"Well we don't have any."

"Says you."

"What else about her?"

"Arms thin, tubelike, muscled, covered in soft skin."

"You like softness."

"Hairless arms."

"I've got hairy arms." I show him. He trembles.

"Ribbed pink sleeveless shirt," he says.

"Of course we make all our garments of hide, fur, hair, and tree pulp. Tell me about her legs and feet."

"I couldn't see them. The bus door was closed."

"Were you not curious enough to open it?"

"A moving image is a record of something that already happened, just as, if you were to write a description of a tree and send it to me in New York, I would not be able to chop down the tree and count its rings."

"Did you make love to her?"

"I've never met her."

"When all you men got off the bus that first day and came to dinner at our place, why did she remain on the bus?"

"She'll never leave the bus."

"Did she die on the trip down?"

"She *was* the trip down."

"And you've bought this trip?"

"We bought it, we built it, it's ours, and we're gonna pay for it."

"My feet itch. I have to go and see my dad."

"Please tell me your name again."

"Pocahontas, but that's not my real name. My real name is a secret. If I tell you it you'll die."

"Aren't you then deceiving me?"

"No. All deceptions keep secrets but not all secrets deceive."

"Do you want to know my name?"

"I know enough of you for now."

And off I march on itchy feet.

Twenty minutes went by in which I had no thoughts, and now I'm having some again. I'm thinking of the grim, ranine sunlight that surrounds and obliquely penetrates this old corn shack I'm climbing into, was climbing into, am sitting down inside of; musty, worn corn shack in a fallow field: my home. The pallet I am sitting with erect posture on is crisp and hard. A gloom pervades the air in here. Can I do the dance the girl that guy described to me did? I would like to meet her. Maybe I'll go to New York one day. Wish I could watch myself dance right now. Where is a mirror when you want one, or a divan or a friend or a dad?

Frank

I bit the one whose ear's already been bitten off. Now he's out half a forefinger due to his dumbness and my teeth. Some guys don't know how not to get bitten down to nothing. He'll be gone in a week at this rate. Or maybe he's one of those guys who won't be what he should be till he's half of what he was. A certain kind of guy wises up only after getting halved.

For biting him they slapped me sixteen times. And they can fucking slap me all they want. Slap away, you pack of fools, and put a finger near my teeth again, and see how long it lasts. Man, it stinks in here. Rain, unbathed men, weeks of indigestion unto death. Which is it, sad or cute, that they haven't figured out we speak English yet? They think I'm their insurance against the eight sample guys they're sending to Sid, two a day for four days, for him to vet: this is partly true. God, I could make quick work of them with a small knife. All but a few. The short, thick guy with the red beard would take some guile to overcome. The muscle guy, one of the two who look alike, would take a little guile. The fat one with one arm moves slow but has the big gun and has been in the rough a hundred times—that would make him hard in the closework. If I could not just trim but shred one with my teeth I'd calm down a bit. Goddamn thin hall of stink on wheels, someone ought to burn this thing. It should take thirty guys a few days to throw up enough houses for them all and they haven't finished one. Pack of weaklings don't have a single skill to live beyond their fortress town up north. I've heard about it: bright green sea on all sides that you'd die to stick a foot in.

He's staring at me now, the one with the red beard, considering me. He's got wounds of his own: healing gash below his hair, livid puffed-up skin around the eyes, broken nose. I bet his own guys beat him. He gives me the quick upward head toss. "Jack Smith." He's the real head of this group. The one who's head in name alone, the weakest one of all, the soft and indecisive one, the one whose job should be to gratefully part his lips and ass when the hunters in the group come home and want a balm, can't stand Jack Smith, had him beaten but he knew he couldn't have him killed, knew the death of Smith would mean the death of all, or didn't know but was told, "Sir, we'll beat him but we won't kill him." Jack Smith takes me in, acknowledges me, recognizes me. He's the me of his side, I'm the him of mine. Powhatan's not like their weak guy but he's old, his decisions honeyed with sentiment. That he would let his daughter talk to him that way and not punish her is proof. To love a girl is no excuse to let her fuck you in public. My eye still hurts where she poked me. I'll poke her back repeatedly till she bears me a son. I yearn to fuck her sentimentally but to let sentiment enter fucking's a deadly mistake in a war. In a war you want to mate with a strong girl, and if she pokes you once or ten times before you can get a seed in, that much better for the future of the town. One day you lie on a girl and fuck her with your feelings and the next you're on your back and your feelings lie on top of you like a fat succubus. Look at Powhatan, who can't move. You can see little of the battlefield from a horizontal vantage. I know no man of war as great as he was in his time, but for action an old man's as bad as an old woman or a girl. We can string these chumps along awhile without detriment, but soon we'll have to act, and if he can't act we'll act against him first, have already started to, Joe and Stickboy and me and a few others. Damn bus, I can't breathe.

Now that the rain has stopped, the bus is empty but for Smith, the muscle, and the guy whose finger I pretended to swallow and will tie into my hair tonight when I get out of this putrid hellhole. The rest are trying to build their fort, which I'd like to see become their tomb. Powhatan plans to soften them up with bad water and starvation, then give them some of what they need in exchange for all we can extract from them. The last part's pretty vague: all, what's that? To me that's the first thing you find out—one thing I was sent here to do but so far their talk reveals squat.

A scuffle on the bus behind me. That scrappy little one who thinks he likes to mete out pain wants to get to me but the big guy won't let him. Guy like that attacks and fails, attacks and fails, a catamite of pain, a gloryhole with teeth, I don't disadmire the undaunted singleness of goal. A throbbing, newly half-gone digit doesn't stop him wanting more from me. A scruple doesn't enter into how he thinks or acts. He's a man of pure ends and needs. Guy knows which big rock is his to try to move up the sheer face of the cliff of his life. Jack Smith's up front with a log book and half-finger-man's still back there straining against the big guy who wears the surprisingly crisp and clean and white and tight tank top and underpants. They've got me strapped to a bolted-down seat with my back to most of the inside of the bus. I face a window so scuffed and smeared I can't see shit from it. Waving brown-red tops of corn stalks like a sea of semi-hardened blood. Jack the pragmatist, big guy into hygiene, little guy in love with pain and death, my admiration grows, the better to kill them with, contempt makes a man sloppy, how helpful it already has been to be in this putrid place.

"Dark savage bastard, let me go over there and bite his finger off and then I'll bite his dick off and then I'll bite the dicks off all of them and then let's see how glorious their cocksucking little civilization is, I hate it down here in the wild, let me go rip his fingernails off one by one, what do you care if I do?"

That's a predictable speech. Jack Smith didn't look up from his log book for it, must be soothing background music to him. He knows as long as you can hear the small guy yell you don't have to keep an eye on him— that's what the big guy's for. I wouldn't mind being on the big one. I bet he's pretty good at taking pain. Of the three, I could make best use of him alive. Smith's too smart and finger man's too wild but with strength like that and discipline and cleanliness the big one'd make a good extension of me. A good commander knows how to make his men prostheses of himself. You feed a guy like that a sturdy balanced diet of dignity and humiliation, you can use him to the combined extent of his capabilities and yours.

Smith's behind me now and sticking something sharp and hard in my back. I've tried to twist my semi-unencumbered head around to bite off anything of his that's there and he's elbowed me in the temple. I respect that. He now has something softer draped across my upper back as well as the hard thing pressed in farther down. I'm semi-blinded by the blow to the head so I pull my strength inward now and won't strike again unless I have to and then will strike hard and not miss, kill him or let him know he'll have to feel a lot of pain to give me some, if that's what he wants, I can't tell. The little guy is very clear in what he wants to do, but Smith knows how to be obscure.

"Just so you know, nothing's stopping me from killing you but whim. You think you matter much to us? We don't need you. We don't need anyone in your town. What do any of you have that we don't have more and better of?" What's the soft thing along my upper back? How irksome! I guess he's leaning on me like a chum, a chum who at all times knows he may need to knife you. My head's clearing. What's he saying this for? It's not gratuitous. It's a bluff and I like him for it. Even an obviously false bluff about a man's dispensability's a little bit discomfiting. I admire him for it. Soften me up. Another nice thing is he knows I speak English or has a hunch. Smart motherfucker and I like him more and more, want to fight him more and more. "We get rid of you we have one less point of resistance is how I see it." Good, keep talking, Jack Smith, and when I can I'll hammer you hard and then you'll retreat to where I can't get at you to recover from the hammering and then you'll come back and hammer me harder than I hammered you to let me know I'm still the one in cuffs but you'll find out that even in cuffs I'm going to be fairly interesting to be messed with if you want to try, and I hope you do.

He's walking away. Come back. He's gone, off the bus. The boredom of confinement now unrelieved by a decent enemy to menace me. Now time, who'll guide me slow or fast to my death, is my comrade. The little man has given up for now. Against the chest of the bigger man he sighs and rests. The big one must not love the pollution of his white shirt with the viscous mix of juices of which the little one's noggin offers a steady supply from multiple holes, some made by gods, others by men and beasts. A cloud stands still outside the window here. Time creeps.

Sidney Feingold

Subjects presented themselves two a day for four days, a representative sampling. Each predictably offered considerable resistance, which we softened with broiled venison in a busthead reduction, a savory meal that combines rich and complex flavor with the obliteration of a subject's inhibitions. After the meal, subjects reclined and were engaged in conversation neither substantive nor heavy, this and that, where are you from, what was that like. When the clinician observed them to be sufficiently pliant he introduced a series of inkblots and encouraged them to comment freely on each without concern for logic or coherency. Transcripts of responses follow, with commentary.

JOHN RATCLIFFE. Subject still has baby fat, a smooth face expressive mostly not by muscle movement but by continual shifts in coloration. The relative amounts of blood in each of the thousand facial capillaries tell a thousand different stories of his moods, of which there seem to be four or five per minute. An earnest face in ongoing rebellion against the cynic's mind that struggles to govern it. A man vying for control of his face and losing every day in every way. Posture: regal, petulant. Clothing: fine, tired, soiled.

Subject's response to image two: "It's that bitch my mother making love to, well, half the Upper West Side—the half that did not include my father. My mother's the one on the left. I called her a bitch but that's just a little joke between her and me. I love my mother. I understand her. I understand that she is the one on the left, someone asymmetrical when not in love. The dark place where the two figures come together is me, an unarticulated pre-larval mass, the cloven single-cell creature produced when a female copulates with a thousand males seriatim, or all at once."

"What about the negative space?"

"The white part? The white part at the very top in the middle is also me—just that very top white portion that looks a bit like a lady's ass or upside-down heart that's truncated, cut off. Just below that, well, sometimes when two dogs fuck you need to separate them with a powerful stream of cold water, so that white shape there's a fire hydrant to separate and cool down the dogs. The white figure below that is a man bound at the waist and falling through the sky helplessly toward earth. Now I'm looking at the black blobs and loops and smudges at the bottom. They are shit. Everyone shits. Some people aren't very discriminating about where; myself, for instance, lately. Do you people have a decent water source or do you just have constant diarrhea all your lives?"

JOHN MARTIN: A small young man with a high forehead. Garments, skin, and perceivable orifices filthy; garments obviously once quite fine and still in possession of a vestigial dignity. Subject unusually battered: left ear half gone, face nicked and bruised, extremities swathed in grimy gauze, right forefinger half gone, walks with a limp. Wounds appear not to be self-inflicted but one is tempted to surmise he sought them out.

Subject's response to image four: Upon being presented with this image, subject wept vigorously for ten minutes, pausing only when unable to breathe. In the fifth such interval of breathlessness, I slapped the subject and reminded him in an artificially broken English that while I am trained as a healer, he was in this context being not healed by me but assessed for his mental state, and that his compatriots were relying on him for the success of their mission to pull himself together. Subject gazed dreamily at the image, at me, at the walls of the room, at the air and a phantasm he seemed to see in the air; I estimate that he was at most half-cognizant of the purpose of the interview and of anything else many of sound mind would refer to as the world.

Subject said, "You're playing heartball, son, that's the name of the game and there's no other game in town, you can bet on it, you don't swing for the bleachers you might as well not come up from the dugout, you can do it, son, elbows high, eyes on the ball, gameface, gameface, in the zone 24/7, don't *be* a pussy, *do* a pussy. Oh Daddy, where are you now? Can you hear me? No, the caterpillar of death has spun you up in its cocoon. The cocoon devours all life in its path, bodies broken down and spun into moth flesh, the moth consumes the sky itself. Winged darkness."

"Is that what you see?"

"See?"

"In the inkblot."

"What inkblot?"

"This inkblot."

"What are you talking about?"

I stared at him.

"Hey, I'm just playing with you, you gaunt, bespectacled Indian fuck, glasses-wearing brainiac rimjob."

I restrained myself from laughing and looked at him with what I hoped would appear to be incomprehension. "Tell me what you see in the inkblot. What does it look like to you? What does it remind you of?"

"Your ass."

Though it was probably in violation, strictly speaking, of the protocol of this assessment procedure, I chose to stand up, turn my back to the subject, pull down my pants, and show him my ass while remarking, "Perhaps this will give you a more accurate point of comparison."

The subject, who had been leaning forward rather tensely in his seat, now leaned back, extended his legs, cupped his genitals, massaged them briefly through his pants with his bandaged right hand, ran the same hand down and up from high hairline to chin as if to erase his face, dropped both hands limply to his sides, tilted his head back, opened his mouth, closed his eyes, wept again, stopped himself from weeping moments later, sighed. "All right, all right, it's like a half-man, half-autobus creature that roams in the night. Its eyes are also headlights, its function is to crush. You can see two guys' legs oozing out from under it, one on either side. Its tailpipe is its dick. Two giant flaps open up in its rear to expose the penis for, you know, various penile functions. It backs up into its mate. Right now it has a probe in its urethra and it isn't liking that too much. It doesn't feel pain the way we do because it's half-autobus, but I think you'll agree there's no getting around how much a probe in the dick is going to hurt even something that's half a machine or whatever. The man-autobus is enormous, even bigger than the autobus we arrived in. I think it's safe to say that the entity that's doing the probing can expect violent retaliation and I don't mean an eye for an eye but I'd have to guess somewhere in the neighborhood of a hundred eyes for an eye if I'm making myself at all clear."

Philip Habsburg

This morning as I sit atop this watchtower situated on the highest point in Fort Greene Park and gaze down upon my brethren in the struggle who scurry along Myrtle Avenue as if not to scurry would be to die—and it could—I contemplate the trouble; not the trouble of the world, which is coincident, coextensive, and will be coterminous with it, but the trouble of another dear and finite entity, my son, John Martin. Someone blundered, maybe his mother, if a force of nature could be said to blunder; one cannot fault and cannot but love a woman who mates like a man, fuck and move on, fuck and move on. Where is she now? Myrtle Avenue, Flatbush, DeKalb, the long view down to Coney Island, Myrtle, Flatbush, DeKalb, I am spinning around in an ancient wheeled office chair spinning around in an office chair spinning in an office chair spinning in a chair spinning my beloved son are you dead or alive? What had happened when you came home from school on that first afternoon of your thirteenth year and wept and continued to weep past nightfall? What did it mean when you came home afternoon after afternoon and wept? The torn bedclothes, the marks on the wall, the cuts on your thigh and forearm and wooden floor, the episodes of swollen feet and hands and lips, the hours in the basement, the diaries written and burned, written and burned? In week four of your daily weeping I deployed a strategy of unwavering irritability to see you through the crisis. Your stepmother, the first official Mrs. Philip Habsburg, may she remain deceased, chose as her strategy incomprehension and oft-articulated impotence. "I'm scared," you eventually shrieked, to whom I forget, "I'm scared of the other boys. They are horrible, horrible creatures," as if that explained anything. I hadn't yet defected from Manhattan then. I put you in the finest school and when you squirmed and wailed I held you there. And now you are a vicious, willfully stupid twit, weakling, and my mortal enemy, as is Jimmy Stuart your boss, as is Penny Ratcliffe my erstwhile concubine, now his. Manhattan's finest schools produce Manhattanites and for that reason must be destroyed. At this moment multiple phalanxes of assassins are moving across the Williamsburg, Manhattan, and Brooklyn Bridges in what I hope will be a decisive maneuver in our peaceful ongoing diplomatic exchange with the people of that fetid isle. And here up the side of the tower comes a Manhattanite in skintight black jumpsuit and mask. I steady my rifle down the tower's vertical wall, sight him, pull; a liquid wad of red springs up from a hole in the black mask, dissipates, and falls in separate droplets to the flagstones below, followed moments later by the Manhattanite himself. He is swept up by the tattered remains of the patrol he hasn't killed and I shout down to them, "Someone relieve me!" Expert work by this assassin, he seems to have dispatched ten of my men; slightly more expert work by me. I stroll now down the hill to the tented outdoor command center on the erstwhile tennis courts. These are the few last fine days of spring. In a week we'll move in out of the beastly sun to our bunker in South Portland Street. Johnny Martin, where are you, and are you my fault? Before I die I'd like to see you, hail you, hug you, kiss you, love you, plumb your depths, and kill you.

Sidney Feingold

JOHN ROLFE. The "communications officer," this should be interesting. Looks more like an aesthete—a worn-down aesthete, a sad and angry aesthete, is there any other kind?—than someone who can communicate or accomplish anything. His long greasy brown hair adheres to his skull and neck; they all have greasy hair but one senses the present subject's hair would be styled the same even were he not on the rag end of nowhere. Dark and sunken eyes with a crepuscular lividness to the skin surrounding them. Dark purple lips of medium thickness coming to two sharp gynecoid points beneath the nose, ever pursed as if to kiss or make a remark so subtle only a listener with a self-endangering degree of empathy for the speaker would discern its full meaning. Skin in the same deplorable condition as that of his comrades, though one suspects in his case he's let a quarter-inch paste of grease build up atop the skin as a form of shield for an organ twice as sensitive as that of an average man. Posture: snakelike, wound around his own body as if to strangle and consume himself.

"This chair is uncomfortable," says the subject.

"Apologies."

"Say something else."

"What would you like me to say?"

"You speak English perfectly well, don't you, only with that same odd emphasis and inflection as the girl we discovered you with in the corn shack when we arrived, Poke-a-huntress."

He blushes. I shrug. Under the languor and grease he knows what's going on.

"So then what the hell was the charade with the translation software?"

I shrug again. To be seen through and yet maintain a nearly expressionless psychiatric neutrality is so delicious I'm getting a bit of a junior erection that I hope the subject can't detect from where he sits.

Subject's response to image two: "The two main dark forms are horned and hunchbacked beasts. They're holding hands and very much in love. And each had been alone for many years. And each had been vicious and felt doomed. A standard night for either beast had been to wake up late in a cave that was its transient home, bathe in a nearby stream, dry itself with leaves, gallop to the closest town, kill as many humans as quickly as it could with its diamond-hard teeth and sharp claws; when fatigue began to cramp its back and arms and legs and jaw, it dragged a last girl—always a young girl with smooth skin, blonde hair, a throaty scream, and much to live for—off into the woods to sodomize and eat her; in the wee hours, a crushing melancholy came, for the goal of all the death—especially the death that was the meal—was revenge, the dish that leaves the belly wanting more.

"And who do you think, Dr. Find Gold, had wronged the beasts?"

"I don't know, tell me."

"God. Do you know who I mean when I say God?"

"Well our culture is not monotheistic, and therefore—"

"Shut up, it was a rhetorical question. God had made these beasts to kill, and made their minds to need revenge. They killed to get revenge against the God who made them need revenge."

"Isn't that self-defeating on the part of your God?"

"No, that's what God calls 'creativity.' And then the beasts met. Funny story. It happened in a town not far from here. That night the beasts moved toward one another, unaware, from opposite ends of this town, from house to house, slashing little children through the heart, biting the heads off the moms, and then, in some unknowing schmuck's backyard, each saw the other. They stood still. They thought, Am I dreaming? Looking in a mirror? And each, for the first time, felt love, as strong or stronger than the urge to kill. They ran at each other and crashed, like two moons that collide in cold, dark space. And here's an interesting anatomical fact about the beasts. Each one had both a vagina and a penis, but one's penis was located six inches above its vagina, while the other's vagina was located six inches above its penis. At the moment of impact, the penises slid into the vaginas. Each beast, having paid scant attention to these body parts till now—despite the sodomy of the human girls, which was reflexive, a bodily function if you will, like shitting, or murder—each beast sank its many pointed teeth into its lover's neck, but not deep enough to kill. While the intended human victim of both looked on from the back porch of his house in horror, bewilderment, and, let's tell the whole truth here, unwished-for sexual arousal, the two beasts were rolled up in one delicious ball of black fur on the lawn, pleasure mounting and mounting and mounting until, with a long and thunderous double-beastly roar, they came into each other with violent contractions of their planet-moving muscles, and came as they came, which made them come again, which made them come again.

"And so began a beautiful friendship, Dr. Find Gold. They no longer felt the urge to kill. They switched to eating grasses, mosses, fungi, leaves, and grains. They settled in a cave that got lots of late-afternoon sun. They planted a garden of flowers and herbs. They frolicked through the forest hand in hand. Pictured here, each transforms the other's ugly face with love's gaze. Playfully they stick their tongues out between sets of teeth made to snap the thickest human bone but no longer used for that purpose.

"And now I call attention to the darker blobs of ink within each large, dark form. These represent the overflow of love from the beasts' breasts, a soft, black, oozing love that spreads beyond the body of each beast, beyond each beast's inherent, God-given capacity for love, a blob of dark ink that stands for love's power to transcend destiny, for all that's good in life, and is released in each beast by its only beloved—a blob of ink which, in a sense, became the world by blotting out the world.

"And now I would like to call your attention to what is asymmetrical in this picture, namely, the long, thin line of goo that's coming out the right beast's ass. It's a shit, but not an ordinary shit, as you can see. Woven into it are elongated blobs of mucous and blood. The right-hand beast, in its old, murderous life, while sodomizing some nice young lady before devouring her, contracted dysentery from the excreta that clung to the inside of her anal canal, for though she herself was not infected, she carried the germs. Both beasts had had stomach cramps and runny bowels before. Both had had fevers. Neither made much of the illness. When the right-hand beast could not get out of bed, the healthy one brought back berries for it, though the right beast's appetite was gone. The beast of sound body, being a beast, knew nothing of medical science, and so made little of its companion's dehydration, the tenderness of its abdomen, the referred pain in its right shoulder, and, toward the end, the yolky yellow fluid that poured from the abscesses in its liver, and down and out its alimentary canal, and again I refer you to the picture if you don't believe me.

"I don't know how to tell the rest of this. What can be said about the pain the left beast felt when the right beast died? Nothing, at least not by me. I don't have the words. Nor do I know how this beast grieved. Did it return to killing girls and men? Did it try to kill itself, or God? I can't say. What I can say is that it lived for many more years in a state of undiminished grief. And do you know what the living beast is called?"

"No."

"Nor do I, but I suspect it's a name we both know, a common name, the name of something ordinary you'd find around the house."

BUCKY BRECK. Fatigue, the stress of testing foreigners all day, my body's aches and pains from sex with Char, and what the evaluator has unequivocally determined is a wicked contact high off the busthead have rendered his remarks in this space more freeform than he'd intended or than is useful given his pragmatic goal. Psychological evaluation is a young man's game. I'm stiff and tired and sore and wan. Lately when I have time for thought I choose pleasure instead, and one can't choose both for the two curdle when mixed. I need to think, but not right now. Evaluator, evaluate thyself, but not right now, not when I have their strongest man in a chair in this room with nothing between him and me but a cheap desk and a stack of psychiatric prints. But he wouldn't hurt a squirrel in mid-flight toward his face unless ordered to. Oh to be young and strong and mindless! You think one thing at a time and between that thought and what you know to be true there lurks no intermediary of doubt.

The evaluator is a gnat on the neck of a flea. The man who sits across from him is sheathed in the pale armor of his skin. The evaluator believes the cut on his own knuckle must have brushed against some dust of uncut busthead and wonders just how fucked up he will become.

"Looks like you've been sampling your own sauce," the subject says. The evaluator is trying to hold it all together but some of it flies round the room, out the window, and toward the tops of trees, where passing gulls catch it in their beaks, chew it, swallow it, digest it halfway, fly back to their nests, and vomit it into the disproportionately large and obscenely open mouths of their infant children, who then fly from their nest and, taking the first aerial crap of their lives, let it fall on the head of the evaluator to whom it once belonged, restoring this part of himself to himself, but not in a dignified manner. But dignity is just a lie the living tell themselves about the seriousness of their own lives.

"Are we supposed to be doing something here or just staring? Wow, your pupils are mad dilated."

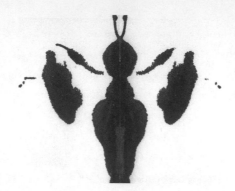

Subject's response to image number seven: "Tell you what I see? I see, you know, a bunch of blotches."

"No, what does it look like, what does it resemble?"

"I'm not following you."

"What does it look like?"

"It looks like some black ink blotches on a—"

"All right, follow my lead here. One might say about this that it resembles a fly with its wings plucked off."

"Plucked off? Why would someone pluck the wings off a fly?"

"To study it, or to be cruel, I suppose, or some combination of the two, but I was just giving you an example."

"If you plucked the wings off it, it wouldn't really be a fly any more, would it? I mean think about the word *fly,* seems like if you take the wings away you can't call it *fly* any more. Maybe the wings are the part that's really the fly, so whoever did the plucking really plucked the *fly* off the fly."

The evaluator is holding back tears.

"Anyway I see more of a mother and her two babies," the subject says.

"Excuse me?"

"A mother and her two babies."

"Tell me more."

"The mother is flinging the babies away from her and now they have to fend for themselves."

"Why would she do that?"

"Because she loves them."

"The mother flings away her own babies because she loves them?"

"So they'll learn how to get along in the world. That's how most decisions are: like you've been flung and you haven't hit the ground yet and you're thinking real fast about how to land with the least amount of pain."

"So the two larger, uh, blotches on the left and right of the central blotch are the babies?"

"Yes."

"And the two lines extending out and up from the central blotch?"

"The mom's arms."

"They're not attached to her body?"

"That just shows how much she loves her babies."

"How so?"

"Well I didn't make the drawing or anything, but it seems like the person who did was saying that flinging away the babies makes the mom feel like she's flinging away her own arms."

"But she does it anyway."

"She has to, even if the babies will hate her from the time she flings them until just a little bit before they die."

"That's a big sacrifice, giving up her children's love for their survival."

"Has to be done."

"You said a little bit before the babies die they'll stop hating their mother. Why?"

"They will understand that she was preparing them to accept death with a calm heart, and they will forgive her."

The evaluator tries to look at the subject's face to see what he might be feeling, but the air in the room has grown dark, and the subject's face is a part of the darkness. No, the subject's face is the source of the darkness.

"Hey, Doc, do you need a glass of water or something?"

"No, I'm fine."

"Why you lying face-down on the floor?"

"Resting."

"Rough night?"

"Rough decade."

"I hear you, man. What was in that sauce, anyway? I'm feeling weird."

An observer—say, the ghost of the august medical man who was my mentor, Dr. Ronald McKelty, whose job is now to float behind my left ear and shake his vaporous head in disapproval of everything I do—might think the evaluator has lost control of the interview. Not so. He feels the only way to maintain control is to give in to the wish to lose control. That is why the evaluator is now rolling around and moaning softly on the floor of the evaluation chamber, a floor of dirt the tread of many feet has made shine like gold.

"Am I done? I don't feel so good," the subject says. Whoever sweeps this floor does a great job. There's not a spider web or speck of dust, at least not in the corner of the floor my face now occupies.

"Doctor, let me help you up," the subject says.

"What's it feel like to be you?" I say.

"I don't know."

A Couple of Fops

"What's happening now?"

"They're thinking it over."

"Thinking what over?"

"Whether to tear us new assholes."

"We'll need them if the bad water and rancid food keep using the old ones at peak capacity. Speaking of which, do you have any extra bottled water?

"Are you kidding me?"

"That brackish water the Indians gave us in exchange for that non-working motorcycle is not agreeing with me and it might be nice to clean this infected arrow wound in the thing that was my hand before this big and purple and amorphous mass replaced it. Not that one can blame the Indians. Imagine how sore we'd be if they were to arrive unannounced in New York in a large armored vehicle and park it at 42nd and Broadway."

"My wounded knee sympathizes with your wounded hand."

"Yes, I've seen your knee. Dreadful."

"COULD ANYONE SPARE ANY CLEAN WATER? DON'T FORGET US SICKIES, WE'RE HUMAN TOO!"

"That was decent of you. I've always liked you."

"Same."

"Same."

"Same."

"Where did Jack Smith go? I feel better when he's around, not that I think he can save us but he seems less likely to get us all killed than the other gentlemen in whose hands our fate rests."

"He left on *an expedition of trading and reconnaissance,* as he said, after giving John Ratcliffe crap vis-à-vis building our fort here on this swamp and, in fact, starting to build it at all, since, as he said, if we were to wait a few days for the Indians to give us permission to build, it would then appear as if we were building because they'd permitted it rather than simply because we wanted to, which is the real reason we're building it, but perception is reality, as he says, or some other boldly pragmatic catch phrase, I do like his phraseology and bearded grin. I wish he were here too. He went off with, among others, the communications officer, Johnny Rolfe. Not that Rolfe's not a decent-enough fellow, but one doesn't ever know what he's really thinking despite the sort of earnest face he presents to the world; it's the *communications officer* aspect of Rolfe I find comical I guess I mean to say. In any case, he and Smith and three others have assembled our remaining all-terrain vehicles and have gone off to *investigate the area and its impact on our options* or some other admirably utilitarian phrase from the mouth of Smith, whom I trust and will trust a whole lot more if he comes back with clean water."

"I beg your pardon?"

"I beg your pardon?"

"Would you repeat what you just said?"

"Which part?"

"The whole thing."

"Dude, my mouth was next to your head when I said it. Where were you?"

"Oh dude, I must have faded out."

"That's all right, I don't feel in tip-top shape myself. At this point I wouldn't mind if someone were to come and move us out of the sun. I feel my skin is melting off."

"WOULD SOMEONE MIND MOVING US OUT OF THE SUN? OUR SKIN IS MELTING OFF!"

"Very kind but I'm not sure anyone heard you. I barely heard you myself."

"And yet it sounded so loud inside my head."

"I'm angry, I confess."

"About what?"

"Dying here."

"I got an awful feeling in my stomach when you said that."

"How can you distinguish between that awful feeling and the awful feeling given to your stomach by the rancid food and water, or any of the terrible events that have happened since we left New York?"

"I don't know."

"I know it does no good to repeat it but I'm pretty angry about dying here."

"Would dying elsewhere be better?"

"Yes!"

"Where?"

"New York."

"Why?"

"My mother."

"She's alive?"

"Yes."

"Is she nice?"

"She would kill for me."

"That *is* nice."

"Did kill."

"Who?"

"A few fellows."

"What for?"

"Meaning me harm."

"Meaning or doing?"

"Meaning with intent to do. Mother. Mother, though, has not lost her softness in hard times. She would treat you nice."

"Would treat *me* nice?"

"Would treat you *very* nice."

"I'd love to meet her."

"She's an excellent cook, can do a lot with a little in the kitchen. I'd love for you to meet her. You and I eating a meal with Mother that she had just prepared. It makes me angry to think it won't happen."

"Don't dwell on the anger."

"Hard not to."

"Hard not to."

Jack Smith

We came up the bank of this creek with a dirt bike and a crude car made from a kit. We'd hauled the car and bike down from New York on the top of the bus and it's paid off, especially now that those asses back at the camp can't even get it together to forage for food. Have to do it all myself. Bastards are good enough at having a guy locked up in chains and punched in the face but don't know food unless some poor idiot in livery brings them a mound of it on a gleaming platter, for the privilege of doing which he's sold his soul and that of his mother. Reminds me of the time I was captured by the president of Pittsburgh, who would have cut off my head had his wife not stopped him. Later she helped me escape from jail, and wished to return to New York with me, and took my refusal with admirable grace, but prevailed upon me in a nightlong swiving that, to judge by her cries, pleased her greatly, but left me cold as swiving always does. By which I mean the act left me cold but not the tender heart of that lady. That most of my sex will sell out their friends and beliefs to soak their dicks I am by no means the first to observe. And though some ladies I know will do the same, on the whole they're a finer lot than the men—and since the urge in me for sex is scant or nil, the fineness of which I speak is of the mind and not the flesh. I don't think that ladies have fewer vile thoughts than men, only that they've learned to inhibit them for the sake of the good, which they've taken pains to let take root in their minds, and for which the minds of most men make rocky soil at best. I sometimes think I glimpse a lady's mind in Johnny Rolfe, a mental fineness, I mean, which I am drawn to and creeped out by in equal measure, and can't afford to think about right now.

Up the bank of the creek we went to trade for food and drink and find the tit of oil we hope is in these parts, else why go to the trouble. Tit of oil and, it would seem, food and water purification technologies, since they seem to eat dead animals and plants and not drop dead themselves. In addition to the booze long since poured into the earth north of here due to Mangold's death, a great strategic loss—the booze, I mean—I'd procured some trinkets from those tough nuts I punked up there in Delaware, and when we parked our dirt bike and car by the creek to make camp before the sun set, and a group of local kids came timidly out from behind trees and concrete half-walls to investigate the strangers and their marvelous machines while their dads hid ready to arrow us in the knees if we got cute with their kids, I took out some colored beads and mottled marbles and copper coins and sundry things and passed them out among the little ones, who laughed and liked them and wanted more, and I gave them more and they scattered along the wooded bank to play and fight among themselves and furtively watch these strange new men who came down from the north with trinkets and a car. It's good to get a strange town's kids to like you as a means to entice its grownups to, unless the grownups think you're out to harm their kids, in which case they'd as soon rip your arm from its socket. But here it worked and the kids' dads crept from behind the trees, bows down, arrows at rest in their quivers. Not that I wouldn't have shot one in the hand with my gun if he'd gone for his bow, but a guy wants not to shoot a potential partner in trade until not to do so would bring about the guy's own death or the death of one of his men.

The dads met us at the bank of the creek, a half a dozen of them. I held up another sack of trinkets and with body English showed I wished to trade it for food and water. They laughed with what I hoped was glee, as jolly savages are said to laugh by some who've met them and some who've not, though I myself have not met anyone, savage or not, who is jolly. One of them took from a small sack around his neck a short stick of bread, which he broke in two and half of which he popped into his mouth. The other half he broke in half again and let one of those halves drop to the hard dirt path we'd been riding on, and pressed it with his foot until it cracked. The last half of a half of a stick of bread he held out to me while he raised his brow and smiled and laughed. This was a lean, red man—all of them are red—with no shirt and the barest apron covering his genitals, which were large, which, I've noticed in passing, most of these Indian guys' genitals seem to be. It burns a man's gut to be mocked when he's not had more than one good meal in a month and a half. Like some of them, this guy had a small green snake that hung down from a hole in his ear on the left side of his head, the side with the hair, and I took out my gun and shot his snake in two as if to say *You're not the only one who can make jokes about halving things*, the sort of joke that isn't meant to make its hearer laugh, though I sensed he understood its meaning.

Of the men who were with me—Rolfe, Lohengrin, Mankiewicz, Gosnold—two, Rolfe and Lohengrin, had guns, and I hoped the Indians didn't calculate the odds of our three guns against their six bows as I did, and evidently they did not, or did and felt pride and bread not worth dying for, and when thirty more red men stepped from behind trees with straw baskets of corn and bread I understood the six we'd seen had been at least half messing with us the whole time, and with body Indian they said they'd give us all the bread and corn for a gun, and with body English I said no way but how about a few hatchets I also happened to have, and classy beads I hadn't shown the kids, and they subtracted a basket each of bread and corn for the deal and said they'd need at least to *try* a gun and I said as long as you promise to give it right back, which they did, and they did, and we sat on the bare earth and all ate bread and meaninglessly looked each other up and down since body language is hard to conduct idle dinner chat in and we needed to save our oomph for the rest of our trip up the bank of the creek and they needed to save theirs for whatever they needed to save theirs for—though I'd also add fuck them because I think they can speak English anyway—but all in all I said to my guys as the sun went down and the red men built a fire that I thought the first day of our trip up the creek was not too bad a day, but I should have known that that is not the sort of thing a man should ever say.

Eventually, and thanks to Rolfe, we did get down to talk, or body talk, and though the body's talk is coarse and inexact, we guessed the red men we dined with that night said the big man on the bed, the sad man in the smoke-filled n-shaped hall we went to for the talk-by-machine, the one who seemed to be the king or chief or president, runs a lot of towns in these parts but not all—not theirs—but with him around they have to watch their backs. These guys gave us what we wanted because we've got what they want and by this I mean not just knives and beads but guns that they think if they play their cards right they could count on us to use against the chief and his men next time they try to mess with these guys we ate with, and since these guys seemed to like thinking that, who would I have been not to let them? They live in a town called, if I'm not wrong, Kickotown. The Kickotown guys said not to let our guard down up the creek, since not all people in these parts are happy to see out-of-towners; in fact a lot of them would rather see us die or leave than stay, and if they get to choose between the first two they choose a bit of both. And so with that in mind, and after six rough hours of one-eye-open sleep, we hit the bank of the creek again on day two of this little side trip about which not enough bad can be said.

Half a mile before we stopped for sundown we saw a sight too wondrous to be good. Despite the car and bike we don't go fast since the path along the creek is strewn with roots and beds of soft mud in which a bike or car could get stuck. So we had a lot of time to take in that sight on a spot across the creek—little dumb show no doubt staged for our delectation—nude young ladies bathing. And not just bathing but slowly soaping up their own and one another's skin, and if their soft purrs and ululations were a sign, really liking getting clean. They dumped buckets of cold water on one another's heads and shrieked as they did, and you could almost see the gooseflesh stand up on their skin and you could see their purple nipples come erect, and then they started soaping up again. You could not fault them for carelessness with dirt. More scrupulous bathing in all world I defy anyone to find, a rigorous honoring of the virtues of soap. Not that I notice such things but all the guys in my group achieved instantaneous wood.

"Jack, let's take a rest here," Happy Lohengrin said.

"Absolutely not," I said.

"I haven't had a bath in a month," he said.

"Nor have I" and "Me neither" and "So very dirty," said the others.

I said, "Are you guys out of your minds? Do you not know a setup when you see one?"

"What setup?"

"We're witnessing good old-fashioned wholesome cleanliness."

"Unselfconscious native ladies getting clean the old-fashioned way."

"Wholesome, honest cleaning."

"What could be more innocent?"

"A stab in the throat with a sharp stick could be more innocent," I said.

"What if I cross the creek on that little log bridge there," Happy said, "and investigate what they're up to with great delicacy, using every skill of diplomacy at my disposal, and you three can stay on this bank with your guns trained on the young ladies, who I think you'd have to agree would be very talented indeed if they were concealing weapons right now."

"I've seen women keep surprising things in that sheath," I said.

Happy, who'd used sex to get Chris to stop the bus and let the men drink booze, wandered over and casually draped himself on my arm—he really is a genius of physical comfort—and said, "'That sheath,' Smith, you're very cute. Really, Jack, this is exactly the kind of situation I'm good in. Don't tell me I wasn't brought on this trip for just this circumstance."

Happy's always up for sex and certain of his skill-set in that field, as well he should be given his prodigious accomplishment with even someone as priggish and married as Chris, and despite my own lack of interest in sex, to tell the truth I've sometimes pictured slipping him one, a smooth and pleasant-featured boy with a calming, easy way. But what he seemed not to want to get was that if a woman's hard-won goodness flees her mind, or if she's one of those in whom it never put down roots, and if she then gets bent on murdering a man, he can please her more intensely than she's ever been pleased in her life—four or five or six times if his means to give her love are as great as hers to take it—but that will not change her mind about her task, whose joy may be most profound if it's done at the peak of her pleasure and his, at least that's what I know of humans' double wish to fuck and kill, which when combined make an alloy stronger than either of its simple component parts.

"No," I said.

"Why?"

"I already said why. It's written all over their—you know—everything."

Gosnold said, "Wouldn't be a bad way to go."

"You have no idea," I said.

"I have an idea," he said and glanced, as did we all, at the front of his pants, a pyramid on its side.

"I forbid it."

"And what are you gonna do if we—"

Before he could end the thought the tip of my gun was in his mouth and the hammer drawn back. "Okay, okay," he said around the gun, and gagged and spat when I pulled it out. "Jesus. What the—" He shut up when I made as if to put it back in.

"No, guys, we have to respect Smith, he may very well know whereof he speaks," Happy said, and winked at me. It's hard not to be sympathetic to Happy. Fucksack he may be but he's got a fundamental decency, no pun meant.

"Take one last long loving look at the lathering ladies, lads." That was Johnny Rolfe, who you never know quite what plane he's moving toward you on but I think he kids more than you'd think from out of a sad face that looks as if it wouldn't ever want to kid, or "employs rhetorical devices" as he would say from out of a face that looks too tired to use any device but a toothpick to prop up each eyelid. Rolfe alone among our men said not a word to try to make me think we should cross the creek to soap up with the girls, though he too was sporting substantive wood, nor did his throat fail to make the same moist sound as the throats of his compatriots, as if those low and mournful sounds were iron shards, the glistening skin of those girls the strongest lodestone in the world. I like that Rolfe. It's good to have someone to like in a time and place in which nature whispers to your heart, *Like nothing, care for nothing, respect nothing, believe in nothing, attach yourself to nothing but the wish to live.* But my liking of Rolfe I'm wary of since what good can it lead to? I'd slit even his throat if I felt I had to though I hope I don't ever feel I have to.

And so we rode our bike and car out of sight of the gals and carried on up the creek toward who knew what, while tears of erotic frustration sprang from the eyes of a few of our guys, fell through the unfamiliar air, and disappeared into the new ground into which we've chosen to press our feet and tires, and on which we brace each day for who knows what. We made camp a half a mile hence and broke our bread and boiled our corn in our water and saved the water after boiling it because we don't have a lot and can't waste a drop. Corn, Jesus. Its sweetness, its unique mouthfeel and palate ride, who knew? Corn is huge. Me, I'd sooner spring to wood for corn than girls.

The night was dark and cool, the woods made noise, and we wondered who or what watched us from beyond the demi-orb of light our fire made. We slept in shifts. Rolfe and I stayed up for the first three hours, Lohengrin and Mankiewicz for the next. So tired was I that sleep encased me like a tomb. And so the scream I heard, though it came from far away, was sharp enough to penetrate my deathlike sleep. Neither Mankiewicz nor Lohengrin was in camp. I heard two repeated screams, a greater and a lesser, but both so far beyond all other uses of the human voice I could not tell which belonged to whom. I grabbed one of our flashlights, told Rolfe and Gosnold—who'd also been awakened and were scared—to stay and watch the bike and car, and ran back down the creek bank toward the screams. I dreaded what was causing them and had to work against the urge not to run toward their awful sound. The thick, insistent dark ceded little to my weak light. I stumbled, fell, got up, ran; stumbled, fell, got up, ran in a daze of fear. Both screams grew louder as I ran, one more quickly than the other. I came around a bend and hit Lohengrin hard in the face with my face but didn't know it was his. We yelled, fell back, got up. I stuck my gun in his neck and he held his knife to mine. We saw each other's faces and the knife and gun came down.

I pointed my light at his face. Each of us was bleeding from the brow. His mouth was open wide and his lips fluttered irregularly. He wheezed and uttered sounds that approximated speech. His eyes were all fogged up. He pointed down the trail from where he'd come. "Mankiewicz. Mankiewicz. Mankiewicz. Mankiewicz."

"What about him?"

"They got him."

"Who?"

"The girls."

More inarticulate sounds and waves of movement in his face; wheezing and weeping. Another howl reached us from what must still have been Mankiewicz. "Where are the girls? Same spot?"

"Yes."

"How many?"

"Don't know."

"What happened?"

"Don't know."

I slapped him and he fell down and wept. I picked him up by his shirt and made him look at me. "Lohengrin, you have to tell me what you know because I have to go get Mankiewicz and I have to know what I'm up against. Now!"

"I talked him into going back down the trail to the girls. We took one of the lights and a gun and when we got there we saw one of the girls sitting alone at the foot of the log bridge in nothing but a pair of panties. Look, we've been on the road a month and a half and you get tired of yanking it or having Mankiewicz do it with his mouth, so—"

"Tell me what happened!"

"We crossed the log bridge to where the girl was. Mankiewicz went first and she held her arms out to him. Oh my God, she looked amazing and I could smell her, and—" Mankiewicz howled again and I felt my balls inch up into my thorax. "Save him, Smith!"

"What else happened, fast, tell me!"

"Then something hit me behind the ear, then I ran back across the bridge and kept running."

"Where's the gun?"

"I don't know."

"Go back to camp and come back here with Rolfe and Gosnold and don't leave the bike and car behind."

I ran for three or four minutes and heard no more howls. When I got to the log bridge the first light was up in the east, downstream. I smelled roasting meat. I shone my light across the creek and saw faint flames lick up behind a human form that must have been Mankiewicz. He was tied to two poles stuck in the ground, left hand and foot to one, right hand foot to one. I couldn't see well but I knew he was dead. His head hung down. He was nude, and in the dim green light of dawn his skin looked darker than it should but I didn't yet know why. The weak light made his belly look like a jagged black hole. I saw no one but him, and the fire behind him continued to cook whatever meat it touched. I hid behind a tree along the bank and called to him, I guess I was confused. I stepped from behind the tree and when I heard a gunshot I also heard its bullet hit the leaves above my head. The gun was a six-shooter and damn it if I hadn't asked Lohengrin if he'd brought extra bullets and if they'd been taken along with the gun. I came out from behind the tree to try to make them shoot at me again. Nothing. I leaned against the tree with my gun in my hand till Rolfe, Gosnold, and Lohengrin arrived.

With our guns out we eased ourselves across the creek. The sun was in the sky behind the trees now and warmed us up a bit. Mankiewicz's fingers were gone, the skin of his arms and legs had been scraped off, the dilapidated shell of bone and skin that had been his torso was now filled up with air and blood. Crusted black shriveled shapes the size of disused socks lay in the dying fire. These must have been his guts, lungs, and heart. Sharpened mussel shells to whose edges clung soft and wet red clumps of scraped-off skin lay on the ground around the tied-up corpse. We put the guts back in, cut it down, and hauled it back across the creek. No one shot at us.

In the car we had a mediocre shovel the Indians had given us to bury Matt Bernard. By trading off we took an hour to dig a hole for Mankiewicz twenty yards back from the creek in a sparse stand of trees. We put him in the hole as gently as we could and looked at him and looked away in turn. I told Rolfe to pray for him before we put the dirt back in and he said, "Why me?" and I said, "Because you're the communications officer," and he said, "God has imposed a communications blackout in case you haven't noticed," and I told him to say a damn prayer.

"Lord, keep us from your thoughts, and you from ours," Rolfe said. He stared at me. I don't think Lohengrin or Gosnold heard a word he said.

Johnny Rolfe

We're fleeing down the creek at breakneck speed while Smith continues on alone—well not alone but with an Indian for a guide. Lohengrin and Mankiewicz are dead. Lohengrin was dead before he died. I'm still alive as far as I can tell. I admire Smith insofar as he seems not to long for love and sex as we do, and the absence of desire for another human's flesh, or soul, seems to redouble his acumen in the preservation of himself and even of his kind—his kind being, for now, the fools he took this trip with, i.e., us. But if the penalty for a yearning heart is to have it cut out of your body and fed to a fire, the penalty for the use Smith puts his heart to is to continue to put it to that use.

As I put the last shovelful of dirt on the mound above what had been Mankiewicz, four Indians walked out of the woods. Smith pressed the muzzle of his gun to the nose of one of them before he recognized him as the guy from Kickotown who gave us bread and corn. The four of them were good enough not to mime *I told you so* regarding Lohengrin's death. Instead they pressed their heads to the mound to show their sympathy or grief. Smith said by hugging their necks that he was glad they'd arrived when they did because he needed them. The one whose nose still bore the impression of Smith's welcome said something I freely translate from the language of gesture as "You have a funny way of showing gladness." Smith apologized and offered them his gun to hold and, he said, in the future, have. In exchange for what, they asked. Someone to guide us through these woods for the rest of the trip up this creek, about a week, Smith said.

The crossed arms of distrust, the raised eyebrows of incredulity, the stamped feet of indignation—in short, a mini-lexicon of cross-cultural resistance and outrage—preceded the moment when, shoved toward us wearing a scowl of odium and fear, a young man from Kickotown whose name seemed to be All-Burnt became our guide. After uttering an angry goodbye to his neighbors, the first thing he did in our midst was to wave his hand in front of his nose and pinch his nostrils with his fingers, a sign we understood, inured though we were to our own smell. He brought us to the creek, jumped in, rubbed his head, face, arms, pits, chest, and crotch with force, and beckoned us to do the same. We demurred, having come from an island whose surrounding waters eat away the human skin.

None of us but Smith wanted to continue the side trip up the creek. Smith came to each of us in turn to hug the backs of our necks tightly with his pythonlike arm and whisper words whose characteristically Smithean ratio of collegiality and brute force was persuasive. The one of us he had most trouble talking into the rest of the trip was Lohengrin, whose neck, having turned to goo with the rest of him, kept slipping out of Smith's arm's embrace. Lohengrin, as I said, was in a sense already dead. He died when what he lived for—the pleasure of loving—had its guts scooped out while it watched and heard its own screams. And so the wire that connected Lohengrin to the future was cut, and he was stranded in the present.

All-Burnt, hygienic savage amid putrescent civilized men, led us back up the creek till darkness came. We ate, and he agreed to stay awake through the night while we slept. I woke up at dawn to find Smith and All-Burnt gone, no doubt to show the early bird gets the oil reserves, the point of this trip up the creek and of the larger trip down south, I think, is it? I forget. Gosnold was asleep, and Lohengrin lay apart from us, eyes catatonically open. I happened to be looking right at him when it began. It was as if the seeds of twenty arrows had been planted beneath the skin of his legs, belly, chest, arms, and neck, and now all sprang up to a height of a foot and a half in the time it takes a man to sneeze and be blessed. And so the life of his body ended not long after that of his mind. By the time I finished watching Lohengrin's death, Gosnold was on the bike and hauling ass down the creek. I leapt on behind him. Smith with his oil and Lohengrin with his new non-Lohengrinness would have to understand.

Albert

How did he do this to me and how did I let him? He did it with elastic wrist-bands and a will to live that obliterates consideration. And I let him insofar as my chief skill in life has been to let. At my urging, my friends and I came back to the sad little band of Northerners after the scoundrels of Chickahominy lured one of them across the creek with sex and disemboweled him. I'm known for placing empathy over caution in the affective chain of command; if after I die I'm thought of for having said anything worthwhile, it'll be "How are you?" I accommodate, therefore I am but briefly.

I'd meant for us to stay just long enough to press our heads against the mound of dirt they'd put their murdered man in, to let them know their grief was not lost on us. I hadn't thought Jacksmith, who has since caused what soon will be my death, would ask for one of us to "guide" him. But he did, and I was the obvious choice, and so he and I rode up the creek on these men's car and bike, whose ill-suitedness for this land boded well for mirth if not for life, and whose loud sounds cracked each cubic foot of air they entered into.

All day, in fealty to the people of my town, I kept my English tongue inside my head. That we don't speak English is a ruse my people think both necessary and hilarious, a hundred years' supply of laughs squeezed from one small, hard joke. At dusk, when we stopped and ate, the northerners looked so grim and tired I told them with signs I'd stay awake all night while they slept. Hours later, when the sky turned from black to deep green, Smith awoke, called me "All-Burnt," and said with signs he wanted me to push on with him into the woods. I said we couldn't go till we could see. He took out a small electric torch and yanked me by the arm. Though I didn't want to, I obliged, and as I lie across the shoulders of two men I don't know, who are bringing me to a town near mine but not mine, I reflect again that this has been my life's main work: to oblige another's wish against my own.

A mile into the woods, Jacksmith and I were besieged by men from Werowocomoco, Powhatan's town. I heard their feet and breath moments before I felt their arrows move the air beside my head. None hit their mark, not because of our footspeed, or the dark sky, or thickly planted trees, but because the men meant to take him alive, which makes my death another grim if somewhat modest joke. Jacksmith, not knowing he was surrounded and already caught, slipped the two tight, dirt-browned elastic sweatbands he wore on his right wrist around my right wrist without first detaching them from his, and, as I tried to get loose, he tried to place me between himself and the arrows, which, as I said, were meant at most to graze. The arrows' shooters did not anticipate a target that was doubled, and flailed, and so an arrow pierced me in the neck, another in the chest, another in the gut, another in the groin, another in the knee.

Jacksmith saw what he thought was a hole in the wide ring of men and, holding me, ducked through it. That was when we fell into the swamp. The swamp embraced us and wouldn't let go. Jacksmith squirmed and I squirmed beneath him. My lungs, against their best hope, sucked swamp water even as the pressure of his body on mine drove the arrows deeper into me. By the time more air reached my lungs I was somewhat more dead than I'd ever been, and in the strong hands of Powhatan's men. As they bound Jacksmith's arms and legs with rope, they laid me on dry land, pulled their arrows out of me, replaced them with salves, but I could see by their eyes and feel by the mood of my wounds that I wouldn't recover.

These—the wounds—are the next-to-last gifts I'll ever be given, the salves the last. The salves, as gifts, are of use in the economy not of healing but of feeling, the wounds of use in the economy of dying. The front of me, where the arrows went in, now faces the branches of the trees and the sky, to which I say goodbye by touch, taste, smell, sound, and sight, through my new wounds and through the old intrinsic ones—mouth, nose, eyes, ears, skin. Two men I don't know are carrying me face-up toward their town and my doom, and if I want to see one final time a few last landmarks I know before

I leave for a place, if place it is, whose landmarks I suspect I won't know—unless the punishment for life is more life—I'll have to arch my neck and see them upside down, which makes my neck's new hole stretch, which hurts, and so I see these last familiar sights through an added veil of pain. But because part of what makes pain hurt is knowing it will continue over time, mine doesn't hurt that bad.

We now pass the spot where I killed my first deer, whom, exemplifying how poor a warrior I have always been, I sentimentally named Thomas before he died, and so his name remained as I carried him back to my town—as these men now carry me back to theirs, or maybe mine, since all this looks so known to me—and Thomas he was when I skinned him, when my mother and sister chopped his flesh and stewed it with spices and corn, when we ate him, when we shat him into a hole in the ground, and Thomas he continued to be in the flies that ate the shit and are long dead now too and part of the earth and the air, and Thomas he is to this very hour in me, who am dying, and causing him to die again, but he'll live on in, for one, the sassafras tree that thrives in the spot on the forest floor that once was the hole we shat my first dead deer out of ourselves into.

And there's where I had my first kiss—I wish I had it still, I wished it had been on the mouth of the girl whose neck it was on, I wished her neck had liked the kiss as much as my lips did, I wished her cunt had liked it as much as my dick did. Whose kiss was it anyway? Whose lips, dick, deer, and shit? Not mine, I've rented or borrowed them, am moments from giving them back.

And there on the bark of that tree is the stain of the tears I shed when the girl that I kissed kissed someone else, and beside it the stain of the blood that I shed from the cut I made on my arm to try to get the pain of not being kissed back outside my body, where it had threatened a coup against my brain's rule of law.

And there is the place I was killed by my Uncle Al, not really killed but we called it killed—killed as a boy to become a man, one of the ancient folkways we've tried to adopt from people whose bloodline was cut long before we were born, people whose bloodline we do not continue but whose folkways we try to, though we know them only in fragments and some of them make no sense in the present, as for example the symbolic death of a boy who is then reborn as a man. If you're going to kill a boy don't screw around with symbolic death, do it for real, all but a few of us boys should have died for good back then, save a town a lot of grief, so many adult males competing for extremely limited resources on a blighted land, which leads to perpetual war or constant and vigilant work to avoid it, who wants that? Death and rebirth minus the rebirth: now there's a coming-of-age rite that would wake up a teenager, but this may just be one of the many holes in me talking, though whether mouth, ass, or arrow wound I cannot say. Is there even a me any more, or am I a mere mind being jostled at shoulder height past key sylvan landmarks, defunct farms, disused and crumbling interstate highways and county roads, fallen-down condos and malls, dead pathways and venues I resemble more and more? Death and rebirth? Death and death to all boys who won't take a vow not to kill.

And there's the spot where I killed my first man—look, a drop of his blood on that leaf over there—one of the scoundrels of Chickahominy, they've got metal knives but they favor the sharpened mussel shell and the murder styles of many years past, a touch of nostalgia for good honest old-fashioned violence and death. I was out in the woods looking for berries or my own happiness, a boy with a care and a good eye for wild fruit, when this Chickahominy asshole jumped me with mussel-shell knuckles and tried to gouge out my eyes. He knocked me down and leapt on me screaming. While he was midleap I unsheathed my bodkin and held it straight up. He saw it coming toward him as he fell but by then he couldn't unstick his fate from the planet's gravity field.

And there is the spot where I rushed to my mother's arms with the blood of the dead Chickahominy boy still fresh on my clothes. She slapped me, I fell down, I stood up, she slapped me again, but more softly this time, and hugged me, held me against her breast for a long time, complicated woman, how complicated and difficult to be a woman in these times, and maybe these new holes in my body help me know what it's like to be female; no child will enter the world through any one of them, but they seem to be birthing new thoughts.

And there is the face of the girl whom I finally kissed on the mouth, my wife, nice girl, whose belly's as big as a corn shack with our son, whom I'll never lay eyes on except in outline—bye, Albert Junior, or All-Burnt Junior, or whatever your name will be, I hope you'll be less accommodating than I of rivals, strangers, neighbors, friends, and your own wish to be kind.

And look, there's the spot where I encouraged my unborn son not to be kind, great legacy, thank you, world, for letting me be for as long as I was, peace out.

Pocahontas

"Excuse me, Sir, are you the northern aggressor who ordered the hamburger?"

I said that, about two seconds ago, through a hole in a wall of the n-shaped room where my father put the captured man from the bus who looks impregnable to arrows, knives, and doubt.

"Who's talking to me? Where are you?" He stands with his back to the wall through whose one dot of not-wall I speak to him. He is short, and so my mouth, whose height the wall's hole is at, addresses the small, sad spot of scalp around which his manly red mane swirls. I spied him through a side window a moment ago, his legs slightly bent at the knee, arms not quite touching his sides, never unready for an attack on his life though his feet be tied to the floor.

"You want a side with that? The chef would also like to recommend her delicious turtle-meat bruschetta, at no extra cost."

"How many of you speak English?"

"How many of me do you imagine there are?"

"Who are you?"

"Your conscience."

"Come on."

"Call me the voice of the hole in the wall."

"You're the girl we met the day we arrived, you were sitting in a corn field with that old guy, you did that dance, you led us back to that town where all those girls were."

"Those weren't girls, Sir, those were ladies."

"Could have fooled me."

"What is the purpose of your visit?"

"We're here on vacation. Where are you?"

"Will knowing where I am help you tell me why you're here?"

"Yes."

"I'm behind and above you."

He turns—I think, though I can't see him well since his head blocks my view—to look at me as best he can, given the disposition of his feet, and sees, I'd guess, a dark hole, since where I am behind the wall is in the shade, and this is what I am to him for now, a dark hole, as he's a large and darkened head to me.

"How'd you get back there?" he says. "Am I not being guarded?"

"I bribed the guard."

"Is this some kind of psychological torture? What are your plans for me?"

"What would you like my plans for you to be?"

"Seriously."

"Seriously? First fatten you up, then eat you. A soup and salad comes with your meal. I'd recommend the corn chowder and the caprese with tomato, basil, and coon's milk mozzarella."

He's breathing deeply now, I think. He's taking long, slow breaths to dissipate his fear with air. I'm messing with his head, though that's not what I came here to do. What did I come here to do? I came here to know. Know what? I don't know, but I came at peril of my freedom, if freedom only to run from corn shack to corn shack in the margins of night and day. If Harry Parahunt—the muscle at the front of the jail who loved me as a child and spit in my hair to prove that he did—were to find me now, I'd end up like the redhead here, I think: in a darkened room, bound to the floor, or worse.

"Who are you, anyway?" he says.

"I'm the clouds in the trees, I'm the screech of the owl who flees from the sun, I'm the breast of a young man slain by a gun, I'm a drop of menstrual blood, I'm an egg."

"Ah for crap's sake," he says, and adds, softly, as if not for me to hear, "this is like talking to Johnny Rolfe, if he had a sense of humor."

At the sound of the name of the man who broke that thing in me whose breakage maybe made me start to bleed, a little something broke in me again, though it didn't hurt as bad or good this time; more like the slamming open of a door, though door from what to what I know not.

"You still there, princess? I say something struck you dumb?"

That little redhaired bitch, he said the name of the man to get to me, I'll make him suffer if I can. I can't. I won't. The girl who values niceness gets shoved back down my throat each day by bitches like the redhead here, why must they exist? They must exist to test my niceness creed, I guess. I must not let niceness lose, though right now I feel something want to take its place in me that I can't name.

"So let's get back to why all you funny-looking men are here, okay?" I ask the dark back of his head through the hole in the wall.

"Are you asking in an official capacity?"

"Nope, this is just me, the independent minded little princess, asking in an unofficial capacity and even a kind of illicit capacity."

"If you're here illicitly, what happened to that guy at the door with the knife and the bow?"

"I drugged the guard."

"Look, princess, uh, what shall I call you?"

"Pocahontas."

"Look, Poke-hunt-ass, I want something from you, you want something from me, let's see if we can both get what we want."

"Look, Captured Man—what shall I call you?"

"Jack Smith."

"Look, Jackshit, why don't you start by telling me what you want."

"I want to know why I was captured and why I'm being held in this room with my feet tied to the floor. And you want to know about your sweetheart, Johnny Rolfe, am I right? He wouldn't ever say this to me but I think he's pretty gone on you."

"No, you're not right."

"So what do you want to know then?"

Ooh, I regret having revealed to this man that I like that man, just as I regret having inadvertently revealed to those other men—my father, his advisor, and his young warriors who rise up from the ground with penile stiffness—that I had a wireless communications device and a period. I didn't know that I liked that man but the burning I feel in my face right now tells me I do. How do I end up revealing these things I don't know I have or feel? And why must the knowledge of my liking that man come to me from the violent little mouth of this one?

Note to self: Learn how to reveal nothing to men. Corollary note to self: Reveal everything about us to me before conversing with a man or other threatening entity. Self's response: But some self-knowledge comes only through engagement with others; you cannot truly know me if you devote all your resources to defending me against potential threats, for in so doing you also foreclose the possibility of knowing me; you must allow the world to touch you and penetrate you and know you; only then will you be able to know me and protect me from harm. Response to self's response: I wasn't expecting you to talk back. Self: This is what I mean, no communication is one way, how dense are you? Pocahontas: No need to be insolent. Self: I'm just saying. Pocahontas: Am I not, by opening you to the world in order to know you, exposing us to the very sort of danger I hope to prevent by knowing you? Self: Yes. Pocahontas: This is confusing. Self: Tough corn nubs. Pocahontas: Tough corn nubs, that's your answer? Self: Yes.

"Well," Jackshit says, "what do you want?"

"What is the purpose of your trip?"

"Friendly exchange of goods and ideas."

"So y'all done undertook a long and dangerous journey and are in the shape you're in now—which is disgusting, have you no pride?—for the friendly exchange of goods and ideas?"

"Yes."

"Well then you've come to the right place! We is a peaceful people. We believes love is thuh ansuh to all questions, except thuh questions to which the ansuh are 'Relax.'"

"All right we're going around in circles here. Guard!"

"I blew the guard."

"Guard!"

"I shot the guard."

"Are they going to kill me?"

"Now we're getting somewhere."

"Though you've given me squat."

"But, being a man, you've taken what I haven't given."

"Are they?"

"I don't know, they don't consult me."

"Can you get me out of here?"

"No."

"You refuse?"

"I'm unable."

"I thought you shot the guard."

"I pantsed the guard."

He glowers and curses me in his head. Sometimes a part of the back of a man's head as seen in the dark through a hole in the wall is all one needs to know what's going on inside it.

"Since you're considered by my dad and his men to be a hostile extraterritorial, as all extraterritorials are considered hostile until they prove otherwise, and sometimes not even then, and since you're therefore tied up in jail and may be about to die, while I'm free to move around at will and am the daughter of the man in whose mind your fate lies, I'd say you should start being open and honest with me and if I see that you're making an earnest effort to do so I'll do what I can to make sure you (a) don't die, and (b) go free."

"You're Powhatan's daughter?"

"Oops, I did it again."

"Did what again?"

"Revealed something to you by accident."

"What was the other thing you revealed?"

"My love of Johnny Rolfe."

See, Self? This is the new me, the one who opens herself to the world, who gives a lot and hopes to receive a lot in return. It's almost unbearably exciting. My hairs are standing on end, as if they were penises. I'm so scared, too, and sad. I feel like crying. I can't cry, though, in front of him—in back of him, I mean.

"You crying?"

"No."

"Yes you are, I hear you. I see a teardrop clinging to your mouth."

He's turned his head again. I see his eye and ugly, bloody brow. I lick off the tear he saw on my lip and stick my tongue through the hole and out at him. Now my tongue's in jail—whoa, how symbolic—and now I pull it out again and put it in my mouth.

"I can't believe I have to negotiate with a punk girl who's probably yanking my chain, but, listen, what do you want? You want to meet up with Johnny? You get me out of here and I arrange for you to meet at sunset by the second fallen log on the right as you head up the creek?"

"I don't want to meet him—"

"You *don't* want to meet him?"

"Let me finish, Jesus, men are so—ugh! I don't want to meet him *yet*. I prefer to exchange a few emails with a guy before I date him. You can tell a lot about a guy by how he emails."

"So what am I supposed to do?"

"Give him my email address."

"That's it?"

"Well, and make sure there's something he can send me a message on."

"And in exchange for this you'll make sure I get released and not killed?"

"Yes."

"What's your email address?"

"cornluvr@werowocomoco.com"

"Deal. I'd shake your hand but . . ."

"Who you talking to?" That was Harry Parahunt, who's entered the cell whose unintended gap my ear is pressed to.

"The air," my new friend says.

"I'm moving you. Put your arms behind your back and if you try to make a move on me I'll stab you in the heart."

"Where you taking me?"

Harry Parahunt does not reply.

"Don't forget," Jackshit says to me.

"Don't forget what?" Harry says.

"Not to stab me in the heart if I don't make a move on you." Jackshit turns his head to me one more time and shows me his green, bloodshot eye, in which I see enough will to kill a whale.

I can't save his life or ensure his release but I know my dad will let him go, that's his way in these things, and when he's let go Jackshit may think I made it so, or he may not, and I may or may not get an email from that man for whom my feelings scare me very much. If only I can get my hands on a communications device. How hard could that be? Very hard! But I love this day, which has shown that a big wooden wall around a small port of air can serve to make two folks work hard to say what they mean, and that one can sometimes understand what the other thinks and wants despite the great impediment of the matter between two minds.

Penelope Ratcliffe

I like the dark, in which touch, smell, taste, and hearing overthrow sight, their queen in the light. I like that my mattress is firm, the thread count of my soft sheets high. That I live like this I don't know how to justify. On what surface does my son now lie? Does soft cloth surround him too, or do waters, spiders, knives? When can a mother no longer save her son? When she conceives him.

After we had sex tonight, Jim read aloud a haiku he wrote for me, as is his wont, and gave me a copy in his fast and clear and forceful script on company letterhead:

> Manhattan's dirt in Brooklyn's eyes
> my cock in your ass
> orgasm

Great haiku, Jim. The hardest part of my job as executive secretary to the CEO of the Manhattan Company is liking his poems night after night. I like some but must say I like all and do so convincingly, the job never ends, thank God the sex is more consistently good than the haiku.

He's breathing quietly now. Glad he doesn't snore. After drink, food, sex, and art, as his brief interval of pre-sleep languor began, in a room smothered in dark velvet and lit by fifty candles, on our firm, acre-wide bed, I told him I'd intercepted an electronic communication from Brooklyn's ambassador to Manhattan, Pete Zuñiga, to his employer, Brooklyn's CEO, Phil Habsburg, with whom my man is engaged in a struggle to the death, by proxy of course, since they haven't met in years.

"Is it about our meeting yesterday?" he said.

"Yes."

"You have it on you?"

"Yes."

"Read it to me."

"'Cherished Leader—'"

"'Cherished Leader'? How far up his—"

"I know."

"If I had a higher tolerance for bullshit I'd have all my employees—"

"Resist the temptation. 'Dear Mr. President' gets the point across just fine."

"Proceed."

"'As per usual when I have an audience with Stuart, I was met by a group of thugs on foot halfway across Brooklyn Bridge, blindfolded, and shoved into the back of a bike-taxi, as if this were high school and I the unpopular kid being brought to the secret clubhouse for an interview with its leader, who would inevitably rebuff me.'"

"Poor guy, must have had a rough adolescence. Despite myself I've always found his petulant rage, thinly disguised as formal decorum, poignant. I feel another haiku coming on:

> Pete Z.
> annihilation in a thimble
> Brooklyn weeps"

I laughed and continued. "'When the blindfold was removed I found myself in the usual candlelit—'"

"But what do you think of my new haiku?"

"I thought my laughter would signal that I found it funny."

"But I like to hear you say it. I love the sound of your voice."

He said this with half-closed eyes, his naked, lean, middle-aged body limp beneath his pale and massive politician's head, which was half-submerged in organic pillows. His voice broke slightly on the word "voice." For the hundredth time I'm amazed and moved that he lets himself be weak with me. I could kill him now.

"'When the blindfold was removed I found myself in the usual candlelit room with freeform damask wall hangings and futons on the floor, an agreeable room designed no doubt by Stuart's executive secretary, Ms. Ratcliffe, the former Mrs. Philip Habsburg, and, Sir, I hope you don't mind my saying that I fully commend your having married her despite her subsequent perfidy, she's quite a woman, intelligent, artful, astute, wonderful to look at, with excellent posture . . . .'"

"What a mystery that Phil hasn't had this guy fired or executed every day. As most men do, he wishes the seat of your bike were his face."

"Look," I said, pointing, "the vice president has risen to the podium again."

"Come here," Jim said.

I rolled and sat up on the stalwart VP, who gave a short but pithy speech that my body received with brief but heartfelt applause.

"Whew."

"Is that a quote from Zuñiga's communiqué or is that you ejaculating as it were?"

"Me."

"Finish reading the letter so I can think it over in my sleep."

"'Stuart let me wait in this perfumed room for a good forty-five minutes, but waiting is to being ambassador as having your upper lip waxed is to—'"

"My God, he avenges himself for the waiting on whoever reads this. Proceed."

"'I used the time to commit to memory one of the sonnets of Olena Kalytiak Davis, last Poet Laureate of the United States—at the end of the time when there were such things as poets laureate, and states—an endeavor in which I am indebted to you for allowing me free access to the closely guarded underground vaults of the erstwhile Brooklyn Public Library.'"

"Now there's a man who understands the need to undergird statecraft with poetry. This Davis, have you heard of him, Penny?"

"Olena is a woman's name, Sir."

"You sure? What about the middle name, Call-it-a-yak? Is that a woman's name?"

"I don't know."

"Man's name?"

"I don't know."

"Is it a white name?"

"Don't know."

"Black name?"

"Don't know."

"Red name?"

"Don't know."

"Yellow name?"

"No know."

"Lady poet laureate. I guess it could happen. You don't ever write poetry, do you, Penny?"

"No, Sir."

"I like that you call me 'Sir' late at night. It means you know that to be Manhattan is never to be off duty."

"Nor to be Lady Manhattan," I didn't say aloud. "'In any case, my dear Philip, Stuart arrived in his own time and I told him Brooklyn owns Virginia. He said he didn't know that. I expressed incredulity. He said he understood that in Virginia Brooklyn owns a five-mile-wide corridor of land through the center of which runs the largely disused Interstate 95, and not until that road crosses the northern border of Florida does Brooklyn control a wider swathe of land around it, "and anyway," he said, "whosoever commands I-95 commands the world, so what are you worried about?" I suggested to him that I was worried about us both being bound by the real estate contracts we'd signed down through the years and he told me he was "not the i's and t's man of this outfit." I wondered aloud whether, if it were the case that Brooklyn owned only I-95 in Virginia, which it is not, his men's journey down along it, before they veered east to the Chesapeake, would not then have been an act of trespass. He said they hadn't taken that route as far as he knew, though again he averred he was not the detail man. What route *had* they taken, I wanted to know. He said he didn't know and wouldn't tell if he did, and went on to assert that indeed the sense in which any man at all could be said to be "his" was flimsy, and that these so-called men of "his" in the Chesapeake environs were acting not on his word or behalf but of their own will and for their own gain or loss, and if it could be proven that the ground their equipment and selves now covered were that of Brooklyn—which

proof he doubted I'd produce—Brooklyn would then be free to do with the
men what it saw fit. I tried to let him think I lived in this imaginary world
of his in which his fellow islanders are not his employees and had not driven
south on an armored bus in the name of Manhattan. I moved then to build
an argument—'"

"'I moved then to build an argument'?" said my man, sleepily. "This guy
couldn't move to build a fart after spooning down a quart of hummus."

"'—about their intentions. Could they, a group composed entirely of men,
mean to settle this land? No, they could not, else why not bring ladies? And
even if ladies were present, why would anyone settle the most tainted, unpro-
ductive, oil-poor, animal-less patch of the North American continent east of
the Mississippi? My answer: they would not settle it, they would station themselves there to perpetrate cowardly acts of privateering against their neighbors
across the East River. He suggested I no more knew where the Mississippi was
than I knew where my own, well, anal area was—excuse me, Sir, I include this
detail to give you a sense of his vulgarity—and he went on to correct my use
of the word *privateering* with the word *piracy*, since, as he had asserted earlier,
these men's actions were neither caused nor sanctioned by himself. As for my
argument, he felt it was as uninteresting as it was pointless insofar as he'd
already covered what I was saying and probably would say for the rest of our
meeting, which he hoped would be short, under the umbrella of "Brooklyn was
free to do with the Manhattanites in Virginia what it saw fit as long as it
could prove they were there illegally." Very steamed I was at this point as I'm
sure you can imagine, Sir, so I stood to go and told him I'd be sending him
the relevant documentation on the ownership of Virginia with a messenger
who would be holding a 10-by-13 manila envelope embossed with
Brooklyn's corporate logo, bobcat rampant, and enjoined him not to slit the
throat of this man, as he had done to the last several, before he could complete his delivery. He apologized and lamented that he found it difficult to
distinguish between the messengers and the assassins we send, and I replied
that one carries a manila envelope, the other a gun and throwing stars. He
thanked me and I gave him a curt headbow that I think he recognized as the
diplomatic equivalent of the finger. At this point as if by telepathy Ms.
Ratcliffe entered the room and took my arm, a gesture I must acknowledge
as negotiational genius because how can a man maintain the sharp inner

feeling of aggression necessary to any diplomatic interchange when being touched along the length of the arm by Ms. Ratcliffe, if you'll pardon my forwardness on this point.' You still with me, dear?"

"Oh yeah, oh yeah," he said with closed eyes and mouth, "sharp inner feeling of aggression, length of the arm, forwardness, it's all going right in through the portals of my mind sans mediation of consciousness. Continue."

"'She walked me through a contiguous series of equally fragrant and gossamerly decorated windowless rooms until I was met by the enormous Official Blindfolder or whatever he is, at which point I begged Ms. Ratcliffe not to let me be blindfolded. She said I could keep the blindfold off until just before we reached the lobby, but then she'd have to put it on because the lobby had windows. I asked her if she'd put it on me herself. "If you like," she said.

"'In the next room I was surprised to encounter Chris Newport—whom intelligence has confirmed was the captain of the Godspeed, the armored bus in which they transported their men to the Chesapeake—whose left arm, you may recall, Sir, you severed with your Glock on the last day of the Battle of Joralemon Street. He was seated on what looked to be a throne or executive chair, but more clinical-looking, and to his right on a similar contraption was seated a thin teenager, remarkably red in hue, a weird-haired hayseed despite the well-cut suit of lightweight linen, which he wore as if he'd never worn a suit before. As I went to shake Newport's remaining hand, a big, rough-looking woman in a navy smock interposed herself between him and me on a low stool, also clinical in feel, and seemed to be about to service his feet in some way I was surprised to be in the room to witness. At the interruption of our handshake Newport made a face to me that signaled an apology that thinly disguised an arrogance that covered up for a lack of intelligence and competence. The boy next to him, before whom a second rough and besmocked woman had taken up position on a stool, seemed startled by each move everyone around him made. "This is Prince Mammoncock, son of King Powhatan of the Chesapeake," Ms. Ratcliffe said to me, pointing to the boy.

"'I understood this all was being staged for me. She'd counted on my asking not to be blindfolded quite yet so she could bring me to this room for this show, as if inadvertently. This Mammoncock was no prince but a wide-eared, odd-haired bumpkin of the first order. The women on the stools were merely pedicurists, I'm somewhat sad to say, since one always exults in the sexual depravity of one's enemies, of which I'm confident there's an abundance, though none was on display at this time, but only an incompetent charade of a strong southern alliance I'm sure does not exist. The boy, "the prince"— in a panic as the pedicurist removed sliver upon sliver of the calcified skin of his lower foot as if dicing cold cuts—shouted "I need those!" I'd guess these were migrant pedicurists from the wilds of eastern Long Island's north shore, big, square-jawed, strong-armed women with a rough and no-non-sense approach to footcare I can't say didn't interest me. We should consider hiring them away or kidnapping them, Sir. I laughed, and was led from the room, blindfolded, knocked unconscious, and awoke with blood in my mouth and a brutal headache on the corner of Atlantic Avenue and Court Street. All for now. Respectfully,' etcetera.

"You awake now, Daddy?"

"No."

"I guess he didn't buy Namontock as prince."

"No."

"Night-night."

"Night." He seemed to be asleep. "That fat, one-armed, gray-haired, bearded fuck," he said as if in a dream.

"Newport?"

A minute went by. "He hasn't left yet, has he?"

"No."

"Don't let him go back till he talks to me."

"I won't."

"Does he think there's oil down there?"

"Yes."

"He's full of shit, there's no oil. This trip is gonna result in a net loss of oil but I'll be damned if it results in a net loss of everything. That corn the kid brought, they must have some way of eradicating the toxins from it, that we have to find out. And trees. Are there trees down there?" The question oozed like oil from his sleep-softened lips.

"Yes."

"Good. We're running out of trees. Ninety-eight percent of Central Park is denuded and the other two percent is under armed guard. Have Chris hack down trees and send them up. And he should set up a small glass manufacturing plant." He peeled back the lid of one eyeball, which rolled toward me. "Why aren't you writing this down?"

"You're asleep."

"I make my best decisions in my sleep."

"Glass manufacturing," I said.

"We need windows."

"What else?"

"Are you writing this?"

"I'll remember."

"Deputize their guy—what's his name?—Pow Hut Tan, as honorary Virginia Branch vice president of the Manhattan Company. Give him a gray three-season suit, a bed, a desk, a chair, a sink, a set of pornographic shot glasses, and some shoes."

"I assume we'll discuss these agenda items at the board meeting tomorrow."

"Sure, just before the members of the board line up and blow me."

"How will we know what size shoes?"

No response.

"Jimmy?"

Deep and peaceful breaths.

My boyfriend is asleep, has been asleep for hours, while I lie awake and think of my son, about whom Chris Newport made an inscrutable face when I asked after him.

Glass manufacturing and shoes.

Lady poets though there may not be on God's gray earth, I shall now compose a verse, which I'll call "Men":

> Men are shits, say it loud!
> They come on strong, they're never clean,
> they have no rhythm, they're fragile.
> Think of a thousand men at the bottom
> of an ocean. Men are mirrors of women,
> reversed bottom to top, not side to side.

The stars are out—men
are puzzled by their beauty and seeming
lack of organization. You could blow men
over with a mirror. What's that mournful sound?
It's men, trying to put a woman
in the sky as if it were the rind of which she
were the fruit, or she the skin whose wart they were.

A Couple of Fops

"How did we get here?"

"By bus."

"No, I mean how did we get to the end of the world."

"By bus."

"I mean metaphysically."

"By bus."

"Do you ever wonder what did it, finally, what killed civ?"

"What's civ?"

"Civilization."

"You have a nickname for civilization?"

"We were close before it died."

"I really do like you—"

"And I you."

"And I you, but should we not make one last ditch effort to obtain clean water before we give in to lying around and contemplating civilization and metaphysics?"

"When does one need metaphysics more than at the end of the world?"

"I suppose you have a point."

"In any case I can't get up."

"Nor can I."

"Nor can I. Is there even still an I, or am I just a mind that blithely carries on as its former makeshift casing turns to dust? Seriously, what do I look like now?"

"Don't ask me, I went blind on Tuesday."

"What do I sound like then?"

"Don't know, I'm deaf too."

"Or I'm hoarse."

"Nor can I smell or touch or taste."

"What are you then?"

"A quiet ball of want."

"Are you angry still?"

"Why should I be?"

"Look what's happened to you."

"I told you I can't see."

"Think what's happened to you."

"I think anger leaves the body when the senses do."

"Why won't wanting leave it too?"

"Wanting's everywhere, and so has nowhere to go. Wanting's what there is when nothing else is there, the indivisible substance of which the world is made. Before there was a world, there was a want. After the world, the want will remain."

"Shall we contemplate the end of civ, then?"

"I've always liked you."

"I've always liked you too."

"How shall we contemplate it?"

"Don't know."

"How shall we honor it?"

"Not sure."

"It's nice to talk."

"It feels good to talk. Talk takes the edge off the want."

"When it doesn't put it on."

"Indeed, it sometimes puts it on."

"Mostly puts it on."

"Causes it."

"Maybe."

"Maybe."

"It feels good to agree."

"What would you say was the chief cause of the end of civ?"

"Airplanes."

"And its pinnacle?"

"Airplanes."

"Are you just being clever?"

"Never."

"You know who is still civilized?"

"The Indians?"

"You read my mind."

"Your mind is my only reading material."

"The Indians are nice."

"Or not."

"We'd do better to live with them than with the fellows into whose midst we were born."

"Should we go live with them now?"

"Let's."

"Let's."

"Let's."

"Let's."

Jack Smith

At dawn I parked the car at the edge of the dank and malodorous swamp my
guys had picked to build our makeshift town on, had built half or less than
half and stopped. I grabbed a pot of corn from the car and carried it through
the ten-foot-wide gap where the palisade they meant to build around the
town didn't meet itself, so if I'd been a local with a weapon and a gripe instead
of one of their own with a carload of locally grown grain I could have walked
in and killed five of them—us—before the wan guards who lay asleep at the
gap in the wall would have awakened and tried to lift with bone-thin arms
guns they likely hadn't learned to shoot. I'd been gone a month. Summer's
heat and wet weighed down the air, the trees' leaves, the dirt on my skin. I
looked at all the small brown tents whose worn stained cloths might well
have been the souls of the men whom they didn't quite protect from the
animals, other men, and elements; each tent lay in its own soft defeated
concavity on a plot where a hard house should have stood by now. These
men had never been robust or skilled but now they were inert and had done
nothing. Were they dead? I kicked the narrow place where one tent's old
cloth jutted out near the ground—some man's knee or bony ass—and heard
a howl inside: that one wasn't dead. I kicked such parts of other tents and
got the same noise, so some if not all of the guys were still alive. I flicked on
my flashlight and stuck my head inside one tent, then the next, then the
next. There's no word for the stink in them but there's a word for the men
who were the living source of the stink: thin; or half the stink in any case,
the other half the swamp.

I moved the round clay pots of corn one by one from the car to the sad shack they called the mess. They're three feet across and ready to go, is the beauty of them. You put them on fire, add water, and stir. Each one comes with a packet of spice I wouldn't put in my mouth if you paid me, not now that I've seen what they spike a guest's food with if they want him softened up for hell knows what.

In my fatigue I'd left the keys in the car and when I came back through the hole in the palisade to get the third of the eight pots Ratcliffe was in the driver's seat and had started it, with Martin riding shotgun. "Sayonara!" Ratcliffe said, and Martin slapped him in the head as if to say "Why'd you say that?" Ratcliffe jammed it into first and headed down the dirt road toward what's left of I-64—enough if you've got an all-terrain car like the one he and Martin were fleeing in with five big pots of corn. I ran toward them. Martin shot at me and missed. I shot at him and got him in the arm and ran. Martin fell into Ratcliffe, who swerved and hit a tree. A pot of corn burst and swamped them. They jumped from the car with blood on their heads and tried to run but fell down. I took the gun from Martin's hand and held my gun to his head. Ratcliffe sat on the ground in a daze. He had no gun and posed no threat. He'd put on weight, the only man of the dozen I'd seen who hadn't grown bone-thin. And though he hadn't put on weight, Martin looked in good health too, to the point Martin could, which wasn't much, and anyhow to put on weight he'd have had to interrupt his quest to get chipped away by beast, man, and tool, to shed all non-Martin parts till what's left is just the vital him; if he succeeds in getting down to that core Martin under all the excess non-Martin, he'll be a baby-sized beast you'll never want to meet.

I said, "Where were you going?"

"Up your ass," Martin said. He's good to have along for a laugh if you don't mind getting stabbed in the heart when you turn your back. Against his will I scrutinized his arm, from which my bullet had removed a thin patch of flesh and nothing more.

"You pussies meant to go back to New York without telling anyone, and now you're going to unload the corn for me."

Ratcliffe said, "My head hurts," and Martin said, "Fuck you." I put Martin in the driver's seat, sat next to him, and made him back the car up from the tree they'd run it into. While pressing my thumb into Martin's newest wound I aimed the gun at Ratcliffe and told him to stand up, unload the corn, and bring it to the mess.

"I told you, I was just in a car crash and my head is killing me." I shot at the dirt in front of his feet to make it spring up and hit him in the eyes. He got up and came toward the car with a sad look as if I'd said the kittens his cat had just given birth to weren't cute.

The barrel of my gun supervised their work. By the time they'd transferred all the pots of corn from car to shack and scooped up what they could of the corn that had spilled from the burst pot, the fifteen living skeletons that now made up the Virginia Branch of the Manhattan Company were out of their tents and standing around us. Each stared out at the corn from the pair of dark hollows in the middle of his head.

"Smith was about to drive back to New York by himself with all this food," Ratcliffe said, "but we stopped him."

"If you stopped him, Ratcliffe, why's he holding a gun on you?" Johnny, thin as the rest, said.

"Because we stopped him."

"Some of the blood from the wounds on their heads you'll find on the dash of the car," I said.

Ratcliffe said, "That doesn't prove a thing. What's a little blood from my own head on the steering wheel of a car compared to the blood of Happy Lohengrin and Gerald Mankiewicz that Smith has on his hands? He's guilty not only of treason but of murder, too. I say we execute him by firing squad."

Martin said, "I say we preserve our limited number of bullets and hang him instead."

"Have none of you picked up on how fat Ratcliffe is? Only guy I know who's put on weight on this trip. Any of you wonder at all how that came to pass? If you're going to kill anyone, kill him, but not before he tells you where he hides his private store of food."

Father Richard Buck moved out from behind the thin twig that had hidden him and said, "At the best of times our decisions as to whom to punish by death are imperfect, since none of us has the all-seeing wisdom of God. At this moment we're all too weakened and demented by hunger to take the life of a man and be certain we've done so justly, laying aside for now the larger question of whether it is ever just to do so. I say we eat a big breakfast first and then decide whose life we'd like to end."

I don't know whether to admire or be amused by this man who regularly tries to talk to and live as if overseen by a blind and deaf and nonexistent god even when he himself is nearly dead from lack of food, but he's another one on this trip I like.

I told them not to cook a whole pot of corn since more than half would go bad before we could get it down our throats. They cooked a whole pot. Nor had the corn completely cooked when in eagerness they took it off the fire, so the meal we ate this hot and humid day, in chairs that tipped or fell when you sat, on tables rickety and splintered, was a hot thin gruel that featured corn so undercooked ten men broke their weakened teeth on it.

Still it was breakfast enough that almost all who ate it then tottered and farted back to bed—bed in this case the damp and beaten-down roll of foam and cloth each found when he crawled in through the weary lip of his one- or two- or four-man tent, what a man can expect for a bed when he signs up for a trip down south and then splits town when the earth starts to shake.

Ratcliffe and Martin were among those whom eating caused to fall asleep, so for the first time in my life I wasn't beaten and bound to a chair with rope after a meal and could move about the grounds without more than the usual fear of being mortally attacked. Dick Buck and Johnny Rolfe, though sleepy, came with—Buck kept awake by love of God and Rolfe, I'd guess, by love of girl. While I was gone they'd named this place Jamestown after our CEO. That they dared make *town* of this wet and sucking thing that vied with my foot for my boot at every step bespoke the glorious and yearning bullshit of men's souls. And as for *James*, it's just as well he'll never come and see what mud his name was given to.

As we walked, dodging tree stumps and tent poles, and inspected the three structures they'd put up, or semi-up—the mess, Ratcliffe's house, and a meeting hall or hallway—I gave an account of my time away, starting with "Oh and by the way, Rolfe, thanks for leaving me out in the woods with a savage as my only friend when the going got rough."

"And how'd your *friend* make it through, okay?"

I like the way he won't take crap from me, can't stay mad at him long. "So anyway, Rolfe, I got up early in the morning after the night I last saw you, and took this savage guy All-Burnt out into the woods with me to have a look around."

"'Have a look around'?"

I like how insistently he listens but that can get tired. "Okay we get it, Rolfe, you've been wronged and you're justifiably indignant so shut up. So we're out there, All-Burnt and I, decent kid, at the time when the sun lights the sky but isn't up yet, fresh air, as fresh as it gets in these parts these days, morning coolness, some comradely joking which I knew was All-Burnt's way of saying 'Hey, I know you saw your guy with his skin flayed off and his guts scooped out the other night and I feel for you, man,' so he's doing some pretty hilarious squirrel imitations and things when *wham!* I get an arrow in my thigh and *wham!* he gets one in his arm, but neither arrow goes in all that deep, these weren't really death arrows but more like arrows to say 'Hi, how ya doing, we could kill you if we want but won't quite yet,' but still an arrow shot from twenty yards takes a bite out of your thigh, and then *hello*, a hundred guys step out from behind fifty trees so that's *that* situation. Given how Mankiewicz ended up I figured they weren't killing me yet because they wanted to kill me like they'd killed him, so I bound All-Burnt to me by slipping my wristbands over his wrists so I could use him as a human shield or not shield so much as 'Hi, this is one of your fellow savages and if you try to shoot me you shoot him so don't,' but I guess that's not how they saw it because they killed him with arrows. So then I'm shooting at them from behind this dead guy I've got strapped to me, and that's got me distracted enough that I don't see I'm backing into a four-foot-deep puddle in the middle of the woods which I dropped my gun into and then they had me.

"They stripped off all my clothes, tied me up in a hammock-type thing, and paraded me from town to town, where the audience tended to be young ladies who seemed to find the sight of All-Burnt wounded to death and me forcibly inserted into a hammock with no clothes on humorous. We stop a night here, a night there, and I have to say all this time they're feeding me excellent food, gamey and weirdly spiced but not drugged or poisoned, not yet anyway. By the way, that's the core of what they have that we want: untainted food, real food that comes from things that walk on two or four legs or swim in the sea or fly in the air or grow from the ground, real fucking food, it's genius, worth killing and dying for, food, the staff of life, make a note of it, you peacenik dimwits.

"We finally get to the town where we had that e-sit-down with their main guy, Pa-What-Ann, more of a lie-down for him, and he was lying down again this time, I guess this is how the savage CEO greets guests: on his back, with young half-naked ladies all around fanning and feeding him. Even on his back you sense a full alertness in this guy, and massive strength, like if he fell down he'd make a hole in the earth. But I didn't get to see him till they'd roped and locked me in a room a dozen days, thinking I guess that that wasn't practically a form of relaxation for me by now. Oh and Johnny, guess who comes to visit me every day in my little savage jail made of local trees? Don't want to guess? Don't even want to have a facial expression right now, you sullen guy, you? I'll tell you who, Johnny. Poke-a-Huntress, that's who, the girl who made you come in your pants the day we arrived in this place. Remember? You did that beautiful improvised greeting dance for her and then you hugged her and you came? Well that is one flirtatious young woman, let me tell you. That is a woman who likes to come into a man's hot little jail cell with no top on and be demonstratively comfortable with her weirdly but appealingly tattooed young body and just chatter on about all kinds of things she thinks might be of interest to a man from up north who thinks he might get pretty grimly killed at any time, charming young woman who you don't quite know if she's putting you on or what, hard to read the kid or any of them."

The three of us stood at one end of the semi-open-air meeting hall that none of us leaned on the wall of lest the whole thing fall down. The sun had not yet cleared the trees *and maybe won't today*, I thought.

"By the way," I said, "no supply shed?"

"No supplies," Rolfe said.

"Each man keeps his tiny little bit of crap to himself," Buck said. "Bunch of jackals won't see the end of summer."

I said, "Newport's due back with a busload of stuff this week."

"Finish your little story," Rolfe said.

"I know what you like about my story, Johnny."

The face he looked at me with had been made obscure by a chain of disappointments in which there was no weak link.

"So the girl and I bond each day in my cell, nice girl, strong bond grows between her and me, cross-cultural bond that transcends age and sex and geography and skin color and basic assumptions about the world—really sweet girl who seemed drawn to me somehow, and then one day there I am removed from my cell and staring up the nostrils of the big guy on his back, who turns out to be her dad. He sits up a bit with the aid of pillows stuffed under him by a couple of the nubile half-naked women there seems to be an endless supply of in these parts, and I was given some pillows too, and each pillow's embroidered with a little story, like in one the big guy is stabbing some other guy in the heart with a spear, while in another he shakes hands with another big guy across a river, while in yet a third a baby covered in precisely embroidered blood and slime comes out from between the legs of a naked girl while the big guy stands in the background with a fatherly grin on his puss.

"So my hands are untied and I'm low to the ground on these pillows outside the front door of the big room we had the e-sit-down in, with the big guy across from me on his massive indoor-outdoor bed, and we start eating what I hope was deer meat plus a lot of dishes with corn: corn chowder, corn stew, corn pone, corn bread, fried corn, corn grilled without having been removed from the little airy stick it grows on. I guess a group of folks can get pretty inventive with corn if they need to. I eat till I feel it all coming back up my throat and then Mr. Big says something in his native tongue I'd translate roughly as 'Well it's been fun and now you die.'

"He moved his hands and ten guys came out of nowhere with a rock the size of a car. They put the rock on the ground and two of the guys tied my hands back up with ropes and laid my left cheek on the rock. Then they picked up baseball bats and—"

"Baseball bats?"

"—and swung them up above my head and I'm lying there seeing the beautiful face of my mother in the air beside the rock my head's about to get crushed into when suddenly I feel this soft pressure on my right cheek which turns out to be the pretty young Poke-a-Huntress rubbing the stubble of the side of her shaved head against my cheek and shouting what I can only imagine is the savage equivalent of 'Daddy, please, don't! It wasn't his fault! He means so much to me!' I don't know but I guess the girl has the hots for me."

Rolfe's face now looked like a stone at the bottom of the sea.

"Then there's this very long-ass pause in which I can't see or hear shit what with one ear and eye pressed into the jagged rock and the other covered by the ear and thick black hair of the dusky maid whose breasts my back was covered by and who'd jammed her twat against my ass—a touching rescue if it worked, and it did. The big man said something I could barely hear, and down went the clubs, and up went the girl. They untied me, and the upshot is all this corn, which I traded for some guns a couple of their guys are on their way over here to pick up, plus some gas for the bike we gave them before, which can't bode well for the oil-getting part of our trip unless that's their bluff but I don't think it is, though as I said, given the feasts they have over there I'd say we struck oil as far as food goes.

"As for the girl," I said, angling my words directly down Rolfe's earhole, "she wants to see me again real soon but before that I should send her a love letter, from what I can tell from what she jabbered at me in her own weird tongue."

"She speaks English," Rolfe said.

"Didn't sound like English to me. Maybe it's the language of love. But communication's your field, Rolfe, and so's being lover boy, I've got no time or talent for it, so why don't I give you her email address and your wireless back and you write her a mash note and pretend you're me?"

"Or, alternatively," he said with sleep in his voice, "you could shove both so far up your ass they come out your mouth mixed with all the other effluvia that comes out of there"—only Rolfe would say "effluvia"—and then he, too, slept for an hour, as did Buck, which left me with time on my hands and volts in my veins, since on the tour of our "town" we'd also looked at the ten pathetic ovoid mounds of turned-up dirt with sticks on top—graves of men who'd died of arrows, microbes, or despair since I'd left for my upriver trip—and while some men respond with sleep to grief, I respond with none at all. If a bed is a practice grave, my body insists it will know what to do when the real time comes and can therefore skip the rehearsals.

In my town's post-breakfast sleepytime I took apart three chairs they'd made, re-cut each leg to match the other three, planed and sanded all the parts, and nailed them to each other once again.

By then Ratcliffe was awake enough to have me arrested, assigning the task as before to the big underwear-wearing twins Bill and Bucky Breck, whose muscled limbs the air had encroached upon a bit since I saw them last but not enough to let me break their grip.

"Have you not arrested him often enough to make you happy?" Dick Buck said.

"He's committed murder and sedition."

"How so?"

"He killed Lohengrin and Mankiewicz and gave guns to the Indians."

"You wouldn't have had breakfast today if it weren't for him," Buck said.

I said, "I haven't given them a thing. They'll be here any minute now to take what I promised them and if they see us fighting with ourselves they'll know we're that much easier to kill in case that's what they want to do."

"He didn't kill those guys," Rolfe said. "Mankiewicz died by disobeying Smith's order and Lohengrin died in an ambush."

"That's not the way it looked to me," Gosnold said, and was the first to draw his gun, though all the guns came out so fast I can't say whose was first. Gosnold's was pointed at Rolfe, Rolfe's was pointed at Ratcliffe, Ratcliffe's was pointed at Buck, Buck's was pointed at Martin, Martin's was pointed at me.

I think we'd all have died had Newport not come rumbling up the road in the bus right then, back down here from New York. He eased his big and grizzled self down the stairs, followed by ten more men in little better shape than the ones on or in the ground.

"Nice trip?" I said with the barrel of Martin's gun in my face and the Breck twins' four hands on my arms.

"What the hell's the matter with you guys? Put your guns away." All obeyed. "Get your hands off him." The Brecks let go.

"What'd you bring us?" I said.

"These men and a month's worth of food. Ten gallons of water. Some pistols, rifles, and machine guns, five power generators, the gas to run them five hours each, saws, axes, farm equipment. Beads and pearls and silver coins to trade with. A few walkie-talkies. Some other crap. Not much. Jimmy Stuart offered squat, not a huge fan of our little project, says it gives Brooklyn another thing to be belligerent about and hasn't shown itself worth doing so."

"Any communications devices besides the walkie-talkies?"

"No."

"Hell."

"Which would you guys rather do, unload the bus or kill each other?"

"Can't we do both?" Martin said.

"Come here, Martin." Martin went. Newport kissed his high, banged-up forehead. "Now be a man and get up on that bus and haul things down." As Martin climbed the stairs, Newport slapped him on the ass and Martin giggled, a sound to chill a brave man's heart.

We had so little food that what little equipment we had fit next to it beneath the mess hall's roof. The few of us who had the will and strength to work spent the afternoon putting walls on the mess. The rest languished under trees and overdrank the water Chris had brought with him from New York. When evening came we heated up the corn we'd cooked that day. It had a sour taste and two more men got sick than were by now.

When all the men slept I crept in the dark to Martin's tent and eased my hand down inside his bedroll.

"Come to give me hand release?" he said.

"Some other time."

"Be a sport."

"I'd rather not."

"Come on."

It wouldn't have been the worst thing. Martin's got a nice set of brass balls, admired by all, and smooth and creamy skin on his hips and thighs, but knowing him, his dick'd break off in my hand and I didn't want that on my mind. I found the device by his right knee and pulled it out of his bag.

"You're taking that?"

"Yep."

"What for?"

"For us to live instead of die."

"Bring it back?"

"Sure."

"Sure you won't, ah . . . ?"

"Martin, is that really you?"

"Yeah."

"Why you acting like this?"

"Like what?"

"Nice."

"I just dig you, I just dig you."

"Is this a dream of yours I'm in?"

"Mm."

I guess he was asleep, a state in which niceness could descend on even him. If only he would sleep more often, or always.

Next I found the tent Rolfe slept in, and woke him.

"Give me your hand," I said.

"You gonna put it down your pants?"

"Not right now."

I gave him the wireless device. "Why you doing this?" he said.

"I want you to write a love note to the savage princess and sign it with my name."

"Can you please drop the bullshit now?"

"You mean the 'effluvia'?"

"Yeah, the effluvia."

"You like her and she likes you, and that's the story of, that's the glory of love."

"All right let me take a guess as to what a guy like you could possibly want when you steal into my tent at midnight, give me back my wireless device, and sing a song of love, and by the way don't ever sing. And move your mouth away from mine, your breath is foul, it's hot in here. You know what love is because you've studied it, not because you've felt it. You never will. You know what love is? It's this insidious thing that infects your eyes and ears, spreads to every inch of skin, the follicles of hair on the skin, the lips, the tongue, a hundred million microscopic organisms crawling on you. They commandeer the hollow of your thorax and your guts, your arms, your legs, your head, and other extremities. You cease to be yourself. You are now a vessel of impressions and thoughts of the person you love, of wishes for her, of dreams of her. You're jealous of the air she breathes because she takes it inside her all day and needs it to live; it becomes her, as you want to. You cast your thoughts of her and you an hour, a day, a week, a year, a hundred years into the future. No thought has the power to push itself as far into the future as the thought of love—not even thoughts of fame, or wealth, or death. You with me so far, Smith?"

"No."

"Of course you're not, but listen. It can happen—and this is what *you* want to happen—that this same love is extracted from the bodies of the ones it has possessed, and is used as an expedient to link one family to another, one town to another, one corporation to another, and then it follows not the paths of thought and flesh but those of trade and law, and is meant to replace but really just precedes and facilitates the theft, murder, and rape of one swarm of men by another that goes by the name of history. That's why you're giving this back to me."

"Just write your girlfriend a letter, Rolfe, Jesus Christ."

"I will. Thank you for giving this back to me."

"Good night."

Now everyone's asleep but me. No moon or stars light the sky. My hand's in front of my face and I can't see it. The Indians were supposed to have arrived by noon to take the trinkets and guns I promised in exchange for their corn. They could be just beyond my hand for all I know. I'd get my flashlight but it would only serve to light their way to me. If they want to kill us in our sleep they will. Except for me. Me they'll have to kill while I'm awake.

Stickboy

"I can't believe they call this place a town."

"If ten men call a sack of shit a pot of gold it makes it one in name alone."

Spoken by Joe and Frank, who used to be the boys I grew up with, nor has the change improved them: they're worse: their schemes and games, which once harmed only other boys—and sometimes girls, cats, and trees—now harm all, or could. But I need none as I need them, so I must try to think of them as good—like trying to fit the dick of a man with an infant's foreskin hood.

We ran through the woods. The always imperfect air, of which there's not enough in any single breath, rushed in and out of my mouth. My friends—I'll call them that for now; to call them by a truer name would take breath I still can't spare—chatted while I gasped. Their skin was dry and mine was damp with sweat. What a curse to have been born Stickboy, though had Frank or Joe been born Stickboy and I Frank or Joe, Stickboy would then be the name of someone cunning, swift, and strong; a man can purge himself of his name but not his body of its theme nor his life of its fate.

"I still can't take these guys seriously, they're so pathetic," Joe said. "They don't seem to know anything."

Frank said, "We don't want what they know, or are, we want what they have."

"Then we should kill them, take it, and be done."

"If we wait we'll get more."

"Oh, all right, Powhatan."

"I think you know the difference between him and me."

"Yeah, you're the one who'd slip a knife in your best friend's back if you think it would get you 'more,'" I said.

"No," Frank said, "I'd tell *you* to do it, and you would."

This conditional prediction, like a little snake, slipped into my ear and bit my brain, numbing out the band of brainflesh that constitutes the border of what I know and what I'll do. If a man can't purge his life of its fate, he also can't foresee it. I became afraid. Fear is foresight written in the code of mood, but break the code and you break the message too.

We arrived at "Jamestown" an hour after dawn. Their small, tough redhead, Jacks Myth, at the lazy hole in their fortification, awaited us looking like a stone statue with burning coals for eyes. He hadn't slept all night, I thought. He too felt fear but wouldn't let it show. He's their side's Frank and Joe rolled into one, with Joe's big strength in compact form and Frank's cunning and speed, the strategist and foot soldier of their army of one. But he has something Frank and Joe lack: compassion, or so I detect, but maybe just enough to harness to his cunning—that is, no more than is useful. But compassion's best beyond use; its true form is surfeit. In that way it resembles thought, whose true form is surfeit too. The gods invented thought in man not to make him better than the beasts but to drive him to his doom, to be stopped only by its halt cohort, compassion. In other words, the mind of man's the gods' cruel game that now has almost run its course.

"Our guns?" Joe said instead of "Hello," mistaking tactlessness for expediency.

"Come have breakfast," Jacks Myth said, and led us through the wet and sleeping camp or town past a thrown-together shack to an open-air table whose smooth wood top smelled freshly hewn.

"You just make this yourself?" Frank said.

"Yes."

"Nice."

"Thanks."

Myth spooned some nasty-looking corn slop onto four plates of specious cleanliness and put them down in front of us.

Joe said, "Why you feeding us our own food?"

"So you won't shoot us with our own guns."

We'd brought our own dried deer meat but tried to be polite, even Joe, by eating this affront to food. It was hard.

"Joe, now I know what the northerners came down here for."

"What's that, Frank?"

"Cooking lessons."

"So you two speak English."

"What was your first clue?"

"All of you speak English."

"Pretty much."

"You lying bastards." Myth smiled, his slightly green teeth's testament to somehow not having been punched out of his mouth all these years, though one sensed many had tried.

A few of his tribe wandered toward us one by one, each a thin and brittle pillar of odor. I sensed Joe think, "I could punch each once in the heart and kill them all in less than a minute." That's why he'll never be king.

Their king, who shouldn't be, was the only plump one of the lot, but even he had changed. The flesh of his face, which had used to billow out from the bone like a pink cumulus cloud, now was gray and subject, like a rag, to Earth's gravitational pull. "So," he said, "you've come for the guns we promised you," and as the flesh of his face hung loosely from the skull it clung to, so this remark of his hung loosely from the truth, though as with ample flesh that covers bone, his words hid the exact shape of what lay beneath them.

"Where are they?" Joe said.

"Turns out they speak English, Rat Cliff," Myth said to his boss.

"You call that English? This way, gentlemen, through the gate."

"It's true, our English differs from yours," Frank said. "For instance, we wouldn't call that a gate, we'd call it the place where you gave up working on the fence."

Rat Cliff's face grew red from below; the soft folds of skin seemed to tremble as the blood entered them. We walked through the fence and out of their town to a spot of hard ground where their armored bus stood next to the small, open car Myth had driven away from our town in.

"Did a tree jump in front of your car on the way home?" Joe said.

"There they are." Jacks Myth indicated two huge guns mounted on the roof of their bus, and turned back to us, his eyes open wide and sending out a mix of pleasure and defiance.

"We'll need your car to transport them."

"They won't fit in the car."

"We'll take them one by one then."

"Still won't fit."

"We'll dismantle them."

"Do you know how?"

"You'll show us."

"Do you know how to use them?"

"You'll show us that too."

"I don't recall agreeing to that with your boss."

"You've shown us how to use the guns, you've shown us that quite amply, and for that we thank you. You've also demonstrated that using guns is just about all you know how to do, and if there's anything else you'd like to do, like stay alive, you'll need our help, or at least you'll need us not to interfere with you."

"And, hypothetically, what do you suppose would stop us from *interfering* with you and your two friends right now?"

"The promise you made to my boss."

Myth moved his hands to his hips as if to say "That's all?"

"And your own interest in this region, which you have not been straight-forward about."

Myth still did not seem convinced.

"And this."

At that, fifty of Frank's best friends stepped from behind local oak and hickory trees and half-gone walls of erstwhile office parks. Each one held his bow down at his waist as if he'd forgotten it was there. Since, coincidentally, none of the towns we've conquered have been armed with guns, and no men who've passed this way have wanted to trade for them, we've perforce learned to pass an arrow through the eye of a needle from a hundred yards away.

"So you'll give us a demonstration of your guns," Frank said, "and that way we'll know you're not selling us crap."

Jacks Myth smiled again, not as he had smiled before—these northerners have a facial expression for each mood, and their moods are many and varied, with sometimes only the finest shade of difference between one and the next, such that I'm tempted to impute nearly full human intelligence to them. His mouth stayed closed this time; the smile, which did not completely conceal a sense of savage contentment, implied he'd hoped we'd ask him to show us how to use the guns.

"All right. I suppose we'll need a target. I'd hate to destroy another tree,", he said, and looked at me, or, to be precise, at the last trace of the wound on my head caused by the branch the one-armed man shot off the tree I happened to be sitting under at the time his friends were skirmishing with mine. "I know something we can use. You, the big fellow, I'll need your strength, come with me."

Joe looked at Frank, who by his stillness gave assent. Each of ten thousand moments like this in the course of a life are what make Frank a leader of men and Joe a led man, despite the latter's fierce mind and great mass. And what makes me neither leader nor quite led may take more time to know than I have.

Joe went up inside the bus ahead of Jacks. Time went by and he came back down straining, ass-first. The edge of a brown, large, flat, square thing he was carrying with both hands seemed also to be stuck to his mouth, and pressed down on it. His foot hit the dirt. He stepped back away from the bus. The big brown thing pursued and bore down on him, mainly on his mouth. Jacks appeared on the bottom step of the bus, walking forward, pressing on the back end of the large brown square, four feet or so in width and length, which he appeared to be force-feeding to Joe. Jacks leapt off the last step; the square jolted forward into Joe's face. A small and oblong blob of blood squirted from Joe's upper lip or gum and landed on the narrow top edge of the square while a few drops darkened the deep brown field of the square's planed side. Jacks advanced while Joe unwillingly retreated, but only in the way a breach-born baby's feet could be said to retreat from the womb, its head advance, as if feet and head were not the front and back of one thing struggling to be born. By means of the square, Jacks backed Joe up to a bitternut hickory twenty yards from the right flank of the bus. Joe swung right and out to the side of the tree. He and Jacks lowered the large square to the ground, leaned it on the tree, and one thing again became three.

Joe stood with flecks of blood on his top lip, which with the bottom one made a tight seal of his mouth. He seemed to want to lunge at Jacks, but stood as if pinned to the spot by a four-foot square of air. To leap on Jacks and tear his face, as Joe's eyes said he wished to do, would have been to admit he'd been beaten in the moving of the square, which the code of pride of the men of my town precludes, which means I'm not a man, since I'd rather admit nothing more, and nothing would bring me more relief, than defeat.

"Here's the target," Myth said, pointed at the square, and waited.

"So shoot it with your guns," Frank said. When Myth or any member of his crew makes a face or a move I must guess what it means he feels, but Frank might stand stock still and I could read what he feels by how his skin and hair abut the air, and now his stillness—which could mean many things in a body that likes and needs to move as much as Frank's does—concealed bemusement at how adroitly Myth turned the moving of an object into a strategic victory over Joe, and, in amounts calibrated to each other, wariness and respect. "You're waiting for what?" he added after a time.

"This square of wood has been treated with a substance only recently developed by our scientists, expensive to produce, manufactured in extremely limited quantities as of yet, and still in its beta phase."

"What are you talking about?"

"The substance this piece of wood has been specially treated with."

"And?"

"Applied in liquid form, it hardens into armor."

More voluminously meaningful stillness from Frank. Joe spat blood at the dirt. Rat Cliff looked quickly at the small, oblong blob of blood in the dirt, at Joe's face, at Frank's, at Myth's, scowled, and watched a nearby squirrel leap from the thin branch of one tree to the thin branch of the next, scramble up the second branch as it arced downward under the squirrel's weight, and disappear from all our lives, at least for now. The two other men of Myth's tribe let the flank of the bus hold up as much of their weight as they could while remaining on their feet.

"Is this some kind of bullshit to make us think it's great that the bullets from these guns you're selling us can penetrate this ordinary piece of wood? Or, worse yet, to explain in advance why they won't?" Frank said.

"Oh, they can," Myth said, "but I'm hoping you'll see how worthwhile it would be to buy the liquid armor from us—a small quantity of it anyway, which is all you'll need. Not that we have any to sell you right now, but we're expecting a shipment soon."

"There remains the obvious question of how to know everything you've just said isn't bullshit."

"We can make a little test of sorts."

"Talk to me."

"Well, we've learned the hard way that you people can shoot your arrows at great speeds, that they pierce and shatter hard objects we'd want them to bounce off of, like human bone. So why don't you shoot a few arrows at our treated target here, see how it holds up, and then we'll shoot the target with our guns and compare. I think you'll find your arrows won't penetrate and our guns will."

If Frank feared he was being outmaneuvered he concealed it even from me. He gave a sign to Joe to stand by the bus and shoot at the square. Joe marched toward the bus. The two thin men who leaned there moved away in undisguised fear. Joe discharged another blob of spit and blood, strung an arrow, shot it, strung another, shot it, and so on till he'd shot five, all of which pierced the square of wood and stuck halfway out its back, and were grouped within a radius of an inch. Joe, reliably, announced by how he stared at Jacks that he had his pride back. Jacks in turn gripped the top of the bus door and swung himself up onto its roof. Frank seemed to take the roof in one quick leap. They stood side by side on the roof of the bus under a tree, chatting inaudibly as they ministered to one of the guns, like friends who'd joined to pet a lion's head. Jacks held a long sash of thick, horizontally conjoined bullets out to his side with his left arm while with his right hand he did something— pulled the gun's trigger, I suppose—that caused a louder noise than I'd ever heard, twice as loud as the noise of the gun his one-armed friend had used to shoot the tree that landed on my skull. The noise stopped. All of us but Myth stared in wonder at the gun. We looked at what he was looking at, which was the wooden square with Joe's arrows in it, or what was left of arrows and square, which was small and medium-sized splinters of wood.

"Well," Frank said, the strain of shame in his voice, "that's a fine gun, and we'll take it from you now, and leave you to the many other accomplishments—

in addition, I mean, to having destroyed a piece of wood—that you no doubt have planned for the time between now and when the sun goes down."

"It's all yours, as is a car and driver we'll provide for you."

"We'll drive it ourselves."

"How do I know you'll bring the car back?"

"Because I say we will."

"We'll provide a driver, no offense."

"We'll need some tools to unbolt the guns from the top of your bus."

"You didn't bring any?"

"How would we have known they'd be bolted to the bus?"

"They have to be bolted to something."

"May we borrow your unbolting tools?"

"We don't have any."

"Why not?"

"As you've pointed out, we're ill equipped."

"You're telling me you have no tools?"

"That's correct."

"You expected us to bring our own tools for this purpose?"

"I neither expected nor didn't expect, but the guns do need to be unbolted to be moved."

"Let's look at that stack of tools I saw in that shack you keep your food in."

"None of those will work."

"Let's look."

"It'll be a wasted trip."

"Joe, he thinks a walk to his toolshed will be a wasted trip."

"We wouldn't want to waste a trip," Joe said.

Frank said, "We wouldn't want to waste a trip by walking to your toolshed. Goodbye."

Myth said, "I'm sorry how this turned out. Come on back to our town any time with the proper tools and you can have our guns."

"Well I was just kidding about not walking to your toolshed. We'll take the chance of a wasted trip."

"You won't find what you need."

"We'll try. We'd love to try. Give us the chance to see your town once more and its toolshed."

Myth shrugged. We walked back through the hole, or gate. Twenty of our fifty hidden men emerged from the dark sides of their respective trees and filled the space where fence did not meet fence, bows at ease on fingertips like fingernails or waves of air.

"Have your men stand down," Myth said.

"Can't."

"Why?"

"They're here on orders from my boss."

"They're making my men nervous."

"No need for nerves unless you plan to do us harm."

"We don't."

"Or cheat us."

"If cheating were a capital offense we'd already have killed you for giving us the so-called fresh water that made us sick."

"And we'd have killed you for giving us an incomplete disassembled motorbike."

"Exactly."

"They're on Powhatan's orders to be here, but mine to shoot or not to shoot."

"So you won't mind," the plump one, the boss, Rat Cliff said, "if a few of our guys train their guns on you and your bowmen."

"Well, they already have."

It was true, they had. From the gaps in some of their tents, I saw the tips of narrow metal cylinders protrude. Before the last big war, or so I've read, situations such as this were called mutually assured destruction, a phrase used to describe a set of conditions wherein all sides in a cold conflict were considered safe if each had arms enough to annihilate the other no matter who attacked whom first, a sweetly hopeful use of the subjunctive mood which has since been proved naïve.

Frank and Joe and I entered their small shed, the early morning sun ceased to shine on the backs of our necks, and we strolled around the stacks of stuff they called supplies. In the dim light I saw blank CDs, scissors, shears, saws, machetes, boxcutters, utility blades, awls, picks, a hoe, mousetraps and rattraps, staplers, paper, double-ledger accounting books bound in recycled vinyl, wire, wirecutters, matches, planes, hammers, files, portable fans, a box of dusty partial books whose titles were obscured, walkie-talkies, alarm clocks.

"No wrenches or pliers," Frank said.

"Told you."

"Do these work?" Frank held up a walkie-talkie.

"Put that back."

"How much distance can you use these over?"

"Put it down."

He tossed one to Joe. "Head out into the woods and talk to me on this."

Myth made a move to block Joe but he was already out the door.

We went to the door and watched, through a gap in the fence, Joe's large, rectangular ass dart among the trees and diminish in size, while his voice, clung to by clumps of static, came through the little plastic box in Frank's hand. "Frank. Frank. Can you read me. *Can* you read me. Over."

"Roger that, big Joe. How far are you from the gate, over."

"Fifty yards. Fifty-five yards, sixty yards, *can* you read me, over."

"Roger that I can and do big Joe. How's the weather where you are, over."

"Heavy snow. Over. How many more of these do they have, over."

"Roger that question, Big Daddy Joe. Am reconnoitering an accurate response at the present time, over—I mean, how far out are you now, over."

"Hundred yards, one fifty, two, quarter mile, over, the sea, over, Europe, over, the moon, over."

"Ten. Over."

"What. Over."

"They have ten walkie-talkies, over."

"Take them, over."

"I am, over."

"What. Over."

"I am. Over."

"What are you putting them in. Over."

"A bag. Over."

"A what. Over."

"A bag. Over."

"Oh, a *bag*. Over. I thought you said a *leg*, over."

"Where are you now. Over."

"The sun. Over."

"Hey these walkie-talkies are good," Frank said to Myth.

"And if you think you're walking out of here with them, you're wrong."

Frank tilted his head a half inch toward the door of the shed. Myth looked. There stood cousins Rawhunt and Parahunt, arrows in their bows aimed at Myth's ear.

"If they shoot me they'll get shot in the back."

"Not if first the guys who'd shoot them in the back get shot in the back."

"Don't take the walkie-talkies and no one will get shot."

"We won't take them all."

"How many?"

"Six."

"Four, and we keep six."

"How 'bout five each?"

"That makes no sense."

"We'll use the fifth to contact you."

"You're not so stupid after all."

Frank put four walkie-talkies in the canvas bag he'd brought inside his quiver. He added paper, pens, a stapler, some bandages, a portable fan.

"Now you're acting stupid again."

"Don't forget you screwed us over on the guns."

"Did you really think I'd let you have the guns?"

"Did you really think I wouldn't take as much crap as will fit in my bag and still hold a grudge about the guns?"

Joe stepped in and loaded a couple more bags full of stuff. Each of us took a bag—well, they took two each and I took one—and we jogged back to our town. Things were said, plans were made, but my lungs and legs, not as strong as Frank's and Joe's, kept my brain from knowing what it heard. I know I was assured, in whispers too soft to be heard by the fifty men whose footsteps crackled lightly in the cracked concrete and scrub brush by our side, that my friends' ill treatment of me in our town is a ruse to make our boss and his advisor think things are as they've been.

"Then what," I asked, "is the purpose of your ill treatment of me out here in the woods?"

"Oh that's just for old times' sake," Frank said.

This joke, if joke it was, made the dread in me metastasize. Like love, it gobbled up my nerves. It made me want to undermine my friends, and steal a certain thing from them and give it to a girl I like, whose thing it once was anyway, if a thing can be said to belong to a girl, or to anyone, which it can't, since, as has been all but proven for a certitude, you can't take it with you, and even if you could you wouldn't know what to do with it. The girl, like Joe and Frank, has caused, causes, and will cause me great hurt, but unlike them she doesn't do it out of spite. I'll always love the way she looks and acts, no matter how she makes me feel.

I found her by the black cloud that floats above her head at all times these days. She's curled in a ball on the floor of the jail. The wireless device, which I stole back from Joe for her as per my plan, I lay at her sleeping face. When she wakes it'll be the first thing she sees. The second thing she'll see is me, though thing I'm not, technically, though soon I'll be, and soon after many things, then no thing. The jail is quiet and dark. Her left breast lies on the spot where Jacks Myth's left foot stood when he was kept here two weeks in ropes. No guard stands at the door. No foreigner's been captured, no criminal caught. The jail holds no one, as far as those who do the counting know. Its disuse makes it a good hiding place for an exile, who is an inside-out prisoner. The moon in the eastern sky lays a column of light across her face. As ever, I favor the dark part of the room.

She's still curled up into a little dot. A dot of her's better than a line of most. The left side of her face lies on her folded left arm. Her north eye opens, looks at its closed southern counterpart, closes again. What she saw first, if she saw at all, was not, as I'd guessed, the gift I stole for her, or me, but herself.

"You awake?"

"No."

"See what I brought you?"

"No."

"Want to have sex?"

"No."

"See what I brought you?"

"What'd you bring me?"

"Open your eyes."

"Don't want to."

"Then you won't see it."

"Describe it to me. Is it bigger than a cockroach?"

"Yes."

"Bigger than a rat?"

"Yes."

"Bunny rabbit?"

"Same, unless the rabbit's just eaten the rat."

"Is it my wireless device?"

"I thought you said you didn't see it."

"I didn't."

"Liar."

"Takes one to know one."

"What are you talking about?"

"How your whole life has become a lie."

"I don't lie, I scheme, it's different."

"You joke but what you're doing is deadly serious."

"What am I doing?"

"I don't know, why don't you tell me?"

"Nothing."

Her eyes have not yet opened again. She hasn't moved an inch. She may still be asleep.

"How'd you get the wireless back from Joe?"

"He gave it to me."

"Liar."

"I bought it."

"Liar."

"I stole it."

"Liar."

"Anyway, I just wanted you to have it."

"Thanks."

"And see how you are."

"Fine."

"And have sex with you."

"Ugh."

"What do you do all day?"

"What do *you* do all day?"

"Nothing."

"Nothing."

"No really."

"I sulk, and then I fill my mind with light."

"How?"

"I sit in a place where I'm undetected and unobstructed. My legs are crossed, my back is straight, my posture easeful yet erect. It helps me to imagine an enormously long cable attached at one end to the crown of my head and at the other to a helicopter that hovers soundlessly above the clouds. Then the sulking begins. It comes quite naturally: all I have to do is think. To think and be sad are one for me now. 'Thought is the indwelling of the father in the head of the child.' You know that proverb?"

"No."

"I just made it up."

"But how do you go from thinking and sulking to filling your mind with light?"

"I'm telling you how."

"You're not."

"If you'd shut up."

"Okay."

"I see."

"What?"

"I see instead of think."

"How?"

"By seeing as fast as I can."

"But how can you see without thinking? When you look at a thing, isn't your mind naming it and qualifying it for your eyes?"

"Your eyes have to outrun your mind. You see and see and see so fast your mind tries to keep up, gets tired, has a heart attack and dies. Then it's just you and your eyes, and the green air leading the world into them."

"What does that feel like?"

"It feels like the world is getting lighter and lighter and lighter until you can't see it anymore."

"Is that what you do all day?"

"I run a lot."

"How do you eat?"

"I steal food, or get it from Char, or I disguise myself and take my meals among the unsuspecting people of our town."

"Who do you disguise yourself as?"

"Different people. This morning I disguised myself as a squirrel, and accompanied you along the branches of the trees to the interlopers' sad little town. That's how I know about your traitorous heart."

"Is it not treason to love one of them without even knowing him?"

"If the gods had made woman to love a man only after she knows him, no woman would ever love." Her eyes, which have been closed until this time, open. "You brought this back to me so I could contact him."

"Yes."

"You're very sweet."

"Shut up."

"I love you."

"Shut the fuck up."

"Stickboy."

"While you let in the light, I let in the darkness," I say, and shut my eyes. When I open them she's gone, and so am I.

Three

06:01:43

Knock-Knock from: Internet user GREASYBOY

GREASYBOY has sent you an Instant Message not bound by your Terms of Service Agreement. Would you like to accept the Instant Message from GREASYBOY?

☐ Yes
☑ No

06:02:19

Knock-Knock from: Internet user GREASYBOY

GREASYBOY has sent you an Instant Message not bound by your Terms of Service Agreement. Would you like to accept the Instant Message from GREASYBOY?

☐ Yes
☑ No

06:02:32

Knock-Knock from: Internet user GREASYBOY

GREASYBOY has sent you an Instant Message not bound by your Terms of Service Agreement. Would you like to accept the Instant Message from GREASYBOY?

☑ Yes
☐ No

GREASYBOY: Hi.

CORNLUVR: Have you ever dated a woman much older than yourself?

GREASYBOY: But you're younger than I am.

CORNLUVR: Have you?

GREASYBOY: Why are you asking me this?

CORNLUVR: Must we build the wheel before we roll along on it?

GREASYBOY: Yes.

CORNLUVR: Then this is going to take forever and be tedious.

GREASYBOY: No I mean yes, I've dated a woman older than myself.

CORNLUVR: Much older?

GREASYBOY: How much is much?

CORNLUVR: Ugh.

GREASYBOY: I was an undergraduate at the Manhattan School of Communications.

CORNLUVR: I'd never have guessed you went to college.

GREASYBOY: I was going to have an affair with one of the martial arts instructors but then her back went out.

CORNLUVR: Out where? Remember English is not my first language.

GREASYBOY: Apparently bullshit is your first language.

CORNLUVR: And that was that?

GREASYBOY: What was what?

CORNLUVR: That was the end of the affair?

GREASYBOY: I guess it's hard to have an affair with a bad back.

CORNLUVR: Was she beautiful?

GREASYBOY: Yes. She had puffy hair. She was thirty-eight, to answer your other question.

CORNLUVR: What was she like?

GREASYBOY: Sad.

CORNLUVR: How do you know?

GREASYBOY: The back pain.

CORNLUVR: What's that got to do with it?

GREASYBOY: Body pain always has its duplicate in mind.

CORNLUVR: You think you know women.

GREASYBOY: I didn't say that. I think I understood that woman, a little.

CORNLUVR: Maybe less than you think.

GREASYBOY: You're not one of *those* women, are you?

CORNLUVR: Which?

GREASYBOY: Who think men do not and will never understand women, especially herself.

CORNLUVR: It's not impossible, just unlikely.

GREASYBOY: And do women understand men?

CORNLUVR: Better.

GREASYBOY: Why?

CORNLUVR: Because women are more like men than men are like women.

GREASYBOY: Horse dukey.

CORNLUVR: What's dukey?

GREASYBOY: Teeth.

CORNLUVR: Gotta go bye!

GREASYBOY: When can I meet you?

INTERNET USER CORNLUVR IS NOT ONLINE AT THIS TIME

From: GREASYBOY
To: CORNLUVR
Subject: What was that?

Dear CornLuvr,

That thing that happened when we saw each other last night is all the more crazy given that I don't know how to spell your name. Do you trust me? I don't trust you. I want to. It's hard to. I've not been bred for trust, and you're quite strange in almost every way.

Please know I'm not one with all the programs, intentions, wishes, and behaviors of the gentlemen I am visiting your region on business with. They're them and I'm me. I'm with them but not of them. I'll supply specific examples of this in the course of what follows. Here's the first example: the induction or "hiring" of your father as vice president of the Manhattan Company, Virginia Branch. Not my idea. A guy observes a lot of the ideas his fellow humans come up with and act on and he despairs; he wonders how the human race survives; evidently not by the frequency or consistency of its good ideas. I believe survival is predicated on unrelenting will plus aggression plus, of course, how very pleasurable God made fucking, and I hope neither pessimism nor the explicit mention of the great pleasure of sex are taboo in your culture as they sometimes are in mine, but I say these things in the interest of total honesty and transparency, anything less than which, I feel, will be an impediment to the fullest possible understanding between us, and I figure if you like me at all, which you seem to despite not having answered my last half dozen IM's, you like my darkness and devotion to pussy.

Guess I'll stop here for now. Let me know if you want to hear my account of what happened that night leading up to and after our encounter. I'll take a breather and hope to hear from you.

Yours truly,

Johnny

From: CornLuvr
To: GreasyBoy
Subject: No Subject

Jah Knee
Re Lacks
Paw Cunt Ass

From: GreasyBoy
To: CornLuvr
Subject: RE: No Subject

Dear P—

I've got a lot of reason to be tense: the fire that wiped out half our town, the rats that ate the corn your father sent to us last week, other things. But it does relax me to write a girl like you and tell her all I think and feel and am up front. I wish you'd know me all at once, with no need for the slow and unreliable advance of time.

As you've seen, we made a bunch of car trips to your place with gifts our CEO sent for the "induction." I know I said this last time but can we agree the induction was a fuck up? Not least because your dad was not at home when we arrived. And your people's sense of ownership and theft diverges from our own. As our town's officer of talk, I told your dad's VP, Sit Knee Find Gold, what the gifts were meant for as the car made trips back and forth with more and more of them, but that did not make him stop a group of prepubescent boys from spreading out around the growing pile where he seemed to egg them on to pick things up—shoes, clothes, watches, jewels—and run off to the woods with them. We tried to block them from the stuff or chase them down once they had it but they were too fast. A few of my guys kicked their legs and punched their arms and necks as they passed, and when that failed to deter we tried reason, though studies have shown that the male brain does not begin to develop the capacity for reason until the age of fifteen, so our efforts resulted in further theft accompanied by the looks of blank incomprehension that make boys their age so cute. When two of them took buckshot in the thighs, ass, and lower back, that seemed to daunt the rest, but by then they'd denuded us of half the swag we'd meant for your dad.

Sit Knee, who each time I've met him has made me feel I'm a book he's reading a new chapter of through eyes half-covered by their lids, invited us for supper. The acorn-sturgeon salad was humane, the beaver tapenade divine. Your people cook well. We have to come to one of your towns to get a good meal—to get a meal at all, since what we eat at home-away-from-home deserves a name I will not foul this letter with. As laudable as your food is how you clean it, I don't mean gut and skin a squirrel, I mean rid it and all else you eat of the poison that resides in each cell of everything that grows, walks, swims, flies, crawls, or creeps. Such technique should confer greater power than your dad seems to have. It has long been said that who detoxifies the food supply commands the world, or could if he wished, but maybe your dad took a long, hard look at the world and deemed it not worth the bother?

The after-dinner open-air show you know about, having done the mise-en-scène yourself, I'd guess. My guys' response was not as rude as it might have seemed. First, you should know that when we see indistinct figures rush out of the woods at us from all sides shouting and whooping with bows in their hands, we tend to freak out. And I don't know if you caught that exchange of words between Jack Smith and John Martin, but it went something like:

MARTIN: They're gonna slaughter us!
SMITH: No, no! They're girls!
MARTIN: So what? Girls kill too! Shoot them!
SMITH: Holster your guns! Holster your guns!

So I would caution you as a fledgling director of environmental theater to be aware of how much more interactive a performance can get than you might have intended when your audience is a group of frightened, half-starved travelers from a land where parody is chiefly used to wound and kill. And I know you were dressed—or not dressed—to look like the men of your town, but beautiful, topless girls running a circle around a group of love-starved men will cause the sort of open-mouthed, drool-lipped catatonia you witnessed, followed by the violent open-armed lunges at you my guys made. All in good fun for you, perhaps, but you really can rattle a group of fellows like that, and may I add on a somewhat different note at this time that your overall physical conditioning seems to me superb, admirable, and worthy of emulation? And physical control as well. The way you and the older woman—the muscular one, whose not-small breasts still float so unusually high on her chest for a woman of her age, if you don't mind this kind of observation made, again, in the name of honesty and full disclosure of all articulable thoughts in my head and heart—the way you and she mimed lugging down the stairs of a bus that large square of wood to be used as an arrow-and-bullet target, as my man Smith and your man Joe did the other day (how did you know about this?) was so precise that none of us was in doubt what event you were both reenacting and making fun of. And women making fun of how men shoot their arrows and guns, my God, if you did that every night after dinner we'd soon find ourselves so funny and stupid we wouldn't be able to shoot any more. Well, I wish we lived in a world where that were true. Nothing since the start of time has stopped men from killing each other. Art, though sometimes nice, has always been perfectly useless against war.

I liked your skits, your misogynistic jokes and japes—the "Dirty Sanchez," the "Donkey Punch"—though I don't quite understand them. And I very much enjoyed your imitations of us, especially the songs. However, I feel the song sung by "Johnny Rolfe," played touchingly by you,

> I'm disdainful
> I'm disdainful
> I'm disdainful
> of you all,

is not strictly false so much as insufficiently complex.

And then we met behind that tree, a term I use despite how blurry *behind* and *front* proved moments later to be. And then you disappeared, and I awoke in the tines of a thorny bush, its bright red berries burst upon my sleeve, and then your dad arrived. We were led into the high-ceilinged, torch-smoked room he favors for receiving—do you people not believe in ventilation? Again he reclined immensely on a neck-high platform bed, girl on his left, girl on his right, feather fans to keep the smoke from his nose, dog-size chunks of what looked like tofu brought gently to the chasm of his mouth. Again we were led up the length of your dad, again made to touch our hands to his and say our names.

Sit Knee showed us to the blanket we were meant to sit or kneel on. We did, save the aging captain of our bus, one-armed Chris Newport, who stood nearby and said, "My legs no longer bend that way."

"State your business to the man," Sit Knee said.

Ratcliffe, our local chief in name at least, stood. Your dad waved him back down to the floor with his hand, a fan unto itself, and called on Chris instead. And here I must remark on Ratcliffe's bottomless capacity to pout, if only to let you know which man I mean when I say Ratcliffe.

"We'd be honored to confer honorary VP status on you, Sir," Chris said. He don't make speeches much.

"Veepee," said your dad, "is a word in your quaint dialect that our language has not yet absorbed. Please translate."

Smith—whom I gather you've met, I'd like us to discuss that one day soon, fuck you—laughed at the word *translate*.

"Vice president," Newport said.

"Vice president of what?"

"The Virginia Branch of the Manhattan Company."

"You want to make me VP of what I'm already P of?"

Ratcliffe rose halfway up again and said, "If I may . . . "

"You mayn't," said your dad, and waved him down.

"We want you to be part of our team."

"I am part of no one's team. I am the team."

"The job comes with a substantial salary and perks."

"What's the salary?"

"All due respect, Sir, it's inappropriate to discuss money in public."

Your dad laughed, as a deforested mountain might laugh. I can't believe I'm dating this guy's daughter.

"And the perks?"

"There's a pile of 'em outside, to start with."

"All due respect, Sir: I honestly do feel *jackshit* would not be an inappropriate description of the pile of gifts."

Newport, more as military strategist than subtle social creature, I would guess, did not mention your boys' theft of our gifts to your dad, though your dad, strategist and social creature both, probably knew.

"You haven't seen the bed," Newport said.

"You brought me a bed? Why?"

"We've only ever seen you in one. We figured you favored them."

"This? This is no bed, it's a stationary palanquin."

"Sir, all due respect again, I know when my chain's being yanked."

"Show me the bed."

"We'll have to bring it in in parts." Newport turned to Ratcliffe and signaled him to get the bed. Ratcliffe did not stand, and looked back with eyes wide open. Newport opened his eyes more. A competition of degree of openness of eyes equals umbrage versus umbrage in such a context, where I come from, FYI.

"Oh for Christ's sake," Smith said, left, and came back with six men who brought the bed in parts, which they started to assemble.

"Stop. Bring me a plank of it."

A man brought a plank to your dad, which in his hand looked like a chopstick. "Where does this bed come from?"

"New York," Newport said.

"Where's the wood from, I mean?"

"Don't know."

"Bullshit. It's from here."

"How do you know?"

"I recognize the tree this piece of wood was once a part of. I'd know it in any form. I grew up with this tree, and it grew up with me. See the swirl here? See the shape of this knot where a branch was once attached to the trunk?"

"Sir, my sight is dim," Newport said.

"Yes, it is."

"If you owned this tree, then I offer my apology on behalf of the Manhattan Company."

"And if I said I owned all hundred trees you've cut so far and brought back to your boss up in New York, would you then apologize a hundred times? And if you cut a thousand trees near here, will you send me a letter on a sheet of official Manhattan Company stationery made from one of the trees you cut and black with the ink of a thousand apologies? I owned this tree no more than it owned me. After the war, when our forebears came back to this part of the world, they took the grim opportunity annihilation offered to try to live differently than the Americans had. All books on the subject had been burned or lost, all facts were partial, and yet they undertook to reconstruct as best they could the way the Chesapeake's first inhabitants had lived, who'd lived here since the moment man began to measure time, and so we don't own land or anything alive. And so to you and all outsiders we make this promise: if you try to export ownership to these parts you will find in us enthusiastic exporters of deadly arrows."

"So you're okay with owning arrows."

"We give them to our enemies for free."

"So you don't want the bed."

"I'll take the bed. Better me than you. What else've you got?"

"Have you seen the shot glasses?"

"Show me."

A guy went out and came back in with a tray of white porcelain shot glasses whose bottoms were made of murky glass. He held the tray up to your dad, who inspected one and looked at Chris Newport as if to say, "So?"

"Pour some water in it."

The girl to the right of your dad filled the glass.

"Now look inside."

Your dad looked in and frowned. "There's a naked man in here."

"Is that objectionable to you?"

"He's facing me."

"I don't understand."

"If I were to see a naked girl at the bottom of a glass, I'd want her facing me. A naked man at the bottom of a glass I'd prefer to face the other way."

"Oh." The great girth of Newport had begun to deflate under the pressure of this series of embarrassments before your dad. "We would nonetheless like to offer you the honorary office of vice president."

"Make it president."

"Can't. There's only one such man and he's back in New York."

"Make it executive vice president."

"Can't."

"Why not?"

"That's him." Newport pointed at Ratcliffe, glowering on the rug.

"Come here," your dad said to Ratcliffe. Ratcliffe looked at him and did not move.

"Come here!"

His shout made a corridor of air between himself and Ratcliffe that Ratcliffe, it seemed, could not help but go to him along. He stood glumly beside your dad's bed, as if chained to it.

Your dad groaned, pushed himself up off the pillows, swung his legs down over the side of the platform, leapt from it, and landed beside Ratcliffe, whom he loomed above. By inhaling, he grew and made a nimbus of airlessness around himself that Ratcliffe could not escape from and was turning green inside of. "All right, what do I have to do?" he said.

"What do you mean, what do you have to do?" Ratcliffe whispered back, conserving air.

"To be veepee."

"Accept our gifts."

"I accept."

"Put on our company blazer."

"What's a blazer?"

"A jacket, like the one I have on."

"I hope the one you have for me is cleaner than yours. Do you not ever launder or bathe?"

I looked at Ratcliffe's blazer. It was indeed in the Manhattan houndstooth pattern, made monochrome by dirt. The insignia on the left breast, too, had been effaced. The same man who'd brought the shot glass and plank of wood—his name is Bucky Breck, you may have seen or stroked him, almost your father's size, his uniform of underwear not unlike what your men sport each day, or what I moved aside on you the other night to make room for my face—Bucky Breck now brought your dad his houndstooth coat, wrinkled but relatively clean.

"Kneel," Ratcliffe said.

"Kneel?"

"Kneel down, swear an oath of allegiance, we'll put the coat on you, and then you'll be VP."

"I neither kneel nor swear."

"Well then I don't see how we can—"

"I'll promise allegiance, I'll bend my knees a bit. I'd like a fuller tribute in exchange."

"What did you have in mind?"

"Your wristwatch."

"This was a gift from my mother. It's an antique and an heirloom. The band is made of plated gold and inscribed to me."

"Give him the watch," Newport and Smith both said.

Ratcliffe's body then underwent a change more temporal than physical. We all saw creep into his flesh, as he slipped the cherished watch from his wrist, the stark diminishment of time he's got left to live. Your dad, whose wrist was too thick for the watch's band, broke the band, tossed it to the dirt, grabbed the houndstooth coat from Breck, put it on, hung the watch sans band from its lapel, and, to seal the deal, enveloped Ratcliffe's tiny hand in his. The coat did not look right on him—it did not match his long gray hair, bare red chest, or tan skin briefs—and yet he seemed to like it just the same.

By now the bed had been assembled and in came four men bearing on their necks what seemed to be a snake that had swallowed a hippopotamus but was soon declared a waterbed mattress, a gift directly to your chief from ours, who assumes all chiefs to be gleeful and public swordsmen, as he himself is.

The men placed the roiling mattress on its frame. "Were you to lie on it now you'd do us an honor, Sir," Newport said. "Our president has asked us to note your response to the bed and report it to him."

Your dad, who seemed to be amused by how embarrassed Newport was, eased himself, in his undies and new houndstooth coat, a small green snake writhing from the hole in the lobe of his ear, down onto the bed, whose liquid bulk fled from his weight. Soon, though, he lay face-up on it, and the waters rearranged themselves somewhat, and rocked him as the waters of a man-made wading pond would rock an ocean liner that had somehow blundered into them.

And there he lay. The room's quietness revealed the light, high whine of John Martin's ongoing laugh, a sound that had become so omnipresent that one mostly failed to notice it, except at night, when it was a torment. This was followed by a low, rumbling noise, a quick "Oh shit" from Smith, and then the loud explosion of the waterbed, which hurled your dad to the ground beside it, soaking him.

To the ears of your father's archers stationed outside the reception hall, the pop of the bed was no different from the pop of Chris Newport's automatic gun, which they'd all heard not too many weeks before, so when they rushed in and saw John Martin standing above your father laughing, that's whose head a zealous one of them put an arrow through from left to right before he could be stopped, and an explanation of the loud noise made to him.

Again a silence filled the room as we waited for Martin to fall to the dirt. He did not. Your father sat on the floor and gazed up at him with a look more of wonder than concern. Martin had ceased to laugh and seemed to be engrossed in thought. The arrow had gone in behind his left ear and come out slightly higher in front of his right. He lightly touched its tip and tail. "Christ," he said, "I mean what the hell?"

Your dad stood up and clapped him on the back and shook his hand and laughed. The rest of us laughed too, and men from both tribes gathered round to congratulate him. Someone reached to pull it out and Martin slapped his hand away. In a dead tongue, eight of your guys sang a song in four parts I'd guess is your people's "For He's a Jolly Good Fellow," so all in all I think both sides could in subsequent accounts refer to this as a fun induction, except Martin and those of us who had to ride back in the car with him and hear him yammer on about the unfairness of life and his headache, which even so was a relief if you were among those upon whose sleep and nerves his constant laugh—which the arrow had put an end to— had begun to have a deleterious effect.

By the way, what did your dad mean about your forebears? Are you not Indians? You all have red skin.

And as for our post-feast meeting—yours and mine—which began behind that tree after your show and ended in parts unknown to me at I don't know what hour, I recollect it poorly, so full was my delight, so strange the noise you made, so shocked was I that unnamed body parts of mine could be made to join like that with unnamed body parts of yours; so fleeting the duration, so provocative the incompletion, so novel in style, tone, corporeal positioning, geographical location, and time of day was all that transpired. Yours fondly,
Gianni

Pocahontas

"That man does not believe he'll die one day."

"Which one?"

"The one with the arrow in his head."

"How can you tell?"

"He's got an arrow in his head and he's not dead."

"How could he not believe he'll die? What a dope."

"He's not a dope, he's smart and strong, in spite of how he looks and acts and what he says. His unbelief in his own death protects him. His unbelief in his own death is an attack on death that death is flummoxed by. And by the way, you, too, don't believe you'll die."

"I? I know I'll die. I think about it all the time."

"You know and think but don't believe."

"And will my unbelief protect me?"

"There are those whose unbelief protects them and those whose unbelief opens them to ambush, just as there are those who, by practicing for death every day, learn to dodge its spearpoint, while others practice for death only to make themselves readier to receive it."

"Which am I? Wait, don't answer that."

But she'd already answered with her eyes. Oh Aunt Charlene, Aunt Charlene, why'd you answer with your eyes? What sort of auntie behavior is that sort of eye answer and what's a girl of niecely impressionability do to with it and why am I in love with a guy like that who would write a letter like that?

Charlene said, "Write to him" and returned to her mate and rival, Sid, whom she loves and hates more than all the rest combined, even me. Adulthood is complex. I am alone. I am alone in one of the shacks that are and aren't my home post-breakup with my dad. My life is so messed up right now and will be till I die, or that's the way it feels. What consolation is there for living and dying alone, spurned and aggrieved? To live nobly and die for a noble cause? I know no noble cause unalloyed. To feel pleasure? *He* makes me feel pleasure. He made me feel some just the other night. We didn't *do it* or anything, though at one point I was upside down and not keeping precise track of all things going on *up there*, one of which may have been *it*, for all I know. Still, the most intense pleasure's but a splinter of ice on the gallons of lava that gush from my cracked heart.

"Write to him," the ghost of the not-dead Charlene said in my head: the living haunt the banished girl.

"What?"

"Write to him. He's your ticket out of here."

"Don't you think where he's from's worse?"

"That's not the point."

"What is?"

"To love him."

"Like you love Sid?"

The ghost of the living Charlene stared at me worse than Charlene and wouldn't say a mumbling word. Even the spirits of the air sometimes shun the banished girl. It's strange to live alone at age nineteen. Thing that won't go in my next letter to him: since pleasure's no consolation for life, is love? Can love of such a fragile man console? Is any man not fragile? Is any love not fragile? Is any consolation not fragile? Is any life not fragile?

"Write to him!" That again was the ghost of the not-yet-dead Charlene, or maybe the ghost of the not-yet-dead me.

From: CORNLUVR
To: GREASYBOY
Subject: No Subject

>the fire that wiped out half our town, the
>rats that ate the corn your father sent to us last week

Oh no!   :(I know where food is and can show you and help you carry it back to your "town" if you want but don't touch me cuz our whole thing began with touch and we have to make sure it don't stop with touch too cuz in our contemporary political climate plus our *climate* climate one or both of us could get badly wounded and/or disfigured making sex impossible and/or disgusting so I gotta know you don't just want me for the sex and if you look back at your letter it put a heavy emphasis on sex don't be a typical boy don't be a typical boy

>your people's sense of ownership and theft diverges
>from our own.
What you call ownership I call theft. Who do you think was using the place your "town" is located before you? And what's this "your people"? I don't own them any more than they own the ground they put their houses on. The philosophy of ownership is inseparable from the philosophy of "your people" vs. "my people," which is inseparable from war, which leads to the kind of disfigurement that makes a person unfit for sex so please give "town" and "ownership" a re-think at the request of the person who right now would like to continue to be touched by you as long as she is not too wounded or dead to do so.

>When
>two of them took buckshot
Took buckshot like they took the gifts? *Un petit jeu de mots*, Gianni? I don't like those boys. They're dirty, they smell bad, they torture mice and girls, they have no morals, and if they grow up they'll be worse than the men they're instructed by. But don't make puns about their pain. Respect pain. If we could truly imagine pain we don't feel, we would not survive a day, so we don't imagine it, we can't, and that indispensable glitch in the human machine is also ironically what lets us inflict pain on others at little cost to a good night's rest. So though you can't feel the pain of those boys you shot in the ass, you must honor it by not making puns.

>and the
>older woman—the muscular one, whose not-small breasts still float so
>unusually high on her chest for a woman of her age, if you don't mind this
>kind of observation made, again, in the name of honesty and full disclosure

As with ownership, please give "honesty and full disclosure" a re-think, and the woman you speak of is my Aunt Charlene so, you know, eew.

>and then your dad arrived

My dad and I are not on speaking terms, he banished me—will tell you all about it when I see you next—so when you mention him just know that what you say is news to me. And be advised that if you've shown me warmth toward the end of a strategic alliance between "your people" and "mine" you're barking up the wrong tree. But you don't seem the type. Not sophisticated enough. And by sophisticated I mean conniving, and by conniving I mean crass, and by crass I mean unsophisticated.

>fuck you

A strange, nonsensical phrase used frequently by people from New York, who I've noticed also use words to make things fuck that can't, unless where you're from shit can fuck, in which case please don't ever take me there.

>A competition of degree of openness of
>eyes equals umbrage versus umbrage in such a context, where I come from, FYI.
What?! Speak English, fer chrissakes.

>Ratcliffe,
>whom he loomed above.
I love my father's massiveness and strength, yet your man Ratcliffe's smallness makes me feel so sad. He seems to be a walking advertisement for noble ambition encased in an impenetrable shell of bullshit; every good impulse in him is met with the irresistible force of his own weakness. He and my dad standing next to each other, as you describe them, kind of equal one person, or humankind in general. I don't know what I'm saying. I can't believe I'm saying these things to you when I barely know you. Fuck you.

>In a dead tongue, eight of your guys sang a song in
>four parts I'd guess is your people's "For He's a Jolly Good Fellow,"
Don't forget, when people laugh they bare their teeth. And that wasn't no dead tongue, that was a parody of y'all's crude pronunciation of the language we

both speak. We have a cadre of songwriters whose job is to make up humorous songs about current events. The one they sang to you that day goes

> You come to us on your rude bus
> You starve and fart and steal our land
> You say you mean no harm to us
> But now we've drawn a line of sand
> We hope you're not too blind to see
> How very close you all have come
> To making us your enemy
> Your strength won't save you if you're dumb

and is not called "For He's a Jolly Good Fellow" but "Fuck You, New York Shits." The topical songwriters of the Chesapeake are guys and gals too weak to fight and farm, respectively, which, as you can see, is no guarantee they'll write good songs, especially songs of the top-down variety wherein the leadership says to them, "Put this dire warning in song form," but they do make their point, however crudely, which you might want to pass on to the New York leadership, in case they, too, hasn't understood the words.

>Are you not
>Indians? You all have red skin.
You know who I am. What Indians were on this land the Europeans' microbes killed; and who was left the Europeans' microbes' hosts killed; and who was left after that the bombs killed. We're red cuz we smear ourselves each day with SPF 90 red goop to stop the sun from burning us alive, but take a closer look, Mister. You know who I am. I'm the etcetera and the so forth. I'm just an Irish Negro Jewish Italian French and English Spanish Russian Chinese Polish Scotch Hungarian Litvak Swedish Finnish Canadian Greek and Czech and Turk and Injun Injun Injun. My dad's more black than red, my aunt's more yellow than red, my uncle's more tan than red, Frank's more brown than red, Joe's more white than red, I'm more bled than red, y'all are green and not well fed, and some of y'all are almost dead.

Meet me by the thing today at thing o'clock. Big kiss and a hug and fuck you every day in every way,
Poc

23:19:47

Knock-Knock from: Internet user GREASYBOY

GREASYBOY has sent you an Instant Message not bound by your Terms of Service Agreement. Would you like to accept the Instant Message from GREASYBOY?

☑ Yes

☐ No

GREASYBOY: What you doing right now?

CORNLUVR: Scouring pots with my friends.

GREASYBOY: I thought you were banished.

CORNLUVR: Girl still got to help her sisters do the dishes.

GREASYBOY: Does your father know you're there?

CORNLUVR: No.

GREASYBOY: So all the girls you're scouring pots with are acting in defiance of your dad?

CORNLUVR: Girls value the community above the individual.

GREASYBOY: Have they told him so?

CORNLUVR: That would be counterproductive. They'd have to start a war with him to get him to listen to them and girls don't start wars, though often they participate in them. They just welcome me when I come around, and we farm or build a house or cook or wash dishes or fold clothes or put on skits or babysit the little boys and girls.

GREASYBOY: The little boys and girls don't tell on you?

CORNLUVR: The little girls know not to tell because they're girls. The little boys know because they haven't yet learned to be the sort of louts whose asses you filled with buckshot, nor the sort of louts who'd fill boys' asses with buckshot.

GREASYBOY: What if you're found out?

CORNLUVR: Every time a man comes near, a girl will stop him in his path, do a sexy dance, tell him to meet her in an hour by a certain tree. Usually he goes off right away to wait by the tree, a tree of his own sprouting all the while in his crotch. If that don't work she'll suck his dick on the spot, he'll come and fall asleep. Sometimes by the end of a dishwashing session five or six men will be asleep in a pile on the path outside the kitchen door.

GREASYBOY: Speaking of waiting by things, I waited for you today by the thing and you didn't show.

CORNLUVR: *I* waited for *you* by the thing.

GREASYBOY: Which thing?

CORNLUVR: Fallen log.

GREASYBOY: I thought you meant thorn bush. I missed you so bad it hurt.

CORNLUVR: Don't get sentimental on me.

GREASYBOY: I'm not. Sentimentality is when you give more tenderness to a thing than God gives to it.

CORNLUVR: You monotheists, man.

GREASYBOY: So you disagree with the definition?

CORNLUVR: Right.

GREASYBOY: Why?

CORNLUVR: Let's say you're God.

GREASYBOY: Never happen—I've got poor management skills.

CORNLUVR: Then let's say the truth, which is that there's not one God, there are many gods, each with its own temperament, so one god will give a lot of tenderness to a thing to which another god may give none. But that is not the whole substance of my disagreement.

GREASYBOY: What else?

CORNLUVR: Can't articulate it in your meager language.

GREASYBOY: Blow me.

CORNLUVR: Gods aside, I believe the essence of human emotion is excess.

GREASYBOY: What does that mean?

CORNLUVR: It means that it is in the nature of the feeling of sadness, for example, to be in excess of whatever in the world is causing the sad person to feel sad.

GREASYBOY: How can you know this?

CORNLUVR: I know it by feeling it.

GREASYBOY: But you just got done saying feeling is excessive by nature.

CORNLUVR: Ya, and that's what makes it the truest form of knowing, since knowing is excessive too, and awful, and if you don't believe me, believe your own myth of the world's first couple and their life-ruining encounter with knowledge.

GREASYBOY: What do you scour the pots with?

CORNLUVR: Sponges.

GREASYBOY: Where do they come from?

CORNLUVR: Where do what come from?

GREASYBOY: The sponges.

CORNLUVR: How should I know?

GREASYBOY: And soap?

CORNLUVR: What about it?

GREASYBOY: You use it?

CORNLUVR: We use soap!

GREASYBOY: Does it smell like anything?

CORNLUVR: Lemon, sometimes mint.

GREASYBOY: So, fragranced soap.

CORNLUVR: The miracle of dish soap.

GREASYBOY: And do you know where your soap comes from?

CORNLUVR: This is very deep and all.

GREASYBOY: Which do you think is an index of the more advanced civilization, knowing where the soap comes from, or not knowing?

CORNLUVR: Meet me tomorrow by the thorn bush at thorn bush o'clock. Bye!

Johnny Rolfe

I'm just sitting and thinning by this prickly thorn bush. Ow, a spider bit my ass. I wonder if this is the end, just like all those other times I wondered if it was the end, and those other other times when it *was* the end. I borrowed the car. Hope she likes the car. Wanna get her in the car and drive her out somewhere far away and show her the sky as if it were mine. How stupid, to want to pretend to own the sky. Wanna drive her out somewhere far away and cower with her in my arms beneath the sky that would crush us to death. Yeah! Love those pits in her face where the pocks used to be. List of things in her I love: 1. those pits in her face; 2. she's cross-eyed and ugly; 3. rough high cheekbones; 4. big bony calloused feet against my ears; 5. she does not, like New York girls, go "Aaahhh" or "Oooooh" or even "Ohhhh," but "Oh! Oh! Oh! Oh! Oh!" Here comes that clutch of scary boys, the ones who'd spit on me as soon as pull the legs off a spider and pop its writhing thorax in their mouths. But I'm not what they're after now. Among themselves they toss that three-inch hard rubber ball which if whipped against your thigh would raise a welt. They play a game with it I've seen them play before that might be described as a marriage of handball and chess, though into the gap between one English word and the next disappears this game they play: swift, slow; swathe of silent thought, knee to groin. Twenty yards from the thorn bush beneath which I sit and wait for my girl, they bounce the ball off what once must have been the side of an office building or parking garage. But I've got my trusty car I drove in on. Here she comes running from deep in the woods. 6. Hairy arms.

Swiftly do my filthy pants rise. Must not touch her, as she asked. How I regret the filth of my pants. The closer she gets, the more I regret.

"Hey."

"I'd kiss you but you said not to."

"What's in your pants?"

"I borrowed the car."

"You people need *that* much food?"

"We're starving."

"You're stupid. Nice car."

"Let's go for a drive."

"Let's go for a drive."

"What's that game those boys are playing?"

"Handball."

"What's the ball made of?"

"New Yorker testicles."

"I like you a lot."

She punched my arm. My dick went down. She kissed my cheek. My dick went up again.

"Please say your name so I know how to say it."

"Pocahontas."

"Poe car haunt as."

"That's my nickname, not my real name."

"What's your real name?"

"If I tell you, you'll die."

"In what sense?"

"In the sense of starting not to be alive and staying that way."

"How?"

"Sunburn, heart attack, emphysema, poison, gunshot wound . . ."

"I mean how will saying—"

"It's cursed."

"What is?"

"My name."

"No it isn't."

"Yes it is."

"What does that even mean?"

"Anyone who hears it will die."

"Right away?"

"Soon."

"We'll all die soon."

"You pick the wrong thing to mock."

"That's magical thinking."

"I don't care. Thoughts can kill. So can names. Hang a right."

"Here?"

"No, back there."

"But there wasn't any—"

"You have to squeeze between that oak tree and that quondam savings bank."

"You mean that bombed-out hole in the ground?"

"We'll swing by and pick up some sacks of corn and dried fish, then we'll go for a swim, then we'll deliver the food to those poor schmucks your friends, then you'll take me home."

"A swim? Where?"

"The Chickahominy River."

"That's where Mankiewicz got killed."

"You won't get killed if you're with me."

"Okay but I'm concerned you'll see my boner."

"I see it right now."

"Don't look at it."

"Stop."

"I can't."

"No I mean stop the car. We've arrived at the food."

"I don't see it."

"It's buried underground in a special protective container which don't even bother to come back here and try to find it because they move it every day."

We got the food and swam nude in the river where I unexpectedly pronged her from behind and not only did she not resist but (7. hairy thighs; 8. muscular everything) she backed up and backed up and backed up and I came so hard I had to crawl up on the bank and faint. Next I knew she was on me going "Oh! Oh!" I can't stand the feeling of loving her, I want to die, I'll soon get my wish.

We're driving to Jamestown. To continue to insist on calling this a town is to stand on the precipice of hope and stare into the abyss of idiocy, story of my life.

"By the way, when I said those boys took buckshot in their backs I wasn't being cute."

"You'll never be cute."

Midafternoon. Driving with Pocahontas in the open-air car through a series of unintentionally reforested strip malls, air so fresh it stings your nose and burns your eyes. Mint jelly sky. Early autumn sun lasers our napes, bores into our spines. A rabid seagull flies at us, she swats it down, it dies.

Jamestown is a fright. When they hear the sound of the car at the gate, anatomical skeletons—men not long ago, birthnames clinging loosely to their skin like hardened mud—stand up from their homes, tents, and would-be graves to greet us. Some don't stand: they have fresh holes in them.

John Martin skulks by a fire in his slimy three-piece suit. He's shaved his big head and filed the arrow in it to rough nubs on both ends. He turns the crank on a spit of lean meat whose smoke makes my salivary glands open up so fast my tongue aches. The spit itself seems to be the rusted antenna of an antebellum car.

"What happened?"

"Why'd you bring that twat to camp?" he says.

"She got us food and shut up before I put another arrow in your head. What's that meat?"

I look away from the meat and hereby stop myself from guessing what it is.

"Where's Jack?"

"Stealing food from twats like her."

I'd punch him if it didn't bring me closer to the meat.

"What happened?"

"What do you think? We got attacked."

"By who?"

"Bunch of savages."

"Which ones?"

"Don't know. They came here just after dawn with hoods on their heads like cowards and shot the coffee mugs from our hands, then shot our hands, then our guts."

"Where's Ratcliffe?"

"Crying in a tent somewhere."

"Where's Newport?"

"Duh, do you see the bus anywhere? He left this afternoon. Says he'll come back with food, weapons, supplies, and men but I'm not holding my breath."

"I thought we all came to an understanding at the induction. Why'd they do this?"

"Maybe because you're predatory, amoral, and rude," she says.

Martin says, "So are you."

"Less than you."

"Like degree matters."

"Degree is all there is."

"How many of us are left?" I ask.

"Twenty, eighteen, maybe."

"What should we do?"

"My plan is to start an all-out assault on them that won't let up till the bus gets back: slaughter a hundred a day, take what we can get our hands on, meet the bus on its way back into town, climb aboard, leave this place full up with savage blood, don't come back."

She runs at him and hits him in the mouth. He hits her back and she hits him and by now my knees are on his chest and dirt and blood mingle at the back of his head. My position gives me too good a view of the meat on the spit. I look at him and look back at it. "Martin!"

"Oh like I'm gonna observe your little niceties and starve to death."

"We brought food so get it off there and bury it. Is Dick Buck alive?"

"Yeah."

"Get him to pray for it."

"Look who suddenly has a qualm. Hypocrite."

He's got a point but I can't cop to it in front of the lady I love, whom I must lie to about this and a few other things till she figures out the truth.

But, "Don't pretend you wouldn't do the same if it was that or die," she says to me. "We all would. We're made to. Let's just get out front of that *in the interest of honesty and full disclosure.*"

I leave Martin on the ground and take Poc to find Dick Buck.

"I can't," Ratcliffe says and weeps as we enter the tent, Dick Buck's hand on his back. Can't *what*, I don't know; everything, I guess. "I've failed and will fail again. I've let us be destroyed and could have stopped it. I'll step down now and will no doubt fail in that too."

Ratcliffe and Buck look up. "Who's that? Get her out of here. She's got a bodkin in her purse."

"Easy, Ratcliffe. Let's just assume for now you're wrong in everything you say and do. No bodkin, no purse. She brought us food."

"Why?"

"Trust her, John," Dick says. "Trusting her will help your heart to heal."

"Nothing will. I'm lost."

"You know what Martin's doing out there?" I ask Dick.

"Must I?"

"Smell that."

"Christ."

"In a sense, yes."

"I name Martin my successor," Ratcliffe says.

"We won't let you do that," I say.

"I'll do what I want."

"If you want to save your soul, you won't," Dick says.

"I can't believe you talk like that. Do you know what a fool you sound like?"

"John, you brought me on this trip to talk like that. I've risked my life to talk like that and act like that and try to see that you do too, unlikely as that is."

"Why bother?"

"Because God exists."

"Really?"

"Really."

"You're insane."

"And you."

We eat dried fish from a cloth sack as the sun goes down. Poc completes her lightly spiced corn stew at midnight and we eat it and go to bed groaning. On the way there I ask her to come to New York. She shakes her head. I ask her why. She looks at the sky.

"That wasn't my dad," she says.

"What wasn't your dad?"

"Who attacked."

"How do you know?"

"He said they wore hoods. My dad wouldn't wear a hood or let his men wear them. As your friend said, it's considered cowardly."

"Who was it then?"

"My guess: Frank and Joe."

"What does that mean?"

"It means your enemy is two enemies, one unreasonably aggressive, the other more so."

The muck we built on sucks the town down half an inch each night, and if you're one of those who sleep in tents—which I am since our houses have been built by filing clerks—you wake up with half a cup of swamp between your cheek and gum.

Poc is gone. Smith comes back in the other car with corn and dried deer meat. "Fair trade enhancement device," he says, pointing to his gun. He's got a long and dripping gash up his left arm as from a knife.

"What's that?"

"Bird bit me. What the hell happened here?"

Dick Buck tells him. The life has gone out of Ratcliffe. He hands executive vice presidency to Smith without complaint. Martin's loud complaints are quelled by all the rest of us with the net loss of a tooth for him.

Smith says, "We'll eat for a week, get back our strength, and attack."

"Why don't we just leave?" I say.

He looks at me as if I've said *Why don't we just die?* "We can't."

"Why not?"

"You want to leave? Go. Take this car." He knows I also can't.

"There must be something we can do besides kill them."

"Like what?"

"Talk with them."

"Pray with them," Dick says.

"We talked with them, we sang with them, we ate with them, we swapped with them, and some of us have even slept with them. If we don't show them we're strong now they'll wipe us out."

Some of the worst plans in the world get acted on when those who contest them get tired. Some of the second-worst plans in the world get acted on when those whose plans are even worse get tired. So it went with Smith's plan to attack, Dick's and mine not to.

And so we ate and slept and strategized. A bad storm came up. Wind blew down our walls. Wound in plastic sheaths, wedged one by one in local shrubs, self-fed from small bags of malodorous fish held against our flesh, we weathered it for three days. And then we had no fort, no walls, no town, no bus: snails sans shells; slow meat. Wet and full of dread, we moved on them.

Pocahontas

I say to Stickboy, "Step into mah office," and he say, "There's water in it."

"There's water in everything."

"I miss you."

"Miss you too."

"You know the girl who says she misses you is lying when she drops the 'I' and looks at the ground when she says it."

"Ugh, can't a person accidentally drop a pronoun and then try to find it on the ground?"

"Anyway, glad to see you."

"*I'm* glad to see *you*, Stickboy," I say and try to use my eyes to drill through his into the place in his brain where the secret thoughts are lodged, the ones with which he betrays himself and those he loves—a bigger part of anyone's brain than most like to admit. If, as evidently monotheists think, a single god has made the brain, then he seems to have erected in most men's brains a sturdy partition between the part that knows itself and the part that betrays all the other parts.

"So this is pretty weird," I say and point at it all.

"Yeah, who'd have ever thought?"

"Me, I'd have thought."

"Me too."

The sun has dropped halfway below the trees. We're standing in what used to be our town. It's gone. The buildings, somewhat damaged by the storm, remain, but the people left, not wanting to be attacked by New

Yorkers with guns at an unspecified time. They knew they would be coming because I told Stickboy and he told Frank and Joe. Frank and Joe told Dad and Dad moved the town over their angry objections, Stickboy says. Those two expressed the wish to stay, kill them all, and thus be through with them. Sid piped up and said why kill them when they'll soon kill themselves, and in any case to kill them may not be the same as to be through with them since they come from a big town up north whose wrath may be provoked by their death. Frank then used the phrase *talking puppet* to describe Sid, and Dad, for whom the air still parts when he walks and talks, suggested Frank and Joe could stay and fight on their own if they liked but encouraged them not to, and the daughter of that man wonders why he would be firm but reasonable with dissenting and disrespectful officers while with herself he was unreasonable and peremptory and devastating and has misused his remaining time on Earth by using words to exclude her from it. Or maybe no such dialogue took place among my dad and his men but was made up by Stickboy and retailed to me for a purpose unknown, and my unknowing in combination with my knowing cause me to continue to try to bore into his skull with these third-rate tools, my eyes and thoughts and talk.

In the dim, moist light of dusk we watch the thin pond that used to be our town's main square. We're in the doorway of the n-shaped one-room house whose divan was the site of my near-rape. The divan is sodden and sad; no one would try to rape a girl on it now, piece-of-shit divan, poor divan. The whole room is wet. The pond is wetter. We're standing on the driest spot in town.

"Where'd they go?" I say.

"Orapax."

"Lousy neighborhood. Why there?"

"Hard to get to, easy to defend." His face says he means the new me and not the new town. He tries to kiss me and I stop him. We both cry. Poor, sad, sodden, piece-of-shit Pocahontas and Stickboy, to whom nothing good will happen.

The lintel of the doorway cracks in two with a shocking noise. They're here. Stickboy runs and falls down in the mud and gets up and runs. I step out into the middle of the pond and hold my arms above my head and hope to die and feel I won't just yet. Holding guns, they—including my boyfriend—encircle me.

"Where'd they all go?" the red-bearded Jackshit says.

"I don't know nothin." The water is up to my waist. "Lower your guns, bitches," I say to try to be a guy, though to be a guy may hurt more than not.

They lower them. It's dinnertime. They've brought food but can't start a fire when the wood's all wet. I show them a special Indian trick for starting a fire after a rain, which is you go to the woodshed and get the stash of dry wood wrapped in plastic. They didn't seal their food up well before the storm and it's maggoty. I take my boyfriend to my childhood room and have sex with him in there on the wet mattress and it's kind of weird but nice, I like how he seems to be saying "Awe, awe, awe, awe."

The air is dark in this room I grew up in. I hear his loud and snarling voice. I nudge and then shake him.

"What?"

"You were yelling."

"Was I asleep?"

"I hope you weren't awake."

"Why, what did I say?"

"I think your exact words were 'Fuck you, you cunt!'"

"Really?"

"Ya, and I'd like to reiterate that those are all nice things—*fuck*, *you*, and *cunt*—and yet, again, you didn't mean them in a nice way. Your tone of voice was really harsh. Were you cursing me?"

"I think I was cursing me."

"As a sexually active vagina?"

"You make a good point. I'll have to think about that."

"Don't strain yourself."

We hear the loud noise of a voice far worse than the one my beau used in his sleep, and run outside. Four thin men—the New York night watch—lie face-down in the shallow pond that used to be the middle of our town. We can see them by a fire that burns beyond the pond between two n-shaped homes. Beyond the fire and facing it, tied to two stakes four feet apart, is sad Ratcliffe, whose guys called him chief, now call him man, and soon will call him neither one except in past tense. New York, who meant to ambush my hometown, has instead been ambushed by it.

The man beside Ratcliffe, whose knife has not yet touched the latter's skin, is not a man at all but the same boy, Opechancanough, whom not too long ago I couldn't stop from beating up his friend, and now, I'd guess, is being offered this premature ceremony of graduation to mortal violence in recompense for a backful of New York buckshot. Jackshit comes charging gun-up from a nearby house. Joe shoots him with a gun he must have got from a face-down dead night watchman. Jackshit leaps into a bush and is gone, don't know if he got shot, don't know nothing, all that's being done is done too fast for looking to see it and much too fast for thinking to believe it and as for knowing, knowing hobbles miles behind on broken feet. The other guns of New York's dead night watch are held by Frank and Dad and Sid. Sid's got his gun to Johnny's skull. No one cares enough to hold a gun or knife to me, I guess.

"I'm John Ratcliffe!" Ratcliffe says with an indignation that suggests being tied to a stake soon to be flayed alive is one step worse than a fly in his soup. "Do you know who I am? I'm John Ratcliffe! My mother is Penelope Ratcliffe. My father-in-law is James Stuart, Chief Executive Officer of the Manhattan Company."

Daddy, who ignores or doesn't see me, says, "Your own names must taste good to you because you always have them in your mouths and, to judge by your thinness, seem to prefer them to food. But names lose their flavor if you keep them in your mouth too long, and if you swallow them they go down hard and make you sick. Would you like to spit yours out now or die with it in your mouth?"

The tied-up man's eyes widen. Pee goes down his leg. I scream at my dad. He looks at me, looks away, nods to Opechancanough, who moves toward Ratcliffe. I jump on my cousin's back—not for love of Ratcliffe—and am peeled and thrown from him and hit the wet ground hard, my own familiar town a sleepy blur to me of ground and sky. I hear a wail where Ratcliffe is and turn to see the wail is colored red. A small man seems to float down through the air from the top of a nearby tree and impale Joe on a long and shining pole. Joe looks scared and sad and starts to cry as in a dream he once described to me. My dad, with an ax, as if in a hurry to get through his chores, chops at the legs of the man from the sky as he would wood for a fire. And now my eyes can see no more, my mind think no more, no one in here know no more.

Johnny Rolfe

We're on a thing that once was called Route 5. The autumn storms are fierce down here. We've put the rag top up on the jeep but it leaks. I'm driving north without the girl I love. Martin lies across the bloodied back seat and since he now takes up so little room Dick Buck can sit by him and cauterize his wounds. In the shotgun seat, Smith contemplatively holds his own injured left arm with his uninjured right arm. Who among us isn't almost Martin now: woozy, incredulous, legless, enraged? "Who the hell'd you think you were, Tarzan?" Dick Buck says to him—or me—cackles unhappily, zips the back flap up, and turns again to Martin, who is hardly Martin any more, and yet more Martin than before. Bucky Breck drives our other car with four more hobbled or terrified men. Ratcliffe's dead, to say the least. The bikes we threw in the creek. It's done.

High, bright headlights coming toward us blind me through the rain. Behind them I can dimly see a long gray box on wheels. "Who the hell is that?" I say.

Smith says, "That's a New York truck."

"How do you know?"

"How many New York trucks are there? Don't drive past them."

I brake and so does the truck. Out of the truck steps a pimp and layabout—who among us isn't both?—called Sal Argyle in a black rainsuit and matching broadbrimmed hat. I knew him vaguely in New York and may with lots of luck know him only vaguely someday there again. He walks up to the jeep and opens the flap a crack.

"You guys look like crap."

Smith leans over me and says, "Where the hell you been?"

"Got a flat in Dover."

"For a month?"

"They had good weed."

"You have arms?"

"Some."

"Supplies?"

"Some."

"What does 'some' mean?"

"It means I traded some for weed."

The rain that came in through the crack in the flap has soaked me by now and lightly burns my skin. Argyle, tall and thin, clings to the frame of the jeep so as not to be blown down the road by the wind. Smith jumps out. I thought he'd flatten Argyle but he evidently doesn't want to waste the time. They walk back to the truck and seem to be climbing into it. On the back seat, Martin lets out a long moan. Dick Buck and I don't talk but I think we both know what a grim turn of events for us this truck is. He murmurs what I guess are prayers for Martin's erstwhile hacked-off legs. Every prayer has its wound. God made even those of us who give up on Him in our youth hope our wounds will make our likeness to Christ more than skin-deep, but I doubt even Dick harbors such a hope in Martin's case.

Argyle climbs back into the cab of his truck and Smith returns to the jeep. "We're turning around."

"No," I say.

"We have an opportunity."

"The opportunity to lie face-down in a ditch?"

"The savages may not have fuel but they do have food processing technology we need, and somewhere around here they must have a big facility we just haven't found yet. Argyle has twenty men in the back of his truck and weaponry enough to subdue the savages."

"So let him subdue them."

"He's too subdued himself."

"Then let Stuart send down reinforcements. We tried our best."

"We tried our worst."

"Same thing."

"Stuart won't send anyone else. He doesn't care enough about this. If he did he wouldn't have sent a weed-smoking pimp to rescue us."

"He's right not to care. Caring's overrated."

"*Not* caring is your bullshit paper-thin shield against disappointment. You lost the girl you love and you don't want to go back because you're scared you'll lose her again."

"No, I don't want to go back because I'd be going back for your reasons, not mine. You think we deserve to have what they have at their expense. Please tell me what's so good about *us* surviving instead of *them.*"

Against my right temple Smith presses the barrel of the gun he gave me on our way down here, a tender reminder. "I still love you," he says, "but let's have this nice conversation about values and beliefs someday in a dry place in New York over a stuffed pheasant."

I put the car in gear and turn it. Martin says, "We're going back?"

"Yes."

"Good, I want to slaughter them," he dreamily mumbles.

"Tell me you won't be glad to see your girl again," Smith says.

"I don't know if she's alive."

"Don't be ruled by fear, pussycat. When you see her next, sock a seed in there to make you want to stay alive. We need folks like you to balance out folks like him," he says, indicating Martin.

"And who'll balance out folks like you?"

He laughs and taps the side of my head affectionately with the barrel of his gun. No doubt if he were driving I'd put a gun to his head and tell him to go the other way, which supports my belief that who prevails is who has the better strategy or weaponry, a formula for success which virtue not only has no part in but is an impediment to, since virtuous thoughts drain time and force from strategic ones.

There's no town to go back to so we stop the two jeeps and the truck for the night on hard high ground. Smith and I walk through the tapering rain to retrieve a few guns from the back of the truck. He must know I won't try a one-man coup against his one-man rule. The air in the back of the truck is ten percent oxygen, ninety percent marijuana smoke. Hurricane lamps make a dim light. The twenty men jammed in this oblong box recline or sit or stand. Some talk, some play cards, some make love, some oil their guns, some do more than one of these activities at once. They've managed to transport intact their own two thousand cubic feet of New York across state lines, their means and end both being oblivion. I think I'll stay with them tonight, have found a vacant spot, have smoked a bone, and now am thinking this to you. Are you there?

CORNLUVR: I'm here.

GREASYBOY: Where?

CORNLUVR: Don't know.

GREASYBOY: But I didn't even type my message to you, I just thought it.

CORNLUVR: And yet I read the whole thing. So you're back?

GREASYBOY: I guess.

CORNLUVR: What for?

GREASYBOY: To take.

CORNLUVR: Take what?

GREASYBOY: What've you got?

CORNLUVR: Nothing.

GREASYBOY: Nothing—especially nothing—nothing above all else—is worth dying for.

CORNLUVR: Meet me tomorrow at tomorrow o'clock by the puddle.

GREASYBOY: Okay.

CORNLUVR: Bye.

GREASYBOY: Don't say that.

Pocahontas

I'm waiting for my man, twenty-six heartbeats in my hand. The birds have stopped singing, the crickets have stopped chirping, the squirrels have stopped hissing, the leaves have stopped rustling, the rain has stopped need need needling the sodden earth it impinges upon. There is about the forest today a sweetly sad post-annihilation feel, as if I were a smaller version of its heart. Feeling sick and dirty, huh, I'm waiting for my man. Hey white boy, what are you doing by this log? Hey white boy, how come you treat me like a dog? Hey white prince, what if you really are a frog? I apostrophize him in case he's sick or sad or hurt or dead or fled or imaginary. White bitch, I do get weary in my shaggy dress. When I get weary, try a little tenderness. Hold me, squeeze me, don't ever leave me, got to got to now now now, try a little—huh—

"Hey, move away from that log before that caterpillar bites your leg off" is all's he can say when he finally shows.

"Thank you for saving me from the vicious caterpillar."

"No problem."

"Problem."

"Yeah, problem."

"Squeeze me."

"Unh?"

"Squeeze me right here."

"Oh. Watch that puddle."

"Watch *that* puddle."

On a half inch of dry ground we are squozen each to each and each watch a puddle. My puddle is a pretty rainbow of microbes. Somewhere over the rainbow, up my ass.

"Joe's dead," I say.

"So are most people. Your dad chopped off Martin's legs."

"Is he dead too?"

"No, he's taking it in stride."

"Hey, I said no pain jokes. Did you tell anyone you were meeting me here?"

"No."

"Then why is three of your mens behind that tree over there?"

"Which tree?"

"The one by that puddle."

"That one?"

"No, that one. And three more behind that one and three more behind that one."

"Oh crap."

A man I haven't seen before, someone clean for once, with faded, grayish skin and clouded eyes, emerges from behind oak tree number two in a zebra-striped sharkskin suit saying, "Dude, I hope you don't mind I followed you. You bicker a lot but I sense you really dig each other and that makes spying on you an exalted experience so thanks."

My sweetheart, Johnny, seems, even in his stillness, to descend vertically into the rain-defeated earth, like an obelisk built above a sealed-off mine shaft. He stares at me as if he wants to cry. At moments such as this I wish he'd be the commanding, belligerent asshole my father is, and punch or kill or remove the legs of this guy. No I don't really wish that. I always have conflicting feelings when something bad's about to happen to me, and something is, else why would all these guys be here? How unpleasant and interesting it is to be alive! A bomb of love exploding in my head for my guy! I leap on him and press his flesh to mine. He falls and I fall on him. The ground is soft and wet and cold and so am I. Oh Johnny, oh I love your rough and gaunt and sallow skin. Above my head, the sickening clicks of guns being made ready to fire. We may now die—who knows why?—and so I dig my lips and teeth into his cheek, this skinny, dirty man who is my doom. What on earth has made me love my doom so much? What gives? I give—the only way to make my bad life good. But of course I never give enough. I always don't give enough. And since talk and deeds are but the runty brood of thoughts, I'm trying—right now!—to make of my cloven brain a device for the composition and transmission of thoughts and thoughts alone, and send them out to you, Johnny Rolfe, who have and have not earned my trust; to you, Charlene Kawabata Feingold, intermittent docent of my life so far, distracted as you are at every moment by the heroic struggle to have a good life despite being the willing prisoner of a woman's body and a marriage to a man; to you, unknown corporeal inter-locutor who I hope is just kind of out there somehow knowing my thoughts and undertaking your own heroic struggle against the exigencies of having a body made of a trillion cells each with a hungry mouth; and to you, Pocahontas, most unknowable of all and yet so eerily finite. How y'all doin?

"What are you doing?" Johnny—you—says—say.

"Making out with you."

"Why?"

"Cuz you're cute?"

"But we're surrounded by men who are pointing guns at us."

"So? They'd be pointing guns at us if we weren't kissing, and kissing is better than not kissing."

Well, guess what, everyone I'm transmitting my thoughts and feelings to, including you, he's kissing me back! His soft and acrid tongue is in my mouth right now! I knew he was a good egg, a good quail egg with a tired poor huddled baby quail in it yearning to breathe free of its shell.

"On your feet, lovebirds," this new grayish-hued person says. He's bossy for a guy who's barely there.

"I don't like the new guy," I whisper to Johnny.

"Yeah, tell me about it."

"Who is he?"

"Pimp and a pothead."

"He's dressed inappropriately for local conditions."

"Who isn't?"

"Why's he doing the talking and holding a gun while Jackshit's just standing there with his thumb up his ass and an inscrutable expression on his face?"

"Good point. Hey Smith, why you being so weirdly passive?"

"Look who's talking."

"Kidnapping her was my idea," says the gentleman whose skin is the color of the air. "Hey, it's cold in this forest, does anyone have a windbreaker?"

"This guy won't shoot me so I'm going to stomp off into the forest if you don't mind," I whisper to my boyfriend and before he can whisper back I stomp off into the forest and here come some guys with some guns and I feel myself being lifted to the top of a tree and my thoughts now inconveniently flee.

My thoughts are back, hi, I'm on their truck. I think I been here a while but who the fuck knows, shit is happening all the time ain't never happened before. This truck is like an n-shaped house except it's rectangular and cold and damp and made of tin and on wheels and I'm surrounded by idiot white men none of whom's my guy. Their priest, Dick Buck, who thinks I really ought to love his god, says, "Who made the world?"

"I don't know."

"Who is God?"

"I don't know."

"What is man?"

"I don't know."

"Is man's likeness to God in the body or the soul?"

"I don't know."

"How is the soul like to God?"

"I don't know."

"Why did God make you?"

"I'm not so sure he did."

"Of which must we take more care, our soul or our body?"

"I don't know."

"What must we do to save our souls?"

"This question I don't readily see the value of looking to you for instruction in."

"Is this indoctrination working?"

"No."

"Shall we forget it?"

"Yes."

"Do you love Johnny Rolfe?"

"Well I don't, like, *love* love him, but I love him."

"What does that mean?"

"I don't know."

"Do you want to marry him?"

"Eew, no, we're just dating."

"Would you marry him if you knew doing so would put an end to this bloodshed?"

"Only if you could guarantee an end to bloodshed worldwide till the end of time."

"Seriously."

"Could you convince my dad to talk to me again, and not just once, but from now on?"

"If I could, would you marry Rolfe?"

"Maybe."

"I'll see what I can do. Do you have any questions for me?"

"Can you get me off this fucking truck?"

"No."

"If your god has any control over what passes for human activity, what sort of god is he?"

"All the more reason to keep him in our thoughts and prayers and conversations and hearts."

"Who made your skinny ass?"

"God made my ass. Man made it skinny."

"At least you have a sense of humor."

"Who's joking?"

"God, I'd guess."

Johnny Rolfe

Of my two sub-specializations within the field of communications, no news and bad news, I am far better at the former, but today have been called upon and—despite my distaste for this adventure's conception, its goals, its trajectory, its management, its personnel, its scope, its methods, its avoidable failures—feel compelled to practice the latter. I look forward to embarking as soon as is feasible upon a career and a life predicated exclusively on no news.

Before discharging my duty I went to visit Pocahontas. She was in Sal Argyle's truck. How Argyle, who at the wavy border of himself is not so different from the air, so quickly became the leader of this trip I know not.

She said, "How are you?"

"Fine. How are you?"

"How's the Chickahominy River?"

"Angry."

"What's in it?"

"Water."

"What else?"

"Flotsam."

"I've been in this windowless truck for some unknown number of days and this guy's trying to make me believe in his god and you haven't visited and I'm three feet above my homeland but unable to touch it and can't tell except by gut if it's day or night so how the hell do you think I am?"

"I think you're like the Chickahominy River."

"Goddamn right. What news of my father?"

"A meeting with him was arranged for today at his erstwhile town of Werowocomoco which this truck we're in is parked a half a mile from."

"Don't tell me where this truck is parked. I know where this fucking truck is parked."

"Let her out of the truck."

"No."

"Touch me," she said.

I did, with Argyle watching, what the hell, I have to touch my girl.

"I'm not your girl."

"How'd you know I was thinking that?"

"I always know."

"You haven't known me long."

"From here on in I'll always know."

"What am I thinking now?"

"'Why won't she tell me her secret name? I won't really die, she just wants to keep a secret from me because she doesn't trust me. Maybe she's right not to trust me.'"

"Whoa."

"You're cute in a stupid way standing there with your mouth agape but go talk to my dad and tell him . . ."

"What?"

"Tell him . . ."

"What?"

"Listen to what he says and answer as I'd answer."

"So I should talk for you."

"Yes."

"That's a bad idea."

"Why?"

"I'm a man and you're a woman. I'm from the north and you're from the south. I'm white and you're not. I'm me and you're you."

"What are you staring at?" she said to five stoned guys in the truck who'd turned toward her voice as babies turn toward shiny things when looking out to sea. They turned slowly back to their games of cards or bongs or sandwiches or their companions' mouths. "You're not white either."

"Yes I am."

"You think you're the first of your line to be drawn to nonwhite coochie?"

"I still don't want to talk for you."

"If you will not be for me, who will?"

"I'll be for you, not talk for you."

"How will you be for me?"

"I don't know yet."

"Stop saying 'I' so much."

"Okay."

"You know how you can be for me? Leave the door open on your way out. My lungs have memorized every exhaled bong hit in here."

I lifted the door. "There," she said, "is a picture of my life right now: the back of a New York truck framing you, the sky, two oak trees, and a disassembled kiosk of my youth."

"I'll do my best with your dad."

"Poor kiosk."

I leapt from the truck. Sal leapt too. I said, "Keep the truck door open for an hour." He closed it. I punched what I thought would be his face but was air.

"Many finer men than you have tried and failed to punch me in the face. Sorry." He grinned and made a picture of my life right now: gray lips and brown nubs of teeth framing the faint glisten of an otherwise black maw.

Martin would not stay back in the corn shack we've commandeered for his convalescence. As we enter the great reception hall at Werowocomoco, he hangs down Bucky Breck's chest in a papooselike sling, balls front, eyes ablaze, tongue held back by clamped-down teeth. Leglessness has taught him statecraft's secret of restraint. His luminescent alabaster head, made horned by the arrow that transects it, looms more regally than ever before above the rest of his shortened self.

Their same set of men greets us. Powhatan, Find Gold, Frank, a thin and pale and seated Joe, alive, it seems, for now, despite having been run through the gut with a stick of some kind. Fifty archers line the walls in rusted folding chairs. We are Argyle, Martin, Smith, Breck, Buck, me, six potheads with automatic guns, and more dispersed outside among the dampened trees.

Powhatan stands and looks more tired than when lying down, and yet his breathing makes the room itself breathe. "What?" he says.

"Pocahontas is with us," I say.

"'Is'?"

"They—uh—we've taken her hostage, Sir."

Distress and secrecy vie for control of his face, and cause a slight rearrangement of the air in the hall. "What do you want?"

"Peace."

Find Gold and Frank both make as if to object. Their boss quiets them by extending the fingers of his right hand to their full length at his side.

"And if we don't agree?" he asks.

I can't make the threat I've been instructed to.

Sal Argyle says, "I think you know."

Powhatan seems not to notice him. "Where's Newport?" he says to Smith.

"Gone."

"Smith, you'd kill my girl?"

Smith looks at the floor of the hall, which shines like dulled gold beneath the bright lamplight. What Sal has done to Smith to make him mute I don't know, and fear. A quiet noise as of something scraping something else comes from a wall to our right where there hangs, ceiling to floor, an arras on which is stitched a well-known scene of a Moor stabbing a malignant and turbaned Turk beneath whom lies a Venetian the Turk has just beaten. Smith and Argyle have evidently heard it too. Smith's hand centimeters up toward his gun. Argyle undulates. Frank's eyeballs flick toward the noise. And into my gal's dad's neck and head there comes a sad alertness that makes the walls around him sad, and the air, and the floor the air and walls rest on, which is the floor not only of the hall but of the world.

"So, you," Powhatan says to me, "you're now the one who speaks to me because—what?—because you've— you've—"

"Well I wouldn't say I—'"

"Tell me what you people want."

"She wants to speak to her father."

"So you're also an emissary for her. How confusing for you."

"Yes."

"I don't think the man who makes a threat to kill my daughter if I don't accept his terms can plausibly negotiate a peace between her and me, so why don't you tell me what exactly your terms are, and I'll accept them, *because I'm beside myself with anguish over my daughter's safety*, and you and she may take my acceptance of your terms as a sign that I value her life."

"Sir," Frank says, "with all due respect, your judgment is understandably clouded by your concern for your daughter."

"My judgment is clarified by my concern for my daughter," he replies.

"Or," Sit Knee says to Frank, "to put it another way, shut up."

"I'm afraid I can't do that while our lives are being sold down the river by this softening geezer."

"You'll have to," Sit Knee says, and turns to half a dozen of the archers seated on the edges of their rusted folding chairs. "Please remove Frank and Joe from the hall."

They don't budge.

"Please," Frank says to them, "remove Sit Knee from the hall," which they do with a struggle, during which the latter's face remains unreadable by me.

"And now," Frank says to the ones still seated around the edges of the hall, "train your arrows on that man." He points to his boss, at whom the two score men dutifully aim arrows. "And now, won't you all please stick his counterproductive ass with something sharp and let us be done with him?"

No one moves.

"I said *now*!"

They continue not to shoot and all look scared, as if to aim at him were only play, while to speak or even think of shooting him will bring them great ill luck.

Frank screams, and screams again, and each scream lasts as long as it takes his lungs to empty of air. Now that Powhatan's attention is turned to the screams, a young man I recognize as my gal's gentle friend Stickboy is running out from behind the arras. He shoves a knife in her dad's back—the back of his upper thigh. Powhatan is falling to the dirt floor. Stickboy is running knife-first at Frank. Their bodies seem to crash and I can't see clearly. Stickboy collapses to the dirt floor, which, I notice, having been packed down and made smooth, does not absorb but holds, for now, these two men's blood.

"You think when I told you to kill him I didn't know you'd try to kill me next?" Frank says to Stickboy, who lies curled up as if not yet ready to be born.

"You think I didn't know you knew?" Stickboy says.

"Yes, I think you didn't."

"You're right, but now I'm better off than you."

"That's what the losers always say to the winners to console themselves for their loss, and that's why losers lose and winners win."

"Yes, that's right, you've won. You now have power, strength, a chiefdom, the command of an army, what oil there is in these parts, factories to clean the food, even a crude sort of beauty, and the potential to lose each of those things, and you will lose them, one by one or all at once, long before you die, and their loss will cause you exquisite pain, whereas I have and have always had nothing, which I will never lose, even if someday, by an unlikely turn of events, I should have something," Stickboy has said, and is dead.

Pocahontas

Ah kin *not* make mah brain say what it jess hoid. Mah brain it kin not say what it jess hoid. Hoid mah daddy jess got stabbed in he ass. Whea he ass at now? Whea mah ass at now? My ass is still in the truck which belongs to the peculiar motherfuckers of New York but it feels as if it's on a cliff with angry rocks down below which have already been made red with the blood of the sad fools I know have been pushed off of the cliff or have jumped off of it. There is a lock on the door of the truck of the aforementioned motherfuckers and there is the immobilization of my ass on this mattress an ah have come tuh feel that histry ain't nuthin but uh long and uh desolate corridor uh time that lead up to thuh present and ain't got no uhmergency exit. Seems like nothing ever comes to no good out on Chickahominy Creek because that's where my used-to-be-best friend stabbed my father in his ass cheek and then he himself was stabbed and died and that is just some of what I cannot make my brain know or feel or say or do *nuthin* bout. You stupid man I love so bad, why none of this make you feel sad? And wherefore do thy lips so readily drip with the words of interposition and nullification? Howl, howl, howl! O y'all a man uh stone! If ah had yo tongue an eyes, ah'd use um so thuh ska would poe it black ink down onto thuh erf an thuh sea dump iss fish up into thuh ska and thuh ska dump iss fish it jess got from thuh sea back down on thuh heads uh the mens be walkin round on two legs down beneaf it like they know what thuh *fuck* they doin. Muthuhfuckuh you got to take me to mah daddy now.

"Okay."

"*Okay*, you bess say okay, punk-ass bitch."

"Why are you talking like that?"

"Why ahm talking like this? Why you a punk-ass, bitch-ass, greasy-hair, bad-breff-havin, bony-ass, doan-know-how-to-cook-corn, 'Jamestown,' white-ass New York muthuhfuckuh?"

"I don't know."

"Ah talk like this cuz sometime this how ah feel like talkin."

"Wish I'd brought my dictionary."

"Mah daddy jess got stab and you talkin bout wish I brought my dictionary, *fuck* you."

"Why do you always speak to me so harshly?"

"I'm sorry, I'm sorry, I'm sorry, I'm sorry, I'm sorry."

Pocahontas

There he is, my huge and screwed-up dad. My brain can see him all too clearly now. He just lies there almost as he does on state occasions except he's on his side and not his back, on a cot and not a chief-size bed, low not high, in a small n-shaped hut not a great n-shaped hall, naked not clothed, asleep not awake, wounded not whole. It could be that a daughter shouldn't think this when her father's going to die, but my, what a murderously large penis you have, Daddy. How not so very different its natural color is from the color of your wounded purple leg. I'm breathing through my mouth but still can feel the maggoty apple smell of your wound at the back of my throat. Your wound itself I feel right here, right here, right here. "Father Buck, give me that blanket, please. Is this the cleanest blanket you have? Now scram, if you don't mind, Father. Great, thanks, bottom of my foot to your rosy Anglo backside." What was that sandy-haired, bespectacled trick moping in here for anyway, more religious instruction? Hope to make my father want his New York God as he expires? These people ruin what's left to be ruined. Wonder what *that* guy's penis looks like. Wonder what all those guys' penises look like lined up in a row. Oh no wait I already saw that—kind of sweet and sad, like the men they hang from, oh what a cockeyed optimist am I. Lemme put this moldy blanket on your rotten-apple-smelling self, Daddy. Oh, I see, you throw it off, that's why they've got you lying naked here. Now come on, just hold your arm still so I can put this blanket on your big shivering gore-encrusted ass. I said hold your arm still! Massive arm like fifteen eggplants all in one. My father is dying, my father is dying. You awake or you just chuck this blanket on the ground like a soiled hanky in your sleep? Always liked your hair—not the grim white spikes that shoot up on the shaven side of your head so hair don't get caught in your bow but the long, coarse, silver curls, mmm, they feel good in my nose and mouth, block out the shit-and-rancid-watermelon smell of your infected behind. Let's say this gorgeous, musk-rich hair is the loving dad and chief, while the gashed ass is the stupid mean guy who acceded to my would-be rape and banished me. My lips on your hot brow now: let their saliva'd-up selves be balm to your sad head. And hey come on so wake up so we can get this reconciliation over with so I can get on with my life instead of being all neurotic and yelling at my boyfriend every day from now on because I didn't work things out with my dad. "Come on!"

"What the . . ."

"You awake?"

"Who are you and why are you kissing me?"

"Oh well I'm your daughter Pocahontas and I'm kissing you in case restoration hang its medicine on my lips, my kiss repair those violent harms a dozen things done messed you up with."

"When did you die?"

"Die? Watchu talkin bout?"

"Where have I been? Where am I? I will not swear this is my leg. Let's see, I feel this prick."

"Um, Daddy, let's not have this get all weird. You may be suffering from dementia but stop touching yourself in the presence of your daughter."

"I fear I am not in my perfect mind."

"Perspicacious as always."

"All the skill I have remembers not this smelly blanket nor the cheap construction materials of this hut. Where am I?"

"I don't know, some hut somewhere. One of the lesser huts of your kingdom."

"Do not laugh at me, for as I am a man I think this lady to be my child Pocahontas."

"Right, that's what I'm saying."

"Be your tears wet?"

"No, they're fake, plastic tears, duh." (I make my jibes real tenderly, okay?)

"I know you do not love me."

"I love you so much! Daddy! I love you!"

"Don't cry, my dear. I've been so awful to you."

"That may be but I've been a world-class cunt so let's just call it even. Hey, no, don't try to get down on your knees because it'd be too odd and your leg's all messed up and you'll make it worse.

"I can't feel my leg, how bad is it?"

"Well if you can't feel it that can't be a very good sign, can it?"

"I don't know, don't ask me hard questions, I'm all confused. Where am I again? New York?"

"I'd say hallucinationville."

"Hallucinationville, ha! You've always been my favorite."

"You've always been my only."

"Well so we've made up. Now what should we talk about?"

"Do you have, I don't know, retrospective thoughts?"

"How much better not to have been chief."

"What would you prefer to have been?"

"A fisherman, a food service worker, a germ."

"Do germs have chiefs?"

"If germs have chiefs and minds, their chief's mind is doubled as my own. Hard to be a chief and germ or chief and man at once. The chief's a god, the man's a beast. The chief, like a beast, wants war. The man, like a god, wants peace."

"What about girls?"

"Girls keep men and chiefs in check."

"Hardly."

"Without you and Char grumbling at me every day I'd have been worse, made more war, felt less for the sick and weak."

"That's dumb, Dad, to make girls do the dirty work of feeling."

"What would you have done had you been me?"

"I'd have felt, all day every day."

"Is that what you do as you?"

"I guess."

"And how is that for you?"

"Hard."

"One cannot be chief and feel to that degree."

"Seems like lots of things you can't do and be chief. Does chiefdom limit you to be a jerk, or what?"

"You're being tough on your wounded father."

"Sorry."

"No, it's all right. I'll try, I'll try with my remaining time on earth to feel more real, even though I'm not a chief no more." He closed his eyes.

"What you doing?"

"Getting in touch with my feelings."

"You're being funny."

A tear came to each of his eyes, and several more. He cried.

"Oh, Daddy, it's okay, I don't want you to be sad."

"I want to be. I have to be to say goodbye to the world. That's what I want to do in my final time here with you."

"Do what, just hang out here and feel the most?"

"At least until your dad gives up his ghost."

Pocahontas

"He's surviving his big trip, don't know if I'll survive mine," I say to my worried Aunt and Uncle, Char and Sid, who link arms by the shotgun door of the cab of the truck I'll ride up north in away from all I know.

"You sure you trust this schnook?" Sid says.

"No."

"Then why go?"

"Why stay?" Char says.

"To fight Frank," he says.

She looks at him as if to say "Don't be a fool," and he looks back at her with drooping eyes beneath each of which a slender supine crescent moon of red inner eyelid becomes a tiny model of the fifty years of blood and gore the eyes above them have borne witness to. And she looks back at him and he looks back at her, and back and forth a dozen times between each blink of eye cuz such a loving pair they are that bitter spousal bickering is done with looks words are far too slow to parse.

"What will you do?" I say.

Char says, "My Uncle Croatan lives on a little island down the coast. We'll winter with him."

"Regroup to take on Frank," Sid says.

"That you'll have to do alone," Char says as if saying "You spend too much time in the basement making origami instead of helping out with the housework."

"I'll miss you both so much," I say. At that, the kohl Char draws around her eyes to make her look less tired is made liquid by her tears and drops from the stark cliffs of her cheeks, which makes Sid and me cry too. Up runs my guy, and like a man eager to hit the road at the end of a long stay with the in-laws, says, "We don't go now, we won't get out alive."

I'm in the truck, the door is shut, he starts it up, it lurches toward New York, while Sid and Char, feet on the dirt of my hometown, link arms. She waves her left, he waves his right, in unison like a single, unhappy, self-loving beast, or like a wistful mom and dad, bye guys, don't die.

"Whew!" my boyfriend says as we roll up the east coast of what was once known as North America. What a dumb time to say "Whew!" I picture the cuboid of the back of the truck, which contains my new friend the redhead Jack Shit and his beard and his wound. Yes, he, like everyone, is wounded now, on the inside I guess, since no marks show on his skin except that little flesh wound on his arm that don't account for his moldering mood.

"What's up with Shit?"

"He's groggy."

"Why?"

"He's hurt and drugged and sad."

"Shit, sad?"

"Even Shit gets sad."

"Who knew Shit could feel," we say at once. I feel relaxed around this man!

"You seem relaxed," he says.

"I am!"

"Shouldn't you be sad?"

"Yes!"

"How come you ain't?"

"Don't know!"

"Okay."

"Tell about Jack Shit in the back of the truck."

"He fell in love with Sal Argyle."

"He said that?"

"To calm him down so we could get a move on I gave him a big shot of busthead, which as you know acts in some to make them tell the truth."

"He said *love* though?"

"No."

"What'd he say exactly?"

"He said he'd never had sex like the sex he had with Sal Argyle."

"Huh."

"Said Argyle seemed to be all over him at once with hands and lips and skin and teeth."

"Maybe you don't need to tell me all the details."

"Said his orgasms had orgasms, after which he was super-malleable vis-à-vis suggestions Argyle made, such as the one to kidnap you."

"How'd he get hurt?"

"Isn't it obvious?"

"He didn't mean to love, and loved, and lost? Poor guy."

I hear him back there moaning; I hear the light, high whine of the motor of the truck; I hear the moan of the wind in the trees; I hear the soft, grim wail of each tree rise up and fall back as we go by; I hear the sound of all the men a hundred miles back as they breathe, talk, yell, sigh, groan, sneeze, come, die and decay; and each sound I hear I become, and cannot unbecome until every atom of this truck returns to its home in air, earth, sea, or star. Here we go on our great northern adventure!

"You crying?" he says with a hand on my knee. "Don't get dehydrated. Here, have some water from this plastic tube. All plastic comes from animals, you know."

I wept, erstwhile animal in my limp grip, and said, after all, "Shawneekwa."

"What?"

"My secret name."

"What?"

"My secret name is Shawneekwa."

"Shaneequa?"

"That's it."

"That's your secret name?"

"That's your response?"

"And I'll die from hearing this?"

Now I really, *really* cry, can't tell why, not yet.

He stomps on the brake and my ribs hit the dash while a shriek from the back of the truck hits the back of my head. I have occasion at this time, my face smooshed against the glass, to gaze down and out at the cracked and clotted road, gray, windswept, encroached upon by all that it is not: my future and the path to it in one.

"I love you, Shaniekway," he says.

"I think I broke a rib."

"I love you so much."

"You're a funny one."

Johnny Rolfe

"Love is nice and all," she said, "but we'll make lousy time to New York if you slam on the brakes every hour to tell me you love me and shatter my ribs. Who shrieked, do you think?"

"John Martin, I'd guess."

"Just one shriek from him?"

"Yes. I think the thump against the front of the back of the truck that came just before the shriek was also him. He's quiet, compared to how he was on the ride down, doesn't need to let you know he's there each moment of the day."

"He seems almost restrained, almost thoughtful, almost courteous, almost decent, almost human."

"His diminution leaves him more exposed to threat, which has taught him to dissemble."

"Shut up and drive."

I drove along what little road there was. The land's indifferent to all roads, it makes them become itself and not the other way around. I drove and felt my nerves extend down to the wheels, each wheel became an honorary foot or hand or face, and pressing up against them was the earth and its age-old wish to encroach, to take back everything it once was and only for a time was not. How dumb of me to say all plastic had once been animals when each of us has been each, and all of us have been everything, and everything been us. And all of us and everything were once a single dot of stuff that was the world before there was a world, a dot Dick Buck would give the name of God, a

God who could not stand to be alone or less than everything, and now that God is everything He's still alone. I drove and, driving, felt I chose a future for myself.

A break in the drive and we stood at what we figured was the side of the road. The sun had not yet left the sky, it seemed to wait for us to have our break and get back in the truck, that's what we will our sun to do and kid ourselves that it complies, and so successful have we been in this that even since the time of that communications pioneer Galileo Galilei, and despite his gift to our knowledge of the world, we give the name of Nature to our self-deceit.

Trees nearly bereft of their leaves; brown and sodden grass; wind that came from somewhere, chilled us, went somewhere, turned to nothing in our thoughts; illegible former edifices—a wall, a caved-in roof, a porch, a post, a beam, a crumbled shack or store, a desiccated privet hedge; the brown-gray fog; the dirt; the sun we didn't want to leave the sky: that was our world at that time on the side of the road, or the road. Smith, Martin, Buck, Breck, Poc, me: that was our mobile nation-state.

"I'm cold, let's go," the Martin who had legs would have said. The legless one shivered and said nil, his face a hard red rock. That he now did not say or show his thoughts and moods kept us all on edge. Each of us hoped not to wake in the dark to find Martin astride our throats and cracking our jaws with what remained of his thighs. While the rest of us stood on the floor of the earth, he sat, fists shoved down into unforgiving gravel. The sun's slant rays hit the side of his head and seemed to set his welded-looking left half-ear ablaze, but did not penetrate his dark and matted hair. One had to concede his had become a dignified head against steep odds. "He's really come into his own," Dick Buck remarked, and Smith replied, "Or would if it were anatomically possible."

Smith no longer moved through the world like a virgin. Like the rest of the adults I know, he had been imbued with the melancholy that follows intense pleasure as winter follows summer. His beard was thinner now. Its new crooked, thin gray lines made it resemble less those nostalgic still lifes of wildflower bouquets Manhattan Company artists are paid to paint to narcotize a beauty-craving populace than like the leached fields of muck it is the purpose of the wildflower art to distract us from. The facial scars and cuts

Smith had accrued since our trip began had lost their lustrous redness and turned dim and brown. I leaned awhile beside him up against the truck. Why, if a man's not got a fresh wound of his own, must he probe his friend's?

"Did Sal wake up before we left?" I said.

"I guess having his wrists and ankles bound with rope to his cot woke him up, yes."

"I thought the drug was meant to make him sleep."

"Turns out not all drugs you pay too much for on the Chesapeake black market work as advertised. Made him shit at least as much as it made him sleep."

"He would've brought us all down."

"Shut up."

"He would've brought us all down."

"Shut up."

"It's okay to feel something for someone that's not hatred or gruff bonhomie, Jack. You've said in several ways that I'm the aesthete and you're the man of action but I don't think men's temperaments are so neatly defined."

I decided not to broach this theme again once he got done choking me hard and long enough to make me fall to the ground.

My neck being sore, Smith drove the next leg with Martin by his side. Poc and I and Bucky Breck and Richard Buck occupied the back, in which we could see nothing go by and wondered where we were. I wonder if ever before so much brooding had been contained in a such a small space. Probably yes, and often, and far more brooding than this, in rooms of lesser size.

"How's your God today?" said Poc to Dick Buck.

"Stern today, I'd guess, but I don't know."

I was struck, as I had often been before, by the gray delicacy of his features, the parchment skin and scalp that covered up what seemed to me an extra-thin skull, a hen's egg shell to guard, but not so well, the bright yolk of his thoughts.

"Do you ever know?"

"No."

"Do you want to know?"

"Yes."

"But you don't know."

"Right."

"Then how do you believe?"

"That's what faith is."

"Faith, sure, faith I get. But you have ideas, as I recall your brief but scintillating religious instruction of me, about the, um, personality of your God, that he is at times judgmental, at times merciful, and at many other times different shades of both. How do you know all this about this god you don't know?"

Buck looked away from her and seemed to want to look, as we all did, out a window that didn't exist. With the palm of his hand, he shoved back at her what she'd just asked and said, "Not now, not now, not now." He stood and slipped behind the sackcloth curtain that hid our chamber pot. Some of what was inside him now came out, and not as prayer.

He emerged, wan and drawn, and lay on his side on a stained thin foam mat. The fuel the lamps burned impinged upon our alveoli and seemed to eat into my recently attacked throat.

"What is the soul?" she said.

"Now you're the catechist?" Dick Buck, shivering, said.

"I'm a girl who wants to know what the soul is. Here, put this on you." She draped a smelly skin on him.

"Thanks, I think I caught a bug."

"What is the soul?"

"Don't think I can answer now. Got to ride the bug."

"Ride the what?"

"Don't feel so good," he said, bent, unbent, and loosed a thin string of acrid puke from his mouth.

"I think the soul is a passenger in a truck," she said as she mopped his modest pool of puke with a rag and put her grimy, gentle hand to his brow. "I think the soul is a rider shut up in the back of a truck on its way northward, toward safety, toward a life of reduced suffering."

"No suffering," Buck said between a violent shiver and a great antiperistaltic, spittle-producing heave. "Carry on with your analogy."

"Reduced suffering," she said. "My young pragmatic mind, carried lo these months in a girl on the lam, can't conceive it otherwise."

"Reduced then, you're already wrong, go on."

"I see the soul as a soul in a windowless truck heading north toward a place where the back door of the truck will open on a nicer world. A windowless truck, Father Buck, out of which the soul can't see, nor can it be seen from the outside, it's just in there, all holed up, all sealed off, wanting to get out of the truck but patient, too, for the end of the trip. And it must put its trust in the one behind the wheel, who steers the truck toward its northern destination. And the driver knows the temptation of sleep: the hours are long, the night is dark, the road is rough, the back is sore, the eyelids droop, the driver sleeps, the truck veers toward a great, hard, sheer rock bigger than itself, the truck hits the rock, the driver's hurt but not dead. The driver descends from the cab, screams, flaps about for a spell by the rock in the dark at the side of the road, remembers the soul, runs to it, undoes the lock on the back door of the truck. There stands the soul, bruised, shaken, a gash on her cheek, a gash on her knee. She descends from the back of the truck with the driver's helping hand. She takes deep breaths, she looks at the sky, the pitch-black sky in which no stars shine, she looks at the pocked and unsteady earth and she does not know in her eyes and her breast which is earth and which is sky. The driver screams, she slaps his face, he calms down. They whisper now, they need to whisper back and forth, who knows what they say, soft words spoke so gentle now, makes the journey easier to bear. By the light of a torch they look at the wound the rock made in the front of the truck, one headlight gone, the trip dimmer now by half in the night hours, the trip harder in the night hours for the driver to bear, the driver fears for his mind and his life, can he stand to go on? He cries, the soul puts her lips to his tears, puts her lips to his lips, her tongue to his tongue, the soul and mind kiss while the body looks on with one eye gone. Go on back up there now, go on back up to the cab, you must, back the truck up away from the rock, that's a good driver now, put that truck back on that rough and pitted road, that road that is sometimes no more road than the sky is road, now halt that truck while I get back in that windowless place, for put my trust in you I must, for I am the rider and you are the driver and this truck is our imperfect vessel, this bad road our only path, the only way we may ever get to that slightly better life than the one we have never left and are always leaving.

"Well, that's my analogy of the soul. What do y'all think of it?"

No one answered her, for Buck was asleep, and Breck was asleep, and so was I.

The scream woke me. Breck, whose scream it was, sat up, and Poc came in to hug him from the right. He threw her off with his right arm, which was thick as her head. He trembled and groaned. She came in to hug him again and told him it was all right, it was all right, it was all right, it was all right, a lie, since none of it was right. He took her hug this time. She talked to him and left a hand on his arm, and one on the top of his head. To watch her touch him caused a twinge in me I knew was murder's seed, a tiny thing. But I know the best of women give comfort promiscuously; that this fine impulse should have its counterpoint in male rage argues for a God whose chief trait is neither mercy nor judgment but caprice.

"What was it? Tell us. Telling helps," she said, another lie. Breck wept. Each of us, it seems, will weep in turn, or all at once.

Thinned though he was, Breck remained impressive nonetheless. His dark straight hair; his pale, unblemished skin; the sheer muscularity of him, now encased in cotton neck to foot for fall: his form, in short, contained within itself a note of hope. Inside of me, past envy, past jealousy, past dread, past my time-tested understanding of my own inadequacy, was this certain knowledge, caused by Breck: beauty exists. He wailed, shuddered, sighed, was silent for a time. Poc kept her hand on him. "Come on, Breck, tell us, tell it, tell."

"I can't."

"Tell us anything you'd like. Talk to us. Tell about your life. Tell about something nice, a warm memory."

He looked at her as if she'd spoke in tongues. She encouraged him some more. He softened. What was going on here? What was she robbing him of? A guy like that needs not to think of his warm memories, needs not to have them. Memories confuse. Look at me with mine.

"It was Ratcliffe," he said, brought his knees to his chest on a skin on the floor of this windowless truck, hugged them, stared at the dim and fuggy air a foot in front of his face.

"You dreamt of Ratcliffe."

"He was a poor leader but a decent guy," Breck said. "My mom was his mom's pedicurist. She walked down from the Bronx to the Upper East Side one morning a week to do his mom's feet and sometimes I came with. That scared, purple Ratcliffe face at the second-floor window. He was ten and I was eight. He opened the window and hurled the keys down at my head. They stung when I caught them in my hand. We went up to their living room on the second floor of their brownstone and all four sat there breathing in the perfumed air. Mom and Mrs. R. gave each other looks I didn't understand. Little Ratcliffe sat with his slicked-down hair on the edge of a chair made just for him in his dark blue suit with short pants and gold buttons. Everything about him was fake and scared. He sat up straight cause he thought he should but he didn't know how. His hands were composed in his lap the way he thought a boy's hands should be who was better than the person he was staring at. Light, soft, curly-boy hair disguised with pomade as normal-boy hair. Head tilted to say 'I'm the head of a dignified boy' when there can be no dignity for a boy of ten, and his was the head of a boy who would freely piss his pants if you made to spit at him. Mom said, 'Go play, boys.' Why do mothers say that no matter who you're with? Rabid dog on a chair across from you and your mom'd say, 'Go play, boys.' I guess that's what they say when they want you dead. Not dead, I mean, but not alive. 'Wish I hadn't met or fucked your dad, suck you back inside and unconceive you.' Mom loved me and raised me good, but still she sometimes said, 'Go play, boys.'

"So Ratcliffe took me to his room, which was huge and yellow with a rocking horse and clown posters, and said, 'I'd like to see you crawl around and bark like a dog'—not because he wanted me to but cause he thought he should want me to or thought I should want to, which I wasn't having any of, so we stared at each other, him lying on his bed, me standing by the door. That happened for a while and then he rolled onto his belly and read a book that was under his pillow—rich boys have books—or pretended to read it but in truth lay there sensing my location in the room with his back. I left the room, walked down the hall, opened a door, saw Mom and Mrs. R. hugging each other naked, and the next week when we went to the Ratcliffes' John and I were told, 'Go play outside,' despite how deadly that could be for small boys.

"Mom was a country girl from Yonkers who got pregnant by a drunk at age sixteen. He died on a trip to Ohio before I was born. If she liked to hug a lady in the nude she did it simply like a country girl. No thinking about it, no complications, no manipulations, no lying, no pretending you were doing something else, no power structure, no money changing hands, no shame. I take that back, there's always all those things, especially when the poor hug the rich in the nude. I played outside with Ratcliffe cause Mom liked the sex and needed the job, though my mind didn't say that to itself like that at that time. How hard it was for any man, woman, or child not to go out of their way to hurt Ratcliffe! You have to admire how high he rose, given how most people could barely stop themselves from breaking his teeth with their fist all day long his whole life. We went out to the street and he was swarmed at once by every available eight- and nine-year-old. I pulled them off him and we went back inside, him with bloody nose and gums and arms and sad white knees below his short pants.

"I guess the moms had loved each other fast that day, or not at all, were finishing the pedicure, Mrs. R's foot lotioned up on my mother's lap. 'He beat me up,' Ratcliffe said, of course. 'He hit me while my back was turned and threw me on the ground and stomped me.' Didn't cry, got to like the gumption, fuckhead Ratcliffe, ass. Mom smacked me with her lotioned hand, more than one good thing for her at risk here, smacked me again, lotion on my cheek, and again. Mrs. R. stopped her—'Martha, these are lovely boys.' I ran outside and stood on the corner. She tried to hug me when she came down, I wouldn't let her. Tried to lift me in her arms, wouldn't let her. We walked the grim hour back to the Bronx and stopped for ice cream: a counter in the ice cream store that we leaned on looking down. I hated her. How awful that I hated Mom even for an hour! 'Martha, these are lovely boys,' she said in the Penny Ratcliffe rich-lady sex voice. I laughed and my ice cream came back out of my mouth and I went, 'Martha, these are lovely boys' and Mom laughed. We made pouty lips at each other going, 'Martha, these are lovely boys,' and Mom let the ice cream run across the backs of her fingers, which taking care of other women's feet had made red and hard. Mom died a long time ago. Ratcliffe was not a nice kid, nothing was right about him as a kid or a man, he put me in harm's way all our lives and got my boyfriend killed and now his death's on my head."

He wept a little more but not as bad as before. I guess his boyfriend was Bill, the one we all thought was his brother. Mention of the boyfriend made me less scared of how Poc touched his arm, which she continued to do, but not that much less scared. He fell asleep soon after that. His beauty still consoled, in spite of all. And Poc's singular ugliness did more and better than console. She came and put her legs on me, hands, mouth, in silence. We fell asleep right afterwards, or at least I did.

Father Buck got better and Poc got sick. She had the shakes, the trots, red-rimmed nostrils. Love moves the place where you end and not-you starts. I know this because when Poc got sick I got sick too. When she was sad I was sad. When she stubbed her toe I felt it in my thumb. When she thought of yellow I said *sun*. When she came I cried out. I began to crave this undoing of me: when we were apart and I couldn't be sure what state she was in I sneezed, cried, ached, thought, and came again and again to make sure I was still her and vice versa.

The truck stopped. Smith opened our door. Martin sat on his hands on the cold road. Dick Buck and Bucky Breck climbed down. I carried Poc out for her first taste of New Jersey. A green and faded sign said Union City, the name of a place long since dead. Naming inaugurates nostalgia.

We breathed this air that wasn't used to being breathed. We were all a little stunned, by being in New Jersey, by the continued existence of New Jersey and ourselves, by myriad other things. "So this is New Jersey," Pocahontas or Shineequai said.

We looked across the river at Manhattan. The Chrysler Building continued to be gone. Since leaving, I hadn't thought of the earthquake we'd left in the middle of.

"How will we get there?" I said.

"Let's try the Lincoln Tunnel," Smith said. "If it's flooded then we'll have to find a boat. Let me drive, but take Martin, he's creeping me out. I'll take Rolfe and the Indian girl."

We looked at Martin in profile as he gazed, mouth shut, at New York. The wind swept across his voluminous and dignified brow and sawed-off arrow ends. He walked toward the truck on his hands, stopped, pulled himself up into its back, walked toward the cab along its metal floor, spun around, and stared at us. Since he didn't talk this was like watching some highly intelligent trained brute perform a stunt. How had his arms and abs grown so strong in so short a time? We agreed, out of earshot of Martin—unless his ears, too, had grown preternaturally strong—that the Martin who said nothing posed a greater threat than the one who voiced each complaint.

But for debris the tunnel was clear. We were stopped coming out of its mouth by armed Company guards. They knew who we were. One of them climbed the metal stair on the driver's side and signaled Smith to roll down his window.

"Where's Argyle?" he asked.

"Didn't make it back," Smith said.

"Who's in the rear?"

"Father Buck, Bucky Breck, John Martin."

"Who's that?"

"Indian girl."

"What kind of Indian girl?"

"Princess. Daughter of their chief."

"Really?"

"Really."

"Let's see her credentials."

"And, oh, who the fuck might you be?"

The guard contemplated his own identity awhile. "Follow us," he said. He climbed down. He and his pal mounted a pair of bikes and pedaled them ahead of us through town.

"Why didn't the earthquake wreck the tunnel?" I said.

"What earthquake?"

"When we left."

"That wasn't an earthquake, that was a bomb."

"Who's got a bomb like that?"

"Who do you think?"

"Brooklyn? How do we know they haven't already staged a hostile takeover?"

"Because that's not their plan. How could it be? Brooklyn can't afford to annex Manhattan any more than Manhattan can afford to annex Brooklyn. Everyone's strained to the brink. They don't want to own us, they want to destroy us."

"How do we know they haven't already destroyed us?"

He punched me in the arm, friendly but hard. "That's how."

Pocahontas

I don't feel so good, I don't feel so good. This place where I will start my new life—some new life, ha—great new group of guys I'm with—strong one, lame one, holy one, crafty one, one who thinks he's me, love them all, love them all—this place where I will start my new life is dilapidated and forbidding. I don't feel good I gotta cold and am smooshed against the car door by my boyfriend's bony ass and am expelling gruelly poop once an hour and my eyes are red and my nose is red or so say the sideview glass. O gruelly poop I love you so, sad to see you go. "Lemme sip some uh that watuh from that erstwhile animal you got in yo lap, playuh, whilst we led through thuh ugly streets uh this town by those two dudes on bikes. Hey how come ain't no buildings here in thuh shape of uh lowuh-case n, n-e-weigh?"

There sure are a lot of enormous houses here that aren't houses anymore. It seems eight of nine of these is so crumbled and fallen-down and vacant-looking and grim that can't nobody possibly live in them or use them but for scrap or a place to crap. And then you've got that one of nine, it too in disrepair, browned by bad air, windows thick with smudged dirt. Making homes of trees as we do where I'm from is what puts the texture in architexture. Each twig of your home has a grain, a name, a past, a slant, a tree that was its mom or dad, a mark or set of marks that makes it not its neighbor twig. But when you use, uh, "What's this stuff called again?"

"Concrete."

"And this?"

"Steel."

When you use concrete and steel and it falls down it becomes nothing. But that ain't even what happened here cuz they ain't even *fell* down all the way cuz if they fell down all the *way* they'd be a lot uh nothing all around us and a body likes to have a lot uh nothing to roam around in, good to roam around for hours a day in nothing when you growing up to make you feel you free even though you not free, make you feel like you got control over where you go and what you do even though you ain't got it, really, much. But I don't like the half-fall-down state of this whole town, whose canyons trap the air that grays your skin as you wander through them on your bike or in your truck. This here is way too much ugly not-nothing to be bumping up against all the time with no remit. Shesus no wonder all these dudes who grew up here is turned out like they is. Daddy build the building and the building turn around and build the son.

"Are we there yet?"

"Almost."

"Where we going?"

"Don't know."

"What's your guess?"

"Office of the Chief."

"Who dat?"

"Jimmy Stuart."

"What's he like?"

"Priapic."

"What else?"

"Narcissistic."

"What else?"

"Unkind."

"What else?"

"Clever."

"What else?"

"Warlike."

"What else?"

"Charismatic."

"What else?"

"Generous."

"What else?"

"High-minded."

"What else?"

"Poetical."

"What else?"

"Cultural."

"What else?"

"Devout."

"How should I act?"

"Be yourself."

"Who dat?"

"Me."

"I don't feel so good."

"Me too."

"What is that enormous pile of debris, stretched as far as the eyes can see?"

"I don't know. Smith, what is that?"

"That is what I think we once would have called the Chrysler Building."

"It is black."

"It is covered in ash."

"It is ash."

"Chunks of blackened brick and steel and concrete."

"It stinks."

"Smells bad too."

"It seems to smoke."

"There is so much of it."

"It goes on and on."

"We are right next to it and it is huge and we are tiny."

"Look at those children playing jumprope by it."

"They're smiling, but their feet and ankles and knees are covered in black soot."

"It is crawling up them."

"They are becoming it."

"Soon it will reach their brains and they'll be naught but it."

"Soon we'll all be naught but it."

"That's an ugly thought."

"What's a beautiful thought?"

"Gimme a minute."

"You should always have one ready for times like this."

"The Chrysler Building itself was once beautiful."

"That is not a beautiful thought, that is a beautiful building."

"Same thing."

"But many died in the making of it. And many more were spiritually crushed by it."

"At its top it had a stack of gleaming arcs on each of its four sides, eight arcs per stack, I believe, times four equals thirty-two arcs, each arc polished to reflect the sky around it, man's literally highest achievement reflecting God's grandeur. Back when it was built you could stand at the top and feel the clear, clean, cold, blue, crazy-ass air hit your skin like— like— like— like— like— air."

"But each gleaming arc you mentioned had fangs."

"Those weren't fangs, they were the points of a crown, or they were triangular representations of radiant light."

"God gave us light and we have to keep making more."

"Let's not fight by this mile-wide pile of night."

"Little children playing next to it."

"But not in it."

"Oh they're in it. We're all in it."

"We're almost past it."

"We'll never be past it."

"Let's forget it as soon as we can't see it anymore."

"Which will be never."

"Or very soon."

It's good to get a little New York history. I always like to know the history of the places I visit, even though I've never visited anyplace before. Did I mention my father just died and I'm sad and away from home for the first time even though there isn't really any home for me anymore so I'm nowhere and everywhere at once? Look, the bicyclists are slowing down.

"I guess we're here."

"'La Petite Marmite.'"

"'The Little Cooking Pot.'"

"He's meeting us at a restaurant?"

"Disused restaurant."

"Speaking of pot, I could use some pot."

"We left our source of pot tied to a cot, *ach mein Gott*, I love Sal a lot. Chances are that now he's not."

This erstwhile restaurant that we are being led through on foot by those nondescript guys who led us through town on bikes sure is dank and grim. The once-white swathes of cloth that cover the two dozen small tables we are walking past seem to have absorbed so much dust, smog, ratshit, and anguish that they are now dark gray and hard like the bones of the folks who ate off them before they died. Through a dank and grim door, up a dank and grim stair, down a dank and grim hall, up more stairs, some more dank than grim, others the reverse, chipped, mottled, cracked, worn down, worn out, broken through, home repair a vanished art, home décor a distant dream of the people of my boyfriend's town, it seems. A golden door, rimmed by red light, glows at the end of the hall. I continue not to feel so good, I think I gotta puke, would prefer not to go through the door, don't like what I believe awaits me there, must go through the door, not to go through the door that glows at the end of the hall is to shun life, die unfulfilled, haunt the earth as neither mood nor thing. *I'll wait in the hall*: a coward's motto.

"I'll wait in the hall," I say and cop a squat on a cobweb.

"Come on, you have to meet the CEO," my boyfriend says, "and then we'll let you ride the fever out on the prow of a bed of down softer than any dreamt of in your people's bedmaking philosophy." He hauls me up by the arms.

"'Let me'? Let this," I say, and show him the bird that flies from the northern edge of my palm.

We're through the door. The air in this big room is red and hot to the touch. Finally a room that's not the remnant of a room. The degree to which this room is *done* seems to want to make up for how undone the others all across this city are. The walls are covered with a soft red cloth that adheres to them; likewise the couches and chairs. A bouquet of electric lamps—I've heard of these—hangs from the high ceiling and its light's refracted through hard-edged teardrops of glass, each attached to the bouquet by a little hook that lets it dangle and sway with the motion of the air in the room, which makes the light buzz around my eye like a substanceless bright fly. The fuel that lights their chief's electric lamps is what these guys went south to find, and in the end will kill whoever has it, though no one has a lot of it since ain't a lot of it left in Earth, and I must admit these lamps are pretty enough to kill for, as is this rug that is red and clean and soft and soothes my hard and tired and fevered feet.

And there's their main man, the My Dad of Their Side. He's smaller than my dad, but looks strong. He smiles on his soft red chair. He has blonde hair. White suit. His penis lurks egregiously beneath his pants. All men's dicks lurk to some extent, I guess, but some let you know it right away—who knows how?—and he's one of those. He's in the I-have-a-penis camp, the let-my-penis-be-a-central-feature-of-the-initial-impression-I-make-on-a-heretofore-unmet-interlocutor crew. Who hasn't met a ton of guys like *that* before? Oh, the penis, what would the world be like without you? We may never know.

"Hi! How's it going?" he says, marking him further as a "Hi! How's it going?" kind of guy.

Smith says, "This is Pocahontas, an Indian princess. Pocahontas, this is our chief, James Stuart."

"Isn't the communications officer supposed to do the talking?" says their chief.

"He don't like to talk," Smith says.

"How's a guy supposed to run a business?" Stuart says.

I guess I ought to do a greeting dance for him but feel too ill and slow so I just bow. I say, "I think I gotta take a shit," which makes him rearrange the fabric of his whitish suit a little bit.

"Lead her to her shit," he says, and I am taken from the room, and since a lady never shits and thinks at once, suffice to say that for the next while the me that thinks flees down a dark hole.

Johnny Rolfe

"Holy shit, the toilets here are made of gold!" she said from offstage left.

"*That's* their princess?" Stuart said.

I said, "She's grieving."

"I think I'm in love," he said, "and I think the princess just shit in my tuba."

He said *I think I'm in love* lightly, casually, indifferently, and will no doubt pursue her in just that way, and she'll succumb, but a schmuck like me will bust a gut for love and still fuck it up. No, she won't succumb; well, maybe for political advantage; no, she doesn't think that way, and loves me; well, maybe for the wicked sort of thrill a girl will allow herself on holiday; no, she loves me, despite my flawed and gimped-up love of her. The Pocahontas of my mind betrays me every day. The one on the ground, I hope, will not.

"Well, so," Stuart said, the signal that business was to begin. He had been sitting with his taut, lean ass on the left side of the seat of his red armchair, his torso leaning back and to the right, right elbow holding nearly half his weight on the right armrest. He stood now and smoothed down the white arms and legs of his suit, brushed each limb repeatedly with long, brisk strokes of his palm. "So, so, so, so, so. You're not supposed to be here now, are you? You're supposed to still be down there so what the hell happened and how about let's hear it from the communications officer this time?"

"Don't you fucking touch my girl," I said.

"Well then let's hear it from Jack Smith." Stuart nodded to two of his seemingly endless supply of square-jawed men in dark blue clothes, who punched my chest, arms, shoulders, and neck till I fell down.

"Sir," Smith said, "the communications officer's a romantic. Civilization needs its romantics."

"If you mean that a state can make no progress without a modest percentage of civilians bloodied and crumpled on the floor at all times then I agree with you. Your report, please."

"We've lost a lot of men."

"And?"

"What very little oil they have they trade for."

"With who?"

"Don't know."

"What *do* you know?"

"They have trees."

"I've seen the trees Newport brought back."

"How is Newport?"

"Dead."

"Of what?"

"Some disease or bomb or gun, or was pushed into the sea and drowned, I knew how he died and meant to keep it in mind but I've got a thousand worries, each more vicious than the next, and Brooklyn at the door of my ass clamoring to be let in. Trees and what else?"

"They grow crops and catch fish and eat them."

"How?"

"Food purification technology."

"Did you see it?"

"No."

"Why not?"

"They keep it well hidden."

"So?"

"We had inadequate men and supplies. We'll need more to get what we want from them."

"I don't have more. Every man and gun and scrap of food and ounce of fuel I send down south I have to give up here. Habsburg's made massive kills in the past three weeks. He's suddenly outweaponing me, I don't know how."

"A hundred men deployed down south now, Sir, would let us plant crops this spring that we could eat next fall."

"We can't eat if we're dead."

"We could fish and eat this winter."

"Fish where, the East River? The Hudson? There's not a fish alive in either place."

"The ocean."

"I send a fishing boat into New York Harbor, Phil Habsburg will smash it to bits, besides which no one here has ever fished."

"So we could go down south again and bring back truckloads of dried fish, or fishermen."

"No."

"Sir, do you mean to say food is within our reach and you won't commit resources to procuring it?"

Stuart strode toward Smith and stood a foot from him. "I don't have resources to commit!" His spittle reached me where I fell. "Where's John Ratcliffe anyway?"

"He's among the unfortunate majority of our men who died, Sir."

"How did he die?"

"Sir, with all due respect, the world is topsy-turvy when you care how Ratcliffe died but not how Newport died."

"How did he die?"

Smith told him.

"Stop calling me 'Sir,' you sound like an obsequious idiot." Our middle-aged chief had meant to say that loud but said it faltering and soft. His pale peach face grew gray. "Please—" he said, "please wait here." He left the red room by a different door than the one we'd come in.

Smith made to help me to a chair. I let him know I liked the floor. My neck hurt and I watched the worn, scraped, diverse footwear of the corporate guards. Some had cracked jackboots, others ancient rubber sandals fragilely encasing woolen socks smeared and bleared with toil; inside their socks, their actual, put-upon feet. I tried to call to mind the feet of everyone I'd known and everyone I hadn't known, two by two: the beleaguered work appendages of my race; their skin, sinew, and bone, their blisters and calluses, their bunions and corns, their brittle toenails, their arches fallen and erect; those mostly misshapen chief points of contact with the hardness of the world, what we use to haul our fond and petty hopes from infancy to death.

Poc's feet, unshod, came back into the room. "Whew," she said, "I think I crapped out my brain. Hey, what you doing on the floor, oh no." She ran to me; before she could arrive, a long and awful wail came from far beyond the door, and again, and then again, followed by a sob, a rest, another sob—sounds not unlike the ones the son of the woman who now made them had made when he was killed a sliver at a time.

The redoubtable Penny Ratcliffe, wailing, retreated or was carried to a part of the building still more remote from us until we couldn't hear her any more. Poc sat murmuring beside me on the rug. Heat from an unknown source warmed my hurt neck and head. The room was red and dim. We stayed still in wait. Jimmy Stuart reentered absent his phallic poise. His hair and white suit were mussed and he sat in his soft executive chair.

"Martin," he said, sighing, eyes softly closed, his eyelids' engorged capillaries uttering what he could not, "what about Martin?"

"He's here."

"Who else?"

"Father Richard Buck and Bucky Breck."

"Get Martin."

Two sandaled guards left and came back. Martin waddled in on bare hands. "Jesus Christ, get up, would you?" Stuart said to me. I slowly did.

"What happened to you?" he said to John.

"What do you think?" Martin said.

Stuart thought about that. His silence was an apology of sorts. He wasn't on top of things and couldn't pretend to be now that his concubine had grieved so loudly in his ear. He was not an idea, as I'd thought when we came in. He was mortal, and Martin's presence seemed to make him more so.

"Please have a seat."

"I've got one," Martin said.

"Do you want to tell me what happened to you?"

"What good would that do?"

"Well. You've been on this expedition and seen things I haven't. What advice do you have for me?"

"Do everything."

"What do you mean?"

"Do everything at once."

"Can you be specific?"

"Hit Brooklyn hard, with everything you have. Destroy Brooklyn. Send enough fully armed troops down to commandeer Virginia. Send large armed expeditions out to Connecticut, Pennsylvania, Rhode Island, Ohio. Find who's there, conquer them, take what they have. Suck dry a radius of 500 miles. Leave enough forces in each town to control it. Expand your power and land holdings quickly and emphatically. Go deep into Brooklyn, wipe out isolated rebel cells, establish settlements of civilians. Conquer everything, own everything, run everything."

"Martin, how can I?"

"How can you? How can you? Every bullet you have you shoot. Every bomb you have you detonate. Every bus you have you roll through a tunnel or over a bridge. Every man you have you deploy. Every coin you have you spend."

"It was a rhetorical question, Martin."

In three grand knuckled arcs across the floor, Martin had his shoulders pressed to Stuart's knees, teeth not much more than a foot from Stuart's treasured dick.

"Does anything at all about me seem rhetorical to you right now?" Martin whispered.

"Thank you, Martin, for your advice," he said in calm but weakened voice, and eyeballed two guards to come get Martin.

Martin held them off with the force of his voice: "Look at me." He took a half-swing back on his hands and pointed with his half-finger at his ruddy, scar-hardened face, the shaved-off arrow nubs that jutted from his skull, his nonexistent ear, his interrupted legs. He said no more; his pointing alone said loudly that he was not just a strong advocate but the very embodiment of maximizing diminished resources with hardly a thought to the imminence of their exhaustion.

"All right, all right, tell me what you think I should do first."

"Not with these three here."

Smith said, "You're gonna let this ineffectual . . ." He didn't finish, since he knew what had been true of John was no longer true. Smith had many strengths, but top-level statecraft seemed not to be among them. Martin in his new incarnation had just been effectively bumped up to executive VP.

"I'll talk to Martin alone now," Stuart said. "Find Smith a soft bed, he's done an adequate job. Get some fluids into the princess here, and get her a front-row seat at the shooting of our new advertisement in Central Park tomorrow. And scrape her boyfriend off that chair, and drop him in a room somewhere."

Pocahontas

I've skimmed across the earth and here I am in Central Park. What a mutilated place this is! I watch it through a lightly mucoused eye. "Park," I'm told, once meant grass and trees and rolling hills and playing fields and flowering, perfume-giving plants imported from around the world—a place to frolic, jog, rest, work, wild, and sigh. But now it seems to be where beggars come to die, and has no trees nor grass nor sun, has cardboard beggars' shacks and dirt and fences made of chain. Hills it has, which hide still other hills, more shacks and fences, more large and broke-down buildings, more brown and retched and wretched air. They chose this spot to tape a little show. "Tape" means capture in a little metal box all the sights and sounds within an open-ended cube of space, and in a little cube of time, or so I gather by looking. The author of the script that they will act out and tape I met and spoke to for an hour on this selfsame hardwood bench I'm on right now. He's tall, bespectacled, stoop-shouldered, with pale, moledup skin, large and pointy nose, and thin brown hair that seems to continue to thin as one watches it, which is surely less grim than watching his opaque and doleful eyes. "So, you're an Indian princess, what's that like?" If there be a duller man in all God's sick republic let me not ever have to converse with him lest I die of the acute agony of not wanting to be conversing with someone so menacingly dull. Luckily he has become absorbed in the task of interfering with the taping of his script, or advertisement as it's called, which, it turns out, is based on the story the now-deceased Chris Newport told of his first encounter with Uncle Sid and me in a field down south so many months ago. Where is Uncle Sid right now? I wonder and may never know, I feel so sick, eyes hurt, head hurts, skin hurts, ass hurts most of all. But the other me—not my man, I mean, but the gal who represents me in the ad—wow, is she ever robust, look at all that black hair and tight, rosy skin. If that's me, I see how beautiful I am. But what's she doing being me? Is it not enough for them that I'm me? That northern tart with too much hair on her head and not enough hair on her arms and legs, and not enough me on or in her, what a grim little cunt she is as she saws the air with her hands and says words ("Welcome, handsome English-speaking stranger!") I'd rather die than say. Who and why's this me-not-me they tape? The only thing true about their fake corn shack is that it's made of wood they stole from us, but how they made it sucks, all square and straight and held with metal nails and screws and too high off the ground, surrounded by gray-black dirt and painted cardboard urine-yellow corn. And do they think just any hack Jew with gray hair and a tan's good enough to be my Uncle Sid? ("We enjoy cultural and economic exchange with energetic and enterprising northerners. Here, take this barrel of oil for free as a token of our good faith in your intentions toward us.")

"What is this, anyway?" I ask some unknown underling I can't quite see now that my sight's grown dim, and he replies, "This is a reek-rooting film," and I say, "What's reek-rooting?" and he say, "It's when you get people to go on a trip by telling them that it will be far easier and more useful than it ever turns out to be." I'd know that jaundiced worldview anywhere, that's my man saying that to me. "Who are you, are you my man?" I say to him and he say back, "I sho is yo man, Shawneekway, and will be till you die, which, judging by your jaundiced eye, could happen pretty nigh." And no longer can I say for sure which is my life and which the advertisement version thereof, am I living or "living," dying or "dying," talking to my man or "talking to my man"? Is this my consciousness or a voiceover? Help!

"Shaw-knee-quai, wake up, wake up."

"What?"

"Wake up."

"What?"

"Wake up!"

"Oh."

"You were dreaming."

"How you know?"

"You said, 'Oh beautiful English speaker, I welcome you to my humble land' and other bullshitty things people don't say except in dreams or advertisements."

"Where are we?"

"Central Park."

"What happening?"

"They're shooting the advertisement version of our arrival at your home."

"How is it?"

"Inaccurate but compelling."

"How do I know you're you and not the actor playing you?"

"Because he's far handsomer and healthier than I and he's over there in front of the camera saying, 'I love you, beautiful Indian princess, and I love your gentle people too,' while I'm here saying this to you."

"They both sound like something dopey you would say."

"Well then look here at my penis. Has anyone else got one quite like this?"

"There you have an excellent point."

"I'm glad you like my point, it likes you."

"What's it doing now?"

"Coming toward you."

"Going into me."

"I hope you don't mind."

"Well I feel pretty under-the-weather but this is—Oh!—making me forget my aches and pains. Hey, aren't your buttocks getting dirty?"

"Don't care! Don't care!"

"Oh!"

"Awe, awe."

"Hm."

"Uh."

"Wow."

"Ah."

"Good thing these eleven fake stalks of corn were protecting us from sight while we did that."

"And everyone's distracted by the fake me and the fake you over there doing much the same."

"Sex is reek-root-ment?"

"What man in his right mind wouldn't want to meet and enjoy a gal like you down south?"

"A gal like her, you mean. Not sure I like her-me to be used that way. Ooh, the sex exhausted me, I feel sick and sad, I must lie down."

"You are lying down."

"Not on this wet, cold dirt. Somewhere safe and soft and dry and warm."

"Nowhere safe in God's bellicose nation-state."

"Are they done taping?"

"No, taping takes longer than life."

"I'm depressed."

"Soon you won't be."

"I fear you're right."

"Why you say that?"

"Cuz I'll die."

"When?"

"Soon."

"How you know?"

"I'm sick."

"Not that sick."

"Sick enough."

"Live."

"Can't."

"Why?"

"I said my secret name."

"I thought that meant I'd die, not you."

"Um well that's the secret secret of my secret name."

"What?"

"The one who dies is me."

"Don't believe it, won't, can't."

"You might have saved me had you not said it back to me as a question."

"Said what?"

"My name."

"I did?"

"Yes."

"How?"

"I said *Schoen y qua* and you said *Chaud ni quoi?* you know like with incredulity."

"So I killed you?"

"Li'l bit."

"Sorry."

"Luv mean muthuhfuckuhs doan nevuh gotta say they sorry."

"I'm depressed now too."

"But your depression'll last a long time."

"I fear you're right."

"Sigh."

"Ow."

"Want to see and smell the East River tomorrow?"

"If I get a good night's sleep and amn't dead."

"Big state occasion."

"What?"

"Brooklyn-Manhattan cease-fire talk."

"Where?"

"On a barge on the East River."

"It'll never work."

"Could be fun though."

"Who'll be there?"

"Jimmy Stuart, Phil Habsburg, John Martin his son, Smith, armed thugs, maybe Penny Ratcliffe."

"Who you asking me as, yourself or a mid-ranking officer of the Manhattan Co.?"

"Both?"

"Bitch."

"Sorry."

"Love means—ah screw it, what I'm supposed to do there?"

"Just be yourself."

"Who dat?"

"The one over there with the hair."

"Bet she don't got pussy hair like me."

"How could she, she's just a white girl from the Upper East Side."

"No rilly, what I gotta do on that boat?"

"Pretend like you like Manhattan Co."

"Can't do that."

"Then don't."

"That's it?"

"What's what?"

"I help your side, I don't help your side, do, don't, easy come, easy go, all the same to you? No side you're rooting for? Don't care who wins?"

"No."

"You should."

"Both sides stink. All sides always stink."

"Then make one side better by being on it."

"Really?"

"Yes."

"How?"

"You must figure it out."

"So you're saying take action."

"Yes."

"I don't know what to do."

"Figure it out. That is the meaning of *Shunequal.*"

"What is?"

"Figuring it out."

"Really?"

"Sure, why not."

"Huh."

"What was that loud bang?"

"A bomb."

"Whose?"

"Brooklyn's."

"Anyone dead?"

"Looks like the advert's dead, for now."

"It was a dumb story anyway."

"Let's get out of here before another bomb explodes."

"Okay."

"You're not moving."

"I'm tired."

"I'll carry you."

"Hey! Easy on the ribs, ace, they ache. Ugh, how tedious to be carried out of Central Park."

"Sorry."

Pocahontas

What strange fish these are who fear the water that surrounds them. And by fish I mean men, and by men I mean these grim and self-destroying fools among whom I sink down now in illness and despair. But the heck with Shell Knee Craw for uttering the *d* word, even in her mind, and to no one. She—I—might as well say aloud, seriatim, to her worst enemy—and who dat is she think she know but (*ugh!*) will not admit—all her killing secret names, show all her secret selves, leave no wall between her outside and her inside, become, in other words, nothing.

We stand atop the high sea wall that guards the island's long and languid eastern flank from the deadly water it yearns to merge with, and await a boat to take us to a barge where the two big chiefs will meet and talk, not fight and die as they've had men do in their frightened stead lo these past however-many years. Such is their agreement anyway, though in my short life I've come to see agreements as I've come to see girls: soft and leaky vessels of consent, not hard to poke a bigger leak in and make sink.

And the troubles they take not to let the water touch them! The mobile gangway from wall to boat; the gangway's splashguard; the toe-to-head wet-suits; the facemasks; the repeated instruction to walk lightly on the gangway and with excellent balance; the increased alertness and heart rate as shown in the red-ness of the skin around their eyes that can be seen beneath the hard, transparent surface of their masks; all of these subordinated to the prayers—as vehement as they are varied—to their deity, that one widely knowledgeable Ghostman whom they make wear all the hats and who surely died long ago of overwork.

How exciting to take a trip on the sea! Well not sea but river. Well not river but narrow, goopy mass of wet brown stuff that stinks and burps and barely flows, and barely separates two groups of men who keenly wish each other harm. And here we are at the barge, about which even I want to say *Is that all there is?* though I hope if I am ever remembered, described, or accused, it won't be as an Is-that-all-there-is? girl, I'm sure the past is burdened with enough of those. Another splashguard-saddled gangway brings us from small boat to flat and drab and worn-down barge, which makes up in bigness for what it lacks in ornament.

O brave new barge that has such people on it! There's Manhattan's chief, Jimmy Stuart—so gracious about his prized tuba in which I evidently shit, if not about anything else—peeling off his skintight white wetsuit to reveal a skintight white polyester shirt-and-pants ensemble; has ever one man decked himself more ostentatiously in petroleum byproduct? And there's his grieving concubine, Penny Ratcliffe, the mother of the small, inept, and frightened man who nominally led Manhattan's expedition to the territories of my dad (to make those two words in my mind—*my dad*—is to jab my own heart twice with the bodkin of sorrow, to feel my own death spread into my limbs from this oft-gored heart, for what is death but sorrow multiplied beyond the body's modest capacity?) and died there by all-too-tiny increments. What a beautiful and burdened girl this Penny Ratcliffe is with her puffed-up and slightly livid top and bottom eyelids, her regal and gravely erect head. That head don't swivel much at all on that neck but yet the stony, devastated eyes roam about and take in all; she is even in her saddened state a lover of the look of the world. And despite how draped she is in loose black cloth, I, even with my dimming sight, also see, as must anyone with eyes, what a absototalfuckinglutely rocking female form she's got beneath the drapes, and so it's no surprise so many heads of state and other major cheeses of the temporal world have yearned so fiercely to be all up in that.

And there's the admirable fiend John Martin, who's made his wounds his armor and his arms. The hardness and angularity of that massive, permanently blood-reddened head, one feels, makes a perfect shield, ram, cannonball, or bomb. Indeed, his brain seems always just about to blow, and who would want a tooth of that mouth or splinter of that weather-tempered cheek or jowl or brow lodged as shrapnel in one's own soft self? No wetsuit wrapped around his impermeable form, he cantilevers down the gangway on his brownish-purple knuckles and plants himself in the center of the barge's large white main room, whose glass walls let in light that makes the room seem green. That shortened, squattened man is made of stuff so dense he should by rights fall through the white wooden floor of the barge, through its black and river-seasoned hull, through the deadly depths below, through the river's toxic silt and sand, through the earth's crust, through its mantle to its molten core, whose heat would make him shoot like a rocket back up the vertical tunnel his dense mass just made, up and up into the depths of space above the sky, where in a blinding flash he would explode, and each hate-packed molecule of him would mix with air and turn to downy flakes of love, float down, hit us gently on the hair and nose: a little dot of hate in human form made salutary to his race by the forces of the physical world.

And there's his dad, Philip "Brooklyn Phil" Habsburg, who resembles him as fathers often feel they must. Dad lacks his son's advantage of a lack of legs, but compensates with bullet shape that can only have been forged hour by hour down the years in those twin munitions factories of his head and heart, each belching smoke day and night on opposite banks of the river of his neck. He's got his son's funereally martial bearing and big grim red head. That he may have had to kill an assailant with his hands while eating a breakfast of mashed-up oats and rocks is written in the tautness of his neck and arms and chest and legs and rock-hard ass, all concealed beneath crisp, rectilinear gray garb designed and made no doubt by him for speed and force. Gun or spearpoint hurt his hip; he walks with a smoothened, shiny stick; the stick could be a club or spear or sword: Philip Habsburg, man of war, on the barge to do to his sin-sick rival with words what bombs could not get done, or so his eyes and fist in pocket say.

And there's Phil's foot-and-mouthman, Peter Zuñiga, whose letters to his boss, shown to me last night by the solicitous but essentially repulsive Jim, bear the mark of a man whose talk has taken the shape and place of his soul; here's someone who without his talk dissolves, and whom the air of threat of this green day on this drab barge has consequently made a puddle of. Silent puddle, he oozes along beside the man whose head his talk is meant to make an obfuscating bubble around, but that ain't happening, so a girl has to wonder what use the great man keeps him on for, but she won't waste too much time wondering since what transpires between any great man and the pusillanimous toady he shouldn't love but loves is known, if known at all, only to them so whatever.

And that's it for folks on the barge itself. Not on the barge but on the two boats, one on either side, are all of each side's thugs, whose multiple arms make up for their lack of faces.

Oh and me—here's me, Shania Hickway, sickened Princess, having been carried down the gangway on a palanquin by my man and the man who I can see will be his man when I'm gone, i.e., Johnny Rolfe and Jack Schitt, two peas soon to cohabitate a pod, description of whom I let my brain elide right now cuz it got to keep its strength up for the hard knowing that remains its final task. Summit meeting here we go!

There are seven of us seated at a round white table now. Thugs have scoped the barge from prow to stern and disappeared into the boats of their respective teams. John Martin and his father, Phil, at the table's four and twelve o'clock, strain toward each other in their chairs as if they'd smash it with their heads, wade through its debris, and son smash dad and dad smash son, two rock-faced men's heads colliding again and again, and each would crumble, neither bleed. Jimmy Stuart, taut and relaxed at six o'clock, is angled right to left in his white chair and curved at the top, a pose that asks, *Will you regret that?*

"Why's the Indian princess turning green?" Phil says.

"Seasick," Jimmy says.

"She doesn't have a mouth?"

"Ask her."

"Why you green?"

"Why you red?"

The total lack of movement of his leaden countenance says he likes my insouciance. He can blow me if he dare.

"You'll suffer less if you surrender now," Phil says to Jim.

Jim laughs. He seems to have recovered from the grief his girlfriend communicated directly into his body several days ago, though I think my boyfriend's right to say that what awful sentiment the attentive lover's loved one feels the lover also feels with only marginal decrease in intensity, so, to judge by Penny Ratcliffe's face right now, Jim's must be the merest shell to encase the meat of his grief. "I thought we were here to make nice," he says.

"I am making nice by telling you with words instead of guns that you're done."

"I mean I thought we were here to make a truce."

"The truce is you capitulate, hand over your properties, treasury, resources, *branch offices* (he looked at me), step down as chief, and walk into a clean, comfortable, and well-guarded prison cell, where you'll spend the rest of your life without the heavy burden of corporate governance and beyond the reach of its potential harms."

"I could tell you to do the same."

"Have you not noticed how much we kill you every day?"

"I thought you were a more alert and knowledgeable strategist than this. You have a slight advantage in the field right now, and either you are genuinely stupid enough not to see that it won't last, or you're making a bluff whose fatuity is equal to that of the confidence it pretends to be."

"All right, I see your pride is important to you," Phil says with exaggerated weariness, "so let's say I'm stupid or bluffing or whatever you just said, and if that means spending an extra half hour on this barge to play that game because you'd like to believe you won't be waddling back to shore with my dick all the way up your ass, I'll accept that as a reasonable expenditure of time."

High-level talks, I've always known they'd be like this! I'm intoxicated by them and/or by the disease that's killing me awfully fast right now, I feel its hand constrict my heart. I think I'm supposed to know at least one more thing before I die, what could that be?

"Please allow me to enlarge my description of the current state of affairs," Jim says and makes that sound dirty. "The increased violence and frequency of your recent attacks is a sign of your desperation. You need to win now or you'll never win. I'm here, as you imply, because I am indeed burdened and worried by all this fighting. It's unnecessary. I'd like to convince you to stop it. If you do we might even be able to coexist in peace, but we won't know if we can do that if you keep attacking. If you keep attacking Manhattan we will surely suffer grave losses, but we will also patiently endure, whereas you will exhaust yourselves and spend everything you have and be left inert, depleted, with nothing to sustain you. Then it will require almost no effort for us to annex you peacefully, if your self-inflicted decimation and defeat can be said to be a kind of peace for you."

"This limitless patience and these bottomless resources of yours, they come from where?"

"As you know, we've lately made some expeditions to the south." Jimmy indicates me with a slight movement of his head. I roll my eyes, it's all I have the strength to do.

Phil says, "Her eyes would seem to refute your implication of a southern alliance."

I stick out my tongue at him.

"A greener tongue I've never seen," he says.

My skin and tongue are getting green? I must be turning into air.

When Martin loudly asks, "May I speak?" Jim jumps, and Phil sees him do it.

"He's a scary little kid, I'll give you that," Phil says, and stares at his son, and if eyes were rocket launchers Martin wouldn't have a head. "Speak," he says, "right, Jim?"

Martin's on the table now. My eyesight's growing dim, but Martin's body seems to stretch from table's edge to edge, its one hand reaches out to its dad's throat, its other to its chief's, and then great gobs of red blood pour from holes below the two chiefs' chins, flood the table, now not white, and make the two men's necks slack; their heads roll down, their shoulders then, and soon they're but a group of body parts attached to one another, it seems, only to allow an observer to remember these murdered corpses were once men.

"Man, I hate talk," Martin says, still atop the table, a small knife in each hand, his thighs asplatter with the bright arterial blood of two men; well, we all are, and their blood is joined by my puke. He throws the knives across the floor, where the blood they've loosed follows them, making knife-shaped trails on the floor's white boards. "Anyone wants to pick those up and try to kill me, go ahead."

No one moves, that I can see: not Johnny, not Jack, not Penny, not Pete, not the dim and thuggish forms that line the rails of the two boats, one on either side of the barge.

"Well then I'm Brooklyn and Manhattan now," Martin says with a certainty that is not a sign of vanity but of the future it seems we all felt coming in our bones, though only now has it arrived in our eyes, noses, mouths, ears, skins, and brains.

I don't know what or whom to look at now. The air is still; those of us alive in here are still, all retreated from the table now, while the dead, still seated at it, still pump blood from their wounds, though less avidly than before. I see and smell I'm not the only one who's puked. No one speaks. What do Jack and Johnny think, their eyes and faces blank? What does Penny Ratcliffe think? Martin sidles up to her and seems about to speak directly to her thighs. "Get the hell away from me, you lump of foul deformity," she says quietly. He does not answer her in words, but through the black cloth of grief that enshrouds her thighs, he tries to nuzzle them with his asymmetrically positioned wooden antlers, two ends of a stick that's displaced a slender stick-shaped horizontal column of his brain, a stick whose effects on that singular organ can be seen, I think, all over this room.

While she seems stuck to a relatively un-blood-besmirched spot on the white floor, he circles her, leaning now and then to scratch the fabric of her black skirt with the prosthetic antler.

She puts her palm on his forehead and gives a good hard downward shove. That monumental head of his hits the floor with a loud thwack.

"Wow, your angel anger is fantastic." He rights himself with leglike arms. "I know you loved both these men, maybe even at the same time, but I belong at the helm of their companies more than they."

"You belong at the helm of hell."

"Actually, there's someplace else where I belong."

"Prison."

"Your bed."

"I'd sooner die."

"Sleep with me a thousand nights and die the little death a thousand times. I'll make a better lover than either of them ever could."

"You wouldn't even make a better corpse," she says, "though I'd like to see you try."

"If I were to make a corpse of myself—"

"I thought you said you hated talk, so shut up."

"I don't love talk but I love you, and if I have to talk to let you know why you should love me back—"

"Don't waste your breath, unless that results in your death."

"As I was saying, if I were to make a corpse of myself—"

"Looking for ideas? Throw yourself into this river."

"—then that would make—"

"Attach a pair of pliers to one end of the arrow in your head—"

"—then that would make three—"

"—and yank it hard."

"—then that would make three corpses that you've made this afternoon."

"Take a gun from the holster of any of the men on either of the boats, put its barrel in your mouth, and fire. 'Made'?"

"Your beauty caused me to love you, which caused me to kill those two."

"Bullshit."

"You think I don't love you?"

"That's not why you killed them."

"Then you admit I love you."

"So much the worse for both of us if you do."

"I'd kill the world itself to spend an hour in bed with you."

"Have you not noticed it's already dead? And you're the maggot that feeds on its rotting carcass."

"A better, stronger maggot, then, than either maggot I just squashed, a maggot who can mine the corpse's best meat."

"I'd squash you if I could, you disgust me, you horrify me!"

He swings his bulk along the levers of his arms till he arrives at one of the small knives whose blade's still wet and red with blood. He brings it back and gives it to her handle first. He rolls his head back on his neck. His throat is skyward now, and as it strains to hold that molten rock, his head, in place, its veins and tendons pop up to the surface of its skin. She need but make one shallow slice to end his life. She holds the knife a half an inch from it. She holds the knife and keeps on holding it. "I can't. I won't."

He swings his head back up and nestles it between her legs. He lets first one sawed-off arrow end and then the other roughly rub each inner thigh. "I love you."

"You want me."

"I want you."

"I don't want you."

"You do."

"I want—"

"What?"

She weeps. He's won. I can't believe my eyes and ears, and wish I never could.

Johnny Rolfe

I touched her thick and scuffed-up neck as is my wont and barely felt a heart-beat there. I sat and trembled for an hour by her bed in the La Belle Sauvage suite of the Plaza Hotel, in which she was meant to convalesce but wasn't convalescing.

She woke and took a couple rasping breaths and sucked synthetic milk from a sponge at the end of a stick I held to her lips.

"Nice milk," she said.

"Thanks."

"'Where do your sponges come from?' Remember that one?"

"No."

"You said it."

"I did?"

"Some bullshit like that. Fucking *where do your sponges come from?* Good times. Reminds me of a song:

> Oh my
> Father is dead and my
> Mother is dead and my
> Cousin is dead and my
> Brother is dead and my
> Brother is dead and my
> Brother is dead and my
> Boyfriend's a schmuck and his
> Chief has no legs."

"Nice song."

"It's one my people have sung down the years, all the more beautiful now that it's true."

"How do you feel?"

"As if there'll be no tomorrow."

"Don't say that."

"Too late."

Lacking strength to sit on her own, she was propped on a bunch of depleted pillows on the tired bed in the hotel suite.

"I always thought a New York hotel would have more pizzazz than this. You know your civilization's finished when your best hotel's a careworn fleabag."

"You seem in a good mood."

"Won't you be in a good mood when you're soon to depart this slaving meatwheel? Please don't wince every time I mention my death. Stop kidding yourself and help me face it."

"I don't want you to die."

"Oh, Mr. Johnny, I ain't aworried much. If the Lord is ready, 'tain't for me to hesitate."

"Why don't you want to live?"

"Why don't you want to die?"

"Seriously."

"Seriously? You're a good man in some extremely limited ways, occasionally a kind and intelligent man, but in sum our love has yielded me less fun than pain, and because my means are few, my mind poor, and my need of you great in this strange land, the only way I have to pry myself loose of you is to die."

"You've got a weird sense of humor. Why won't you even try to live?"

"I'm trying! But I've noticed I ain't gonna succeed. I'm not willing myself to die, I'm being killed by some idiotic disease I probably got from you or one of your pals. So before you get all moralistic about 'trying to live,' first try dying and see how moral you feel. Anyway, since when have moral considerations affected anything you do?"

"You insult me repeatedly."

"I mean it. After I die, what are you going to do?"

"I have no idea."

"Well get one. I mean it. Despite the oath you've sworn to anemia as a philosophical worldview and way of life, you're a moderately capable young man and you might want to consider getting off your ass and doing something to ameliorate the world you live in."

"I don't feel like talking about this right now."

"How about starting really small by ameliorating, you know, me?"

"How can I if you refuse to ameliorate yourself?"

"No, I mean make the end of my life as decent as it can be, under the circumstances. And stop badgering me."

"So, what should I do, tell you a joke?"

"Do you know any?"

"Why'd the girl fall off the swing?"

"She was dead."

"You've heard that one before."

"You know what else you could do for me? An excellent funeral."

"I'll promise you the finest funeral in the world, only you must get well first."

"I want a long procession. I hope all the wonderful folks I've met in this beautiful town turn out in full, and I hope it don't rain. I want to go to meet my maker with plenty of bands playing. I want to ride up to heaven in a white velvet hearse, silk velvet. Purple satin inside the casket. I wants them folks' eyes to bulge out. And another thang: I want horses to the hearse, I don't like the smell of gasoline."

She hawked and spat a mauve and chartreuse wad of phlegm into a plastic bowl beside her bed, and lay back on her hard, thin pillow in dismay.

"I've got one for you," she said. "Why did the king fall off the throne?"

"He had no legs."

"We are so in synch right now! You know another thing you could do for me?"

"What?"

"Depose him."

"Done."

"He's one of those people whose life I find hilariously funny to contemplate, a little funnier than standing alone in a room looking at nothing, listening to nothing, tasting nothing, smelling nothing, feeling nothing, thinking nothing."

She closed her eyes and her mind seemed to leave me for a while, a thing I'd dearly like my mind to do, but it never can except in sleep, which rarely lasts even an hour.

"For real. What do you propose to do?"

"Do?"

"About him."

"Who?"

"John Martin."

"I propose to endure him."

"Sheesh, who's got legs and who has none? 'Please know I'm not one with all the programs, intentions, wishes, and behaviors of the gentlemen I am visiting your region on business with.'"

"What?"

"I'm quoting you."

"When'd I say that?"

"A while ago in a letter to me. And '. . . my distaste for this adventure's conception, its goals, its trajectory, its management, its personnel, its scope, its methods, its avoidable failures.'"

"I don't remember writing that."

"You didn't write it."

"I don't remember saying it."

"You didn't say it, you thought it."

"How do you know?"

"Says so right here."

"Where?"

"In my mind."

"So now I have to be accountable for all my thoughts?"

"To know and not to act is not to know, Gianni."

She closed her eyes again. To make her open them, I asked her what she'd have me do.

She sat up, tried to speak, and lay back. She coughed and spat and missed the bowl. Her black hair was pasted to her head with sweat.

"Do you want to hear some music?"

"Do you know how to play music?"

"I know how to press a button on this machine that plays recorded music."

"Where'd you get the machine?"

"John Martin gave it to me when he appointed me vice president for communications of the newly consolidated New York Company."

"I thought he considered you his enemy."

"He does."

"So why'd he make you vice president?"

"Because it's worse than jail or death."

"You could refuse to serve."

"Then he'd jail or kill me."

"How'd you get the juice to run the machine?"

"I traded a week of my life for it."

"What song are you going to play me?"

"Beethoven's Fifth Symphony."

I pressed PLAY. A thundercloud of music darkened the room. After less than half a minute she said, "Turn it off!" I did.

A green sunbeam came in the dim window and limned her veridian skin. Sun and skin were one; she nearly disappeared. From within this haze of light I saw her pale mouth move: "That's the worst sound I ever heard."

"It's pretty awful, yes."

"Why do you listen to it?"

"I think it's beautiful."

"What's beautiful about it?"

"That a hundred people sat in a room and succeeded in the complicated and difficult activity of playing a symphony together without murdering each other."

"But people did such things together all the time back when Earth produced a seemingly limitless supply of food and fuel. That can't be all you like about that noise."

"It reminds me of my hometown."

"This?" she said, and gestured toward the dirty window with her eyes.

"That."

"Why would you want to hear the culmination of centuries of blundering and horror represented in your art?"

"Because art that represents centuries of blundering and horror makes them slightly more bearable, if not more comprehensible."

"So you're prospering from this program you find *distasteful* and are *not one with* and *want no part of* by accepting scarce and valuable fuel from your imperial overlord so you can play—who'd you say that music was made by?"

"Beethoven."

"So you can play music made by Bait Oven. Great. I'm not kidding, you know."

"About what?"

"Doing something."

"About John Martin?"

"About John Martin."

"What?"

"I can't tell you what."

"You want a revolutionary leader? Talk to Jack Smith. He's a better candidate than I."

"He's too pragmatic. He's good at making things run, but a revolution needs someone impractical and unrealistic to tell guys like him why and where to go."

"Have you ever done such a thing in your life?"

"Yes!"

"What?"

"I can't believe you have to ask me that."

"I'm not asking to challenge you, I'm asking because I need guidance."

"This is what I'm saying. Someone has to be the one who doesn't need guidance."

"I assure you I'm not such a man."

"All right. Do this. Wait nine months."

"Nine months from now?"

"From when I die. From now, yes. I should be dying in the course of a difficult childbirth, but a single glance between my thighs will demonstrate I ain't. The tiny hope of a nation from my loins does not squeeze forth into the world so it'll have to come from someplace else. I hereby plant a seed in that virgin mind of yours from which a miraculous idea will spring forth nine months hence." She closed her eyes.

"Don't close your eyes! What about the one more thing you said you still had to know?"

"Now it's yours."

"What is it?"

"You know what's strange? I really want to live," she said, and died.

The Names of the Dead

George Kendall, Herb Mangold, Matthew Bernard, Gerald Mankiewicz, Happy Lohengrin, Albert, numerous fops, Bill Breck, John Ratcliffe, Stickboy, Powhatan, Chris Newport, James Stuart, Philip Habsburg, most men's best intentions, Pocahontas, whose secret name you must not speak lest you find your own on this list.

Johnny Rolfe

To anyone willing to act selflessly in service of a vision of world improvement:

I write to you in my capacity as Vice President for Communications of the America Company. That is, I write as no one to no one.

I'm in the study of my ramshackle and dilapidated house—I work from home a lot these days—on a hill surrounded by a barbed wire fence and a moat of hydrochloric acid in Riverdale, the Bronx, one of many neighborhoods in this vast, exhausted land I love that my protector and boss, John Martin, a philosopher king with an enormous head and massive treelike arms, has taken back from terrorists and secured with armed guards. Not long ago, on this momentous morn, I could hear my friend and roommate, Jack Smith, Vice President for Strategic Planning, mill around downstairs before he left the house. Today is one of many days when even hearing him touch two dishes together in the kitchen makes me want to kill him. I think he wants to kill me half the time as well. Murderous rage may be where the passion is in this second, passionless marriage for each of us. But the presence of his body in these rooms is also a great and almost adequate consolation to me. To meet him by the long-defunct fridge and be wrestled off my feet, to have him press my face into the ancient wooden boards of the kitchen floor—boards that lay between dropped cubes of cheese and the sodden earth long before we were born—is a way to spend a morning that I find more bearable than most. With Jack at any rate it beats conversation by a mile. He's boring. He tells in great detail about adventures he's had and ones he plans to have, long stories with no point except that he's telling them and they happened to him, or could. And nights up in the Bronx are long. Once in a blue, Jack goes out late, passes through the three security checkpoints, and roams the streets in search of danger, but to do that he must once again be in love with death, which is to say in love with life, which, like me, he's mostly not, though on those rare nights he tries to be again. On other nights, he wanders through the house, burping and groaning and breaking things. He approaches the study door, which I've locked, and says, "What're you doing in there?" "Working." "On what?" "Communications." "Who you communicating with?" "The dead." "What do they say back?" "Nothing." "Can I come in?" "No." "When will you be done?" "Never."

But recently I set in motion a little something to mark the second anniversary of my girlfriend's death. Every day's the birthday of the death of someone I knew but I liked her more than all the rest so I chose her death among all the deaths to celebrate with a coup against the efficacious leadership of our chief. When I told Jack about it he said, "Jesus, finally, it only took you two years."

"So why didn't you think it up if you wanted it done?"

"Why didn't *I*? You don't know? Have I been talking to a wall since the day we met?"

Four of us VPs—Vice President for Community Outreach Richard Buck, Vice President for Security Bucky Breck, Jack Smith, and me—assembled at our place for a top secret planning session. I had a cubic meter of the finest artificial cheese brought in, and bottles of super-unleaded water—not the premium-unleaded, mind you, I only make a VP's salary, not a king's. And I hauled out my dwindling stash of busthead to put us all in a mood of optimistic relaxation, or at least make us less grim and ill at ease, except Dick Buck of course, our mostly useless conscience, our Vice President in Charge of High-Handed Rage and Despair, who as the evening wore on freaked out and had to be tied to a soft chair—you know you've got good friends if they use a soft chair and not a hard one—and locked in the basement so he wouldn't hurt himself. Who among us hasn't spent more evenings than he'd like in a basement tied by his friends to a soft chair, Dear Interlocutor Whose Nonexistence This Communication Is Predicated On?

So, having meant to convene in the parlor around a platter of high-end artificial cheese, we convened instead—in deference to our good friend through whose veins rage now would take an hour to pass—in the dank, cold, low-ceilinged basement, where eating cheese would have drawn rats to our lips. Each of us but Buck sat at the edge of a crate clutching his plastic bottle of water close to his chest. Buck alone, aggrieved, muted by the wad of rag in his maw, wrists scraped raw in their struggle to be free, had a nice chair to be in. The rest of us endured the sharpness of crate slats on the backs of our thighs. What rags we hadn't used to silence and immobilize Buck we cut to strips and used as wicks for candlelight. In that cold wet hole in the side of a hill in the Bronx two weeks back, amid rats' squeaks and Buck's grunts, I told them my plan and they told me it back; we argued and refined it; Breck and Smith both said they could contribute guns and willing men; I said I knew none of either but would contribute my brain and flesh, or what was left of them. There wasn't much to plan: assemble willing men in stealth, disable Martin's many bodyguards, move in past his most forbidding guards, his arms and head, and slit his throat. Or shoot him. Or blow him up. Or crush him with a bus. Or poison him. Or drown him. And then hold a democratic election. I guess this must be what my gal envisioned two winters ago, who knows, she's dead, what happens now is no concern of hers.

What little bit of plan there seemed to be to make we made, or tried, and then ran out of things to say, and sat in silence waiting for our friend to let off fighting with his bonds. We couldn't leave him down there all alone or he'd have been devoured by rats, so we sat on our hard crates and looked at one another and at him, and through his gag he tried to shout what must have been "Let me go!" or "Quit staring at me," and each time a rat got in his pants leg Smith stabbed it fast and threw it on a growing pile, which we'd later burn in our hearth at our leisure. To eat them would have killed us but to smell them burn was not so bad.

At length, Father Buck got groggy and wept softly—tears of rage, tears of shame, who knows how to name such things? Not English, certainly. We let him go. He hugged us and apologized and asked, "But why'd you have to tie me up?" We looked at him and didn't say a word and he apologized again. We all agreed to keep our revolution lean, and parted for the night, except for Jack and me: he chased me up the stairs.

Since that night two weeks ago the dread has grown in me. Someone less inured to disappointment—can this world sustain someone like that?—might have felt such dread as hope. That the thought to try to make a change had come to me at all, that my body had not then expelled it as it would have done a childish dream or wormy slice of pie, was marvel enough for one life; such a thought would never have found the loam of hope in me, and if it had it likely would have choked in it; no, this thought's best home and hope has been my rocky, arid, stinking lump of dread: where else could murder's seed have grown and bloomed?

Since that night I've left the house more often than before, and when I go the guards, in whose eyes I used to see contempt for me, now nod to let me know they know, which, of course, makes my dread grow. For me to need a guard to walk the streets is relatively new, not just to me but to the company that is my employer, home, and state. And that's because, as this state has enlarged, its borders have become less geographical than notional. On our official map it looks as if we have more land than ever before, its edge limned in ink with bold and indivisible lines. But discontent makes holes a map's ink can't represent. Such holes cannot be seen at all, exist more in air than land, and more in mind than air. And that is maybe why my modest plan can now exist—not to say succeed.

Today's the day. A couple bombs went off at eight as planned on Brooklyn and Washington Bridges, the only two that had remained unbombed in the last war. The empire's most tender cell's now inflamed. Enough of our chief's guards have been drawn away from him for us to interrupt this afternoon's board meeting with our little coup d'état. Before I leave the house, a razor beneath my tongue, I await the final signal, an email to my battery-operated wireless that will say "Happy Birthday, Shaneequa." The email has just arrived but it doesn't say "Happy Birthday, Shaneequa," it says "Plug in the fridge." This is not a code I know. Did they change it and forget to tell me? "Plug in the fridge," what could it mean? I pace our house's second floor and try to think of what it means. Plug in the fridge. I stare out the window at the greenish sky and cold gray ground. It's wintertime, we've been expecting snow and none has come. My study window's view's lone bare tree, which has its own armed guard, is mute on the subject of *Plug in the fridge*, as is the little stream whose edge the tree is at, whose brown and toxic water becomes one with the tree's trunk from the vantage of this window and my eye. Winters come and winters go, as comes and goes the stream; there once was a girl I loved as in a dream. Plug in the fridge. And as the seasons and the waters go, so go the ones who watch them, and as all revolutions know, death awaits the ones who botch them. Plug in the fridge. I guess I'll have to leave the house and go to the meeting and hope to die or not to die, I'm not sure which. Where's my coat? It's in the kitchen, by the fridge. Good old fridge, site of many tender wrestling matches between my roommate Jack and me. When he's got me down on the floor by the always-closed fridge door, he likes to put his face up close to mine and whisper things to me which in my excitement and annoyance I rarely understand, maybe "Plug in the fridge." Got my coat on, and now it's just occurred to me what "Plug in the fridge" means. It means "Plug in the fridge." I do. It hums and vibrates. It's alive. A miracle has happened, everyone. Current flows through wires that have been barren of it all my life. This is so exciting I grow hard, and come! I plugged in the fridge and came just now, wow. The fridge with current in it reminds me of my lost lover, Pocahontas or Shaneequa. She, too, was soft and smooth, and hummed. Oh no wait she was rough and hard, and shrieked. I forget. Coming by the fridge short circuits the memory of love. Coming by the fridge *is* love. I love my working fridge! Oh the walkie-talkie is squawking the squawk of love, that must be Jack Smith, walkie-talkie-ing home to see if I've plugged in the fridge as per his command.

"D'you do it?"

"Yeah, I came."

"I'm coming home right now. Save some fridge for me."

"Is the coup off?"

"Of course the coup is off, everyone's got electricity. Plus Martin's giving away gadgets down at City Hall."

"D'you get anything?"

"A coffeemaker and a microwave. Guess where I am."

"I don't know."

"The West Side Highway, ten minutes from home. Guess what kind of transportation I'm in."

"A car?"

"Yes."

"Ours?"

"Mine."

"What kind?"

"I don't know. You know what else I got?"

"What?"

"Food."

"So?"

"No I mean *food* food, real food."

"Plants?"

"And animals. Ham, I've got sliced ham, and not your fake sliced ham. You know where we can put the ham?"

"In the fridge!" we say together, as if coming.

"I'll be home in nine minutes," he says, and squawks off. Squawkneekwa. Wonder where the filaments of her former self are now. Maybe in my eye, or in that ham. No, I know where they are. They're in our newfound electricity that suddenly runs our fridge. Think of all the energy, total number of joules outputted by a vivacious young female of the species over the course of an unremarkable and foreshortened life: we sucked it all up in a tube, and now it's gonna keep our ham sandwich cold, and will continue to when we're gone from the Earth. And when the Earth itself is gone, on will go the fridge I now stand before in awe, I'd like to think. Its rectilinear form floats on through the black and airless cosmos, and inside, a lit cube of air, and inside that, a ham sandwich on a flat plastic shelf, kept at edible temperature for all eternity by the used-up life of a girl I may once have known.

To the Reader

The foregoing novel is an ahistorical fantasia on a real event, namely, the founding of Jamestown, the first permanent English settlement in North America, in 1607, in what is now the state of Virginia. Following are some of the books I found to be of value in my research.

Philip L. Barbour, editor. *The Jamestown Voyages Under the First Charter: 1606-1609.* 2 volumes. London: Cambridge University Press, 1969.

Edward Wright Haile, editor. *Jamestown Narratives: Eyewitness Accounts of the Virginia Colony: the First Decade: 1607-1617.* Champlain, VA: Roundhouse Press, 1998.

Karen Ordahl Kupperman. *Indians and English: Facing Off in Early America.* Ithaca: Cornell University Press, 2000.

David A. Price. *Love and Hate in Jamestown: John Smith, Pocahontas, and the Heart of a New Nation.* New York: Knopf, 2003.

Helen C. Rountree. *Pocahontas, Powhatan, Opechancanough: Three Indian Lives Changed by Jamestown.* Charlottesville: University of Virginia Press, 2005.

Helen C. Rountree and Randolph E. Turner. *Before and After Jamestown: Virginia's Powhatans and their Predecessors.* Gainesville: University Press of Florida, 2002.

John Smith. *The Complete Works of Captain John Smith.* Edited by Philip L. Barbour. 3 volumes. Chapel Hill: University of North Carolina Press, 1986.

Thank You

Ray Abernathy, Michele Araujo, Nick Balaban, Kate Brandt, Gabriel Brownstein, Linh Dinh, Leslie Falk, Bram Gunther, Anne Horowitz, Neil Levi, Gillian Linden, Michael London, PJ Mark, David McCormick, Denise Mitchell, Bruce Morrow, Richard Nash, Maggie Nelson, Tina Pohlman, Kristin Pulkkinen, Sylvie Rabineau, Ellen Salpeter, Sergio Santos, Carole Sharpe, Myron Sharpe, Susanna Sharpe, Amy Sillman, Adam Simon, Mike Smith, Jacqueline Steiner, "Bob" Sullivan, and my colleagues at Wesleyan University.

I am also grateful to the New York Foundation for the Arts for a 2004 fellowship in fiction.